DARK INTENTIONS

THE HARPER LEGACY

Book 2

By

Catherine M. Clark

Wylde Publishing

Copyright © 2025 Catherine M. Clark

All rights reserved. ISBN: 99781739619503

The characters and events portrayed in this book are fictitious. Any similarity to real persons, living or dead, is coincidental and not intended by the author.

No part of this publication may be reproduced, distributed, or transmitted in any form or by any means, including photocopying, recording, or other electronic or mechanical methods, and not to be used for AI training without the author's prior written permission, except in the case of brief quotations embodied in critical reviews and certain other non-commercial uses permitted by copyright law. For permission requests, please get in touch with the author.

Disclosure

If you see ****** at the beginning of a chapter, it serves as a warning that the chapter includes descriptions of sexual assault. If you prefer not to read such content, please feel free to skip the chapter, as there is nothing else within it that you will miss.

This book contains a spoiler for my title: I Think I'm a Monster – The Bloodlines & Chains series Book 1.

Chapter 1

Splintered Air and Crowded Beds

Reya

The air cracks with the sound of splintering wood, and I gasp as thick, gnarled branches lunge at me from every direction. It's like the very trees have come alive, their limbs contorting into grasping claws, their leaves rustling with a malevolent energy. One, thick as my torso, whips towards my face, and I instinctively use my powers to deflect it, causing it to slam against a tree, the force of the impact shuddering through me.

Panic flares, but my training kicks in as another branch snakes low, aiming for my ankles. With a sharp exhale, a bolt of searing purple fire erupts from my hands. It burns the wood with a hiss and a crackle, the flames hungrily licking at the bark, turning it to ash in seconds. The burnt branch recoils, its charred end twitching like a dying serpent.

They come relentlessly, a whirlwind of wood intent on binding me, crushing me. I dance between the snapping limbs, a whirlwind myself, deflecting some with a flick of my wrist and sending them careening away with a telekinetic shove. Others meet my fiery wrath, each burst of purple a defiant roar against the onslaught. Sweat beads on my brow, my heart hammers against my ribs, but a grim satisfaction grows with each branch

I turn to cinders.

Finally, with a last, desperate surge of energy, I unleash a telekinetic wave, pushing outwards with all my might. The remaining branches falter, their aggressive momentum broken, and then, with a collective groan, they fall still. Silence descends, broken only by my ragged breathing and the faint scent of burnt wood.

I face the woods where she stands hidden, "Well, that was... enthusiastic, even for you, Freya," I say, wiping a stray strand of hair from my face. A giggle echoes from the edge of the clearing, and Freya steps out from behind an ancient oak, a mischievous glint in her eyes. The fallen branches at her feet twitch slightly, giving away their true assailant.

"Just keeping you on your toes, sis," she says, her voice light and airy. "Wouldn't want you getting complacent, would we?"

It's been nearly four weeks since the reapers attacked. Freya's been pushing me ever since, as it was a close call; I need to do better for next time, and what I discovered at the time still sends shivers down my spine. If it hadn't been for the absorption rune—a desperate gamble Cat warned could backfire spectacularly if miscast—I could have destroyed everything, but the rune I secretly put on myself worked. The time since that near-annihilation feels stretched thin and thick, a paradox of unnerving quiet and the gnawing anticipation of the other shoe dropping.

I desperately want to believe the relentless underworld leader I stole Beastie from has finally given up its hunt and retreated to whatever shadowy corner it lives in the underworld. But deep down, a cold knot of certainty tells me this is likely just the wishful whispers of a weary mind in a world increasingly draped in darkness. Lately, it feels like we're perpetually juggling chainsaws while riding unicycles.

Duncan, bless his practical heart, finishes the house and barn renovations with surprising speed. "Barn's practically good as new with a lick of paint," he'd declared, downplaying the extensive work. Fortunately, those *minimal alterations* take only a few days, during which we huddle around the kitchen table, fuelled by lukewarm coffee and sheer determination, to hammer out the layout for our new business. When the barn is finished, Duncan begins transforming the store we acquired into a Café with a combined bookstore. To expedite this process, Duncan enlists the assistance of several industry colleagues, comprising a team of experienced construction professionals, who contribute their efficiency and expertise to the project. Their combined efforts prove invaluable. The section of the Café designated for my use requires meticulous craftsmanship. Consequently, Duncan engages the services of a skilled carpenter renowned for his exceptional carving abilities, ensuring that every shelf looks amazing and far better than I expect, enhancing the aesthetic appeal of the space.

Tomorrow's soft opening feels less like a celebration and more like a high-stakes dress rehearsal. It's our chance to kick the tyres and test the espresso machine, which we all had to practise with for a few weeks; we also got a regular coffee machine for those of us who like a standard cup of coffee.

Any hiccups, and we'll have the weekend to iron them out before Monday's grand opening—a day that feels both exhilarating and terrifying. Thankfully, Duncan only has a minor roofing job lined up this weekend, which he states can be easily postponed if we discover the café's plumbing is powered by angry gremlins or something equally dramatic. Okay, I'm exaggerating as I don't believe we will have issues with gremlins or whatever else is out there that might be gunning for us to make our day end in disaster.

I'm trying to stay optimistic that we'll be serving artisanal coffee and enchanted pastries without a hitch come Monday. But a shadow hangs over me, darker and more persistent than any lurking demon. I know they are out there waiting to attack, even though it's been quiet for weeks. My sisters think we are finally free, *I don't*, so Saturday night is crucial for us to perform the full moon ritual again to give us a fragile shield against the encroaching darkness, which is our only protection.

The complication, as it so often does lately, involves Duncan. His increased overnight stays and the smile he has put on our sister Maya's face is a testament to their blossoming relationship, which is both heartwarming and deeply unsettling. While I'm thrilled Maya has found happiness after our mothers' death, which hit her like a physical blow, her newfound romance has thrown a rather large, magical wrench into our carefully constructed secrecy. In her desire for normalcy, Maya hasn't told Duncan we're witches. The thought of his eventual discovery fills me with a dread that tastes like ash. It's not the witchcraft itself I fear his reaction to, but the potential hurt and betrayal he might feel at Maya's lack of honesty.

Jenny, ever the optimist, *sometimes to a fault*, keeps reassuring Maya that Duncan will take it all in stride. After all, he grew up steeped in local folklore, tales of witches whispered by their grandmother, which they'd dismissed as childhood fancy. That changed for Jenny the day she nearly tripped over the couch when she saw Pickle, our mischievous pixie. The revelation that those stories weren't just stories hit her like a rogue spell, especially when we explained everything. The fact that she could even *see* Pickle is proof enough that the witchy bloodline hadn't completely thinned out in her family, but weak enough that she doesn't seem to be able to do anything like us.

My worry is that Duncan won't have the same wide-eyed acceptance, especially as we already know he can't see Pickle, so we know the witch bloodline wasn't passed onto him. I'm terrified Maya's heart will be broken, not by the magic, but by the perceived deception. I can only hope Duncan's reaction mirrors Jenny's initial shock, followed by an almost immediate, "Well, that explains a few things." This whole situation feels like walking a tightrope over a pit of sharks who are ready to rip out our hearts.

Jenny's been practically living here lately, a semi-permanent fixture on the other side of my bed. She claims her apartment above her hairdresser's is too quiet, a void she can't bear. While I know loneliness plays a part, I can't shake the feeling that her worry for us is the real anchor keeping her here. Ever since the demon attacks started, her usual breezy demeanour has been replaced by a near-constant state of low-grade anxiety. It's almost comical, the irony of it all. This whole demon mess started because of me, a *harmless* joke gone spectacularly wrong after Pickle was targeted by what she calls nasties that are actually fairies. We so got them wrong in fairytales. So, I wanted to lighten the mood after Pickle was attacked, my misguided attempt at levity that backfired with the force of a rogue lightning bolt.

Despite my monumental screw-up at summoning a hellhound, my affection for Beastie and Pickle has grown into something fierce and protective. They've become my family, an unexpected and utterly chaotic unit, along with Jenny. The only downside to this unconventional family dynamic is that my bed has become a nightly game of Tetris. Four of us crammed onto a king-sized mattress, which has led to some… interesting mornings. Jenny has a tendency to starfish, often ending up draped across me like a particularly clingy vine, which inevitably triggers Beastie's jealousy. He then attempts to wedge himself between us, a possessive barrier determined to reclaim his prime protective spot. It sometimes becomes a nightly wrestling match, *okay*, I exaggerate, maybe a few times a week.

To solve this slumber party pile-up, I bit the bullet and called Michael, Duncan's dad, a few days ago. He's ordered me a custom-sized bed, something akin to a small continent. Thankfully, our bedrooms are spacious enough to accommodate my growing need for personal space—both literally and figuratively.

As much as I adore our little menagerie, I'm drawing a line in the sand at any more nocturnal additions. While my heart goes out to any creature or person in need, my spine is starting to object to the nightly acrobatics.

Cat, my enigmatic dream visitor, the one who dropped the bombshell about my inherent power attracting others, isn't kidding. I never imagined that *'magnetic pull'* would manifest as a fiery hellhound and a sassy pixie. To be honest, since Pickle and Beastie burrowed their way into my life and heart, my sleep has been surprisingly restful, despite the overcrowding. Even Jenny's post-wine crash landings don't disturb me; their presence is a strange sort of comforting weight.

However, this newfound intimacy has thrown a rather large wrench into the already rusty gears of my romantic life. It's been four weeks since that picnic with Jacob, a day that should have been filled with sunshine and easy conversation, a chance to finally get to know him better in more ways than one. Yet, something deep within me, a primal instinct I suspect is tied to my magic, has been screaming *wrong* whenever I'm near him. Beastie, my fiery barometer of bad vibes, shares this unease, his low growls a constant reminder of my own internal conflict. It's becoming increasingly clear that Jacob might not be the right fit, no matter how charming and handsome he is, especially in his deputy uniform.

The moment of truth, the unexpected gut punch, came after that picnic. I saw Jacob on his phone, his expression discerning, which caused a cold dread to wash over me. Something felt fundamentally off. Later that day, the reapers attacked—figures that moved like smoke and wielded scythes that hummed with malevolent energy. One of them, in its dying breath, hissed a chilling revelation. They'd been hired to kill my sisters, so they were not just random agents of the underworld but hired.

Mercenaries.

My first instinct was to point the finger at Sandra, a local witch with covetous eyes on our property and a grudge against our family that stretches back further than I know, as we don't know anything about our family, as our mother lied to us right upto the day she died. But the singular focus on my sisters baffles me. If Sandra was behind this, why target them and leave me untouched? The question gnaws at me, a persistent itch beneath my skin, overshadowed only by the growing sense of danger closing in around us.

I've deliberately kept Jacob at arm's length until I can unravel this tangled mess of motives. My distance hasn't gone unnoticed. Initially, his anger takes me by surprise, and a sudden wall of icy resentment is erected between us. But he finally opens up during a subsequent, albeit awkward, conversation. He confesses his anger stems from past hurt, a previous relationship where he'd been deceived and manipulated. He sees my hesitation as a repeat performance, another girl playing games for attention. Hearing his vulnerability is disheartening, especially since I'm about as good at playing games as Pickle is at resisting watching witchy Tv shows and movies.

I try to be as honest as I can, explaining that my emotional baggage could fill a small U-Haul and that opening up feels like navigating a minefield. Jacob seems to soften, acknowledging that my sisters and I are clearly swamped with the café launch. He even offers to wait, a sentiment that fills me with a confusing mix of relief and lingering suspicion.

Now, I'm adrift in a sea of uncertainty. The shadow of the reaper's blade still flickers in my mind, and the possibility that someone else is pulling the strings complicates my already tangled feelings for Jacob. It's a Gordian knot of emotions I desperately need to untangle, but the truth remains stubbornly out of reach.

Today, we're embarking on a decidedly reckless adventure. New Orleans. A city practically vibrating with history, culture, and, hopefully, some magical books, which is my mission for going. To unearth ancient texts, forgotten grimoires, anything that can give us an edge in this paranormal arms race. Everything so far has been a terrifying experiment in trial and error.

Freya has been our go-to for sourcing supplies and ingredients; her knowledge of plants has started to become surprisingly extensive. And to my utter astonishment, my recent attempts at rune casting have been… successful. In fact, that absorption rune didn't just work; it saved my life when I foolishly decided to tango with the reaper's scythe. An act of sheer idiocy that should have turned me into a pile of sparkly dust when I grabbed it, and as I suspected, it would have ripped my soul out of my body. Instead, I think I inadvertently absorbed its power, which my sisters might have as well, as they, in my reckless act, grabbed hold of me to try and pull me away from the scythe and couldn't let go of me, so they might have absorbed some of its power as well, a terrifying thought. But the full ramifications of that encounter remain shrouded in mystery for me and my sisters.

After that night, I noticed something… off about the absorption rune etched onto my body. It takes a few days for the unsettling truth to sink in. When I finally catch sight of it in the mirror, the intricate patterns are blurred, spiderweb cracks snaking through its design like fissures in ancient pottery. It still faintly resembles its original form, but it is undeniably broken, a useless tattoo on my skin. My frantic attempts to recast it, to try and fix it so it can continue to protect me, have failed, so it remains broken. *Lesson learned.* I must try to avoid grabbing glowing, otherworldly weapons when you have absolutely no idea what they do. My future survival might depend on it.

When we prepared for this trip, a knot of anxiety tightened in my stomach. Freya's coming with me, which is a comfort, but it also means leaving Maya alone. Well, *mostly* alone. She'll have Pickle and Beastie, who genuinely believe he's the alpha of our little pack, to keep her company. We drill into her the importance of staying indoors, and she's promised to be good—still, the thought of leaving her vulnerable tugs at my heart. Here's hoping this foray into the possible magical underbelly of New Orleans yields the knowledge we desperately need.

Lying in bed on this early Thursday morning, a wave of unease washes over me, heavier than the usual pre-trip jitters. Leaving Maya… It's a gnawing worry that's kept me tossing and turning all night, the first truly restless sleep since we moved into this place. A glance at the clock confirms my fears—time to get moving. The drive to New Orleans should be relatively smooth at this ungodly hour, the roads blessedly empty, unlike the inevitable traffic jam on our return. My plan is to make this a swift in-and-out mission. Lingering in New Orleans, with the constant threats we face, feels like tempting fate, a recipe for spiralling into a vortex of anxiety.

My immediate challenge is extricating myself from Beastie, who is currently pinning me to the mattress as he sprawls out over my legs, his surprisingly heavy head resting on my thigh. Pickle is nestled against my neck, her surprisingly warm body a comforting yet precarious weight. The delicate ecosystem of the shared bed makes even the slightest movement feel like a potential avalanche.

Taking a deep breath, I carefully turn my head away from Pickle, trying to bridge the gap with the duvet, tucking it into the space where my neck once resided. My hope is to create a duvet pillow that will prevent her from rolling off the main pillow she shares with me. As I manoeuvre, a wave of tenderness washes over me. Their peaceful slumber starkly contrasts with the anxious whirlwind in my head. Each tiny adjustment is made with excruciating caution, acutely aware of how easily I could rouse my barbie-sized roommate.

"It's fine. You can get up," Pickle says suddenly, her voice, surprisingly clear for someone who looks like a sentient dust bunny, cutting through the stillness. I jerk slightly, startled.

"Sorry if I woke you," I whisper, my voice barely audible.

"You have been fidgeting all night," she replies, a mix of sleepy grumpiness and genuine concern. Apparently, my attempts at stealth are about as effective as a banshee trying to whisper.

"Was I? I didn't realise," I admit, mentally replaying my restless night, the anxious thoughts manifesting as subtle shifts and twitches that have clearly not gone unnoticed by the tiny, magical creature glued to my neck.

"You must be worried about something," Pickle states matter-of-factly, her perceptive little gaze seeming to pierce right through my carefully constructed facade of normalcy.

"I am. I'm worried about leaving Maya here," I confess, the words tumbling out, heavy with the weight of my responsibility.

"She will be okay. I will protect her, and so will Beastie," Pickle assures me, puffing out her tiny chest with an endearing and surprisingly reassuring confidence.

"I know you will." I sigh, a mixture of resignation and lingering worry. "I can't help but feel anxious, though."

"You always worry about all of us," Pickle continues, her voice softening with an understanding that belies her size and mischievous nature. "But we haven't been attacked for ages now, so going on a magic book hunt while it's quiet is what's best right now. This will hopefully help you become even stronger." Her words, surprisingly wise, are a soothing balm to my frayed nerves.

"You're right," I acknowledge, a glimmer of relief breaking through the clouds of worry. I carefully slide my leg out from under

Beastie's surprisingly heavy jaw, causing him to let out a soft snuffle and curl deeper into himself. Then, with the grace of a newborn giraffe, I climb out of bed, ensuring Pickle doesn't take an unexpected tumble.

She watches me intently as I gently tuck the duvet around her, a gesture that feels as natural as breathing. The look she gives me is one I've seen frequently lately—a blend of shock and something akin to awe. It's as if the simple act of being tucked in is a foreign concept, a kindness she doesn't expect. I often think about asking her about the look, curious about the story behind it, but the question always seems to get stuck in my throat, a fear of the unknown holding me back.

"Try to go back to sleep. It's only 5am," I gently encourage her, knowing how much she treasures her rest.

"I love my sleep, so, of course, I will," she replies, her voice filled with a casual certainty that borders on smugness that always makes me smile.

I lean down and press a soft kiss to the top of her head, a familiar gesture of affection. Like always, her eyes flutter shut in bliss, but when she reopens them, I catch a fleeting flicker of sadness, a shadow passing over her bright gaze. It makes me wonder about the memories it stirs, perhaps echoes of a mother's love intertwined with the inevitable ache of loss.

A part of me considers stopping the head-kisses, not wanting to trigger any pain inadvertently. Yet, deep down, I have a feeling that if she genuinely dislikes it, Pickle, with her blunt honesty, will tell me to bugger off by now. So, maybe, just maybe, she cherishes it, even with the bittersweet pang it sometimes brings.

I then shift my attention to Beastie, letting my fingers gently trace the tip of his nearest ear. Surprisingly soft, like warm soft leather, it's an unexpected tactile pleasure. This little ritual has become a cherished habit, especially when we are curled up on the couch, lost in a movie or Tv show. The charming juxtaposition of his bat-like ears and their velvety feel never fails to captivate me. You'd think bat ears would feel leathery and unpleasant, but you'd be wonderfully wrong. I've developed a rather embarrassing obsession with this simple, soothing gesture.

Eventually, I manage to pull myself away before I risk fully waking him, planting a soft kiss on his head as well. Then, I slip into some clothes, the cool fabric a contrast to the lingering warmth of the bed.

With a sigh that combines resignation and anticipation, I head towards the bathroom, the first hints of dawn painting the sky outside. As I reach the door, the sound of running water stops me short. For a fleeting moment, I consider retreating to my room, my mind already sketching out potential renovation plans for a second bathroom—and maybe a permanent soundproofing ward when I remember what I did in the bathroom after a date with Jacob to relieve some frustration when things got a little hot between us.

Just then, the water shuts off, startling me from my architectural musings. Moments later, the bathroom door swings open, and Freya steps out, her hair slightly damp and a mischievous glint in her eyes. "You're up! I was starting to think I'd have to resort to tickling you awake or just drag you out of bed," she teases, a wide, cheeky smile spreading across her face.

"Haha, it's just... difficult to leave the gravitational pull of that bed, especially with, you know," I reply, gesturing vaguely towards my bedroom, the warm haven of my duvet and the still-sleeping forms of Beastie and Pickle.

"Oh, I know. Your bed guardians, or strange little harem as I like to call it, is quite the sight," Freya laughs, leaning against the doorframe, her amusement evident.

"Do you really watch me sleep that often, sis? That feels a bit... stalkerish," I ask, raising an eyebrow, trying for a light tone despite the genuine curiosity.

Freya offers a slight shrug, her playful demeanour softening slightly. "I just worry about you. I know Beastie wouldn't intentionally hurt you, but sometimes I can't help but think he might accidentally... You know... roll over in his sleep and crush you. So, if I have to get up early or go to the bathroom during the night, I peek in to check on you," she admits, a hint of discomfort flickering across her features.

"Thank you, sis. Honestly, if you had a demon beast the size of a small pony sleeping in your room, I'd be checking in on you too," I say sincerely, appreciating her concern, even if it's slightly overprotective.

"Thanks. Now hurry up and move your arse before we start running late. Then you'll only worry even more than you already do," Freya urges, giving me a playful shove.

"I won't be long! I took a shower last night, like a responsible adult," I assure her with a mock-offended tone. "Could you please pop two pieces of bread in the toaster for me?"

"Sure, and of course, I'll whip up some coffee, too," she says readily, already turning and heading for the stairs, her usual boundless energy kicking in.

"Like I even had to ask," I chuckle in response, shaking my head with affection before closing the bathroom door behind me, ready to face whatever mayhem New Orleans has in store.

Catherine M. Clark

Chapter 2

Whispers on the High Street

We successfully made our way out of the house without encountering any problems, which is a relief. I anticipate that Beastie might throw a fit, as he always has a tendency to want to accompany me wherever I go. The night before, I repeatedly reassured him that I would be leaving today and that he needed to remain behind to keep an eye on Maya and Pickle. His absence as we depart is a reassuring indication that he has understood me, and it seems he is dutifully staying behind. Still, as we drive away, a prickle of unease lingers. I keep glancing back at the house, half-expecting to see a shadowy form materialise on the lawn or perhaps catch a fleeting glimpse of his eyes in the window. For a moment, I could have sworn I felt a faint chill in the air, a whisper of a growl that might have just been the wind.

Freya spontaneously decides she will drive to New Orleans, and I agree to take the wheel for the return trip, hoping that the long drive will distract me from my worries about Maya. Or perhaps it will just exacerbate them, as my mind races, leaving me vulnerable to distraction and the potential for disaster. I settle into the plush leather seat, adjusting the seatbelt and sinking into a comfortable position for the journey, feeling the sun's early rays filter through the windshield.

As we cruise through our sleepy town so early in the morning, the deserted streets give the entire scene an eerie cinematic quality reminiscent of a disaster movie. The radio crackles to life, a news anchor's voice reporting on a series of unexplained power outages in a neighbouring town, a detail that feels strangely ominous in the early morning quiet. But in a way, we are living in such a narrative; the world is increasingly unsettling, riddled with violence perpetuated by paranormal activities that have surged in recent years, and of course, we didn't know what was going on was caused by the paranormal till recently.

Just as we approach the main high street, I catch sight of Jacob standing outside the sheriff's department, engaged in what appears to be an earnest conversation with the sheriff himself. The building looms behind them, solid and imposing, a reminder of authority in an increasingly chaotic world. As we roll slowly past, I notice how they both turn to watch our car, their expressions a mix of curiosity and caution.

Unable to resist the impulse, I lift my hand and give a small, tentative wave. To my surprise, Jacob's face breaks into a slight grin, though his eyebrows knit together in confusion. The sheriff, however, remains still, his gaze fixed on our car. It feels like his eyes bore into me, a silent accusation hanging in the air. For a moment, I think he might even step forward, his hand perhaps instinctively reaching for his sidearm. The tension hangs in the air as we drive away, leaving the scene behind but carrying the unsettling feeling with us.

As we leave town, my phone buzzes with a text message. Looking over with a mischievous glint in her eye, Freya places a dramatic hand on her chest and says in a mock-romantic voice, "Oh, could it be? The call of destiny? The handsome lawman yearning for your body?"

I chuckle, knowing she's right. "I'm sure it is, considering neither Maya nor Jenny would be up at this hour," I reply, retrieving my phone from the cup holder where I placed it when I got in the car. I open the message from Jacob, a genuine smile breaking across my face. I knew Freya would want to know what he wrote, so I read out his text aloud, *'Hey, beautiful, where are you off to at this time of the morning? The sheriff thinks you're both off to commit a crime.'* Ah, yes, committing felonies before breakfast. Just a typical Thursday morning for us witches.

With a light-hearted smirk, I type back, *'We are going book hunting and doing some shopping. Will be back this afternoon.'* I add a playful kiss at the end, a habit I can't shake off, even though I'm uncertain where Jacob and I stand anymore.

Freya turns to me, her tone shifting to something more serious. "Sis?" she begins, her voice tinged with curiosity and concern. I can tell she is gearing up to ask something deeply personal.

"Yeah?" I respond, bracing for the inevitable.

"Why did you decide to put the brakes on things with Jacob? You seemed genuinely interested in him, and then you started making excuses to avoid seeing him out of nowhere. I know you've said you're unsure about him, but it feels like there's something more going on," Freya presses, her eyes narrowing as she glances over at me again, trying to study my expression.

I let out a long, resigned sigh, feeling the weight of my thoughts pressing on me. Freya deserves honesty, especially if something is lurking in the shadows that can jeopardise her safety. "What is it?" she leans closer, her demeanour shifting to genuine worry.

"I can't shake this horrible feeling that he might be connected to the reaper's attack," I confess, bracing myself for Freya's likely explosive reaction.

Her eyes widen, and she exclaims, "You what!!! Why on earth would you think that? They were sent by whoever is leading the underworld. You know this as you ticked them off by stealing their hellhound!" Her confusion is palpable, and I can see the gears turning in her mind as she processes my words.

"That's the thing," I continue, my voice lowering to a conspiratorial whisper because I'm nervous about telling her this truth. "One of the reapers said something that made me think someone else orchestrated the attack."

Freya's expression shifts from confusion to anger, as I'd anticipated. "Why the hell didn't you tell us this right after you got the chance? What exactly did they say?"

I take a deep breath, feeling the gravity of my words. "They mentioned something about being paid to get rid of the witches' sisters, but he seemed confused about something to do with me. It makes no sense—whoever or whatever is running the underworld wouldn't have to pay anyone to do it. And why would they specifically want to kill you and Maya?" I explain, the anxiety curling in the pit of my stomach.

"I guess, but why would Jacob be responsible?" Freya asks, her brow furrowing in confusion.

"Well… after my picnic with him, something just felt off. As soon as he left our place, he whipped out his phone and glanced back at me with an expression that definitely wasn't friendly. It left me feeling uneasy. And then, what Sandra said only deepened my suspicions," I reply, my voice faltering slightly as I realise how silly it sounds. Even I can sense the absurdity of the scenario I'm painting.

Before I could gather my thoughts to elaborate further, Freya erupted into laughter, the sound bubbling from her like champagne. I shoot her a look, an incredulous mix of disbelief and annoyance, silently questioning why she is finding this so amusing. "You don't want to take anything that old crone has to say seriously? For all you know, she could be the one who sent them," she points out.

"Yes, I did consider that at first, but honestly, why would she want to keep me around? Plus, my magic has been acting weird whenever I'm around Jacob. Every time we kiss, I can feel this surge of power rising within me, a dizzying rush that sometimes leaves a metallic taste in my mouth and a faint tremor in my hands. It feels less like a protest and more like a volatile force struggling to break free. I can't quite explain it," I continue, attempting to convey my bewilderment, but I can't shake the feeling that I sound utterly ridiculous.

"That's definitely strange," Freya replies, her tone shifting to one of concern. "But I still don't see why Jacob would want to hurt us. He seems like a genuinely good guy. If anything, I think the reapers were sent by either the underworld or Sandra. She would need one of us alive to sign over the land to her, but we can't sell or hand over our property for ages unless she has some other scheme up her sleeve," Freya says. She takes a breath and then adds, "You deserve to be happy, sis. It's been so long since you let anyone in after everything that happened with your ex. You can't be that unlucky, right? Maybe your magic's acting up around him because you're scared and anxious; it's just reacting to your emotions," Freya says, sounding so wise that I can't help but feel a wave of shame wash over me for not considering that perspective myself. Maybe I've been viewing this all from the wrong angle.

I take a deep breath and sigh melodramatically, contemplating her words. "Maybe you're right," I admit. "Nothing catastrophic has happened since then. If he was involved in anything sinister, he would have made a move by now, especially after I've been keeping him at arm's length," I muse, trying to dismiss my earlier fears with logic.

"See? It doesn't make sense for it to be him," Freya affirms, giving me an encouraging smile.

"Fine," I concede, a hint of annoyance in my tone. "But I'm going to take things slow. If my own insecurities are causing my magic to go haywire, I need to confront them and finally move past everything," I declare, a newfound determination rising within me.

"Good girl," Freya says, her tone lightening. "Once you get him into bed and clear away those cobwebs, I'm sure you'll relax and stop worrying about the past." She punctuates her statement with a chuckle as she playfully nudges me.

"Ha, ha, very funny," I retort, rolling my eyes but unable to suppress a smile.

"I know I am. It's one of the reasons you love me so much," Freya declares, her grin widening to the point where it seems to illuminate her entire face.

"Can you believe that Maya is the only one of us with an actual sex life?" I say, feeling that familiar twinge of jealousy rising again as my mind wanders to vivid images of Jacob, his bare skin stretched against my bed sheets.

"Yeah, thank goodness we can put up wards to block out all those sex sounds," Freya replies, laughing. "The walls are definitely thin, so I'm glad I don't have to listen to her happiness."

"That's one of the perks of magic that I really appreciate," I remark, a smirk tugging at my lips.

"I prefer using mine to make my plants grow," Freya says, her expression turning dreamy. I can imagine her conjuring images of her lush garden filled with vibrant blooms and impressive plants, which she manages to grow so big within a day or two.

"You're lucky you can do things like that. You and Maya both have skills that are not just practical but also so creative," I say, a tinge of envy creeping into my voice.

"Sis, what you can do is nothing short of amazing," Freya corrects, her tone sincere. "Without your abilities, we might not even be here. You're our powerhouse, our protector," she adds, sounding almost envious of my strength, which leaves me momentarily flabbergasted. As I absorb her words, I yearn for something practical, something tangible that can help improve our lives. I'm grateful for my ability to protect my family, especially with our circle continuing to grow since we moved here. I can't help but wonder where we would be now if we had gone on the run. Would we have managed to learn enough about our magic if we were hiding out in run-down motels instead of facing our challenges head-on?

Catherine M. Clark

Chapter 3

The Quarter's Unseen Eyes

As we approach the outskirts of Jackson, anticipation courses through my veins. Freya navigates southward, joining the familiar rhythm of Route 55, which promises to lead us to the vibrant heart of New Orleans. A mix of anxiety and excitement bubbles within me at the thought of finally stepping into the city we have dreamt about for so long. Even before we discovered our identities as witches, we often reminisced about visiting the French Quarter, indulging in its culinary delights, and embarking on one of those intriguing midnight graveyard tours steeped in history and mystery – a place where the veil between worlds supposedly thinned, a detail that always holds a particular allure for those of us that wish we had abilities, now I have those abilities with a touch of magic in our blood it feels so different going to New Orleans now. For now, however, our focus is on finding magical tomes while Freya hopes to gather supplies we might need—things we perhaps don't even realise are essential. She is particularly keen on locating seeds for various plants that can benefit us in the future.

The journey unfolds pleasantly at first. The highways are mercifully clear, allowing us to make steady progress. It only takes us two and a half hours to reach the city limits. However, as we near New Orleans, the traffic begins to thicken, creating an almost palpable buzz in the air, a low hum that vibrates with the promise of a city teeming with life.

After a bit of searching, we find a parking lot conveniently located within walking distance of a tram stop, well, streetcar as they call them here, but the swell of people navigating the streets fills me with a creeping sense of unease, a claustrophobic wave that tightens my chest. It's just after 9am, and the sidewalks are awash with locals and tourists alike, far busier than I anticipated. The throngs of people press around me, each face a potential source of danger, their hurried movements and loud chatter amplifying my anxiety until it feels like a swarm of buzzing insects beneath my skin.

"Hey, sis, it's going to be okay," Freya reassures me, her voice soothing as she pulls me into a comforting side hug. "We'll get lost in the crowd here. Just try to relax and appreciate this experience. Remember, Maya is missing out on this trip, and we've been planning for years to make it here someday." Her words are a balm, stirring a flicker of excitement beneath my apprehension.

"Yeah, I'm sure you're right," I reply, breathing out slowly. "I suppose I'm just not accustomed to being around so many people since we moved to Luna Falls. It's like going from a quiet pond to an overcrowded beach."

Freya nods, understanding evident on her face. "That's definitely part of it, but I bet you're also worried about being followed, like what happened back in Jackson when you went book hunting on your own. But I promise you, in a place like this, we'll blend into the crowd." Her unwavering confidence helps to ease my nerves, if only slightly. *Though a nagging thought whispers that we will be followed anywhere we go, right?*

"So, where do we head to first?" I inquire, eager to shift my focus from my anxiety to the adventure ahead.

"Let's check out Bourbon Street first," Freya suggests, her eyes sparkling with enthusiasm. She points down the road just as a streetcar approaches the stop ahead. "Look! That one is going to the French

Quarter—let's hop on!"

We exchange brief glances, nodding in agreement, and quickly jog across the street to board the streetcar before it departs. I pull out the tickets while we make our way to it. Once aboard, we manage to find two seats together and plop down, our excitement palpable. As the streetcar rattles toward the French Quarter, I put away our prepaid tickets, tucking them safely back into my bag. We purchased them online and printed them out at Michael's hardware store since we don't have a printer.

The rhythmic clattering of the streetcar, combined with the vibrant atmosphere buzzing outside, ignites a sense of adventure within me. While we travel down Canal Street, I look out at all the fancy stores, and even at this time of the day, there are people dressed like I have never seen before in person. This place feels magical to me; for some reason, I feel at home and can see myself living here. Of course, if there were fewer people, I couldn't live with this every day now. *Perhaps it's the city's long history with the supernatural, a resonance that my own magic can sense.*

We actually looked at the crime statistics online, and as far as we could see, New Orleans is the only city where the crime rates haven't gone up as they have around the rest of the country—well, the world, really—so that helped me make the decision to risk coming here. However, reading statistics online is one thing; being surrounded by this many strangers still feels like a gamble.

It doesn't take long to reach Bourbon Street's vibrant hub. As the streetcar comes to a halt, we hop off eagerly, the intoxicating blend of music and laughter beckoning us forward. The air is thick with the scent of beignets dusted with powdered sugar and the tantalising aroma of Cajun cuisine wafting from nearby restaurants. We begin strolling down the lively street, our eyes darting from one colourful storefront to another, each adorned with eye-catching signs and twinkling lights.

My sister Freya tugs at my arm, pulling me into a shop that seems unrelated to our quest. I follow reluctantly, the fear of losing her in this throng a constant companion. It feels as if she has transformed into a shopaholic as soon as she stepped onto the street, enthusiastically scooping up every trinket and bauble that catches her eye. *Honestly, if she buys one more sparkly thing, I might have to stage an intervention.* If she continues on this shopping spree, it won't be long before we'll need to hire a small brigade to carry her many bags.

After an hour of Freya dragging me from shop to shop, we finally stumbled upon a quaint little shop with an enchanting name, '*Magic Corner.*' I feel a rush of excitement surge through me, and without thinking, I push the door open with exuberance. The impact is a tad forceful, nearly colliding with an unsuspecting patron on their way out. I manage to catch the door just in time, allowing them to scurry past with a surprised look. *Oops. Maybe I should work on my entrance.*

Inside, the shelves are crammed with an array of mystical items. I immediately zeroed in on the towering bookshelves, eager to discover the hidden literary treasures between the covers. Freya, meanwhile, wears a wide smile as she begins exploring the shop, her footsteps light and curious. As I survey my surroundings, I'm disheartened to find no immediate sign of the books I crave, as the bookshelves are filled with jars. Standing in the centre of the store, I turn slowly, scanning the shelves for any sign of books, hoping to find even a few tucked away in a forgotten corner.

"Sis!" Freya calls out, her voice carrying a hint of excitement. I spin 180 degrees to figure out where she wandered off to. When I finally spot her, she's nestled beside a cosy nook near the counter, her gaze fixed on a collection of books that fill the space. My heart races as I dash over to her, eager to see if any of the volumes can satisfy my thirst for knowledge of magic that can keep us safe.

Freya practically radiates joy as she thumbs through the titles, but my enthusiasm falters as I scan the spines. Every title seems to delve into the realm of plants and recipes, leaving me uninspired. With a hint of disappointment, I cast my eyes around the rest of the store and realise it's primarily a haven for supplies—a trove of witchy paraphernalia, judging by Freya's delighted expression.

I take a step closer to examine the curiosities on the shelves. Scattered among the various jars are strange contents—some are filled with peculiar insects, their legs twitching even in their preserved state, while others contain what look disturbingly like animal parts, things I'd rather not dwell on for too long. I even spot jars of seeds, their labels tantalising in mystery, hinting at potent properties and forgotten lore.

Freya, in her element, begins selecting a hodgepodge of books and small jars, her excitement palpable as she enthusiastically fills her arms with a delightful assortment.

I watch her in amusement, bittersweet thoughts swirling in my mind. Perhaps I should venture into the city alone, allowing her to explore without my distractions. Just as I'm lost in thought, I feel a familiar vibration against my left boob—a message from Maya, maybe? I tucked my phone safely in my bra to prevent anyone from snatching it away, ensuring I can feel it if she calls in case of an emergency, instead of keeping it in my bag, where I wouldn't hear it.

Opening the message, I read Maya's cheerful words. She's awake, all is well, and she wants to know if we made it in one piece. A wave of guilt washes over me—perhaps we should have texted her the moment we arrived to let her know we were safe.

I quickly draft a reply to Maya, my fingers dancing over the screen of my phone, *'We made it! Freya has gone full shopaholic and is buying everything in sight.'* A moment later, my phone vibrates with a message full of laughing-out-loud emojis. Her infectious amusement brings an instant smile to my face, lightening the atmosphere around me.

I tuck my phone back into my pocket and turn my attention to

Freya, who is now approaching the checkout counter. It's quite a sight to behold—the sheer amount she is about to buy will mean she will have so many shopping bags, she is going to start to struggle with them and know she will begin to thrust some onto me if she continues like this. Each bag seems fuller than the last, bulging with her morning finds as the cashier, a middle-aged woman with a look of mild disbelief, stares wide-eyed as Freya continues her spree, adding even more items to her ever-expanding collection as she rings up the items and filling three bags she decides is needed for everything on the counter. The woman's brows shoot up in silent astonishment while Freya, beaming excitedly, reaches for yet another item on a nearby shelf. It's clear that this shopping trip has become a memorable one, and I don't think I will ever see it again.

    As we step out of the store, the street is a dynamic tapestry of life, more vibrant than when we walked in. The number of people weaving through the thoroughfare has doubled, creating a palpable buzz that fills the air with excitement and energy. Laughter echoes, voices mingle, and the sound of footsteps creates a rhythmic pulse that matches the quickening beat of my heart. I pause momentarily, allowing the heady atmosphere to envelop me, and take a deep, steadying breath, inhaling the mingling scents of street food, fresh coffee, and the crispness of the summer air.

    Suddenly, I'm overcome by an eerie sensation that seems to pulse around us, an intangible vibration that sends a shiver down my spine, raising the hairs on the back of my neck. It feels like an unseen force is weaving through the crowd, an almost electric energy that heightens my senses, making the sounds around me sharper, the colours more intense. In that instant, a prickling awareness blossoms across my skin, merging with an unsettling feeling that something isn't quite right. It stirs memories of the discomfort I experienced back in Jackson. This shadowy intuition whispers of being observed, of eyes lurking just out of sight, scrutinising every move I make, a feeling I can't seem to shake.

With my heart racing faster, I swiftly open my eyes, scanning the throng for any hint of an inquisitive gaze, for the presence that seems to linger beyond my awareness. But, mirroring my experience in Jackson, I find nothing remarkable amidst the sea of faces; no one appears to be watching me, at least not overtly. The crowd continues, blissfully unaware, while I stand there with an inexplicable tension in my chest, grappling with the growing sense of unease that refuses to dissipate. "Hey, what's up?" Freya asks, her voice suddenly breaking the silence, causing me to jump slightly.

"What?" I respond, my heart racing as I turn to look at her, still a bit on edge.

Freya furrows her brow, concern painted across her features. "You look worried. What's going on? Did you see something?" She scans the throngs of people around us, her eyes darting about as if searching for a hidden threat, just as I had been doing moments before.

I sigh, hesitating for a moment before deciding to be open with her. "I've been feeling the same way I did when I was out in Jackson—like someone is watching me," I confess, my voice barely above a whisper, *and there's this weird energy in the air, like static electricity, but… more intense.* But I don't say that part to her.

She nods thoughtfully, her demeanour shifting as she acknowledges my unease. "Okay, well, we did anticipate that this might happen, which is why I came along. Remember, with all these people around, I'm sure we'll be fine. Let's focus on our search, and once we're done, we can get out of here and head home," Freya says, her tone reassuring and steady, reminding me that she is the level-headed one between us.

"Yeah, let's get going," I reply, glancing cautiously at our surroundings one last time. I try to shake off the lingering sense of apprehension as we continue down the bustling street. The air is thick with the chatter of voices, the smell of street food wafting from nearby vendors, and the vibrant colours of shop displays competing for attention. Freya surprises me as we continue down the street and towards many more stores. However, this time, she ignores them. *Maybe even her shopping urges have a limit,* I think with a wry smile.

When we reach the end of the street, we approach a store that stands out from the rest—Voodoo House. Its darkly painted exterior contrasts sharply with the bright, cheerful facades of the neighbouring stores. The sign hung askew above the entrance adds an air of mystery that piques my curiosity.

Chapter 4

Secrets Behind the Counter

I step inside, taking my time as I push the door open, a knot of apprehension tightening in my stomach with each creak of the hinges, making sure I don't collide with another customer. The moment I cross the threshold, an enveloping darkness greets me, a stark contrast to the previous stores' bright, almost aggressively cheerful ambience, making my eyes struggle to adjust. This place feels less like a shop and more like a hidden realm of curiosities, the air thick with the scent of dried herbs and something indefinably ancient, evoking memories of a slightly unsettling Harry Potter shop named Borgin and Burkes. Shadows in this store seem to dance with secrets.

As I gaze around, my senses are assaulted by an assortment of bizarre items that seem to belong in a macabre museum rather than a retail establishment. Shrunken heads dangle ominously from the ceiling, their vacant eyes forever closed in a silent, petrified scream that sends a fresh wave of goosebumps down my arms. Creepy, bandaged hands are prominently displayed as if they are reaching out for the living, their decaying fingers seeming to twitch in the dim light, a morbid fascination pulling my gaze. A row of peculiar little dolls lines the shelves, their glassy eyes, unsettlingly human-like, seemingly follow my every movement, sending icy tendrils of fear crawling up my arms, as each one radiates an aura of forgotten magic.

Despite the unnerving atmosphere, a shelf overflowing with books, their spines promising untold knowledge, draws me in like a moth to a flickering flame. I turn to Freya, who has just entered. Her initial disbelief quickly morphs into wide-eyed wonder, her breath catching in her throat. "Wow," she exclaims, her voice a hushed whisper that reverberates against the store's shadowy walls.

"This feels like we stepped straight out of Harry Potter," she comments, her eyes darting over the eclectic offerings that fill the room with an air of enchantment and unease, a mixture of thrill and trepidation dancing in their depths.

"That's exactly what I was thinking," I reply, a nervous chuckle escaping my lips. However, as I continue scanning the space, my gaze lands on a woman nearby, meticulously stocking shelves. Her sharp scowl etches deep into her features, suggesting that she is less than pleased with our Harry Potter comparison. I quickly decide it's best to remain silent, swallowing any further light-hearted remarks. *No need to antagonise the keeper of this strange place,* I think, a prickle of caution raising the hairs on the back of my neck. The last thing I want is for her to retaliate against our amusement comparisons and decide to overprice whatever treasures I might find.

I go to the book section, hoping to avoid further scrutiny and the woman's piercing gaze. The moment I reach the shelves, I observe something peculiar. The spines of the books all look old and worn, showcasing an eye-catching look that hints at ancient wisdom.

Curiosity piques, and a familiar yearning for knowledge stirs within me. I reach for one of the volumes, pulling it from its resting place. As I hold it in my hands, the first thing that strikes me is the unsettling realisation that, despite its worn and old appearance, it's intentionally aged; it is, in fact, a new binding crafted to mimic the charm of an old tome while betraying its true nature, a clever deception that leaves me disappointed.

I start to lose hope, a familiar wave of frustration washing over me, until I turn and, as my eyes fall on the counter, see a few books on a shelf. One stands out to me; its leather cover is darker and more genuinely aged than the others. It reminds me of the old diary I found at the estate sale, a flicker of recognition sparking in my mind, but its name is still very visible, a clear title amidst the surrounding mystery.

I turn to the woman who is still stocking the shelves, her movements deliberate and precise. She is adding a simple doll, crafted from what looks like rough fabric, to the line of vibrant, magical items on display. The doll reminds me unnervingly of voodoo figures, its expression eerily blank, its stitched smile somehow both innocent and sinister. I take a deep breath to steady my nerves, the air feeling heavy with unspoken energy, before speaking up. "Excuse me, can I please look at the book you have on the shelf behind the counter?"

The woman pauses, her hands still hovering over the shelf, glancing at me with a flicker of curiosity in her emerald eyes as she tucks a loose strand of dark hair behind her ear, a gesture that somehow seems both cautious and assessing. "Which book are you talking about, cher?" she asks, her southern drawl thickening the air around us like warm honey, each word a slow, deliberate drawl.

I hesitate for a moment, aware of the weight of my request and the intensity of her gaze. "Erm, the one called *Golems, Protection and Wards*, please," I reply, my voice wavering slightly under the scrutiny, a nervous tremor betraying my inner unease. A small part of me worries she might judge us for our interests, wondering if she perceives us as witches—something I'm not sure how I feel about sharing with a stranger, a secret we guard fiercely.

"Why would you be interested in that, darlin'?" she inquires, her gaze sharp and probing as she sizes me up with a sceptical look, her lips pursed in thought before glancing at my sister briefly. Freya has stopped her exploration of the store, her attention now locked on our interaction, her brows furrowed in a protective stance.

"Why does it matter to you? Do you question every customer why they want to buy something in your store?" Freya interjects, her tone laced with an edge that emerges when she feels people are being unfair or condescending, a spark of defiance flashing in her eyes.

"Now, hold on a minute, sweet pea," the woman counters, as she crosses her arms defiantly over her chest, standing firm and unyielding, not even budging towards the counter. "I'm interested because, in the wrong hands, somethin' like that can cause a whole lotta damage and hurt people, and of course, stir up trouble in the paranormal world. So yes, I reckon I need to know before I sell somethin' like that." Her gaze holds a hint of warning, a silent reminder of such knowledge's power.

Feeling a mixture of vulnerability and determination, a surge of protectiveness for Freya rising within me, I decide to be partially honest. "We need help to protect ourselves," I admit, my heart pounding a frantic rhythm against my ribs as I reveal this sliver of truth to a complete stranger, even though it's just a phrase that anyone can say.

"What would two cheerleaders need protection from?" she scoffs, tilting her head slightly, her eyes narrow and eyebrows raised in disbelief, a smirk playing on her lips that ignites a spark of irritation within me.

Freya's irritation flares at the remark, her cheeks flushing with indignation, which only fuels the fire of my own annoyance. "As I said, we don't have to explain ourselves to you," she shoots back, crossing her arms in a stance of defiance, her chin tilting upwards, and I relax, thinking she would say more than I felt comfortable saying. "We were recently attacked by demons. Is that a good enough reason for you?" I drop my head in disbelief, a groan escaping my lips at my sister's blatant honesty.

The woman's green eyes widen in surprise, a flicker of shock momentarily softening her features, before narrowing again, scepticism still etching her face. "Why would demons be after two ex-cheerleaders?"

she asks, a hint of incredulity in her voice, her gaze shifting between us with renewed curiosity.

That comment marks the culmination of all our frustrations for Freya. With a fierce determination, her eyes blazing with righteous anger, she declares, "We would never lower ourselves to be mere cheerleaders. We are witches—powerful witches, for the record—but our mother was murdered before she could impart her knowledge to us." Her voice surges with emotion, echoing the weight of our struggles and the dire circumstances that envelope us, a raw vulnerability underlying her defiant tone. As she speaks, I feel a rush of liberation wash over me; it is invigorating to finally assert our true identity, even when surrounded by scepticism, but alongside it, my fear also rises in equal measures, a cold dread settling in the pit of my stomach at the potential repercussions.

I can't help but wince, my eyes widening in alarm at Freya's impulsive declaration. I deliberately hoped we could navigate this conversation without directly revealing that we were witches. It feels safer to suggest it subtly, shrouding it in mystery, instead of confronting it head-on, and bringing up our mother. That feels like a reckless risk, a sharp pang of grief twisting in my chest at the memory, and yet, something inside me also feels a surge of strength as Freya asserts our identity, a sense of finally standing in our truth.

The woman listening to us narrows her eyes, as a sly smile, both knowing and slightly unsettling, creeps onto her lips as she leans forward, her gaze intense. "Is that so, cher? Then what, pray tell, is your coven name, girl?" The question hangs in the air, thick with impending judgment, a silent challenge.

Panic surges through me, a cold wave of fear washing over me, and I shoot Freya an urgent look, my eyes wide with unspoken warning, silently pleading with her to think twice before answering. Disclosing our name can expose us to untold dangers, and now, it feels as though we are teetering on the edge of a precarious cliff, the wind threatening to push us into the abyss. But it's too late—the moment has slipped from my grasp, and Freya has already taken the bait.

With a hint of misplaced pride, a naive confidence shining in her eyes, Freya responds, "We are the Harpers." The name rolls off her tongue as if it's a cherished mantra, a symbol of our newfound identity, despite the fact that we have only recently embraced it. Strangely, since adopting the Harper name and aside from that initial slip with the sheriff, it feels surprisingly natural to claim it, a sense of belonging settling within me despite the lurking dangers we know are heading of us, a fragile shield against the unknown.

To my astonishment, the woman's reaction to our name is immediate and intense. Her face contorts with anger, her eyes flashing with a dangerous light, and she takes a few menacing steps toward us, her posture radiating hostility. This causes my instincts to kick in, every nerve ending screaming danger. I instinctively take a step back, bracing myself for a confrontation that feels all too imminent, my magic thrumming beneath my skin, ready to defend us. It appears my worst fears are about to materialise.

"How dare you use that name and pretend to be a part of the great Harper coven!" she exclaims, her voice a low growl of fury, her fists clenching tightly at her sides, her body language radiating threat. I can see the fury bubbling beneath her surface, a volatile energy that feels ready to explode, and every instinct screams that she is prepared to strike. When I think things can't escalate further, Freya, in her usual impulsive fashion, chooses that moment to engage with the woman even more, her own anger flaring in response.

"Our mother was part of the Harper coven but escaped when it was attacked," Freya declares, her voice loud and defiant, echoing through the silent shop. I feel irritation building at her reckless words, a desperate urge to silence her rising within me. I'm acutely aware that she is saying far too much, potentially jeopardising our safety with every syllable.

"Freya!" I hiss, barely managing to restrain my frustration. The words grinding out between my clenched teeth are a silent plea for her to stop. The woman's eyebrows knit together in surprise, the anger in her eyes momentarily flickering with confusion, but this time, there's a flicker of uncertainty as her aggressive stance shifts ever so slightly.

"What was your mother's name?" she demands, her voice edgy with curiosity rather than outright hostility, a hint of something else, something akin to… recognition?

"Elspeth Harper," Freya replies, an air of pride lacing her words, a defiant lift to her chin, even as my anger at the situation boils beneath the surface, a knot of anxiety tightening in my stomach.

The transformation in the woman's expression is quick and startling; the anger seems to melt away, replaced instead by a wave of profound sadness that crests over her features, her eyes suddenly glistening with unshed tears. Confusion grips me, a whirlwind of questions swirling in my mind, and she moves unexpectedly before I can process the shift. In an instant, she surges forward. I'm too slow to react, my mind still reeling, but I instinctively engage my power, ready to strike if necessary. She envelopes both my sister and me in a fierce embrace, the force of it knocking the breath from my chest, a surprising warmth emanating from her.

She then abruptly pulls away, her hands still resting on our shoulders, and I notice her eyes grow wide with fear, a raw, visceral emotion that mirrors the alarm surging within me. Can she sense the latent power within me, the magic that always feels like a volatile storm waiting to be unleashed? Surely not. Yet her following words fill me with unease, a cold premonition settling in my heart.

"I'm sorry. I didn't mean to startle you. I'm not a threat to you," she stammers, her gaze darting nervously between us. An almost panicked look creeps into her expression, and her hands tremble slightly on our shoulders.

"What did you do?" Freya whispers, her voice barely above a breath, her eyes wide with confusion and a hint of lingering fear.

In a hushed tone, I reply, "Nothing much, just my power reacted to the sudden closeness, a faint hum beneath my skin."

"Do you think she felt it?" Freya whispers back, her brow furrowing in anxiety as she glances at the woman, her gaze searching for answers.

I shrug, glancing at her too, still trying to assess the situation, my mind racing to understand this sudden shift in her behaviour. "I can hear you, and yes, I felt your power building; you are very powerful. I'm sorry I took you by surprise. I'm just shocked that Elspeth Harper's daughters are standing here in my store." Her voice is thick with emotion, a mixture of disbelief and something akin to reverence.

The woman pauses, taking a shaky breath before continuing, her demeanour shifting again, a melancholic sadness settling over her features. "I met her a few times. There were always whispers that she was expecting a child, but then, when the coven was attacked, we all thought everyone had perished, swallowed by the darkness that is creeping over the world. And then, several months later, more attacks start on our people. We've been left in a state of fear and restlessness, constantly looking over our shoulders, wondering whether we will be next."

"Wait, you met our mother?" I ask, surprise in my voice with a whisper, struggling to absorb the weight of her words and the more profound implications of her statement. A sudden ache of loss, sharp and poignant, resonates within me.

"Of course, I did, ma cherie. Elspeth was the head of the Harper coven and would visit New Orleans at least once a month," the woman replies matter-of-factly, a hint of warmth returning to her voice, then pauses as realisation flickers across her features. "I'm sorry. Where are my manners? I'm Priestess Marassa." She offers a small, hesitant smile.

"Priestess, does that mean you practice voodoo?" Freya asks, her curiosity piqued, her initial fear now replaced by a thirst for knowledge. When we looked into New Orleans, we actually read all about voodoo. It's the one area of the paranormal world we know a little about, just a little, and only what we can find online, so what we read could be all wrong.

"Yes, dear, I practice voodoo, but I am weak compared to your family line," she says, a hint of sorrow in her voice, her gaze distant as if remembering a brighter past.

"Well, it's nice to meet someone who doesn't want to kill us finally," I say, a nervous chuckle escaping my lips, the tension in the room still palpable despite the shift in Marassa's demeanour.

"I'm sure you are and know just how much danger you are in. I'm surprised you are out in public and not hiding as the world falls into the clutches of evil. I fear we don't have much time left, and can't believe you are still alive," Marassa says as she gives us another once-over, her eyes full of a mixture of concern and awe.

I can't help but ask, a desperate need for answers driving my question, "Do you have any idea who is behind the recent attacks and the myriad of issues we've all heard so much about on the news lately?"

Marassa pauses. I see she is in deep thought, her gaze clouding with worry. "I wish I could provide you with a clear answer, ma cherie. Unfortunately, I don't know who exactly is orchestrating these attacks. However, persistent rumours are circulating that a council has been formed, comprising the most powerful and influential groups that remain in the world today. It seems that whoever is behind these events possesses extraordinary strength and resources, as unifying and controlling such a diverse array of paranormal factions is no small feat. The implications are daunting, to say the least." Her voice holds a note of grave concern.

As she spoke, a memory, sharp and unsettling, came to mind, and I couldn't help but blurt it out, "A fairy mentioned something about a council before I killed them." A shiver runs down my spine at the recollection.

Marassa's eyes widen again in surprise, a gasp escaping her lips. "The fairies are part of it as well?"

"I believe they are being used for hunting down those who are left on the side of good," I say, a grim certainty settling in my stomach as I remember Pickle telling me this, her voice filled with fear.

"Those disgusting creatures, but if you can capture them, they can be used for some dark spells, I've heard. I hope you made them suffer, did you?" she asks, a flicker of grim satisfaction in her eyes, starkly contrasting her earlier sadness.

"I did," I say with a forced smile, a hollow victory echoing in my heart. Then, the memory of Pickle curled up into a ball, her small body trembling as the fairies tried to hurt her, and the ugly purple bruises they left on her delicate skin flash in my mind. This causes the smile to leave my face instantly, a wave of protective anger washing over me as the sound of their cruel laughter echoes in my memories. "Did they hurt someone you care about, cher?" Marassa asks, her voice softening with empathy, looking at me in understanding.

I can't seem to answer her, the memory still too raw, so Freya takes over, her voice firm with conviction, "Yes, they did, my sister made them pay."

"Good, and I hope whoever they hurt is okay," she says, her eyes showing genuine concern.

"They are, thank you," Freya replies, a small, grateful smile gracing her lips.

With her look of understanding, the woman moves gracefully behind the counter, her hands reaching for the book I enquired about. She places it on the polished wooden surface before me and offers a reassuring smile. "Of course, you can purchase this book from me. I wish I could provide you with something more substantial that can truly aid your journey, but every little bit might prove helpful in its way."

"Thank you," I reply, feeling a flicker of gratitude amidst the uncertainty that still clings to me. Turning to Marassa, I pose a question that lingers in my mind, a desperate plea for guidance. "Do you think we'll be able to uncover any other books that might help us understand our powers better?"

She considers my words, her gaze distant as if searching through old memories. Standing behind the counter, she takes a deep breath, a sigh escaping her lips before responding. "You might be able to find something, but a few years back, a group swept through this city with a singular, destructive purpose." Her voice drops to a near whisper at the end, a shadow of pain crossing her features.

She starts to explain and takes a deep breath, the air in the shop seeming to grow heavy with unspoken sorrow before she continues, "They began to buy all the significant texts, the ones that held knowledge of our kind. Before we realised their intentions, they gathered up as many books as they could find, piling them high in a local park. They lit them on fire, watching them crumble into ashes, a deliberate act of destruction meant to erase our history and the ability to fight back." Her voice trembles with a mixture of grief and anger. "If any important volumes are left, I can assure you they won't be on display for anyone. And since you're outsiders, I fear that most sellers won't trust you enough to part with their precious books."

Her words hang in the air like a heavy cloud, extinguishing the sliver of hope I have held on to since entering the shop and leaving a bitter taste of disappointment in my mouth.

"God damn it," I blurt out, my frustration spilling over before I can contain it, the weight of her words pressing down on me. I glance at Freya, who mirrors my concern, and her usual optimism momentarily dims.

"I'm sorry to deliver such grim news, ma cherie," Marassa says, her voice softening with empathy, her eyes still showing genuine sorrow. "The only option I can think of is to ask around discreetly for you. If I manage to find someone willing to sell, I can help arrange a meeting."

I weigh her offer in my mind, my hope battling with the inherent risk. The prospect of seeking out the books we desperately need is enticing yet fraught with danger, the fear of exposure a constant companion. Freya's voice breaks through my troubled thoughts with a hopeful suggestion, her unwavering optimism shining through. "What will it hurt?"

I can't help but feel a deep unease settle in my stomach, a cold premonition whispering of potential consequences. "More people finding out where we are," I say firmly, my tone resolute, the fear of attracting unwanted attention a tangible weight in my chest. The last thing we need is to attract unwanted attention to ourselves in this precarious situation.

"The whole of the underworld knows where we are now. What's one more person going to change things? Anyway, we don't have to give our address, just a phone number," Freya states, making a very good point that chips away at my resistance.

"Fine," I say, a sigh of reluctant agreement escaping my lips. Then, the woman hands me a piece of paper and a pen. I take them, my hand trembling slightly as I scribble down my mobile number and hand them back to her.

"Are you sure you want to do this for us?" I ask with a mixture of gratitude and lingering suspicion.

"Yes, I am willing to help protect the daughters of Elspeth Harper," she says confidently, a genuine warmth in her eyes that finally eases some of my apprehension.

"Thank you."

"I have one question," Freya says as she shifts her weight, clutching her bags tightly, a hint of suspicion in her voice.

"Ask away; what is it, dear?" Marassa replies, her voice warm and inviting, a hint of curiosity sparkling in her eyes.

Freya takes a deep breath, her curiosity piqued. "If no one is willing to keep their books on display anymore, why are you?" she inquires, her tone laced with genuine concern.

Marassa chuckles softly, a knowing smile dancing across her lips, a hint of mischief in her eyes. "Ahhh, but that's just it, ma cherie! I didn't display them for all to see. I actually cast a special glamour over the collection, so only someone with the sight can perceive them for what they truly are." She leans closer, lowering her voice conspiratorially. "Those who came for the books were shifters, after all."

Freya's eyes widen, absorbing this new information with a gasp of surprise. "Oh, okay, so shifters can't see everything magical, then?" she asks, her voice reflecting the surprise that mirrors in her expression.

"Exactly! They are limited in that respect," Marassa explains, her gaze growing serious, but still with a hint of sadness in her eyes. "This is one of the reasons some packs harbour distrust towards other magical groups and choose to resort to violence instead of seeking understanding."

Freya nods slowly, her mind racing with implications. This valuable knowledge can reshape our approach, especially since we might encounter shifters who can pose a threat at some point, as our mother did. A shiver of apprehension runs down my spine at the thought.

We paid for the book, and to my surprise, it turned out to be more expensive than I had anticipated, costing us one hundred dollars. While this is quite a hefty sum, a small gasp escapes my lips at the total. I remind myself that when it comes to the safety and well-being of my family, no price is too high. The woman at the shop mentioned she had given us a slight discount, a gesture of kindness that I deeply appreciated. After completing our purchase, the heavy book felt significant in my hands, so we decided to explore the local food scene. It would give us a chance to unwind a bit, let the tension ease from our shoulders, and discuss the pressing issues raised by the book and what Marassa told us.

Catherine M. Clark

Chapter 5

A Taste of Doubt

We managed to find a small, cosy eatery just a stone's throw away, perfect for grabbing a bite to eat. The air inside is thick with the comforting aroma of simmering tomatoes, garlic, and a hint of something sweet, like cinnamon. Sunlight streams through the lace-curtain windows, illuminating the rough-hewn wooden tables and the mismatched collection of vintage pictures adorning the brick walls. The low hum of conversation mingles with the rhythmic clatter of silverware against ceramic plates. Freya, with her adventurous spirit, decides she wants to try a Po'boy sandwich—the way the crispy fried shrimp spills out from the crusty baguette doesn't sit well with me, and frankly, it looks like my worst culinary nightmare. I decide to stick with something simpler and go for a hearty chicken jambalaya because of my deep-seated aversion to anything that once swam.

As I dig into my dish, the complex flavours of the seasoned rice, tender chicken, and a medley of vegetables dance on my palate, momentarily distracting me from the weight of our earlier conversation. "What do you want to do now?" I ask Freya after swallowing a mouthful.

"What do you mean?" she replies, her brow furrowing in confusion as she pushes a stray strand of hair behind her ear.

I feel a twinge of dismay as I explain, "If we are to believe her, then we won't find any books."

Freya shrugs, seemingly undeterred. "We found a book at her place, so you never know; we might stumble upon another one. Also, since we're here, we should take advantage of it and see what else we can find. You never know what might be useful to us down the line. I've been meticulously recording shop names and what they sell on my phone, which will make ordering supplies easier," she says, her tone brimming with optimism, starkly contrasting my growing pessimism.

I sigh, reluctantly acknowledging her point. "I guess if what she said is true, then I'll have to delve deeper into estate sales, garage sales, and antique stores—like the ones I'm planning on visiting this Tuesday. I'm really hoping that coming here would guarantee we'd find an old grimoire," I muse, taking another hearty mouthful of my jambalaya, savouring the comforting warmth that spreads through me.

"Sorry about that," she replies, a sympathetic look in her eyes. "I'm sure you'll find one eventually. But if you think about it, we might not even need a grimoire, especially since we seem to manage just fine without casting any spells," she points out, offering a valid perspective that I can't ignore.

For a moment, I consider her words, weighing the practicality of our current situation against my hopes of uncovering magical tomes. "Yeah, I guess, but runes are a form of spell; they have really helped us. There must be so much we don't know that a spell can help protect us," I say.

"I'm sure there is a solution somewhere," Freya replies, her voice tinged with a hint of annoyance as she looks at me. "Just try not to fixate on it too much; if you do, you'll end up stressing yourself out. And believe me, that will lead to mistakes you definitely want to avoid."

"Fine, but I'm still going to search for answers," I state resolutely, my determination shining through.

"That's perfectly fine. Just remember to keep it in balance. By the way, while we're here, do you need to pick up any books for *The*

MoonTree?" Freya inquires, her tone softening a bit, making it clear she's trying to redirect the conversation.

"Not really," I reply, shaking my head slightly. "I managed to gather everything I needed from my old contacts back when I was at the National Library. Did I mention that my former boss reached out to me? She asked if I'm willing to do some restoration work for her if I have a secure, insured place to operate. She mentioned that ever since I left, she hasn't been able to find anyone as competent as I was, and she's currently facing a backlog of old books and manuscripts needing restoration."

"No, you didn't tell me that! That's fantastic news. You loved working there," Freya responds, her eyes lighting up with enthusiasm.

"It is! I did. But if I decide to take her up on this offer, some changes will need to be implemented. For starters, I'd have to install a robust lock on the basement door and secure proper insurance to cover it as a workspace, especially considering that some of these books are valued at astronomical prices. As part of the insurance, no one else can access that space. Well, as long as no one finds out others have gone down there. My other option might be to construct a studio with top-notch security," I elaborate, sharing my thoughts and concerns with my sister.

"I'm completely fine with whatever you choose. I'm sure Maya will feel the same way. You can start with the basement for now. We have enough funds at our disposal now, so if you really want to move towards building that studio, the option is definitely there. My only concern would be if we ever faced an attack; what if the studio got caught in the crossfire?" Freya says, momentarily lifting my spirits until her words about potential danger flicker doubts in my mind.

"Thank you for your support. It's genuinely something I would love to pursue. I still can't wrap my head around the fact that we sold our old house for just over six hundred thousand dollars. If I can get Duncan to draft some plans and cost estimates, I will definitely want to ensure that you and Maya approve before committing to anything," I explain, feeling a mix of anxiety and excitement about the next steps.

"Sis, we divided the money from the sale, so we each ended up with around two hundred thousand dollars after the agent took her fees. I'm confident you'll have enough, so there's really no need for you to seek our approval," Freya points out wisely, making a valid argument that I can't easily dismiss.

"That's true, but I'm still not comfortable making any significant changes to our property without either of you on board," I state firmly, crossing my arms in determination.

"Fine, Miss Stubborn," Freya replies with an exasperated shake of her head, a playful smirk tugging at her lips.

"Me, the stubborn one? I think you need to take a good look in the mirror," I shoot back, unable to suppress a smile at our familiar banter. However, the warmth of the moment soon dissipates as a prickling sensation dances across my skin, like unseen fingers tracing my spine. The feeling of being watched intensifies, bringing with it a faint, metallic tang in the air.

"What is it?" Freya asks, her brow furrowing as she catches the sudden shift in my demeanour.

"I feel like someone's watching us again," I murmur, my eyes darting around the bustling restaurant, taking in the lively atmosphere full of the soft clinking of cutlery and the murmur of conversations.

As I scan the room, I observe the various tables where diners are engrossed in their meals, their laughter and chatter creating a comforting hum. Yet, just as I begin to relax, something catches my eye—a flicker of movement in the shadows of a corner booth in the restaurant. I turn my head sharply in that direction. There, nestled in a secluded booth across from us, sits a lone woman. Her beauty is arresting, almost unnerving, with sharp, angular features and waves of dark hair that seem to absorb the light. But her eyes hold me captive – an unnervingly intense gaze that feels like it can see straight through me. Freya must have noticed her, too, as I can see the curiosity mirrored in her expression. The atmosphere shifts subtly, the jovial noise around us seeming to dim as the weight of that gaze settles heavily in the air.

"Wow, she is stunning," Freya exclaims, her eyes practically sparkling as she glances toward the woman sitting across the restaurant. I shoot her a look that clearly says, *'What the hell are you thinking?'*

"She may be beautiful, but she's staring directly at us," I remark, trying to rein in my sister's enthusiasm.

"I mean, I would stare at us too if I were her," Freya replies with a playful glint in her eye, unabashed by the attention.

"Seriously, put it back in your knickers, sis," I say, shaking my head at her once more, a mix of exasperation and amusement at her boldness. *Honestly, sometimes I think Pickle has more sense than she does.*

Freya's expression shifts; a mischievous grin spreads across her face. "Maybe I should go over there and see what she wants," she suggested, her demeanour taking on the predatory quality of a lioness ready to pounce on her unsuspecting prey.

"No, don't," I warn, firmly grabbing her arm to prevent her from making any hasty moves. "She might be dangerous."

"Only to my heart," Freya says, her tone light but her gaze unwavering. "Not everyone is an enemy, sis."

I can't help but roll my eyes. "They pretty much are, considering we have no way of telling who's magical and who isn't."

Freya shrugs, undeterred. "I'm going by the rule, *if they aren't attacking us, then they aren't an enemy*," she reiterates, still watching the woman, who hasn't diverted her gaze. The mysterious lady now wears a subtle smile—a soft curve of her lips that lights up her eyes, as they sparkle, making her look even more stunning.

"Well, that seems like a ridiculous rule to me," I reply, shooting my sister a look that mixes scepticism with concern.

"I can't see myself meeting anyone in Luna Falls, so I need to keep my options open when I head out if I'm ever going to find a date," Freya counters, her voice tinged with a hint of desperation.

"I know, just be careful; I'm sure you'll find someone. What about Jenny? She's flirted with you a few times now," I suggest, trying to offer a semblance of hope.

"She does flirt, but it's clear she's only into guys, trust me," Freya says, her tone laced with disappointment as she fiddles with the edge of the tablecloth.

"Sis, you will find someone eventually. I'm just not convinced this woman is the one for you," I say, my attention drifting back to the booth where the woman is still seated, her gaze still fixed on us.

"I know you're probably right," Freya admits, her voice becoming soft as she sighs. "But part of the excitement is in the hunt, isn't it?"

Once we have finished our meals, I stand up and walk over to the main desk, where the waitresses input orders on a small screen. I decide to pay the bill immediately instead of waiting for them to bring it to our table. I can feel Freya's reluctance to leave without saying something to our uninvited admirer, but I manage to coax her out of the restaurant.

We step back onto the bustling street, I take a deep breath of the crisp air, which carries the faint scent of river water and fried dough. The sounds of jazz music spill out from open doorways, competing with the lively chatter of tourists and locals alike. Wrought-iron balconies drip with vibrant flowers, and the colourful facades of the buildings seem to lean into each other, creating a sense of vibrant chaos. We begin our quest down Decatur Street, searching the many shops for any magical oddities that might catch our eye. I pull out my phone as we walk to update Maya on our progress, and she confirms that everything is still fine back home, alleviating some of my worries.

Freya is in her element when we enter each interesting store; she bustles through the aisles as she enthusiastically continues to acquire supplies. Her phone is constantly buzzing with notes and reminders about everything we might need in the future. Among her list of finds is a quaint shop where we have previously purchased items essential for casting runes and preparing for the full moon ritual. Freya instantly gets on with the shop's owner; their exchanges are filled with laughter and familiarity. Meanwhile, I feel a pang of discomfort in the pit of my stomach—a sensation that something isn't quite right. It's as if the air is thick with an unseen pressure, and I can't shake the feeling that we are still being watched.

With a sigh, I turn my attention away from the shelves full of strange items and glance out the window, hoping to spot anyone lingering nearby or peering curiously into the store. My instincts are on high alert, even as Freya becomes absorbed in her shopping spree and, of course, flirting.

Eventually, we stumble upon a store that I'm interested in, as it's overflowing with books. Towering shelves, packed so tightly it seems the spines might burst, lined the walls, their leather and cloth covers whispering tales of forgotten times. The air hangs heavy with the comforting scent of aged paper and the faintest hint of dust, and a single shaft of sunlight illuminates swirling motes as it pierces through a high window. As I peruse the spines, feeling an exhilarating pull toward the worn covers and yellowed pages, I notice Freya skimming the titles with an air of indifference. I'm engrossed, fully immersed, while she seems to wander aimlessly among the shelves, her boredom obvious.

After about thirty minutes of scouring the bookshelves, I feel a presence approaching. A melodious, captivating voice breaks through my concentration. "Ladies, how's the shopping going?"

Turning toward the sound, I first glimpse Freya's face. Her

expression is one of disbelief; her jaw drops slightly, and she looks utterly astonished. My confusion quickly morphs into a jolt of unease as I recognise the strikingly beautiful woman before us—the same one who had been watching us intently in the restaurant earlier. *Great. Just great. Like I need another complication in my life.*

"What do you want?" I shoot out, irritation simmering beneath the surface as fear creeps in.

"Sis, be nice," Freya interjects, casting me a disapproving glare that suggests she is more intrigued than defensively inclined. It's obvious she finds this woman stunning, and it annoys me—this enchanting stranger can easily be our adversary.

"I want to introduce myself. I'm Madiya, but you can call me Madi. I assure you, I'm not a threat to you," she says, her eyes flicking between us as she gauges our reactions.

Now, it's Freya's turn to appear wary instead of infatuated. Under her breath, she curses softly, "Damn it," the words barely audible but enough to entice a soft laugh from Madi. Her hearing is astoundingly sharp for someone so graceful, and I feel a tingle of surprise at the situation unfolding before us.

Madi's gaze shifts back to Freya, a playful smile forming. "I would be willing to go on a date sometime, Freya." Her voice carries an effortless charm, and I can see Freya's expression shift to one of delight, like a cat that has just licked cream from a bowl.

"How the hell do you know my sister's name?" I demand, my protective instincts kicking in. Simultaneously, I begin to access the magic within me, a familiar hum building beneath my skin, prepared for any escalation this exchange might take.

Madi raises a hand, palms outward in a gesture of peace. "I wouldn't do that," she replies, her demeanour calm yet slightly teasing. My suspicion flares—can she sense my power, just as Marassa could? If she possesses that ability, it can open up an entirely different realm of complications. Being able to detect magical beings is a skill I consider immensely valuable yet undeniably troubling.

"Full disclosure, ladies," Madi begins, her tone a blend of seriousness and amusement. "My boss sent me here specifically to keep an eye on you and ensure that you remain safe while you're in his city." She leans in slightly, her dark eyes glinting with intrigue. "I'm not quite sure why he is interested in witches from out of town when we have local practitioners in abundance."

Curiosity nibbles at my mind, and I can't help but ask, "Who's your boss?"

Madi meets my gaze with casual confidence. "Papa Legba," she responds as if it's the most normal thing in the world.

I blink in confusion, processing the name that feels more like folklore than reality. I scoff, then say, "I don't understand," my voice betraying my disbelief.

"What don't you understand, Reya?" Madi asks me, using my name so familiarly that it sends a wave of unease through me.

"Papa Legba is a myth. He isn't real," I insist, my skepticism growing. I wonder if Madi is some eccentric who wants to keep Freya firmly in her sights, away from whatever mischief lies ahead.

But Madi's expression doesn't falter; instead, it turns serious. "He's no myth. He's very real, and he would like to meet you. He specifically mentioned that he means you no harm and that he's eager to meet the daughters of Elspeth Harper," she declares, her words hanging in the air and leaving both me and Freya momentarily speechless.

Panic surges through me. All I want is to escape this city as fast as possible, to retreat to the safety of the familiar. Yet, I can feel Freya's determined gaze upon me, silently conveying that leaving isn't an option she is considering.

"I would love to meet him," Freya says, her excitement bubbling to the surface as she leans forward, her eyes shining with eagerness. "Will you be coming with us?"

Madi smiles, a playful twinkle in her eye. "Of course I will be; I need to make sure I get your number," she replies, winking at my sister. Her light-hearted demeanour contrasted sharply with the weight of our conversation, but it only added to the worry and fear swirling in my mind. Seriously, Freya? *Now is not the time for flirting. Though I guess for her, any time is flirting time.*

I feel a wave of nausea wash over me, nothing to do with her clumsy flirting, but rather from the deep-seated anxiety gnawing at my gut. I hope my magic reacts like it does with Jacob, so I can find an excuse to get out of here—my mind races with the implications of encountering Papa Legba.

As far as I understand, he is a Loa, a god who travelled from Africa, summoned into existence by the prayers of enslaved people seeking protection for their loved ones in the afterlife. This history looms large in my thoughts, especially after all our research about New Orleans and its rich tapestry of magic and spirituality. If he truly exists, the stakes are immense, and I fear we will be utterly defenceless against him.

"Freya, I really think we should turn back. I can't shake this feeling; I genuinely don't like where this is heading," I say, desperation creeping into my voice.

But Freya, ever the optimist, has other plans. "He assures me he doesn't mean you any harm. He might always be interested in bringing new talent into his fold, but recruit you? It's not like that," she counters confidently.

"What do you mean by recruiting us?" I blurt out, my pulse quickening with a mix of fear and confusion.

"Oops, I guess that was a bit too much information," Madi replies, looking flustered. "He's never specifically mentioned wanting to recruit you. Traditionally, he recruits magical beings that won't be missed, but lately, he's taken an interest in others, even a human woman," she reveals, her gaze darting nervously between us as if fearing she'd revealed too much.

"Sis, maybe meeting him won't be such a bad idea," Freya suggests, her voice taking on a thoughtful tone. "If he is as powerful as those stories make him out to be, he might have valuable insights or aid to offer us."

While I want to believe Freya's perspective, a troubling realisation hits me. "Wait, doesn't Papa Legba have control over demons?" I ask, an uneasy knot tightening in my stomach.

As the words leave my mouth, I watch Freya's expression shift from contemplation to alarm. "Oh, I completely forgot about that part. Isn't he traditionally seen as on the side of evil?" she questions as she shifts away from Madi very slightly, looking at Madi in a new light.

"Yes, he does command demons, but it's not quite as simple as that; he creates his own demons, they aren't like the ones from the underworld," Madi interjects, her tone blending caution and conviction. "He offers a service—demons operate on the whims of those who seek power, fame or wealth. He never forces anyone into a deal; it's always a matter of choice for the weak humans."

Her comment about humans being weak doesn't escape my notice and sparks a burning question I can't suppress. "So, what exactly are you, then?" I ask, curiosity mixed with an edge of apprehension.

Madi hesitates, glancing at Freya with a look that screams for discretion, before turning her eyes back to me. "I'm a crossroads demon. I don't grant wishes anymore. I'm now more of a guardian protecting this city and those he wishes to meet with," she confesses softly.

A lump forms in my throat as I process her revelation. My gaze shifts to Freya, who is now visibly uncomfortable. She picks at her nails as uncertainty flickers in her eyes.

"Are you two willing to meet my boss, or would you prefer not to? If you choose to refuse, I won't impose. I understand if my presence is unwelcome now," Madi says, her scrutiny landing heavily on Freya, who has lapsed into an uneasy silence. The atmosphere thickens with tension as the weight of our decision looms over us.

Chapter 6

Crossroads and Consequences

The prospect of her leaving and the two of us escaping this city seems enticing. As I contemplate it, Freya surprises me with a light-hearted remark. "Fine, take us to your leader," she says, a chuckle escaping her lips as though she is sharing a private joke only she understands. *I think she sometimes enjoys these brushes with the bizarre a little too much.*

"Are you really sure about this, sis?" I question, my concern lacing my voice as I shift my gaze toward her.

Freya's expression turns serious as she leans towards me, her voice dropping to a conspiratorial whisper. "So far, we've faced attacks from demons and reapers. What can it hurt to see if we can persuade some demons to join our side?" Despite her low tone, I feel Madi's attention sharpen, like a predator sensing prey.

"Do you genuinely think we can trust demons?" I ask, my scepticism evident as memories of our previous encounters churn in my mind, bringing with them the acrid smell of sulphur and the chilling echo of demonic growls.

Freya rolls her eyes at me, feigning disappointment. "I'm surprised at you, sis, we already trust a demon. Or have you conveniently forgotten about the hellhound we left with our sister to protect her?" As she spoke, I noticed Madi's eyebrows arch in surprise, her interest piqued by the mention of the hellhound.

"Wait, hold on. You have a *hellhound,* and it didn't turn on you?" Madi asks, disbelief evident in her tone.

I feel momentarily stunned, caught off guard by the realisation that Freya is right. My Beastie, a creature from the depths of hell, is indeed a demon, and I have come to rely on him for my and my family's safety. Maybe Freya has a point after all; *not all demons are inherently evil.* "Yes, we do have a hellhound. I accidentally summoned it when I was trying to lift someone's spirits. I guess the only thing to say is, *take us to your leader,*" I reply, my voice steadier now, and I can't help but chuckle, a nervous sound that mirrors Freya's earlier amusement at using the phrase.

"Well, it seems you are not just your average run of the mill witches after all," Madi remarks, a hint of admiration breaking through her earlier guarded demeanour. "Follow me, then, ladies," she instructs, turning on her stylish heels and striding confidently toward the exit of the store.

We hesitate for a moment, exchanging glances of uncertainty, but as Madi steps out into the bustling street beyond and the sounds of a distant saxophone drift into the store on the humid air, we silently agree and follow her. With a mix of curiosity and apprehension, we venture out into the unknown.

As we step out onto the street, Madi confidently leads us toward a narrow alleyway. I pause at the entrance, a sense of unease settling over me like a damp shroud. The air here is still, carrying the faint, unpleasant tang of stale garbage and something else... something and earthy. "I don't like this," I say firmly, grabbing my sister's arm to prevent her from following Madi into the encroaching darkness of the alley.

Madi turns, her expression shifting from anticipation to mild annoyance. "You can't get to where we need to go by standing out on the street. The place doesn't have any doors," she explains, her voice steady yet urgent. "And we must ensure that no humans see us when we vanish." The word 'vanish' adds a chill to the knot of anxiety twisting in my stomach, making my breath catch in my throat.

Despite my trepidation, I can't entirely grasp what Madi means about our destination. However, her mention of being unseen by humans resonates deeply with me. Swallowing my fear, I reluctantly step into the alleyway, my sister trailing behind me.

The alley is noticeably cooler than the sun-drenched street, the air thick with the scent of damp asphalt and lingering city smells—a strange mix of exhaust fumes and blooming jasmine. As we move deeper into the shadows, the brick walls on either side seem to close in, and I feel an odd sense of claustrophobia begin to wrap around me. Eventually, we reach a small alcove that offers some degree of protection from the prying eyes of the outside world.

"Okay, what now?" I ask, my voice slightly shaky. Madi turns to face us, her demeanour transforming completely. A broad smile breaks across her face, a flash of something wild and powerful in her eyes. In this moment, I feel a chill run up my spine—a signal that something extraordinary and possibly dangerous is about to unfold.

Without warning, Madi rolls her shoulders back with captivating, graceful fluidity. Suddenly, her back erupts with large, magnificent wings that unfurl majestically at her sides. They are a breathtaking sight—glistening in the low light, their texture reminiscent of my favourite Beastie's soft bat-like ears, which I'm obsessed with. I wonder momentarily if her wings feel just as lovely if I trace the intricate veining of her bat-like wings with my eyes as they open to their full span.

Freya is visibly enchanted, her eyes wide with awe as she takes in Madi's stunning transformation. When Madi extends her hands towards us, Freya doesn't hesitate for even a moment; she reaches out and slips her left hand into Madi's right hand, an eager expression illuminating her face.

Madi's smile grows wider at Freya's reaction, but when she turns her gaze to me and shakes her hand, a flicker of hesitation washes over me. I feel a whirlwind of emotions—curiosity, fear, and uncertainty swirling in my mind. *Well, this is certainly one way to travel. Hope she has good travel insurance.* My instincts urge me to trust Madi, so I finally take her hand, my grip tentative and trembling, apprehensive about whatever comes next.

The instant my fingers intertwine with hers, the alleyway seems to dissolve into nothingness. Darkness envelopes us like a thick fog, pressing in from all sides. For a fleeting moment, I feel weightless, as though we are suspended in an endless void. Suddenly, flashes of light begin to bloom around us—glimpses of busy streets, towering buildings, and then a fleeting sight of a graveyard, its stones weathered and solemn.

Before I can fully process the chaotic sights or let panic take hold, we are abruptly thrust into a room. The stark shift leaves me gasping for breath. Freya and I stumble, instinctively leaning against each other for support as we regain our balance.

"I'm sorry," Madi says, her tone apologetic yet reassuring. "The first time travelling through the shadows can be disorienting. You'll feel fine in a second." We exchange a bewildered glance, still trying to steady ourselves from the strange journey that brought us to this space.

"That was weird," Freya remarks breathlessly, confusion lining her features. "I didn't think the darkness would ever end." I open my mouth to ask her what she means, wondering if she hadn't seen the same fleeting images I had, but I'm abruptly interrupted by a voice that lingers in the air, full of promise and intrigue.

"Well now, welcome on in," a deep, resonant voice booms, with a pronounced Southern drawl that wraps itself around the words like a warm blanket on a chilly night. The moment I regain my balance, I turn to find the source.

As I turn, the dimly lit bar envelops me. It's nothing like the sleek, pulsing lounges my sisters favour – all polished surfaces and vibrant noise.

This place breathes history; dark wood panelling absorbs the low light, and faded photographs cling to the walls, hinting at forgotten faces. The air itself feels heavy, layered with the scents of old timber, ghosting pipe tobacco, and spilt liquor's faint, sweet decay. A slow blues melody, unearthed from decades past, snakes through the room, creating a strangely hypnotic, almost sepulchral calm.

Then, my gaze snags on a figure commanding an open booth. He's an immediate paradox. Death seems to have sculpted him; dark skin pulls drum-tight over high cheekbones, outlining the stark architecture of his skull with unnerving precision. He has the haunting quality of a perfectly preserved cadaver, yet radiates a potent gravity – a stillness suggesting immense age and resilience, like a weathered monolith defying time.

And then he smiles. The shift is electric, reshaping the harsh lines into a startling, almost predatory handsomeness. I feel the baffling pull of his presence, magnified by his attire: an impeccably tailored, old-world suit and a polished top hat perched jauntily on his head. He seems less a patron steeped in the bar's nostalgia and more a fragment of time itself, momentarily paused in the smoky light.

"Bloody hell," Freya gasps, breaking the spell of silence that has enwrapped us since we arrived.

My eyes shot over to her, annoyance flooding my expression. I nudge her gently yet firmly, hoping to convey the urgency of silence. *Seriously, Freya? Show some respect. This guy might be a god, for crying out loud.* What is she thinking? Did she want to provoke a possible god? This is unreal; part of me clings to the hope that I will soon awaken from this bizarre dream, realising we haven't even set off for New Orleans yet.

"Come on over here now, chère. Have a seat," the man—Papa Legba, the name surfaces unbidden in my mind—invites. He gestures with those unsettlingly long, bony fingers toward the plush velvet seat across from him. His voice rolls out low and slow, a deliberate Southern drawl where each word sounds steeped in time, like fine old whiskey left to age.

With a mix of trepidation and curiosity, we approach and carefully place our bags on the floor next to the table—thankfully, we haven't lost them in the void getting here. We slid into the booth, each movement full of an electric tension. I deliberately chose to position myself first, settling in between Freya and this mysterious figure, instinctively wanting to protect my sister in case the situation turns sinister.

Clearing my throat, I decide to cut through the veil of uncertainty. "Why do you want to see us?" The question hangs in the air, sharp and clear.

Before Papa Legba could respond, Madi, whom I'd almost forgotten in my focus on the strange man, spoke up. "I should leave y'all be. Call if you need me."

"Now hold on there, Madi darlin'. You stay right here with us," Papa Legba insists, his tone firm yet surprisingly gentle as he gestures for her to join him at his side. Her startled expression is fleeting, vanishing as quickly as she complies. I watch, captivated, as her magnificent wings fold seamlessly into her back, disappearing as if dissolving into smoke. The sight is breathtaking, a stark reminder of the otherworldly reality I've stumbled into.

"Now then," he continues, turning his gaze back to me. "To answer your question, Reya Seraphina Harper. I wanted to meet the daughters of Elspeth Harper. The ones Hec— *ahem* —the ones Cat seems to think are gonna save us all." His ancient eyes twinkle, his voice rumbling with amusement at his near slip-up.

I'm stunned. Not only does he know my full name and our mother's, but he's also mentioned Cat, the enigmatic woman from my dreams. That he almost let slip a different name—*Hec?*—feels significant, unsettling confirmation that 'Cat' might just be a convenient disguise. "You… you know Cat?" I manage, trying to keep my voice steady.

"Course I do, child," he replies, his voice rich with familiarity, carrying a hint of nostalgia like the warm crackle of an old vinyl record. "Known that woman a *long* time. She can be awful serious sometimes, y'know? Used to make it my mission, tryin' to coax a little fun outta her. But lookin' back," he pauses, stroking his chin thoughtfully, "I reckon she had her reasons to stay wound so tight. Maybe more reasons than I gave her credit for at the time."

"What do you mean by that?" I probe, curiosity growing like a flame in my chest.

He sighs, a deep, resonant sound carrying the weight of his words, like the mournful cry of a distant train whistle in the night. "She knew them attacks was comin', child. Knew it long before they ever got here. Could feel that trouble brewin' on the wind, clear as day." He shakes his head slowly. "But even knowin' all she knew, wasn't much she could do to turn things aside, not without breakin' bigger rules than she dared."

"Cost her, though," he adds, his voice dropping lower. "Cost her somethin' fierce. Led to what looked like her end, for a time. Now…" He leans forward slightly, his ancient eyes holding mine. "Now, she's lyin' low. Still somewhere tryin' to wrestle her own story straight, y'see? Still tryin' to steer things, even if her grand plans ain't quite panned out the way she reckoned they would."

"So, she's a ghost now?" I ask, my brow furrowing as I try to comprehend what he was saying. I find it difficult to understand him with his strong southern drawl.

"That's a very human way of lookin' at it, darlin'," he replies, a faint glimmer of what might be intrigue sparking in his ancient eyes. "What's left of her now, well, that's her soul. Her spirit." He leans back slightly, steepling his long fingers. "See, most times, when her kind-the Powers, the old gods, whatever name you got for 'em—when they used to meet their end, they just… *poof.* Gone. Winked right outta existence entirely."

"But," he continues, his drawl thoughtful, "then they started… well, *mixin'* with their own Creations. Started matin' with you humans. And somethin' fundamental changed." He taps a long finger on the table for emphasis. "Seems like gettin' that close, tanglin' up life that way with the beings they fashioned, it gave their own spirits… *weight*. Anchored 'em somehow. Gave 'em souls that *stick*. So now, when they pass on—the ones who mixed their blood with yours—'stead of just vanishin', they linger. Stick around awhile, much like what y'all might call a ghost." He shakes his head slowly. "Curious thing, ain't it? That kind of bond, that connection born from gods lovin' their own handiwork… Somethin' I won't never understand firsthand, mind you. That sort of creatin', that tanglin' up… it ain't somethin' I was built for."

Chapter 7

Echoes of the Past

The complexity of what he is sharing confuses me. I feel I should be a little repulsed by the implications, yet a strange sensation of denial washes over me. I decide to let it pass. "I understand what you mean about Cat being a bit too serious. She's always been tight-lipped with me, refusing to share anything of substance."

"That's 'cause she made a mistake once, a bad one," Papa Legba begins, his voice steady now, serious. "She was honest with a young girl when she shouldn't have been. Been carryin' the weight of that mistake ever since, feelin' responsible for how it all turned out. Ain't surprised she's holdin' back certain truths from y'all; the *whole* truth... well, that could bring a world of hurt down on you." He pauses, looking thoughtfully at Freya. "Still, I reckon it's time you heard at least a little piece of it."

Finally seeming to regain her composure, Freya straightens her posture, that familiar stubbornness surfacing. "And what truth is that?" she inquires, eyes narrowing with curiosity.

"Did you know," Papa Legba asks, his gaze sweeping between us, "you were born right on the stroke of midnight? With a big ol' blood moon hangin' in the sky, castin' its eerie light down on everything?" He watches our reactions, a subtle smile playing on his lips as if he's relishing the moment.

"Why is that important?" Freya queries, looking just as confused as I feel, both of us trying to grasp the significance.

"Ah, well now, maybe it don't seem like much at first glance, dear," he continues, his tone turning enigmatic again. "Time tends to reveal things. But did you also know there was a powerful earthquake shook the land the very night you came into this world?" He leans forward slightly. "Matter of fact, just hours after you were born, your mother and her newborn daughters… they just vanished. Into thin air."

Freya's confusion deepens. "Wait, are you implying the earthquake was *connected* to our birth? That sounds ridiculous." I mirror her disbelief, but I can't help noticing Madi's eyes widen, her entire demeanour shifting as she processes this revelation.

"Who's to say, now?" Papa Legba muses, that knowing smile back in place, like he's savouring a fine secret. "Could all be just… coincidence. But ain't it fascinatin'?"

"If you say so," I challenge, annoyance sharpening my tone. "But why is any of this *vital* to us right now?"

"Just paintin' a picture, child. A glimpse of the circumstances 'round your birth I thought you oughta know," he replies smoothly. I begin to suspect Cat isn't the only ancient being around here who enjoys playing games. So much for straightforward answers.

"Did you really just bring us here to toy with us?" Freya asks, echoing my thoughts, her voice laced with exasperation.

"No, no, that ain't my intention at all," Papa Legba insists, holding up a hand. "But I did promise Cat I wouldn't just spill *everything*, not the things that could bring trouble down on y'all directly. Still, that don't mean I can't offer up a few hints here and there. It's up to y'all to puzzle 'em out." His tone shifts then, gaining a new urgency. "Now, we got somethin' important we need to discuss."

"What might that be?" I ask, irritation still bubbling just beneath the surface.

"For the past few weeks, Madi here," he gestures towards her, a flicker of admiration in his eyes, "has been workin' mighty hard keepin' you safe. Successfully blockin' more and more demons they been sendin' after you." He looks us over. "When y'all decided to go and steal that hellhound right out from under the nose of the underworld's new boss... well, you really stirred the hornet's nest somethin' fierce. Kinda impressive, really," he adds, a chuckle rumbling in his chest, "that you all still standin' – even the human and the pixie."

"They did *what?*" Madi exclaims, shock etched plainly on her features. "These... these witches stole a *hellhound*, and they weren't instantly obliterated? How is that even possible?"

"Ah, but they ain't *just* witches, Madi darlin'," Papa Legba replies, giving me a long, meaningful look. A lightbulb goes off in my head – *this* is one of the hints he mentioned.

"Right," Madi murmurs, realisation dawning on her face as she pieces it together. "Now I understand why you were so interested."

"Wait a minute," Freya interjects, her voice sharp as she homes in on his earlier point. "Are you telling me whoever's been sending those demons after us *hasn't* stopped?"

"Lucky for y'all, we managed to keep our part in things quiet," Papa Legba says, a sly smile dancing on his lips. "So, I'm fairly certain your enemies believe *you're* the ones who took out their latest little hit squad all on your own."

Freya furrows her brow, curiosity and concern warring in her expression. "Why would you do that? Why interfere and hide it?" she asks, her voice steady but clearly sceptical.

"Because you summonin' that hellhound, Reya, well... it introduced a wrinkle none of us planned for," he explains, his tone shifting back to serious. "My original thought was to give y'all some breathin' room. Time to get used to them new powers bloomn' inside you, let you grow stronger. And I am pleased," he casts me a sidelong glance, "to see you took to your trainin' so serious." He pauses, meeting my eyes directly.

"But you got abilities inside you, child, powers you ain't even touched yet, goin' way beyond what you currently understand."

Freya frowns again, confusion clouding her face. "What do you mean, more abilities? Our mother only mentioned we might have one or two abilities, and we've already found those," she says, trying to mask her frustration. I focus intently on Papa Legba's words, searching for the hidden meanings I'm now certain are woven through everything he says.

"That kinda small thinkin' is what's holdin' you both back," Papa Legba asserts confidently, pointing a long finger right at me. "Y'all need to aim higher, especially *you*, Reya." He softens his gaze slightly as he looks towards my sister. "Freya, I reckon you'll find some surprisin' talents waitin' inside you too, in time. Same goes for Maya. But it might take y'all a bit longer to take hold of them gifts proper," he adds, his tone shifting to encouragement.

Freya crosses her arms, impatience practically radiating off her. "Could you maybe offer just a *few* hints about these other abilities we supposedly possess?" she presses, annoyance colouring her voice.

"Well now," Papa Legba begins, and for the first time, a hint of hesitation touches his voice, "truth is... I ain't exactly *sure* what else y'all might hold. See, there ain't never been nothin' quite like y'all before, not exactly. I can only make educated guesses, speculatin' based on the feel of the power I sense rollin' off you."

Freya's frustration visibly peaks. "Well, what *are* your guesses?" she demands, her eyes narrowing as if she could physically pull the information out of him.

"Mm, I think it's best I keep them notions to myself for now," he replies, that sly, mischievous smile returning to his eyes. "Tellin' y'all straight out would likely break my word to Cat. Besides," he adds, leaning back comfortably, "y'all need to find your own way, carve out your own path. That's how it works." His refusal hangs in the air, only making my irritation prickle hotter.

Unable to hold it back, I interject, "So, you're nothing like Cat. You just *hide* information instead of lying about it. Got it." The sarcastic words slip out before I can stop them. Seeing his unchanging smile, I take a breath, shifting gears and leaning forward with genuine curiosity this time. "Okay. Can I ask you something else, then?"

"Go on now, child. Ask what's on your mind," Papa Legba replies, a definite glimmer of interest lighting up his ancient eyes.

"When I first learned I could make fire," I begin, feeling both curious and anxious, "it came out purple. But lately… now the flames are black. Why did they change?" As I speak, I feel Madi's intense gaze fixed on me, her shock almost a physical presence in the air beside us.

He appears genuinely intrigued by my question. "Hm. Interesting," he muses, tilting his head slightly to the side. "Tell me, would you mind now if I placed my hand right here?" He gestures vaguely towards my forehead. "Might help me get a better feel for what exactly is stirrin' inside you, with them powers of yours," he proposes, his voice steady and calm.

I hesitate, a wave of uncertainty washing over me at the thought of letting this ancient, unnerving being touch me. Still, the need to understand outweighs my caution.

"Sure," I reply, my voice softer as I steel myself for his touch.

He moves closer, his approach deliberately slow and measured. Raising his right hand, he lets it hover just above my forehead, a clear pause giving me a final chance to pull back. I remain frozen, rooted in place, allowing him to make contact. The moment his palm presses flat against my skin, heat radiates from it, far more intense than I anticipate, sending a tingling, almost burning sensation sprawling across my forehead like electricity.

Instantly, an overwhelming energy washes through me—a charge uncannily similar to the electrifying feeling that surges through my veins whenever Jacob is near me. It's as if the core of magic within me awakens with a roar, stirring violently to life and igniting something deep and primal. A fierce heat builds, pulsating and swirling until it feels dangerously concentrated right inside my skull. Panic jolts through me, sharp and sudden, and I flinch instinctively against the overwhelming intensity. Yet, I find myself physically unable to pull away; his hand anchors me like a brand even as every instinct screams for escape.

Freya senses my distress immediately. She grasps my arm with urgent determination, trying to wrench me away from him. "Let go of her!" she demands, her voice rising sharply, mirroring the frantic worry in her eyes. It's then that I notice Madi shifting abruptly in her seat, muscles tensed as if preparing to leap across the booth to intervene.

Before anyone can react further, the very air in the room seems to tremble; the booth beneath us vibrates slightly. Papa Legba snatches his hand back as if burned, his eyes flying wide with sheer astonishment. He stares down at his trembling fingers, shaking his hand vigorously as if trying to dislodge something unseen. The enigmatic calm is shattered; the look washing over his ancient features is one of profound shock, bordering on actual fear, leaving me both bewildered and deeply unsettled.

"Sis, are you okay? Did he hurt you?" Freya's voice quivers with alarm, her eyes darting between me and Papa Legba, demanding answers.

"No," I manage, my voice tight with adrenaline, "he didn't hurt me. But whatever's inside me… it really didn't like that." My gaze stays locked on Papa Legba, whose expression remains a staggering mixture of disbelief and something that looks terrifyingly like awe.

"What is it?" I press him, desperate for any kind of explanation, but he remains utterly silent, his mouth hanging slightly open as he seemingly struggles to process what just occurred. He appears rooted to the spot, stunned into stillness by whatever realisation has struck him.

Concern creases my forehead. I tear my gaze from him to my sister, who looks equally troubled, then to Madi, whose protective anxiety now shifts entirely onto me. "What did you *do* to him?" she demands, her tone sharp, accusatory, laced with irritation.

"I didn't do *anything*," I shoot back defensively, "at least, not that I know of!"

After what feels like an eternity of thick, charged silence, Papa Legba finally speaks. His voice, when it comes, carries a resonance, a weight it hadn't held before. "She didn't do nothin' to me, Madi." He slowly lowers his hand, his wide eyes finally focusing back on us, though they seem distant. "I'm just… stunned. By what I just witnessed. What I *felt*." He takes a slow breath. "Seems our friend Cat done surpassed not just her hopes… but all our expectations as well." His words hang heavy in the air, laden with intrigue and undeniable wonder.

As I try to process his earlier statement, the confusion only tightens around me like a shroud. "Now, 'bout what you was askin'," Papa Legba continues, his expression turning serious once more, "the reason that fire of yours turned black… it's 'cause you're lettin' one part of your power swamp the other." His explanation lands like another puzzle piece, but the complete picture of my intertwining abilities still eludes my grasp.

"You got two different wells of power inside you, Reya," he says, his voice steady and insistent now. "That purple fire, that's your witch side; it's finer, maybe got less raw *oomph* behind it, but it won't drain you near as fast. Let's you handle it with more care, y'see?" He pauses, studying my face intently as if gauging whether I'm following along before continuing. "Them black flames, though… they come from somethin' deeper, somethin' *older* inside you. Got way more strength, that fire does, but it's a sight harder to truly master."

We all stay quiet, sensing he hasn't finished – or at least, I desperately hope he hasn't. After a moment where he seems to collect his thoughts, he does continue. "You gotta journey *inward*, child," he says, his gaze intense. "Search deep down in your spirit 'til you find the right door to open. Most folks, untrained like, they look for answers right *here*"—he places a hand flat over his heart, a gesture heavy with meaning—"But truth is, you gotta dig deeper'n that. Go past just simple feelin's and surface notions to touch the real *heart* of all that power you hold." His words resonate deep within me, igniting a spark of urgency, a fierce determination to delve into the enigmatic shadows of my own essence and uncover what lies hidden there.

A palpable tension fills the air as he leans closer again, his gaze intense, holding both deep concern and unwavering conviction. "Your power lives in your blood, child," he begins, his voice steady yet somehow softer now, "and the biggest pool of it sits right there in your heart. But reachin' it proper, controllin' it… that takes more'n just *knowin'* it's there." He sighs lightly. "You been lucky so far, mighty lucky. But luck? Luck's a thin thread, easily snapped." His brow furrows as he speaks, a shadow of unease crossing his features, hinting at the unspoken weight behind his words. "You gotta journey deeper inside yourself, find your way back to summonin' them purple flames when you mean to."

I can't help but frown, the vagueness of his words pressing against me like a physical weight. "Okay, that's still incredibly vague. Are you going to actually share whatever else it is you saw or felt?" I press, studying his expression for any crack in his carefully constructed evasiveness.

Instead of answering directly, he shifts gears abruptly, leaning forward again. "Lemme ask you somethin'. A favour, maybe?" he asks, a sudden urgency entering his tone that catches me completely off guard.

A spark of distrust flares within me—favours from beings like him rarely come without a steep price. "And what, exactly, would this favour cost me?" I inquire, narrowing my eyes.

He seems entirely unfazed by my scepticism. "Y'all 'bout to meet a young woman, very soon now. And I need you to place your trust in her when you do." His voice grows earnest. "Somethin' 'bout her spirit… it calls to me, y'see. Feel this powerful need deep down to keep her safe. Right now, I'm searchin' for a particular weapon, somethin' that'll help her fight the darkness she's bound to face down the road. When I get my hands on the right tool for her," he locks his gaze onto mine, "I need *you* to pour some of your own power into it. Lend it your strength. Make it formidable enough for her human hands to wield proper." As he speaks, his eyes sparkle with an undeniable conviction, betraying the depth of his intentions.

"Who *exactly* are we about to meet?" Freya's voice cuts in, sharp and laced with irritation, clearly fed up with his relentless vagueness.

"Y'all find out soon enough," Papa Legba replies, his voice deliberately weaving that same cryptic thread Cat often used for delicate matters. My mind spins with questions, each more confounding than the last, but one thought surges forward, demanding attention with an urgency that drowns out the rest.

"I barely know how to handle the power I have *now*!" I exclaim, frustration bubbling up despite my efforts to contain it. "How do you expect me to just… perform some specific magic to infuse a weapon? I have no idea how to even begin!"

"You'll know what to do when the time comes, child," he replies, his words still dripping with that infuriating vagueness. "It'll come to you natural, in the moment." It feels like another riddle I'm supposed to solve, and I can feel my already thin patience wearing away.

"Whatever!" I snap back. "And *if*—a big if—I somehow manage this magic trick you're asking for, what do I get out of it? What's the exchange?" I probe, suspicion wrapping around my words as I question his motives.

"Fair enough," Papa Legba concedes with a slight nod. "I'll grant you this, the ability to summon Madi here whenever you truly need help." He glances meaningfully at Madi, whose expression flickers with surprise and confusion.

"What?" Madi exclaims, her voice rising in disbelief.

"You'll help the sisters when they're in *real* trouble, Madi," Papa

Legba commands, his tone soft but leaving absolutely no room for argument. "And I mean *real* trouble, not for every little snag they hit, mind." There's a weight to his words that underscores the gravity of whatever situation we're all entangled in.

"My primary duty is to protect *this city*," Madi interjects, looking genuinely worried by his order as her gaze darts between us, processing his demand.

"This *is* more important right now, Madi. Trust me on this," Papa Legba insists, that serious, weighty look passing between them seeming to seal the urgency of his request.

"Fine," Madi relents, though reluctance still edges her agreement. I watch, fascinated, as she lifts one hand to her dark hair. Her fingers seem to shimmer, then sharpen before my eyes as long, wickedly sharp claws extend from the tips. With a swift, precise motion, she uses one talon to slice a small lock of her hair free. Laying the severed strands in the centre of her palm, she places her other hand flat above it. A brilliant white flash erupts between her hands, momentarily blinding. When the light fades, a shimmering, ethereal ribbon has materialised, wrapping itself elegantly around the lock of hair.

Madi extends her hand toward Freya, offering the ribbon-bound hair. Freya hesitates, eyeing the strange token with obvious uncertainty. Curiosity, however, wins out. She reaches to accept it, but as her fingers brush the offering, Madi firmly grasps her hand. Another, softer flash pulses between their joined hands, bathing the booth in a brief celestial glow. When Madi releases her grip, Freya turns her hand over. Inked across her palm in intricate, shimmering detail is a phone number.

"That's my number, if you need to get in touch the mundane way," Madi explains, her tone so matter-of-fact it feels almost surreal after the display of magic. "In a true emergency, though, just hold tight to that lock of hair and call my name out loud. I'll hear you, and I'll come." She looks between Freya and me, her expression serious. "You should be more careful about things like this, you know. Leaving pieces of yourself—hair, blood, even strong emotions—behind can be dangerous. Witches, other beings… they can use that connection, exploit that vulnerability." Her practical caution settles heavily in the air, a warning I'd never considered but one that now looms large in my mind.

"Thanks," I manage, genuinely hoping we never face a situation dire enough to use that lock of hair. "We'll try not to disturb you unless it's absolutely necessary."

Papa Legba leans closer then, his entire demeanour shifting, becoming heavier, more focused. He's clearly preparing to address a matter of great importance, and the intensity gathering in his eyes makes it evident that whatever he's about to say weighs heavily on him. I nod, feeling a sense of anxious anticipation mixed with curiosity, urging him silently to continue.

"That book y'all made," he begins, his voice low and grave now, his gaze unwavering, "it's a mistake, child. A grave error. It never shoulda been brought into existence." The air crackles with the weight of his declaration. "Cat was wrong lettin' you go ahead with it. Oh, I can guess her reasons—maybe she figured it'd be some kinda safeguard? A weapon, maybe, if y'all stumbled on your path." He shakes his head slowly. "But make no mistake. I don't know a single soul, livin' or dead, could truly *handle* that thing proper if they got their hands on it."

His words hang there, thick with unspoken worry about what could happen if someone else found our Book of Shadows. A rush of defensiveness for our creation surges through me. "But our mother left notes… instructions… saying every witch is meant to create a Book of Shadows! What's so different about ours?"

He regards me with a look that's equal parts solemn and profoundly mysterious. "Now, tellin' you *that* would give away far too much," he replies cryptically. "All I can tell you is this: what y'all put together, it ain't just no ordinary book of shadows. Y'all gotta guard that book with everything you got. Understand? As your power grows stronger, the protections you weave 'round that book gotta grow stronger too. If not," his gaze hardens, "it's gonna draw even more trouble down on you than you already facin'."

Having delivered this heavy warning, he turns his attention back to Madi, his tone shifting once more, becoming lighter, almost dismissive. "Madi darlin', if you wouldn't mind now… could you take these girls on back to our lovely city? Let 'em get back to their day."

"Of course," Madi replies, her cheerful agreement almost jarring after the intensity of his warning.

We gather our belongings, gripping the handles of the numerous shopping bags piled beside us. As we move to stand beside Madi, I notice the air behind her shimmering again. Her magnificent wings, ethereal and vast, slowly unfurl, catching the dim light in patterns that momentarily distract me from the seriousness of everything just said. The sight is breathtaking, a silent testament to the strange world we inhabit, even as a whirlwind of unasked questions keeps swirling in my mind.

Once we're settled, linking hands with Madi for what I brace myself will be another jarring, instantaneous journey, I catch Papa Legba's eye one last time. "Hope you like that diary I left for you, Reya," he says, his voice unexpectedly tinged with genuine warmth. "Hope it helps some."

"WAIT!!!" The word tears from my throat. I lift my free hand urgently, trying to pull back from Madi's grip, desperate for just one more question, one more clarification, but it's already too late.

The dim light of the bar dissolves around me, the world blurring into streaks of colour and sensation, images flittering past like leaves in a gale. I catch fleeting glimpses – us standing before the weathered gates of a shadowy graveyard, the air cold and still – before the familiar, vibrant city rushes back into view, streets and buildings snapping into focus with dizzying speed. The very last image burned into my mind's eye is of Papa

Legba, sitting alone in that booth, a broad, knowing smile gracing his ancient face, infused with a warmth that offers the strangest kind of comfort.

Then, in an instant, we materialise back in the gritty city alleyway, the transition dumping us unceremoniously onto the pavement. As Freya and I scramble to find our footing against the brick walls, the abrupt silence is shattered by the sharp, insistent dinging of our phones, both suddenly bombarded by a flood of text message notifications.

Catherine M. Clark

Chapter 8

Agents of Uncertainty

Ava

We arrive at the quaint motel we booked early Thursday morning, just as dawn breaks around 7am. Located on the eastern outskirts of Jackson, our choice allows us convenient access to the bustling city and Luna Falls, making it an ideal spot for our needs. Similar to our previous trips, the guys opt to share a room, which leaves Rose and me with the delightful perk of a room equipped with a cosy, super king-size bed of our own, and we manage to get rooms that are just one room apart. This arrangement marks a significant change for us; we no longer feel the need to conceal our relationship. We took the opportunity during our drive here to have a candid conversation with Sam about our situation, and he assures us, with a reassuring nod that he seems to understand the underlying depth of our connection, he is also perfectly fine with our relationship as long as it doesn't cloud our judgment during cases.

Understanding the potential complications that lie ahead with trying to find the sisters, we need to split up for this stay to start with. Our plan is to divide and conquer, covering more ground until we can better assess the situation we are about to encounter. I can feel a subtle shift in Rose's usual bright demeanour, a flicker of unease that I know stems from the thought of being separated. Our bond, though still mysterious in its workings, makes me wonder how much she can sense my emotional state when I look at Rose. Hence, I wonder if the demeanour I'm seeing in her might be because she is sensing my emotions as I'm anxious about heading to Luna Falls, but as I study her. I start to realise she is just as worried as I am; she doesn't need to feel my emotions about what Sam and I need to do. We feel it because we aren't sure if shifters are roaming around Luna Falls as we expect. Given the possibility that shifters are here for the sisters and have come from the formidable pack back in Chicago, we worry that the scent of Rose and Luca can attract unwanted attention, putting us all at risk.

After the long drive to Jackson, Mississippi, we are utterly exhausted. We decided to take advantage of the quiet hours and get some rest after the long journey. The nap will refresh us, giving us just enough time to recharge and freshen up before Sam and I head to Luna Falls.

The sun is high enough to make our room bright as I stir at the sound of my alarm going off. My body feels heavier than usual from the drive and lack of sleep. *I should have slept during the drive here*, I mentally chide myself, but the underlying anxiety about the sisters, a feeling Rose likely shares, keeps me on edge. I ended up paying for it as I became too tired to carry on; the others wanted time to freshen up anyway, and it was too early to find the sisters when we arrived in Jackson.

Usually, long hours and being on my feet would be no issue for me, except I'm also now dealing with the mental aspect of learning about the paranormal world. Since I've been put in charge of this small team and have a new partner with a lot of energy, I feel I've been burning the wick at both ends. I manage to peel my eyes open in search of my phone to turn off the alarm, and the bright room hurts my eyes. A soft chuckle fills the air as my eyes start to focus, and then my alarm turns off.

"Hey, sleepyhead," Rose murmurs against the top of my head. Her voice is warm and laced with the familiar comfort of our ancient connection, which makes us feel like we have always been together.

"Hey," I croak, my voice raspy as my throat feels parched. My body feels unusually hot, reminiscent of dry desert sand. I suddenly become aware of my position—once again, I'm sprawled atop Rose. *It seems like a twisted mystery; I distinctly remembered falling asleep lying next to her, yet here I am, inverted in our usual morning embrace. I can't fathom how I end up in this position every single time.*

Rose chuckles softly, a musical sound that breaks through the fog of my sleepiness. I can sense a deeper layer of affection in her touch as she gently runs her hand over my back, a pleasant, soothing gesture that doesn't do much to expedite my awakening. "How do you feel? Have you had enough sleep? If you want, you can still catch some more, and we can put things off until tomorrow," she offers, her tone laced with extra care, a subtle reflection of the worry I know she carries for me.

"Nice try," I reply, stifling a yawn that threatens to escape. "I know you're not entirely comfortable with just Sam and me handling this. I'm going today. We can't postpone; they could be in imminent danger," I insist, hoping my strong resolve will convince her to support my decision.

"I know," she says, her voice slightly heavy with concern, a tangible weight resonating with our bond. "I'm just worried. You know how perilous shifters can be. The thought of you walking into a pack's domain without backup rattles me. What if these three sisters are just ordinary human girls, completely oblivious to the *paranormal* world surrounding them?" Rose's words hang in the air, heavy with the weight of the unknown, and I understand the intensity of her fear for my safety.

"True, there's always that possibility, but I have to find out," I state firmly. "It's part of my job. Ever since I turned eighteen, my mission has been to step in and rescue those in dire need—innocents targeted by malevolent forces who seek to exploit them for their own twisted purposes. These sisters fit that description perfectly, so I can't just ignore the situation."

Rose's arms tighten around me, pulling me closer against her warmth as if to shield me from the impending dangers. I can feel the strength of her protective instincts, a familiar comfort in our intertwined destinies. "I know. But you better get up before I decide to keep you here with me, right where it feels safest," she says lightly, though her green eyes hold a deeper flicker of seriousness, a silent plea for me to be careful.

"I'm worried too, you know," I murmur, glancing at her. "You and Luca are heading into Jackson to investigate the recent attacks and those unsettling reports of people behaving strangely. You could also be walking into danger with shifters lurking about here." *The weight of my concern surprises me*; it feels foreign since I haven't had anyone to worry about like this since losing my parents. But with Rose, it's different; this bond seems to amplify every emotion, making her safety paramount.

"I guess," Rose replies softly, her gaze dropping momentarily. The unspoken tension mirrors our conflicting emotions—her worry for me, a palpable wave that washes over me, and my anxiety for her safety.

I turn my head to face Rose, my heart racing as I lift myself just enough to meet her gaze. Her captivating green eyes sparkle with a mixture of surprise and delight; every time I look into them, it feels like I am falling deeper into an enchanting abyss. "*I love you*," I declare softly, my voice full of sincerity, before capturing her lips with mine.

She had been about to say something, her words lingering on the tip of her tongue, but my kiss silenced her intentions. The warmth of her lips against mine is electric, a familiar surge of energy that always accompanies our physical touch. Though her response comes out muffled, I'm still able to catch the sweet melody of her words, "*I love you too*," a sentiment that resonates deeply within me, I still wonder if what I'm feeling is really my feelings because of this bond, ever since I met Rose I found it hard to not stare at her and think about her. I may never know, but I'm happy I decided to accept this bond.

The kiss feels timeless, stretching on for what seems like hours, a beautiful intertwining of hearts and emotions before I finally pull away. Unable to suppress my joy, I chuckle softly as I gently disengage from her embrace and land back in the spot where I initially started. I lean over, planting a light, playful peck on her lips, savouring the moment before rising from the bed.

With a sense of giddiness, I make my way to the bathroom, my laughter bubbling up. "That wasn't fair," Rose calls out playfully, the hint of a pout in her voice as she watches me retreat.

"It's not my fault you're too *slow*," I tease back, closing the bathroom door behind me with a satisfying click. A deep growl echoes through the air, reverberating off the floors and walls, creating a rich, resonant sound that fills the space. I can't help but laugh, the unexpectedness of it all sending more laughter spilling out of me. *Even her playful annoyance feels comforting*. The cat's mighty roar only heightens the absurdity of the moment, leaving me in a fit of giggles as I splash some water on my face, still feeling the warmth of our kiss lingering on my lips.

Thirty minutes later, I'm ready for the day ahead. I've opted for a pair of well-worn jeans that hug my figure comfortably and a simple black top that perfectly balances practicality and style. With my weapon harness on and with all my usual weapons attached, a knife tucked into my boot and two at my waist, with one at my lower back, a small handgun is also concealed at my hip, and of course, my sword is in its sheath on my back. Each item feels like a crucial part of my persona, a reminder that I'm ready for whatever the day might throw my way.

The early afternoon sun glints off our dark Tahoe as I step outside. Sam is already behind the wheel, his expression a mix of determination and focus. The boys insist we take our primary vehicle because it's loaded with all our gear—the equipment we might desperately need if things turn dicey. For Luca and Rose, this is a no-brainer as they have their own built-in weapons.

I glance back at our room as we pull away from the motel. Through the window, I spot Rose framed in the doorway. Her posture is relaxed yet watchful; it's almost like I can sense a lingering thread of worry emanating from her; maybe I'm starting to feel more through our bond. She stands there, her eyes following us as we disappear around the corner of the building.

Settling into the soft leather seat of the Tahoe, I feel my body relax as the familiar hum of the engine fills the air. Sam insisted on driving today, which I don't mind, as taking the passenger seat allows me to prepare my mind for what we might be up against in Luna Falls.

When we enter Luna Falls, I can't help but notice how picturesque this small town is. We don't know where the sisters live, so we head to the sheriff's department to see if they can help. Being a small town, I'm sure they would know if anyone new has moved in.

"Ava," Sam calls out, his tone slightly hesitant, perhaps sensing the underlying tension of our mission.

"Yeah, what's up?" I reply, glancing over to him.

He shifts his weight in his seat, a hint of nervousness in his demeanour. "I just want to give you a heads-up. Rose made me promise I wouldn't let you do anything *stupid*," he confesses, his expression a mix of seriousness and embarrassment, likely amplified by the knowledge of the deep connection Rose and I share.

I can't help but chuckle at the mental image that forms. "And what exactly did she define as doing something *stupid*?" I ask, my curiosity piqued as I cross my arms and sit waiting for his answer.

"Pretty much everything," he answers sheepishly, a slight blush creeping up his cheeks.

This makes me burst into a full belly laugh that catches you off guard and makes your sides ache. "Don't worry, I don't plan to do anything reckless, and if I *do*, I'll make sure to shield you from her wrath," I tease, a playful glint in my eye. I know Rose's protectiveness stems from our bond, and it's a comfort, even in its intensity. His response is a chuff of laughter, echoing the absurdity of my assurance. I realise then how lightheartedly I'm treating the situation, and for a moment, I feel a sense of camaraderie in our shared understanding of Rose's expectations. Deep down, I understand her worry, but a part of me can't help but wonder if how worried she gets is just the bond making her feel like this. Either way, if something happens to me, I will worry for Sam's safety.

Catherine M. Clark

Chapter 9

Small Town Scrutiny

When we pull up outside the sheriff's department just before midday, the morning sun casts a warm glow over the brick façade of the building. I take a deep breath, savouring the crisp air, and we step out of our vehicle. As we approach the entrance, a sense of anticipation flutters in my stomach, but I remain calm and collected. This demeanour is crucial in my line of work, where maintaining composure is essential, especially when navigating potentially hostile environments.

I'm the first to walk through the heavy wood doors, glancing back to hold it open for Sam. Upon entering, I'm immediately struck by the organised atmosphere of the sheriff's department. To my left is a receptionist's desk, manned by an older woman whose keen eyes follow us intently as we enter. She is wearing silver-framed glasses that perched near the tip of her nose, and her hair is pulled back into a neat bun, emphasising her no-nonsense demeanour.

My gaze quickly scans the open space of the setup. To my right, a row of plastic chairs lines the wall, accommodating visitors awaiting their turn for whatever brings them here. Directly in front of me are two desks; the occupied desk is cluttered with papers and coffee cups, where a deputy in the typical brown and cream uniform sits, typing intently on a keyboard.

In the far-left corner, I catch sight of an office enclosed in glass walls, giving it a contemporary aesthetic reminiscent of an FBI workspace. I assume the man sitting at the desk in the office is the sheriff, his focus also absorbed in paperwork sprawled before him. He appears to be middle-aged, with salt-and-pepper hair and a furrowed brow that suggests he is deep in thought, perhaps contemplating the day's challenges or the cases that lie ahead.

Next to the sheriff's office, a narrow hallway stretches out, dimly lit due to a burned-out bulb. This hallway leads to several essential yet unremarkable areas: the restrooms, a storage room, and, of course, the jail cells. I can't help but wonder if anyone is currently being detained in them.

We walk over to the receptionist, and I notice the sheriff glance up from his desk, his expression shifting to one of mild surprise. His deputy turns momentarily from his tasks, seeing the badge and gun on Sam's hip. The receptionist, a woman whose nameplate reads 'Cheryl,' looks equally taken aback by our appearance. I step forward, pulling out my badge and flashing it for her to see, "Hi, I'm Agent Bekke, and this is Agent Miller."

Cheryl blinks, momentarily speechless, before recovering enough to respond. "How can I help you, Agents?" She looks at my appearance, looking confused, as I'm not dressed like an agent, like Sam likes to be in his crisp black suit.

"We're hoping you can assist us with an address," I reply, keeping my tone professional yet approachable.

Before I can elaborate, the sheriff, whom I notice out of the corner of my eye, has left his office and heads over to us and interrupts, clearly ready to take charge of the situation. "Cheryl, I'll handle this," he says with a wave of his hand, the authority in his voice making it clear that he expects us to follow him. "Agents, why don't you come into my office? I can see if I can assist you."

"Sure," I reply, grateful for his willingness to help. Before I follow him, I turn back to Cheryl and say, "Thank you, Cheryl." She still looks surprised at, I presume, why we were here in her small town. I then turn away from her and follow the sheriff to his office.

As we pass, the deputy, still seated at his desk, casts a glance our way, mirroring Cheryl's astonishment at our presence. His curiosity is evident, but he quickly returns to his work as we enter the sheriff's office.

The interior of the sheriff's office feels more intimate, with its worn wooden furniture and the faint smell of old paper lingering in the air. The sheriff gestures for us to sit in the two chairs facing his desk. Once we are settled, he takes his own seat, his gaze scanning us thoughtfully.

"You know," he begins, looking at Sam with a hint of amusement, "You really look the part of an agent." His tone shifts as he turns to me, adding with a slight smirk, "But I have to say, you don't."

"Agent Bekke is actually our boss and doesn't like wearing suits, not that our team is expected to," Sam says before I can say anything. *I guess this will be one of those times when I do or, in this case, say something stupid, as I would have reacted negatively to what he just said and challenged him,* but we need help, so I remain silent for now.

"I see, so there are more of you, then?" he inquires, his eyes widening in surprise at why there would be so many agents in his town.

"There are," Sam confirms with a nod, a hint of seriousness in his tone.

The sheriff leans back in his chair, a faint smile playing on his lips. "So, what exactly can I do for you in my small, peaceful town?" he asks, his voice laced with an unexpected eagerness.

I glance down at his nameplate, which reads 'John Radshaw.' It feels odd to be in a position to ask the sheriff for help with something so simple. "Can I call you John? I'm Ava," I introduce myself, trying to gauge his demeanour. He shrugs nonchalantly, so I continue, "John, we are looking for three sisters." I watch his face intently for any signs of

89

recognition or surprise.

A look of realisation crosses his features, and he leans forward intently. "I *knew* those sisters were trouble. I could feel it in my bones," he confesses, his voice dropping to a conspiratorial whisper. "Since they arrived in town, all sorts of strange happenings have been going on. Unexplained lightning strikes near their property when there is no storm, and there are reports of the sounds of a lion roaring, but they claim it was just their dog, which is huge; god knows what they feed that thing. I'm considering looking into the laws to see if a dog that large is allowed. I also have a missing man who left his home in Jackson in the middle of the night and was last seen driving towards the Harpers' property, but we found the car abandoned on the other side of town. So, are you here to arrest them? Because I will certainly be willing to help," he exclaims, his eyes gleaming enthusiastically.

His unexpected eagerness to assist takes me by surprise. Given the nature of most small-town sheriffs, I anticipated a more cautious and guarded response, but instead, he seems almost thrilled at the prospect of involvement in arresting the sisters. *I exchange a quick, almost imperceptible glance with Sam. This was… unexpected.*

"Why would you assume we would be here to arrest them?" Sam asks, his tone carefully neutral.

The sheriff looks puzzled by Sam's question, "I just assumed with what I've been dealing with, they must have been into something in Chicago and wonder if they had something to do with their mother's death," he says, still sounding excited with the hope of arresting them.

I'm stunned and unsure what to say. It seems strange that he would look into the sisters and know what happened to their mother, but based on everything he has just told us, I have one question, "So are you telling me these sisters caused the lightning? How?"

The sheriff shifts uncomfortably before he answers, "Well, I didn't *mean* to suggest they caused it. I just mean it's strange, and we haven't had anything like it before they moved here, especially when there was no storm," the sheriff says, then changes the subject as he continues to look uncomfortable. So, what do you want them for?"

"We just need to speak to them about what happened to their mother," Sam states firmly, keeping to our planned story about why we want to find them. His tone conveys the weight of the situation.

The sheriff, a burly man, looks surprised as he glances between us, clearly bewildered. "So, you do think they are responsible for their mother's death?" he replies slowly, processing the implication.

Sam shakes his head firmly. "No, we don't think they had anything to do with it. We've seen a few cases with striking similarities in other states, which has escalated this into an FBI matter. I want to clarify that we do not believe the sisters had any involvement in her *death*. Our goal is to discuss the days leading up to her passing to jog their memories; perhaps they noticed something unusual, something they might have missed or didn't think was relevant at the time, we read the reports made at the time, but we want a first-person account, just in case the detective at the time may have missed something."

The sheriff seems to absorb this, his expression softening somewhat. "Oh," is all he manages in response, a hint of realisation dawning in his eyes that he won't get to arrest the sisters.

"So, can you please tell us where they live?" I interject, my voice carrying a sense of impatience mixed with concern. I fix him with my most annoyed look, hoping to communicate the situation's urgency as clearly as possible. "We're also worried about their safety in light of these new attacks."

"Oh," he said again and started to fidget. He stretched behind him, grabbed a piece of paper from his printer, wrote something on it, and passed it to Sam. I lean over to see what is written on it. Sam tilts the piece of paper towards me so it's easier for me to see. It's an address. "Thank you, sheriff," I say, then stand. Sam follows suit and chases after me after my abrupt exit from the office without saying another word.

As we leave the building, the late afternoon sun casts a warm glow on the pavement. Just as we make our way toward our car, a police cruiser glides to a stop beside us. A man exits the vehicle, and I can't help but notice his striking resemblance to Luca. Not with his facial features, but with his similarity to his build, which tells me he is well built and has an air of confidence that radiates from his every move. I can also tell from experience that he knows how to handle himself.

He scrutinises us with a sharp gaze as he starts scanning us. He seems shocked when I see his eyes drop to Sam's hip. A flicker of concern crosses his face as he takes in our presence. He leans casually against his cruiser, arms crossed, but the tension in his posture betrays his composed demeanour. Unfazed, we climb into our car, and I quickly punch the address into the satnav. The screen lit up, revealing a route that isn't long—thankfully, our destination is just a short drive north of the town. The satnav's digital voice chirps with directions, guiding us. We pull away from the scene, the deputies' figure fading in the rearview mirror as he continues to watch us.

When we reach the turn-off for the house, we almost miss it because the entrance is a little overgrown. As we drive up the long driveway, I feel a rush of excitement with a prickle of unease. *Rose's apprehension about this encounter seems to echo in my own gut.* Before we arrive at the house, Sam pulls over and retrieves his service gun from his hip to check it while I ensure that all my blades are secure and that the weapons I have on me are loaded and ready for whatever we might encounter, the same as Sam.

Once we are all set, Sam releases the handbrake, and we set off toward the house again. As we round what I hope is the final bend in the road, my jaw drops while Sam whistles at the sight before us. The yellow house with grey shutters looks stunning, especially with the lake beside it on the left. We don't see any vehicles outside, which makes me worry that no one is home. We pull up to the property and leave the car, the crisp air enveloping us with a fresh scent of earth, a sweet flowery scent, and something else with a strong aroma, which could be coffee, so someone might be home after all.

As I begin to scan the landscape, my eyes comb over every inch of the sprawling grounds, searching for anything that might raise a concern. The first thing that catches my eye is the vibrant red barn. It looks recently painted, which can be good news for us as it tells us that if the sisters are bothering with basic maintenance of the barn, then they might not be in danger as we thought. Beyond that, fields stretch out in a patchwork of greens and browns, and I notice a glimpse of what appears to be a vibrant field of mixed plants tucked away behind the house I caught a glimpse of as we drove up to the house, I was only able to see part of it as I glanced down the right side of the house. The whole setting is unexpectedly picturesque, bathed in warm sunlight that highlights the beauty of the rural landscape. I find myself momentarily enchanted, forgetting my initial belief that there might be ominous signs indicating the sisters' rumoured witchcraft.

While I'm observing the property, I feel Sam move beside me, his presence a comforting reminder that we are in this together. "Let's do this," I say, keeping my voice steady and hiding my anticipation. Just then, before we have a chance to take a single step toward the inviting front door, a deep, menacing growl echoes through the tranquillity, slicing through the calm like a knife. The sound sends a shiver down my spine, instantly reminding me of the formidable growls Rose and Luca have emitted on other occasions. I glance at Sam, and I can see the recognition dawning in his eyes, mirroring my own unease. *I think about why we were here, and the protective instincts I now have for Rose wash over me, a familiar sensation that comforts and spurs me on as I want to help and protect these sisters if they are in as much danger as we think.* Ignoring the instinct to retreat at the sound of the growl, I feel a surge of determination, while concern for the sisters propels me forward. With my heart pounding, I make the decision that Rose will likely deem reckless, so I quicken my pace, striding purposefully toward the front door, driven by an unwavering instinct to uncover the truth.

"Ava!" Sam exclaims, but he still follows me.

Just before I'm about to ascend the steps to the front door, I feel something unusual; the air seems charged, and I get a tingling sensation in my hand where the ring is. I'm not sure what it means, but I don't let it slow me down. As soon as I ascend a few steps, I notice the curtain covering a pane of glass next to the front door twitch, and then the door opens.

The first thing I see is a huge dog—really huge, the sheriff wasn't joking about its size. It's the source of the growling as it appears, and then I notice a woman trying to hold him back. "Beastie, no! We don't know if they're bad," I hear her say as Sam and I take a step back. I'm unsure how to interpret her words, but they make me think she suspects someone might be after her, which also might confirm our fears that they are in danger.

"Who are you? What do you want?" she asks, her voice sounding strained, laced with a fear that resonates with the unease I'm already feeling.

I pull out my badge while Sam makes sure the one on his hip is on show, the metallic gleam catching the afternoon light, and flash it toward her while I keep a wary eye on the enormous dog by her side. I can't help but wonder what kind of diet has produced such a massive creature—unless, of course, it's a shifter. The thought crosses my mind. Are there shifters that turn into dogs? I introduce myself, "I'm Agent Bekke," trying to maintain an air of professionalism despite the unease bubbling just beneath the surface. "This is my partner, Agent Miller. We hoped to have a word with you if that's all right."

As I spoke, I observed the woman's expression shift from surprise to cautious curiosity. She is strikingly beautiful, her brown hair accented with vibrant blue highlights that catch the light in a way that makes it almost appear to shimmer. Her health seems robust; she stands tall and composed, which eases my worry that she has recently been in a situation where she might have been attacked.

Quietly, she leans down and whispers something to the massive dog, and as if on cue, it ceases its low growl, settles into a sitting position, and fixes its intense gaze on us. "What is it that you want to discuss?" she inquires, though her voice is still taut, hinting at an underlying tension.

"Would it be possible to come inside? We'd like to talk to you and your sisters," I propose, using my friendliest tone, hoping to create a sense of trust.

The woman scrutinises me, her eyes darting over my features before landing somewhere just beyond my shoulder and then shifting to my waist. I instinctively turn to see what has captured her attention, but there is nothing out of the ordinary. When I pivot back to her, her eyes widen as if she has chanced upon a shocking sight. For a second, I wonder if she can see my weapons. *No, she can't, as the ring hides them from everyone.*

"I... would prefer it if we spoke out here. Besides, my sisters aren't currently home," she replies hesitantly, her voice wavering slightly and betraying her fear.

"Do you know where your sisters are?" Sam interjects, his tone calm yet probing.

"They're in New Orleans," she responds almost too quickly, her hand instinctively flying to her mouth as if she has just let slip a secret meant to stay hidden.

"When will they be back? We'd really like to talk to all of you together," Sam presses on, closely observing her every reaction as I am.

"Later," she answers, her demeanour still laced with concern. "But why do you want to talk to us?" Her question hangs in the air, heavy with suspicion and apprehension.

This time, I answer her, "We would like to talk to you about what happened to your mother." As soon as I mention her mother, shock and fear wash over her face, a raw vulnerability that tugs at something within me as I remember the same loss I have experienced and makes me wonder where their father is, as we couldn't find any reference to him.

She falls into a heavy silence for several long moments. She looks sad as she screws up her face, she looks like she is struggling to control her emotions and I feel bad for having to bring her mother up as we don't really need to talk about her. She wrestles with her thoughts. I can decipher the turmoil behind her eyes, but a flicker of movement catches my attention from behind the woman. I squint, trying to see clearly, and then I'm caught by surprise when a fox darts out at the side of the dog and sits down next to it, its fur a vivid orange against the muted darkness of the inside of the house. It sits as if it has every right to be there, drawing my focus away from Maya's troubled expression.

But the fox's appearance is only the prelude to something far more astonishing. A tiny woman flitters into view almost as if conjured from thin air. She lands gracefully on the back of the dog, her presence both ethereal and commanding. What captivates me most are her wings; they shimmer like the surface of a clear lake, each movement revealing radiant colours as if reflecting off water.

I glance quickly at Sam, hoping to share in this moment of wonder, but he is entirely absorbed in watching the fox, oblivious to the extraordinary sight unfolding right before us. The tiny woman, displaying an air of authority, addresses Maya with a voice that is both melodic and urgent, "Maya, what's going on?" However, Maya appears unresponsive, lost in her turmoil.

After a beat of silence, she finally finds the strength to articulate her thoughts, her voice trembling slightly. "There's nothing to talk about," she declares, but her words bear a weight that implies otherwise.

Sam, sensing the gravity of the situation, steps forward. "I'm afraid there is; we've dealt with similar cases related to your mothers, and we are genuinely worried that you might be in danger." His tone is steady and calming, meant to reassure her.

All the while, my attention is divided. With her delicate form and glistening wings, the fairy is now studying me intently, suspicion creeping into her expression. I instinctively averted my gaze, desperate not to reveal that I could see her, so I diverted my focus back to Maya and could see the palpable tension in her body, fear flickering across her features before she spoke again. "You will have to come back another time," she insists, the finality in her voice indicating that there is nothing she is willing to disclose.

Before either Sam or I can respond, the distant rumble of an approaching vehicle interrupts our exchange. Maya's expression shifts, a flicker of relief crossing her face as she catches sight of the car. But that relief quickly morphs into dread as the vehicle comes into focus, revealing a police cruiser that pulled up behind our Tahoe.

A large man exits the cruiser, and the resemblance strikes me immediately. He's the deputy we saw outside the sheriff's department, his stature imposing as he strides past us without a word. I watch as he approaches Maya, his tone even and concerned. "Is everything okay, Maya?" he asks, his presence seeming to carry the weight of authority.

"Hey Jacob, I'm not sure. They want to talk to us about our mother," Maya tells him, sounding nervous instead of scared. The arrival of this deputy seems to have calmed the woman's nerves, so she must trust him to a degree.

"Is Reya still out?" he asks, and I recognise the name from the police report.

"How do you know she's out?" Maya asks, her eyebrows knitted in surprised confusion.

"They drove past me this morning," he replied. "She also texted me saying they were off shopping and hunting for books for your new business," he adds, attempting to keep his tone casual.

"Oh, okay," Maya responds, her surprise softening into understanding. "They'll be back later. Apparently, Freya has become a shopaholic," she continues, a hint of amusement flashing across her face. Her first genuine smile breaks through the tension that has gripped her since we arrived.

The deputy, who has been quietly observing us, asks, "What exactly do you want with the sisters that you can't find in the police report made at the time, agents?" His voice is steady yet laced with tension and scepticism.

"It's none of your business, deputy; this is a private matter and an FBI investigation," Sam replies firmly, his tone leaving no room for argument.

"Well, Maya doesn't want to speak with you without her sisters present, so I suggest you leave and come back another time if you absolutely must," the deputy retorts, the edge in his voice turning a touch aggressive.

"We'd be happy to do that; if you can provide us a number, we can then arrange a more convenient time," Sam suggests, glancing sideways at me. Something in the deputy's presence reminds me of Luca again – a protective, almost territorial aura.

"It would be best if they had Reya's number," Maya chimes in, her voice calm but assertive as she addresses Jacob.

"Sure, go inside. I'll handle this," Jacob replies, his tone assuring. Maya then leans down to whisper something to the dog that seems to understand before they all vanish back into the house. Just before the dog follows her inside, it pauses and gives a low growl at Jacob. In response,

Jacob shoots the dog a warning look, quickly masking any reaction as Maya says, "Thanks, Jacob," just before the door clicks shut behind her.

The deputy steps past us, subtly nodding his head as a signal for us to follow him. We comply, not out of obedience but rather because our path leads us to our car. He halts next to our vehicle, glancing back to ensure we are keeping up, his long strides making it clear he has no patience for slowness.

"I know you want to talk to them about their mother. Is that really necessary?" he begins, his voice lowering slightly as if he is trying to keep the conversation discreet. "Bringing all that back up when they've just started to move on isn't exactly fair, is it?" he asks, the hint of concern in his words suggesting he genuinely wants to protect the sisters from further pain.

"That's none of your business," Sam replies curtly, crossing his arms as he leans against our car. "But we will need to talk to them. If this Reya decides we should leave, then we will—though we need to have that conversation first."

The deputy sighs, his frustration evident. He reaches into his pocket and pulls out a business card, scribbling something down with a pen before handing it to me. As I glance at the card, I note it bears the deputy's official information. When I flip it over, I find a mobile number scrawled in neat handwriting—Reya's number?

"Reya is the one you should talk to," he advises, his tone a mixture of professionalism and something unspoken. "But I hope you'll consider leaving the sisters alone."

"Thank you," I reply, though my mind is racing with questions. *The deputy's protectiveness feels familiar, a trait I see in Rose.* Curiosity gets the better of me, and I can't resist asking, "Are you dating one of the sisters?"

The deputy's expression darkens slightly, annoyance flickering in his eyes. He hesitates before finally responding, his voice tinged with reluctance. "Reya and I are kind of dating," he admits, but his words have an unmistakable edge of insincerity, as if he is hiding something beneath the surface.

"Okay, again, thank you," I say, though my intrigue only deepens. I turn away from him and open the driver's door, eager to head back and contemplate everything we have learned and seen.

Chapter 10

Beyond Human Sight

The weight of the situation settles heavily on my shoulders as we drive back to the motel. Sitting in the passenger seat, Sam focuses intently on the Satnav screen, inputting the motel's address as we leave Luna Falls. It seems like our only option right now.

"Sam, can you do me a favour?" I ask, my voice steady despite the whirlwind of thoughts racing through my mind. "Please text Reya on my phone and ask her for a meeting." I can't shake the unsettling image of the deputy who arrived and swiftly took charge, his demeanour commanding yet oddly perplexing. And then there's the bizarre reaction from the dog—how it growled at him as if it sensed something that the rest of us can't. *My unease about that deputy now echoes within me, adding to my disquiet.*

As I drive along the highway back to Jackson, my mind can't get past the odd scene I just witnessed. The fox's presence and then a *bloody* fairy—a sight so outlandish that it feels like something out of a fever dream. Sam didn't seem to notice her for reasons I can't fathom. I also think the deputy failed to acknowledge her existence.

The silence in the car is punctuated only by the soft tapping of Sam's fingers on my phone, crafting the message that I hope will lead us to answers if she agrees to meet. I tighten my grip on the steering wheel, feeling the weight of the unknown pressing down on me.

I remain silent, I drive, but finally, I can't contain myself any longer and remark, "That was strange, right?"

"It was. The deputy reminds me of Luca and Rose, don't you think?" Sam says, and I can see out the corner of my eye that he looks worried.

"Yeah, I noticed that too," I say, my mind racing through what I saw again. "But I'm talking about the fairy that appeared and landed on the dog's back."

"What are you talking about?" Sam asks, a hint of disbelief creeping into his tone. It sparks my curiosity; he sounds genuinely confused.

"The fairy! She was much larger than I expected, and her wings were incredible; they shimmered like droplets of water catching the sun," I explain, stealing a glance at Sam when I'm sure it's safe.

He looks utterly perplexed. "Ava, I didn't see any fairy. All I saw was the fox that showed up. It was astonishingly tame, but there was definitely no fairy."

"It was there; believe me," I insist, my heart racing with the possibility I'm seeing things. As my mind races for answers, I wonder if the magic ring I wear is why I saw the fairy, so I suggested it to Sam. "Maybe the ring allowed me to see it. If that's the case, the sisters are indeed magical and likely in danger. Plus, Maya let slip that her sisters had gone to New Orleans. Isn't that considered a—what's the word—witchy place?" I inquire; my curiosity piqued.

"Yeah, I caught that slip, too. But it's not typically seen as witchy; it's more known for its voodoo practices. I think you're onto something. They must be magical. I'm just hoping Reya messages back and agrees to talk to us without the deputy hovering nearby," Sam says, a note of urgency creeping into his voice.

"Absolutely. I still can't shake this eerie feeling about that deputy," I admit, a shiver running down my spine. *My continued unease about him seems to amplify.*

"Have you thought about how you'll approach the sisters about being witches?" he asks, his eyes narrowing with concern.

"Honestly, I'm at a loss. We can't replicate what you all did to me for obvious reasons. *My mind went straight to that farmhouse as I watched Rose shift into the panther, scaring the hell out of me.* The only plan I can think of is to blurt it out. *Hey, are you witches? We think you're in danger!*" I chuckle at the absurdity of it.

"That would definitely get their attention," Sam laughs with me, but I can sense that there is a shared apprehension about the path ahead beneath our humour.

When we reached our motel, we can hear voices coming from the guy's room; it sounds like Rose is freaking out. Sam opens the door, and we find Rose waiting for us, her expression etched with worry.

"Thank god, I've been so worried," Rose says, passing Sam and pulling me into a tight hug, a tangible expression of the anxiety I know she has been feeling.

"How did it go?" Luca asks, remaining seated on the floor with several police files spread out in front of him.

"It was strange," Sam replies as he sits on the edge of the bed.

"How so?" Luca inquires as he looks us over, which I'm sure is to see if we have any injuries.

After Rose lets me go, we sit on the floor and lay everything out for them. "That's peculiar," Luca remarks, looking concerned as he thinks on what we tell him and Rose. "Are you absolutely certain that what you encountered was a fairy? I've never had the chance to see one myself, but I've always heard tales of their bald heads and that they are considered really ugly looking, especially with their sharp razor teeth."

"It looked like a fairy," I reply, recalling the enchanting figure.

"She had cascading, fiery red hair that shimmered like spun copper, and her beauty was simply captivating."

Luca shifts in his seat, a glimmer of thoughtfulness crossing his face. "Also, what you described about that deputy who showed up—he very well might be a shifter," he suggests, his voice trailing off as a contemplative silence envelops us.

"What is it, Luca?" I prod, sensing his internal conflict.

"Yeah, you seem to have something weighing on your mind," Rose chimes in, her curiosity piqued, likely also sensing Luca's unease.

After a brief pause, Luca finally speaks up, and I see a hint that he has thought of something but is unsure whether to tell us. "I have an idea, but... it might be a long shot," he admits, still looking somewhat hesitant.

"Am I going to like this?" I ask, a ball of unease forming in my stomach, with how he looks at me.

A sly smile creeps across his lips, a flicker of mischief dancing in his eyes. "Maybe not," he replies cryptically.

"Come on, just tell me," I urge, my heart racing and a knot of anxiety tightening in my stomach as I await to hear his plan. The air is thick with tension, and the quiet hum of the room seems to amplify my unease.

Luca pauses for way too long for my liking, which feels like an eternity—a good twenty seconds—before finally telling us, "Well, I'm wondering if you can show Rose what you saw today; you seem to have this psychic connection. Would you be willing to give it a try?" he asks, his voice a mix of hope and uncertainty.

The idea of sharing my thoughts with Rose sends a shiver of apprehension down my spine. What if I reveal glimpses of things I want to keep hidden? The thought of me inadvertently showing her tender yet painful memories of watching my parents die always creeps into my mind, and of course, past lovers, as I used to hook up with strangers after my deployment. The prospect of revisiting those feelings is unsettling, not to mention re-living the kills I made for my job, start to make the walls of my composure begin to close in.

"Ava, you're suddenly feeling very anxious," Rose remarks. It's not her observant gaze piercing through my façade; it's the bond betraying how I'm feeling. *Great! Just what I need.*

Swallowing hard, I forced a smile, attempting to mask my turmoil. "I guess we can try; what do I do?" I ask, trying to keep my voice steady despite my swirling emotions.

"We don't know how this works, so the only thing I can think of is for both of you to sit facing each other. Then try to picture in your mind what you saw today and try thinking about showing Rose it," Luca said, shrugging.

We follow his instructions and adjust our positions to face each other more directly. But I do something he didn't mention. I reach over and grab Rose's hands, holding them between us, and then close my eyes.

"You got this, Ava," Rose said, squeezing my hands. Her reassurance is a comforting anchor in my anxiety.

"We'll see," I reply as I try to focus my mind.

We sit there for what feels like hours, but it doesn't bother me. I'm used to remaining still for long periods while tracking a target. But I'm unsure how long Rose is able to put up with sitting still. So far, nothing seems to be happening as I repeatedly replay the day's events in my mind.

I'm trying to show her what I saw from a third-person perspective, but after failing for the hundredth time, I decide to try something different. I just ran through everything precisely as I saw things through my own eyes. Suddenly, Rose surprises me. "Wow, I see what you saw... damn, it's gone," she said seconds later, her voice filled with astonishment.

"Sorry, you made me jump, and I lost focus. Did you really see what happened at the sheriff's department?" I ask.

"Sure did; he really doesn't like those sisters, does he? Anyway, try again. I want to see the rest," Rose encourages me, her curiosity now fully engaged.

I refocus and start again. This time, Rose stays quiet. I run through everything, hoping she is seeing it all. When I'm finished, I open my eyes to gauge her reaction. She remains still for a few moments longer, and then her eyes pop open.

"Wow," she finally says as she looks into my eyes and squeezes my hands lightly, her gaze a mixture of awe and concern.

I'm impatient, and the guys are too. "So?"

"I saw it all. You're right; it does look like a fairy. I guess our old stories about them are wrong. Also, that dog seems like a shifter, considering its size and how it sounded. That growl didn't come from a regular dog, but I've never heard of a dog shifter before. Have you, Luca?"

"Nope, as far as I know, they don't exist. What about the deputy?" Luca asks.

"Now, he screams like a shifter, but his scent is off; he doesn't smell like one or anything else. It's best we keep an eye on him. Maya seems to trust him, so maybe he's nothing to worry about. That whole situation feels weird," Rose said, leaving me confused.

"Interesting. Ava, if you manage to arrange a meeting with all three sisters, you and Sam will have to go alone again," Luca remarks, prompting an immediate reaction from Rose, whose worry washes over her face instantly. I'm still focused on what Rose has said about the deputy's scent. I don't remember smelling anything, and I'm about to ask her about it when Rose continues.

"It was strange; it was like I was really there, looking through Ava's eyes and smelling what she could, too. As I've mentioned, the deputy didn't smell like anything. My senses are far superior, so I could pick up on things she couldn't.

"Interesting," Luca replies, and I can see he's now deep in thought again.

"That sounds freaky. What did you smell that I didn't?" I ask, reflecting on the moment and only recalling the crisp air from the lake, which had a sweet, flowery scent with a hint of coffee.

"I could smell sulphur," Rose states, leaving me confused and a little unnerved.

"I don't understand," I question.

"Yeah, I don't either," Sam adds, looking equally puzzled.

"The scent of sulphur usually indicates the presence of a demon," Luca explains to us, now looking worried.

"And there is a strong smell of blood coming from within the house," Rose adds before anyone can comment further, her expression troubled.

"Are you saying there was someone dead inside the house?" I ask, alarmed, a chill running down my spine.

"No," Rose replies, as she and Luca now look so worried that it's making me just as worried. "The blood came from an animal." I instantly relax at hearing it's animal blood, but I have no idea what it means.

"That's strange. So, you're saying that either Maya or the deputy is a demon?" I ask, skipping over the reason for the blood for now, as I'm concerned it might be the woman who is a demon, not that I know what a demon looks like.

"Maybe. You mentioned that the sheriff talked about a man who went missing from Jackson, and his car was found in Luna Falls. The case files we collected today, while you were gone, suggest we are dealing with demons that can possess people. It's possible that the man who went to Luna Falls has possessed someone and is now in the woman or the deputy," Luca explains, his voice grim.

"So, we're dealing with demons here in Jackson?" Sam asks in his usual calm demeanour, but it's clear he's slightly shaken.

"Looks like it. We have a couple of cases that seem more like shifters or vampires since demons don't usually rip people apart. Instead, they tend to manipulate humans to feed on their souls or possess them for amusement, especially if they don't have a corporeal form, like shades," Rose said. Luca nods in agreement, his gaze distant as he considers the implications.

"And how do we kill demons?" I ask, the weight of this new threat settling upon me.

"You can remove their heads like most things, but that generally just sends them back to hell. To truly kill a demon, you need a witch or another demon nowadays. There used to be beings with the ability to kill demons easily, but those abilities vanished a very long time ago, so we have had to rely on witches to keep demons at bay," Luca said, his tone serious.

"That sounds like the sisters can help us if we can enlist their help. It's part of our mission to recruit others for our task force," I say, a spark of determination igniting within me.

"That could work if we can get them to admit they are witches. You need to get back on that as soon as possible, Ava, with arranging a meeting," Luca instructs, his gaze meeting mine.

"I'm already on it," Sam said, as he had already sent a message on my behalf, but Reya hadn't responded yet.

Rose is upset again because she is dissatisfied with the situation. "Luca, we can't let them go off on their own again. The situation is more complicated than we expected, and it can be more dangerous with demons involved, not just the shifters we believe are here."

"Rose, there's no other way. If either of us enters that town without decent intel, it can endanger us all. It might also force the shifters to accelerate their plans for the sisters because they will sense our presence immediately in such a small town," Luca says in his authoritative voice, his tone brooking no argument.

"How about this? If Ava can arrange a meeting with the sisters, maybe you can maintain a live connection. That way, Rose can see what's going on and determine if you're in danger," Luca suggests. The idea seems impossible to me, especially since with how much I had to focus to get this connection between Rose and me to work.

Rose glances at me, her green eyes looking concerned, catching Sam's attention. I ignore both of them and say, "I'm not sure I can do that while also trying to talk to them; it took so much concentration to get this thing between us to work." I explain and see Rose's face fall, Luca shrugs, and then his shoulders slump.

I hope the number the deputy has given me truly belongs to Reya. It has crossed my mind that he might have given me a fake number because of the way he was trying to get us to leave and not talk to them.

Catherine M. Clark

Chapter 11

Panic and Phantoms

Reya

Freya and I scramble for our phones. My mind is racing to the worst possible scenario: Maya is under attack, and I can't shake the guilt of leaving her home alone, especially after being informed that Papa Legba has been keeping the demons at bay and can no longer do so. *Did he really mean he was withdrawing his protection while we sat there?*

As my phone screen lights up, my heart continues sinking at what I see. There are four missed calls and a lot of text messages. I quickly open the first one, dreading what it might contain. *Was my life about to change in the next few seconds, forever?*

"Crap!" Freya exclaims.

Freya's reaction confirms my fears. My heart is pounding so hard I fear it might burst from my chest as I read Maya's frantic text messages. My legs buckle, and I collapse to the ground, my hands igniting in a blaze of onyx fire. The ground trembles beneath me, and I struggle to regain control.

When I get to a message in which Maya seems to have finally calmed down and explained what is going on, I realise Maya is okay.

Relief washes over me, and I'm able to start taking deep breaths to steady my racing heart, which is beginning to make me feel dizzy.

"Interesting," a voice says beside me.

I have to focus, as my brain isn't functioning correctly right now. What I did notice was Madi staring at my hands. I quickly regain control and extinguish the flames as the ground stops vibrating. After a few more deep breaths, I get back on my feet and search for Freya. She appears as pale as a ghost... wait a minute, that's not Freya. I spin around and find Freya sitting with her back against the wall, trying to control her breathing. Weeds are growing all around her, wrapping her in what looks like a protective blanket. Then my attention snaps back to the other person I had mistaken for Freya.

"What the hell?" I exclaim, taking a wobbly step back.

"Can she see me?" the woman asks Madi.

"It seems she can," Madi replies. "What brings you here, Doris? You don't normally spend time in the alleyways."

"Normally, I wouldn't, but I was window shopping on Decatur Street when I was pulled here. It felt like a distress beacon went up; it came from her, Madi. Who is she?" the woman says, pointing at me. An actual ghost is standing next to Madi, talking about me.

"She's a witch, Doris; it seems she can see death," Madi states as a matter of fact, which makes me cringe.

"Reya, who is Madi talking to?" Freya asks, looking concerned as she climbs back to her feet.

"Can't you see her?" I ask, my gaze still fixed on Doris as I take in every detail of her appearance. She doesn't seem as see-through as I would expect a ghost to be. Maybe she isn't a ghost after all.

"See who?" Freya asks, looking confused.

"I think there's a ghost standing next to Madi," I explain to my sister.

"How rude," Doris interjects, shaking her head at me.

"Sorry, I didn't mean to be rude." I stammer, trying to find the right words and feeling awkward, "What are you?"

"I'm Doris Sullivan, of course. Who taught you manners?" Doris responds with a hint of annoyance, reminding me of Pickle.

"Sorry, I've never met anyone like you before—I mean, in your position," I say, stumbling over my words.

"Reya, do I need to get you help? Are you hallucinating?" Freya asks, looking worried about me, when I glance in her direction.

"Seriously, Sis, I'm telling you, there is someone else here," I insist.

"There is, Freya. Let me introduce you," Madi says, waving her hand towards Doris. To me, nothing happens, but Freya suddenly gasps.

"Oh… my god!" Freya exclaims, pressing her back against the wall as she tries to distance herself from our unexpected visitor.

Doris tuts and shakes her head. "Well, that isn't very ladylike. Did both of you grow up on the streets?" she says disapprovingly.

"No, Doris, they didn't. It's just that girls aren't raised like you were anymore," Madi explains.

"The world is falling apart. I'm glad I'm dead, so I don't have to put up with this kind of behaviour. Anyway, I'm going to get back to my window shopping. Please don't drag me into any more alleyways," Doris says, looking around disdainfully before walking toward the exit back onto the street. Once again, I expect her to float, but she walks like anyone else would.

After she's left, Madi turns to me and asks, "Did you not know you could see the dead?"

"Nope, our mother did mention that it might be a possibility since it's in our bloodline," I say, unsure how to feel about this new development.

Freya, though, had a question that didn't even cross my mind.

"Does this mean we can see our mother again?"

Madi looks at my sister with a sad expression before replying, "I'm not actually sure. I know someone was asked to keep your mother safe, but we've heard that this person has been lost to us, and we're uncertain whether she managed to hide your mother in time."

"So, our mother is out there somewhere?" Freya asks, and as I study my sister, I notice she is looking like her heart has been ripped out again, like it was when our mother died. There must be something wrong with me, as I feel nothing.

Madi shrugs in response. *I didn't want to deal with this after everything our mother has done to us.* Madi tilts her head, then turns to face us again and says, "I need to go. I am being summoned." She then begins to roll her shoulders again but stops and asks, "Before I leave, why did both of you look like your world was falling apart?"

"We thought our sister was in danger because she was being attacked. After Papa Legba said he couldn't keep the demons away any longer, we assumed they were already invading," I explain.

"Ahhh. He wouldn't have let that happen while you're here. Also, I'm the one protecting your little town. The demons I have guarding your town are instructed that they can leave when they see you are home and not before. I'm not sure when the demons in Jackson will try again. They have been sending shades out now and then to test whether they can get near your town since we have been taking them out before they can get close." Madi states.

She studies us for a moment before she continues, "You better watch your backs after you return home and keep practising and pushing yourselves to get stronger. Now I know you are more than just plain old witches, I'm sure you will be able to handle the demons," Madi says before vanishing from sight. The last thing I hear is the sound of her wings beating.

After she left, my thoughts turned to Papa Legba. This whole meeting was just to get me to help this human woman. He's like Cat because he doesn't give much away.

Freya and I looked at each other, and then we both sent messages to Maya saying we were okay and would be heading home soon.

"What the fuck does the FBI want with us?" Freya asks.

"Maya didn't say. She's clearly too panicked to think clearly. You can call her, as it's my turn to drive," I say.

"Yeah, let's go," Freya said, grabbing her shopping bags. We dropped them when we heard our phones screaming, and then we headed for the nearest streetcar to get back to where we parked.

On our way to our car, my phone dings again. I expect it to be Maya; she has already messaged us back, going off on one, saying how scared she was. When I open the app, though, the message is from a number I don't know. When I open it, I read it aloud as we walk for Freya's benefit, "Reya, this is Agent Bekke from the FBI Can we please arrange to meet up with you and your sisters as soon as possible? We have something important to discuss with you, and it is very private, so it must be with just yourselves. We mean you no harm. We are friends."

I turn to see Freya's reaction. She looks as confused as I feel.

"Wasn't that last bit strange to say?" I ask.

"Very strange; you don't think they know about us, do you?" Freya asks me while looking worried, which causes both of us to pick up our pace.

"No, they can't," I say, not believing it.

"They are the FBI Do you really think the government knows nothing about the paranormal world?" Freya says in response.

At first, I say, "I guess," then add, "Let's get home and discuss it; too many ears can hear us right now."

It takes us much longer to get home, so it's gone 5pm when we pull up outside our house. Before I've even exited the car, Beastie appears through the front door and races over to us. I can't help but shake my head at the sight. I've been telling him for weeks that he can't do that; he's been finding it hard to wait for someone to open doors for him. So, I will let this time slide as I haven't been away from him for this long before.

Beastie is by my door by the time I open it and get out, and as soon as I do, I start to scratch the top of his head. "Hey boy, did you miss me?" He then begins to show me images of what happened earlier today, and what I see shocks me. Why would an FBI agent have a sword strapped to her back and blades in full view? Something about this doesn't seem right.

Freya and I grab our bags from the back seat and head indoors. Maya is waiting for us as she stands in the open doorway of the front door. Before we get to her, she gives Beastie a dirty look and steps aside so we can enter. She gives us each a dirty look as we pass her.

"Looks like it was a productive trip," Maya says as she follows us into the house.

"In more ways than one," Freya says, "You won't believe who we met today, and we have news about Mum," Freya adds. I wish she hadn't, as I'm worried about how she will take the news. As soon as Freya mentions our mother, Maya trips over her feet and falls into my back, which stops her from hitting the floor. When I help her regain her footing, I can see the mention of her as really affecting her, while also looking confused. She follows us to the kitchen table, where we deposit our bags.

Maya's voice quivers with urgency as she presses Freya for details. "What do you mean you have news about Mum?" Her eyes, wide with anxiety, search Freya's face for answers. I feel a pang of sorrow in my chest, knowing how deeply this revelation will impact her.

Freya finally realises her mistake and looks at me worried. Then her expression turns serious. "You better sit down for what we have to tell you," she replies gently, sensing the weight of the moment.

In an attempt to diffuse the tension, I turn my attention to something else. "Where's Pickle?" I inquire, hoping to redirect the atmosphere just a bit.

Maya inhales deeply, her chest rising and falling with a palpable tension. "The moment she spotted you were home, she bolted outside, eager to conduct her usual daily search," she elaborates, her voice quivering under the weight of her emotions. I can see the conflict in her eyes, a mixture of fear and determination that speaks volumes about the gravity of the situation as it presses heavily on her heart. I can tell this will change things for Maya, as I'm worried she will become obsessed with trying to find our mother's ghost and put herself at risk doing it.

I try to distract Maya by saying, "I truly feel a deep sympathy for Pickle. Every day, she ventures out with the faint hope of discovering signs of others from her race, yearning for the connection and companionship she's been missing. Sadly, her search has yielded nothing so far, and it pains me to watch her struggle. I wish she would exercise a bit more caution before going out; she doesn't realise that the information we need to share could also directly impact her. With the impending threats we face, she could be in grave danger. I don't want her to be attacked again," I say, hoping that what I'm saying about Pickle, Maya takes to heart and uses her brain to think before she acts.

Catherine M. Clark

Chapter 12

Baking, Bonding, and Burdens

We all settle down at the other end of the kitchen table as the bags fill the other end. We then told Maya what happened to us in New Orleans. Maya sat there with her mouth wide open, catching flies the whole time. When we got to the part about our mother's ghost being out there somewhere, it didn't seem to affect her as I expected it would. I expected her to look like her heart would break again, but she didn't, for some reason. I did expect a reaction about the fact that I could see ghosts in the first place, and even this didn't seem to faze her.

"How do we find her?" Maya demands, her voice tinged with urgency and worry.

"I honestly have no idea," I reply, shaking my head. "From what I can work out from what we were told, there is only one person who truly knows her whereabouts, but that individual has apparently gone missing. I can't tell if that means they're dead or not."

Maya's eyes widen, a flicker of panic crossing her face. "So, we have no leads? Do you know who this person is? Maybe we can track them down somehow," she insists, her concern evident. Maya has always been especially close to Mum, and in this moment, it's clear just how much she feels the weight of the situation compared to Freya and me; we have always been more self-sufficient and tend to handle things on our own.

"If Cat ever decides to show her face again, I intend to ask her about the person who was supposed to protect her ghost, soul, whatever you call it," I say, trying to offer a sliver of hope.

"That sounds like a solid plan. Do you think it's possible that she might appear tonight?" Maya looks at me intensely, her wild, wide eyes imploring me for reassurance as if the answer can change everything.

"I really don't know, sis. It's been a while since she invaded my dreams—long before the last attack," I say, my voice trailing off. "And speaking of attacks, we need to stay on guard. We've started to let our guard down, thinking we might finally be in the clear and letting our defences start to slip."

"This just sucks!" Maya exclaims, her frustration boiling over. She crosses her arms over her chest and slumps deeper into her chair as if the world's weight rests on her shoulders.

Freya chimes in, her voice steady despite the tension. "We've already told you everything about what happened to us. Please tell us what happened with your run-in with those FBI agents," Freya asks, trying to redirect the conversation.

Maya hesitates, her reluctance evident as she fixes her gaze on the floor. After a moment, she huffs, "They want to talk about Mum." This leaves Freya visibly exasperated.

Sensing the need to shift gears and provide some clarity, I decide to take charge of the discussion. Beastie has revealed everything to me, and I feel obligated to share. Freya listens intently, her expression growing more astonished as I narrate the events.

"Seriously, this agent Bekke was armed like some medieval warrior," Freya exclaims, her eyebrows knit together in confusion. "She has a sword strapped to her back, right out in the open! What kind of agent does that?"

"Exactly! But what strikes me as strange is Jacob's complete lack of reaction to her presence. You'd think a deputy would notice and question it, especially since she looks nothing like a typical agent. The other guy only had a handgun like you'd expect, but her? She was a whole different story," I explain, trying to make sense of the peculiarities I observed through Beastie.

To my relief, Maya seems to perk up at this information. Maybe she thinks the agents know something we don't. "Well, you can always ask him about it," she suggests, relief washing over her face. "I'm just so glad he showed up. I was really anxious about dealing with them all by myself."

"I could, but what happens if he didn't see them, so I sound like I've lost my mind when I start talking about swords?" I ponder aloud. "And did it look like that agent noticed Pickle?" I ask.

"Honestly, I can't remember. I was too stressed out during the encounter," Maya shrugs as she talks, her eyes drifting off as she tries to recall the moment.

"What are we going to do about these agents if they're actually who they claim to be?" Freya presses, concern etched into her features.

"If they're real agents, then we're going to have to confront them. It may actually be best to take the plunge and talk to them on Saturday," I reply, feeling the weight of that decision settle over me.

"I suppose that can work, but let's make it early. We have the full moon ritual that night and Jenny will be at our place after work," Freya reminds us, with a hint of agitation in her voice. I'm there with her as the timing of these agents turning up isn't ideal.

"I'll go ahead and message Agent Bekke and see what she has to say," I decide, pull out my phone with a newfound resolve, and message the agent back.

We talk for a little longer, and Maya starts to ask questions about Papa Legba and Madi. Then Freya takes the bags of supplies she has bought and heads out to the barn, where she has converted the small office into a storage room for her seeds and cuttings. Duncan built some basic shelves for her in there. She also put the supplies for the full moon ritual and other items in a cupboard and warded it so if anyone snoops around the barn, they won't notice it, similar to the Doctor Who Tardis and its perception filter, which is also what I did to our basement and the clearing in the woods.

Maya is still obsessed with the news about our mother, so she plants herself in front of the Tv after we follow Freya out to the barn. We are now on high alert again, so we have to hope the barn's wards and the protection surrounding our property are enough to protect her while she is out there.

After returning from the barn, I head down into the basement because I have something on my mind. I sit at my desk, and Beastie lies down by my feet. I open the safe and pull out my notepad, and I can't help but look at our book of shadows and wonder what Papa Legba is so worried about regarding it. After locking the safe, I took the notepad I used to write my translation of the old diary, which I now know Papa Legba left for me to find and started to skim what I wrote. The question on my mind is why he left me the diary. Yeah, it gave me the history of paranormal beings, but is that the only reason? His look as he sprung that news on me at the last second hints there is more to it.

I finally translated the rest of the diary over the last few weeks; what was left wasn't very informative as I had already guessed where it was leading, that all paranormal beings were descended from the original gods, well, except demons and the Fae. I continued scanning through my notes, looking for anything I missed when translating the diary and why Papa Legba left it for me. After an hour, I was interrupted when Maya called down and said she was ordering pizza because she couldn't be bothered to make anything.

I just called out, "Sure," then flipped to the next page and came across a sketch I made of a series of runes. I quickly read my notes, and a light bulb went off in my mind.

One of the gods of the underworld, who had a few powers similar to mine, had created the first demons, shadow people, and lethal vampires that he lost control of. He created these demons to help protect him. I read my notes in more detail; I had written that the god had just drawn out the runes with chalk, and like a lot of the runes in the book we have, you have to mark each rune with the blood of the person who is to command the shadow demon.

I ponder whether I should do this for just a few seconds. We are still in danger and need all the protection we can get. I have enough time before the pizza arrives to do what it says. Everything we used for the other runes we cast and some of the supplies we needed for the full moon ritual are still here, so Freya won't miss the chalk I use, as she bought more today.

I quickly grab the chalk and the knife we used before. We left the knife down here because no one wanted to use it for food anymore, so Maya bought a new one. I then stand under the basement light until my complete shadow is at its clearest. I'm unsure if this is needed, but I won't risk doing it with only part of my shadow visible.

Beastie watches me as I get down on my hands and knees and sketch out the runes where my body will be when I stand again. Once all the runes are sketched out and I make sure they all look correct, I stand and adjust my position until they are all within my shadow. I make a cut on the side of my hand, hold it out in front of me, and allow my blood to drip onto the runes one at a time. When I'm done, I pinch the cut and hold it for a moment to stop the bleeding.

When I'm done, I take a deep breath. Apart from funnelling my power into the runes like I've had to do before, I'm unsure if there is anything else I'm supposed to do, and I can't be sure if the diary has everything listed to perform this. I'm also unsure if I have to think of anything in particular, as our mother said in her letter, intent is key when using magic, so I think about what I want to happen. I hold out my hands, so they hover above the runes that are now covered in drops of my blood and funnel my power out of my hands, so it covers all of the runes at once.

Almost immediately, the runes flash red, and my shadow seems to darken for a second and shimmer a little, then returns to normal just as my power stops on its own. Beastie raises his head and tilts it to the side as he stares at my shadow and lets out a soft growl, then lowers his head back down and closes his eyes.

I stand there, stare down at my shadow, and wait for something to happen, anything to happen, so I know it's worked. Except my shadow doesn't move unless I do, like a shadow does, except I feel something. A connection, I can feel my shadow, whatever I've done, looks like I'm always going to be able to feel it now, as I try to feel this new connection I'm suddenly aware I get a slight hint from Beastie too almost like I've created a connection to him too, or maybe I've always had one to him with how I feel about him but now I'm aware of it.

After a few minutes, when nothing else seems to be happening, I clean up, put everything away, and head back upstairs. I check on Freya to ensure she is still okay and find her in her garden tending to her plants. She is safe and sound.

We all woke early Friday morning for our soft opening of The MoonTree. I dressed a little smarter than usual. Even Pickle dressed to impress, as she wanted to come with us. I think she is more excited about our big opening than we are, as we are distracted with other things on our minds, especially after I heard back from the agent during dinner yesterday that they agreed to come Saturday lunchtime.

Our only issue today is Beastie, but Jenny came up with a solution. He isn't going to spend the day with us because we are serving food; he will spend time with Jenny in her store. She also has open fields behind her business, so Pickle can spend time with him out there. She can use the opportunity to look for clues or signs that any of her people have been in this area.

Also, now that we know we can be attacked again at any time, I wasn't happy with leaving him at home. He would try to defend our home even if he was outnumbered, and we might need his help if we were attacked in town.

After breakfast, we load the back seats of our car with trays of Maya's baked goods; we also decided to deliver some trays last night after dinner. Maya has really gone out of her way to bake as much as possible, but baked goods have a short shelf life, so she has to make as much as she can over the last couple of days.

Maya stated last night that she would be driving this morning, as she doesn't trust us to drive carefully enough to ensure her food doesn't squish against the side of our car if we take a corner too quickly. She did the same last night.

I sit in the passenger seat while Pickle sits on my shoulder so she can see out of the front windscreen, which she likes to do as she has only experienced our world from hiding places while Freya and Beastie travel with Jenny.

"This is exhilarating!" Pickle exclaims, her eyes sparkling with a mix of thrill and a hint of mischief as she clutches a thick chunk of my hair, her grip firm enough to prevent her from falling.

"I suppose it's exciting for you," Maya replies, her voice tinged with apprehension as she shifts slightly, clearly trying to steady her nerves. "But if I'm being honest, I feel rather uneasy about all this."

"I can relate," I admit, my heart beating a little harder with my nerves on edge. There is something both daunting and thrilling about the entire situation, and I don't want to let my fear show. I know Maya is nervous because, for this to work, basically, it all rests on her. I'm sure it will be fine, as her food is fantastic, as is Freya's bespoke coffee. I'm nervous because I fear we will be attacked while in town.

I also know Freya is nervous about her coffee mix; she spent two weeks trying to get the balance between the beans she bought and the ones she grew. She can't use too many of her beans each time, or she will run out too quickly, even though she can grow a new plant in a day, but she said if she does, the plant seems weaker, so she can't produce them too quickly.

All three of us have been on a coffee high these last two weeks; we have even noticed it affects our magic during practice, as we can't focus properly. At this revelation, we agreed we would restrict the amount of coffee we usually drink each day, which didn't go down well with us. Now that we know we aren't out of danger, it's more important that we stick to it so we always have complete control over our magic.

Freya is also growing ingredients for Maya to use so her food tastes the best it can. This will also help if she needs us to prep food, as we can't make the food taste like she can. We discovered that if Freya and I used the plants Freya grew, our food would taste better, but not as good as Maya's. Being a kitchen witch, Maya has started negatively affecting my waistline, so today, I decided to wear one of my summer dresses instead of spending the day in jeans that are now a little tighter than usual.

Freya follows suit, but she must wear her hair up as she will serve food. Maya, though, is wearing her chef's outfit, making her look competent and professional.

We also told Pickle she isn't allowed in the kitchen or near the food counter because we have no protective gear small enough for her. She said she plans to stay with me or Beastie to keep him company. She wants to start with me so she can spend some time going through some of the books. She hasn't had a chance to look at the books, as I arranged for them to be delivered to the store.

As we approach the main high street, the anticipation in the car is palpable. Suddenly, Maya breaks the silence with a question that sends a wave of unease through me. "Have you contacted that agent yet?"

"Oh, yeah, sorry about that. I messaged her during dinner," I reply, my voice slightly strained with annoyance at myself for forgetting to inform them, as I was distracted by the fact my plan seemed to fail with regard to creating a shadow demon and the fact I can now feel my shadow. "She has agreed to meet us at lunchtime tomorrow. I hope that's okay."

"Yeah, that's fine," Maya says, but her tone is flat, lacking its usual enthusiasm. Then, with a half-smirk, she adds, "I guess we'd better be prepared to hide two bodies tomorrow." Her words hit me like a jolt, and I stared at her, shock written all over my face, as this was not something I expected Maya to joke about.

"Why would you say that?" I ask, incredulous.

She shrugs casually, a hint of mischief in her eyes. "This Agent Bekke doesn't sound like your average agent. As I see it, this might be the enemy we came here to escape from." My heart sinks at the thought; I hadn't even considered that possibility.

"Crap!!!" I blurt out, the weight of anxiety crashing down on me.

"Now you know where my mind has been since I saw the agents," Maya said, her voice shaky with concern.

"I never thought of that," I interject. I'm sure my expression is one of intense unease as we pull into the parking area at the rear of our business, a space designated for staff and deliveries only. "I just hope they are who they say they are and that the meeting is about something routine—just some standard questions. Then they leave, and we never have to deal with them again," Maya states as she parks near our rear entrance.

When we parked, I glanced out and saw Jenny, Freya, and Beastie waiting for us by the door. They didn't have to drive as slowly as we did, so they beat us by a mile. Once we stopped, Jenny and our sister came over to help unload the food trays.

"I see everything made it in one piece," Jenny said in her bright and cheerful voice; she has been just as excited as Pickle about our soft opening today.

"I wasn't sure we would make it here in time," I say, trying to use it to ensure they don't see the worry on my face. However, the tension in my voice betrays my calm facade.

"Nervous," Jenny asks. "It will be fine," she reassures us with a warm smile as I leave the car. I notice Maya fumbling with the keys to unlock the door to our business as the familiar scent of coffee and pastries wafts through the air. Still, the underlying anxiety makes it hard to appreciate the moment.

After we've finished carrying in the trays of Maya's food. I hand Jenny a cooler and a bag, the bag contains Beastie's bowls, "Is this what I think it is?" she asks while she screws up her nose a little as she looks down at it.

"If you mean some blood and a large steak, then yes," I say with a smile. She reluctantly takes the cooler and bag and gives me a look that makes me chuckle.

Jenny walks to the front of our business, and I unlock the front door, follow Jenny over to her building, and then help unlock the door to her business. "Come on, Beastie. You know you're spending the day with Jenny," I say, waiting for him to follow us across the road.

"Good luck today," Jenny calls out to my sisters, who are standing by our door watching to ensure we are safe.

Once we enter her building, she puts the cooler and bag down, then Jenny turns to me and looks nervous about something.

"What's up?" I ask.

"Is it okay if I come tonight and stay over?" she asks.

Crap! I say to myself, *I didn't want her there when the agents came.* "Don't you have work tomorrow?"

"I do, but I want to talk to you about something," Jenny said, still looking nervous.

"Do you want to talk now?" I ask, worried about what is wrong.

"Not right now. You have more important things to worry about," Jenny said.

"Okay, if you're sure, yeah, it's fine; I'm intrigued about what you want to talk to me about?" I say, giving her a good look over to see if I can see anything off with her that might give me a clue. I also make sure I don't give off my slight panic about tomorrow, and hope she has a busy day, so she doesn't return when the agents are with us, she knows we are going to be talking to the agents but now that Maya has put into my head that they might be our enemy has me a little rattled. Hence, the last place I want Jenny is at the house when they arrive.

"Thank you. I'd better start getting set up. You'd better go and do the same, as it's your big day. Come on, Beastie, I'm your partner in crime today," Jenny says, then hugs me before she picks up the cooler and bag again to take out to her mini kitchen and office out back.

Beastie brushes against my leg, so I scratch his head. He shows me images of him watching our building and tells me he plans to watch over us today. "Thank you," I say to him. Then, we are all surprised when Pickle flies over to Jenny and hugs her neck.

"I will come visit later. Maybe you can cut my hair as it's getting a little long now. This is the longest I've ever had my hair. If I'm not careful, it might get tangled in my wings," Pickle says.

"Sure, I can do that. See you later, then," Jenny said as I turned to leave.

"Look after Beastie, please," Pickle says just before she flies back out the front door with me in tow as we head back to our building, and I can't help but wonder what Jenny wants to talk to me about. When we entered our business, we found my sisters filling the counter and noticed the coffee machine was already up and running, so I joined them and started to help make sure we were ready to open at eight-thirty.

Chapter 13

The MoonTree Opens

The alarm on my mobile blares at 08:25am, we all take a breath, trying to tamp down the jitters. Ever the early bird, Freya heads over to the front door, ready to flip the lock right at half past. I stroll over to the window on the left, the morning light still soft, and yank the cord to raise the privacy blind.

As soon as the street outside comes into view, I do a double-take. A gaggle of four women, who look like they are pushing sixty, are waiting by the door. When they see the blinds go up, they start craning their necks, practically pressing themselves against the glass, chattering amongst themselves like a bunch of excited squirrels. I hope their excitement is the good kind.

I go ahead and raise all the other blinds, letting the morning sun flood the shop. We'd only had a couple of lights on while we were setting up, so Maya flicks on the main lights and our little haven is now on full display for anyone moseying down the street. I turn and take in my area, letting my eyes drift over the beautiful panelling that separates my book nook from the café's seating area.

I can't believe how beautiful the panelling is, chest-high with these cool toughened glass panes, so it isn't all closed off, lets everyone see clearly into my side and the killer bookcases Conner, Duncan's buddy, whipped up. He is a wizard with wood, I swear I can't believe he got it all done in time, he also did the panelling and creates small scenes on each one. Duncan's got his fingers crossed that Conner would join him for real when he finally gets his business fully off the ground, when he's got the cash for an office and enough construction gigs lined up. I'm really pulling for him; I don't want him to lose a talent like Conner.

    I decided on just one joint entrance and exit for my book area. And get this, I got these awesome, what I like to call, cowboy doors for folks to wander through – if I even get any customers, seeing as how everyone's glued to their screens these days. There's this little alcove to the right as you come in, tucked against the wall that backs onto the back area of our building. Right there, smack-dab, is where people will see the books they can actually buy—top forty of the month, comics, graphic novels, the whole shebang. And of course, we have a manga section, which is blowing up these days. The rest of the downstairs is all about rentals, like a regular library. So, you got your dramas, your thrillers that keep you up at night, mysteries that make your head spin – the whole nine yards. Can't forget the comedy, got to have a laugh, right? Upstairs is where I've stashed the spooky stuff – horror, fantasy, sci-fi – along with the real gems, the rare books. And get this, on the shelves up there, Conner has carved these little pictures of mythical creatures. We're talking fairies – which we totally told Pickle were pixies and it seems we have got away with it, there are also Unicorns, a Pegasus, even a freakin' Kraken and dragons! It's pretty sweet, and he even carved a Robbie the Robot for the sci-fi section.

    In the middle of my area, I've got this comfy couch and a little table, and in two corners, I plop down these aged brown leather armchairs. It gives the whole place this cosy, old-school vibe. Well, I think.

    At the time we looked at the property, we hadn't even realised it, but there was an entire apartment upstairs as well. You can access it from the inside, in the horror & fantasy section, through a door at the far end that leads to the area over the café. Alternatively, there are stairs in the back of the building. The previous owner used the space for storage rather than as a proper living area. Currently, the apartment cannot be used as a residence unless we undertake significant remodelling.

I'd been kicking around the idea of setting up my book restoration gig up there, but that would mean being away from my sisters, and that's a no-go for now. It might be an option down the line, though, if things take off and it's safe.

Once all the lights are blazing, Pickle zips around my section, her little face practically glued to the books. She hasn't seen the finished look or the carvings yet, but I've been gabbing about them. I watch her with this goofy grin plastered on my face as she buzzes around, her eyes wide with wonder, soaking it all in. Then she spots the upstairs, zooms up there, and instantly zeroes in on the carvings. She starts making these happy little chirping sounds that make me smile, a broad, toothy smile that makes my cheeks actually begin to ache.

When Freya finally unlocks the front door at 8:30am, the four women practically tumble in, their eyes darting around like they are in a candy store. I can hear them clearly, "Oohing" and "aahing" about how great everything looks. Then they bee-lined for the counter and ordered coffee and Maya's fabulous apple turnovers and muffins.

Once they are seated and those apple turnovers and muffins hit their tongues, they all start making these low, drawn-out groans of pure pleasure, their faces going all red from the intensity of it.

Then, Freya got her moment when they tried her coffee. More groans! We all exchange grins, and I watch Freya's face show relief. She'd been sweating bullets about her new blend. Before the women left, they cornered Maya, practically begging for her baking secrets, and grilled Freya about her coffee magic. Of course, my sisters played it cool, said it's a trade secret, which got a good chuckle out of everyone.

They all promised they'd be back for lunch, but didn't seem interested in my books. I did catch them sneaking peeks at my section a few times, though, and they gave me the once-over, whispering to each other as they did. Made me wonder what *that* was all about. It went quiet for a spell after they left, but we can't help ourselves and burst out laughing at their over-the-top reactions to the food and coffee. We even joke about rigging up a camera and sending the footage to those home video comedy shows. "Imagine," Maya said, wiping a tear from her eye, "Woman Has Orgasm Over a Muffin!' We'd be famous!"

Around 09:20am, a few more folks start trickling in. Some just want their caffeine fix, others are after Maya's grub. I even snagged my first official bookworm! This lady spends a good chunk of time browsing, then comes over and signs up for a library card. Mrs. Lindsey, a sweet little old lady with a mischievous twinkle in her eye, went back to the shelves and returned with three books – the max I'm letting people rent at a time, for up to a week. I'd paid for this library system that prints cards on the spot. It was expensive, but I figured it would be worth it; nobody likes to wait for stuff anymore. So, Mrs. Lindsey walks out with her books and new card, happy as a clam.

We have a steady flow of customers until noon, then BAM! It's like the floodgates opened. Every table is taken, so not everyone can eat in; the café is buzzing with a symphony of happy groans. I even got a steady stream of customers, and a few of them even used the comfy chairs to read while drinking their coffee. One of the little perks I'm offering is that it's free if they want to read in-store. That's why I only put in a few chairs—sold a couple of books too! Not bad for a soft opening.

Pickle parked herself behind my counter with a fantasy novel, flipping through the pages with surprising focus for a pixie. But then her attention span starts to run out, and she takes off, zipping over to Jenny's place. I see Beastie sprawled out by the front window, keeping an eye on us until Pickle flew over and then both moseyed out back. I figured they were hitting the field behind Jenny's shop so Pickle could do her usual treasure hunt for any sign of her people. I hope the sheriff doesn't show up; it wouldn't surprise me if some busybody calls in a "beast on the loose" complaint.

As the lunch rush winds down, I get a visitor I'd been expecting. Jacob saunters in and grabs some lunch with the other town deputy. I watch their faces as they tuck into Maya's sandwiches. Jacob, of course, has tasted Maya's cooking before, but the other deputy looks like he'd just discovered the meaning of life with every bite. When they finally polished off their sandwiches and coffee, Jacob, smooth as ever, came over to see me.

"Hey, beautiful," Jacob says, a little louder than necessary, which, naturally, sends the nearby customers into a frenzy of whispers and stares. *Jeez, Jacob, subtle much?*

"Hey Jacob, food good?" I ask, playing it cool.

"Maya's food is still out of this world, also, how'd Freya manage to make that coffee taste like angels cried into it?" he asks, his eyes twinkling.

"You really think Freya's gonna spill her secrets to me?" I say with a chuckle, and he throws his head back and laughs. He really does have a nice laugh.

Looking at Jacob, all handsome in his uniform and genuinely kind to my sisters, I decide to take Freya's advice and give him the benefit of the doubt. Had he really been behind that reaper attack, wouldn't he have tried something else by now?

"Thanks again for yesterday. Maya was a little freaked out when those agents showed up," I say, genuinely grateful he'd been there for her.

"My pleasure. I knew you were out of town, so when the sheriff told me why they were here, I was worried they'd upset her," Jacob says.

The fact that he was thinking of Maya's welfare instantly makes me like him even more. "It did a little, so thanks," I say, trying not to let my guard down completely, but I did think about planting a kiss on him right there in front of everyone, but at the last second, I bottled it as I remembered how the previous few times we kissed went. It may sound like a porn film in here today, but I didn't think it would go over well if I turned it into an actual porn film.

"Anything to help. You got any idea why they want to talk to you about your mum?" he asks, his brow furrowing slightly, and I can tell he's watching me closely for my answer, which is strange.

"Nope, not a clue. We're meeting them tomorrow, so I guess we'll find out then," I say, and Jacob's expression clouds over.

"You want me to swing by? Offer some backup?" he asks, his voice laced with concern.

I reach over and lay my right hand on his forearm, giving it a gentle squeeze. "Thanks for the offer, but we'll be alright. I'm practically a pro at being grilled by the cops after everything that happened. Besides, what we know isn't gonna change; we weren't even there, so we saw nothing," I say, watching his reaction closely. I can't help myself; I feel like I've been doing it with everyone since the last attack.

He doesn't look thrilled with my answer, but plasters on a smile in the end. "If you're sure, beautiful."

I feel awkward with this sudden tension between us, so I try to explain my recent standoffishness. "Look, I'm sorry if I've been a little…off lately. Our whole future's riding on this place working out, and with everything else – the move, what happened to Mom – it's all been a bit much. Just…bear with me, okay?"

He listened intently, and when I finished, he smiled, his eyes crinkling at the corners, lighting up his whole face. Then, out of the blue, he leans down and gives me a hot, fast kiss. Cue the immediate reaction around us as the chatter increases maybe twenty decibels, and a few people start whooping and hollering. One comment I do catch, which is loud and clear, "I told you! I said he was seeing one of the sisters. I don't know what she's got that my Emma doesn't." *Oh, for Pete's sake.*

"Of course, I'll give you all the time you need. I get it," he says, his gaze soft. But as I look into his eyes, I see something I don't think I noticed before. There's a slight red tint around the edge of his eyes, before I can comment on it, he says, "I better skedaddle before the sheriff comes looking for me and slaps you with an interfering with police business charge," he has a cheeky grin that actually makes me laugh as it sounds exactly like something the sheriff would try to pull.

"Go on, get out of here. The last thing I need is him to blame me for something else," I say, giving Jacob my best smile.

"See you soon," he says, then, bold as brass, he leans in for another quick kiss, which, predictably, causes another round of amused gasps and whispers. Then he heads out, and yeah, okay, I totally watched him walk away. And no, I absolutely did not check out his…posterior in that uniform. Nope. Didn't hear that woman say, "He does look good in that uniform; she is one lucky woman," either. Nope.

About an hour later, I checked on my sisters when the lunchtime rush had really died down. They both look like they'd been run through the wringer. I glance over at the counter and am shocked to see that it is practically empty. "Need a hand restocking?" I ask, surprised.

"With what?" Freya says, looking genuinely confused.

"The extra trays we put in the fridge," I reply, pointing towards the kitchen.

"All gone, sis," Freya states, matter-of-factly.

I stare at her, my jaw practically hitting the floor. "Seriously? All of 'em?"

"Yep. If things keep going like this, we might actually have to hire someone. Good thing we aren't planning on staying open all day at first," Freya says, looking exhausted and thrilled.

"It'd be amazing if it stays this busy. I'm surprised by how many people I've had who are interested in books. I might have to think about hiring someone for the days I wasn't planning on opening," I muse.

"Yeah, I noticed you've been busy kissing your customers! That's one way to drum up business," Freya says with a sly smirk.

"Ha ha, you're such a smart arse. He caught me off guard, alright?" I retort, feeling my cheeks heat up.

"So, you're giving him another shot then?" Maya enquires, leaning against the counter and looking thoughtful.

"Yeah, I guess. You two might be right; maybe he wasn't involved. What you both said made a lot of sense," I admit.

"Of course, I'm right. I'm the brains of this operation," Freya declares, puffing out her chest.

I can't help but snort. "If you say so, sis. How are you holding up, Maya?" I ask, turning my attention to our perpetually busy baker.

"I've managed, but man, I've been slapping together sandwiches so fast my hands are cramping. If it stays this crazy, I don't know how I'm gonna keep up with demand. Thank goodness we're closing in forty-five minutes," Maya says, looking like she is floating on cloud nine but also completely wiped.

"I really hope this keeps up; that money from the old place won't last forever. We need this income," I say, the reality of our situation sinking in.

"You got that right," Freya agrees. Then I see her eyes widen, her gaze fixed on something past me, and her face goes all soft and dreamy. I turn to see what had snagged her attention, and it's immediately apparent why she'd reacted that way.

A seriously gorgeous woman has just walked in with amazing black silky hair and caramel-toned skin. You can tell she is mixed race, but there is definitely some Asian in there – Freya's kryptonite. When the woman glances over at us, her eyes landing squarely on Freya, she almost trips. I look back at my sister, and she's smiling like I haven't seen her smile in ages. It's that same goofy, smitten look she has when she saw Madi yesterday, but without the predatory edge. I'd only seen that look once before, when she was nineteen and thought she'd fallen head over heels for this girl named Simone back in Chicago.

Maya and I subtly back away, giving our sister some room to work her magic. Luckily, Maya catches on quickly, so I don't have to devise a lame excuse to pull her away.

"H…how can I help you?" Freya stammers, a slight crack in her voice. *Smooth, Freya, real smooth.*

The woman smiles right back at my sister, that same look of instant attraction in her eyes. "Well, that's a loaded question," she says, a playful glint in her eyes, "but for now, I just want to try this amazing coffee I've been hearing about but I think I've already found out why its amazing," she adds, her voice a low purr that almost makes me choke on a laugh. She sounds just like Freya does when she's lying on the charm.

Freya has been all doom and gloom about not meeting anyone in this one-horse town. Guess she was wrong! I head back to my book section, trying to look busy but totally eavesdropping, while Maya slips back into the kitchen, probably to hide her own amusement. Freya seems so flustered, it's actually cute. When she went to pour some coffee, she almost dropped the mug! After Freya finally hands over the coffee, the woman doesn't even bother finding a table; she just leans against the counter, totally engrossed in conversation with my sister. Makes me happy to see her looking like that after everything we've been through, even if it might throw another wrench in our already complicated lives.

Everything I do is for them. I want to make sure they have a good life, even if it costs me mine. Just before closing time, a bunch of kids pile in, fresh from school, and make a beeline for the comics. Bought a few too. Once they clear out, I start shutting down the computer system and pull the till tray so I can stash it in the safe in the office. We got another safe just like the one back home, but this one's a little bigger – for all our newfound riches, ha!

Then, I help my sisters clean up after the front door is locked and the blinds are drawn. Working together, it only takes about thirty minutes to wipe down the counters and put away the leftover muffins and a few other things in the fridge.

I head over to Jenny's to collect Beastie and Pickle while my sisters lock up and plan to swing around in the car to pick us up. When I walk through Jenny's front door, she is just saying goodbye to a customer, so I wait until they leave before saying anything. "Did those two behave themselves?" I ask, nodding towards where Beastie and Pickle lie by the window, people-watching.

"Yeah, they were fine. I even managed to feed him without gagging this time," Jenny said, wrinkling her nose in that adorable way she does.

I can't help but laugh. "That's progress! You'll get used to it," I say, though even I still sometimes felt a little queasy.

"It looked like you had an amazing day! Any hiccups?" Jenny asks, her eyes bright with curiosity.

"Nope, smooth sailing, apart from almost running out of food. We might actually have to hire someone if this keeps up," I say, still a little stunned by how busy we'd been.

"That's fantastic news!" Jenny exclaims, genuinely happy for us.

"Alright, I better get these two out of your hair; it looks like you've got another customer heading your way," I say, spotting a woman approaching the door.

"Yeah, that's my four o'clock. I'll see you later!" Jenny says, giving me a quick hug. Then, I head out to the back area of her building and grab Beastie's bowls and cooler.

"We've got a whole lot to tell you when you get to ours," I say.

"Ooh, I can't wait!" Jenny replies, then turns her attention to the woman who'd just walked in. The woman gives Beastie a wide berth, her eyes widening a fraction as she passes us.

Once we are outside Jenny's, and I'm sure no one is around, I turn to Pickle, who is perched comfortably on Beastie's back. "Find anything interesting on your little expedition today?"

"Nope, we didn't find a single thing. I'm starting to think maybe none of my kind ever made it to this world. Maybe I'm the last one," she says as her voice drops to a whisper. I can see a deep sadness in her eyes that tugs at my heart. I really hope she is wrong.

As we wait for my sisters to pick us up, I gaze across the street at our new business. It still feels surreal that we'd actually pulled it off. Our first day is a bona fide success. And I still can't get over our sign. Freya really knocked it out of the park. I'd been floored when I first saw it; she'd even incorporated the image from our book of shadows. So, after the stylish font spelt out "The MoonTree," there's this beautiful picture of a tree with branches that twist and morph into the moon, like it's growing right out of the wood. Then, two other branches curve upwards, turning into these elegant wings that cradle the moon perfectly, just like on our book cover. I'm still not a hundred percent sure it's a smart move, advertising our witchy side like that, but hey, what's done is done, right? Anyway, who is actually going to know the image has anything to do with witches?

Catherine M. Clark

Chapter 14

A Deputy's Kiss

As Freya navigates the road home, I turn to her and ask, "So, what was her name?" The car sways unexpectedly when I speak, causing Maya and me to grasp the handles above our seats instinctively, our startled voices echoing in unison, "What?"

Freya looks flustered but quickly regains her composure and responds, "Sorry, whose name?" Her playful tone suggests she is feigning ignorance.

I sigh, shifting in my seat as the afternoon shadows deepen outside. "Freya, *don't* play this game. You know *exactly* who I'm talking about," I press, trying to keep my tone light while digging for information on her new mystery woman.

"What game? I'm so confused," Freya says sheepishly, glancing quickly at us before focusing back on the road.

Sitting in the back seat, Maya shakes her head, a wry smile playing on her lips. "She must think we're stupid," she murmurs, her tone dripping with playful sarcasm.

I lean forward in my seat, a teasing grin forming. "I'm talking about the woman you flirted with today for about half an hour at work," I say, shooting Freya a knowing look. Despite her attempts to appear calm, I can see the tension in her grip on the steering wheel.

Freya's eyes widen in mock innocence. "I…I wasn't…what are

you talking about?" she stammers, her voice rising a pitch too high, revealing we are on track.

Maya couldn't resist the opportunity to poke fun. "Are you both going to start dating?" she asks, an exaggerated evil grin spreading across her face, her eyes twinkling mischievously. I can't help but stifle a laugh at Freya's flustered expression.

"I *don't* have a girlfriend!" Freya shoots back defensively, her cheeks flushing a light shade of pink as her irritation mixes with embarrassment. The sight is almost too entertaining for Maya, whose grin widens even more, relishing Freya's discomfort.

"Has Freya met someone? I'm so jealous!" Pickle chimes in, crossing her arms over her chest as she repositions herself against Beastie, where she had nodded off just moments after we had set off. Even in her drowsiness, she can't help but join the teasing.

"Don't you start! There's nothing to be jealous of because I don't have a girlfriend, got it!" Freya exclaims, the frustration in her voice evident as her blush deepens. It's clear that her indignation isn't quite matching her state of denial.

I lean back with a satisfied smirk. "Sure," I reply, savouring the moment. "So, what is your new *friend's* name?" I ask, emphasising the word 'friend' to fuel the playful banter further. The tension in the car is conspicuous, a delightful mix of teasing and camaraderie. Freya's eyes narrow, and for a fleeting moment, I think she might actually break the steering wheel with how hard she is gripping it.

"Do you want a beating?" Freya growls at me.

"My team is bigger than yours; try again!" I say with a cheeky smile, knowing full well that the playful threat has lost its edge. Beastie lets out a slight growl in response, which only fuels my amusement. The sound sparks genuine laughter from Maya, which causes the rest of us to join her.

Freya shoots me a dirty look, her irritation simmering beneath the surface. After a few moments of silence, she finally breaks the silence with a flat and somewhat distracted tone. "Dhara."

"That's a lovely name," I reply, recalling the striking woman who walked in and smiled when she saw Freya. "She was quite pretty, too."

"If you say so," Freya mutters under her breath, her eyes flicking away, clearly avoiding the conversation and looking at me.

Maya, ever curious, leans in. "Did you exchange numbers?"

Freya's response comes a little too quickly, and the defensiveness is evident. "No, why would I?"

"Ah, but she did, didn't she?" Pickle pipes up, glancing between Freya and me, her eyes sparkling with mischief when I look back at her.

"Absolutely," I confirm with a sly grin. I can't help but steal a glance at Freya; her expression is one of resigned defeat, the flush in her cheeks giving away her embarrassment.

"Why doesn't she want us to know she likes this Dhara?" Pickle asks, genuine confusion etched on her face.

"Because she claims to be a very private person," I explain, "but she has no qualms about meddling in our romantic interests. So, we return the favour—it's a sister thing, Pickle. You know, a little playful payback."

"Oh, I see." Pickle's expression shifts, her thoughts clearly drifting. "I didn't have any sisters growing up. I do miss my friends, though, the races we used to have," she adds, her gaze drifting out the window, lost in her memories.

"I hope you'll share those stories with us one day," Maya encourages softly, her tone gentle and sincere.

"Maybe, one day," Pickle replies, curling back against Beastie, her eyelids fluttering as though she might slip into slumber, though I sense she is merely pretending to rest.

As we approach our driveway, Freya's voice breaks the stillness. "Fine! Yes, I exchanged numbers. I hope you're all happy about it," she says, her tone a mixture of irritation and begrudging acceptance.

Maya and I exchange glances, a shared understanding and a smile passing between us, but we remain quiet, content to let the moment linger.

As we head indoors, Freya walks past us and says, "I'm going to get you back," accompanied by an ominous look. I can't help but gulp; she always finds a way to get back at me. Sometimes, I can't help myself when it comes to teasing my sisters.

We are all exhausted, so we have a relaxed evening aside from taking a long walk with Beastie and Pickle, which Pickle uses to search for her people. After ordering dinner from the local diner again, I spend some time in my room reading while Maya has an early night as she's shattered from the first day of our new business and all the hours of baking she has put in.

Before I finish an entire page, I recall what Papa Legba said about my original purple fire still being a part of my power. So, I set my book back down, leaned against my headboard, and closed my eyes.

I spend nearly an hour delving into the depths of my body, trying to search and connect with what he mentioned, but all my efforts yield nothing. The only sensation I can grasp is a familiar pulse in my chest—a concentrated surge of power that throbs like a galaxy erupting into life whenever I tap into my latent power. Just as frustration threatens to overwhelm me, it dawns on me that perhaps none of us has truly searched the depths of our minds. Like Papa Legba mentioned, we focused on what we feel in the location of our hearts; he said that's wrong to do, so I redirected my focus.

As I try to focus on my mind, I start the exploration again, but still, no vivid images or sensations linked to my power materialise; only fleeting memories flicker to the surface, each one planting seeds of doubt. A peculiar feeling interrupts my thoughts when I'm about to concede defeat. It's as if something is beckoning me from the corner of my consciousness—a door, I see a door, dark and creepy.

I fix my focus on this door, feeling an initial resistance as I attempt to move towards it. When I reach the door and manage to open it, my mental landscape shifts, and I'm suddenly standing at the edge of a valley, staring at a building that looks like where I used to work, the national library. Surrounding the building is a strange landscape, like a fierce storm is in the distance and a night sky full of stars with a bright moon that feels like it is shining only on me.

With a mixture of trepidation and curiosity, I enter the building. The experience is surreal; at first, it feels like I am suspended in a weightless state. Then, as I fully cross into the building, I gasp in awe at the sight that unfurls before me. Three statues are in the foyer of the building, and they look just like me. The first one, I'm holding out my hands, and sticks and stones hang in the air before the statue. This must represent my ability in Telekinesis. The next is me holding out my hands and coming from my hands in one massive sphere of black fire, its swirling tendrils mesmerising and chaotic; however, my attention is irresistibly drawn to a smaller, radiant ball of purple fire that dances in my other hand. The colours shimmer with their own life, and an inexplicable pull urges me closer. I carefully approach the statue; driven by instinct, I reach out and touch the purple sphere of flames. The moment my fingers make contact, a surge of energy courses through my body, igniting a tingling sensation in my hands that feels both exhilarating and empowering.

My eyes snap open, and a smile breaks across my face, illuminating my features with a newfound vitality. From my fingertips, vibrant purple flames flicker to life, swirling and intertwining with a grace I have missed. For about five captivating minutes, I'm lost in the dance of the fire, mesmerised by how they grow and shrink in response to my will. I feel no drain or fatigue from the exertion—a testament to the untapped reservoir of power within me.

When the *thrill* begins to fade, I extinguish the flames and close my eyes again, a sense of urgency guiding me back to that door. This time, I reach it with surprising ease, as if a part of me has always known its existence. Once inside and having re-entered the building, I survey my surroundings and, to my astonishment, discover a row of books sitting upon display cases positioned in a horseshoe shape, flanking the statues. Each book seems to beckon me, whispering promises of knowledge and possible new abilities waiting to be unveiled.

A fleeting shadow catches my attention as I stand staring at the row of books, curling like smoke near me. Its shape is eerily similar to my silhouette, a reflection that stirs curiosity and unease. Tentatively, I approach the shadow, extending my hand to touch it. To my astonishment, I find it feels insubstantial, almost as if I'm brushing against the delicate threads of a spiderweb. The moment my fingers make contact, the shadow shimmers and pulses, a wave of darkness rippling across its surface, yet it remains frozen as a statue. I'm sure the shadow has deepened, enveloping itself in a more profound darkness.

Determined to quell my unease, I turn my attention to the book beside the shadow. Its ethereal form is nearly transparent, resembling a ghostly apparition that flickers in and out of focus, making it difficult to discern any details. A sense of otherworldliness surrounds it as if it belongs to another realm entirely. Scanning the books, I soon spot some that appear wholly solid. Their covers look robust and inviting, beckoning me to investigate further. I feel a pull towards them, eager to uncover what secrets lie within their pages, contrasting the fleeting mystique of the shadow beside me.

However, something else catches my eye, to my right, there's a strange room that is devoid of colour, and the entrance to the room seems to shimmer and swirl, like a veil hanging over the entrance to a room. I approach this strange room, when I step in from of it I see myself in the room looking back at me, it looks and moves like I do and as I do, I wave at the other version of me, it's waves back at the same time, this different version on me though looks just like Doris, does this mean this room represents my ability to see the dead and when I look closer to the details of the room I see it's not a room at all, it's actually outside and in the distance is in fact a graveyard which cements that this is indeed my ability to see the dead. Unable to resist, I try to touch the other version of me, as soon as my hand touches the veil, my ghost-self vanishes from view. However, as soon as I touch the veil again, my ghost-self returns, maybe I am turning the ability off and on. Curious, I move back to the books, as I approach the first one, which looks like a ghost itself, I try to touch it, but my hand goes straight through it, and nothing happens.

Frustrated, I give up on that book and notice there are a lot of books that look just like this one, which causes a shiver of curiosity to run through me—can these books truly represent the abilities I'm destined to acquire? My gaze drifts to the last book in the line, and it draws me in. It flickers in and out of existence, never quite becoming fully real. A second book nearby strikes me as also being caught in an in-between, a tenuous balance of faded and solid.

As I study the books, I catch sight of another statue, this one much smaller. There is something on its pedestal that also looks faded. I approach the small statue, and when I reach it, I see that the item on it is small. I lean in closer to examine what it could be. As I study the ghostly image, it begins to take shape before my eyes. I have to concentrate hard, as it's barely visible. What I do see makes no sense; it looks like an egg, with a delicate and intricate design etched faintly on its surface. Confusion swirls in my mind. I hesitate, then reach out tentatively to touch it.

The moment my fingers make contact, a jolt of pain shoots through me, far sharper than I expect. I recoil instinctively, drawing my hand back as I mutter to myself, "Ouch," in disbelief. The initial sting flares suddenly within my mind, leaving me breathless. For an unsettling instant, I think I hear a roar, then it turns into laughter as it echoes in the distance—a light, mocking sound. I glance around, half-expecting to find Freya has somehow found a way into my mind, except I'm the only one here in this building as far as I can see and notice for the first time the walls inside thought they look like where I used to work, the rows of bookshelves look fake like they are just an image on a wall. I continue to look around, but of course, how the hell would Freya appear in my mind in this building?

I notice lots of doors around this library, each one looking real and each secured with a padlock. I walk over to one and try the handle; it feels solid, but the door won't budge. The padlock is cold and unyielding to my touch, and I realise there's no keyhole for a key to unlock it. As my fingers make contact with the handle, a tingling sensation travels up my back, sending a shiver down my spine. What could be behind these doors?

Without warning, a soft but sudden weight lands on my lap, making me scream in shock and causing my eyes to snap open with fear. The laughter I previously sensed is now ringing louder. I think it's coming from outside my bedroom door, a mirthful chorus that momentarily distracts me from whatever landed on me while I scramble awkwardly off my bed.

Once I'm off my bed and look down at my mattress, I see my Drake sitting there, looking up at me with those enormous, sorrowful eyes, his sleek tail swishing rhythmically. "What the hell?!" I exclaim, bewildered and still reeling from the shock of what I'm witnessing before me.

My bedroom door creaks open, and a head pokes into my room. It's Freya. I know it's her as soon as I see her bleached blonde hair appear before I see her face adorned with that familiar mischievous grin that always signalled trouble. Just behind her, I spot Pickle, barely able to contain her laughter, her wings fluttering as she struggles to stay hovering in the air.

"What... have you done... to my... DRAKE!?" I demand, my voice laced with confusion, irritation and, of course, bewilderment and then anger at the end.

Freya feigns innocence, a glint of mischief dancing in her eyes. "What do you mean?" she replies, her ridiculously casual tone only prompts Pickle to burst out laughing uncontrollably, collapsing to the floor in a fit of giggles. Seeing Pickle's reaction warms my heart and softens my annoyance just a bit, but then I shift my focus back to Freya, determination etching across my face and plant my fists firmly on my hips, the weight of my stare bearing down on her.

"Freya Ariel Harper!" I say through gritted teeth, my tone firm.

"Oh, oh, I may have gone too far," she whispers, attempting to edge away. But I know her tells, too well, every subtle movement betraying her. Drawing upon my power, I lock her in place, a wave of heat surging through me. Like a predator closing in on its prey, I lunged at her.

Just as I reach for her arm, a fleeting shadow catches my eye, darting in and landing on Freya's limb, grounding her wild movements as she tries to fight my power that holds her in an unexpected stillness. My hand grasps her arm in the very spot where my shadow had landed ahead of my hand, securing my hold right where I intended.

"Hey! sis, that's cheating, and that hurts; you don't have to grab me so hard," Freya calls out, her voice a mix of exasperation and humour.

Her reaction snaps my attention back to her, and I look down at where I'm gripping her arm; my fingers are digging into her skin, and around my grip, her skin is turning red. I quickly let go and step back; I can't believe I hurt my sister as I watch the pale hand print I left behind start to turn pink again.

Freya shakes her arm and looks down at the marks I left. "Ouch, how the hell have you become so strong?" she asks, giving me a funny look.

"I'm sorry. I didn't mean to hurt you," I say softly, my voice barely a whisper as a cascade of memories rushes back. I remember Freya's words about strength—their weight lingering in my mind like a haunting melody. Suddenly, the image of carrying Beastie without straining came to me. At the time, the ease of it had startled me, but with everything else happening around us, I had pushed that moment away, buried beneath layers of distraction.

"It's okay. You don't have to take it all so personally," Freya says gently, her brows knit together in concern as she searches my face for understanding.

"To be honest, I think we're growing stronger. This isn't the first time I've felt it," I confess, glancing down at my hands. They feel different, more capable than before.

Freya's eyes lit up with recognition. "You've noticed it too! I thought I was imagining it. Your grip is definitely stronger than I remember. It's going to be really handy when Maya struggles with those stubborn jars. Anyway, I'm heading for an early night. See you in the morning," she adds, attempting to walk away with an air of casualness.

"I don't think so," I say, blocking her path. A sudden worry surges within me. "What have you two done to my Drake?" I demand, my heart racing as I eye their expressions.

Both Freya and Pickle exchange guilty glances, shifting nervously. "Come on out with it," I press.

"It was her idea," Pickle blurts out, pointing a shaky finger at Freya, who gasps in mock betrayal.

"Traitor!" Freya shoots back, her cheeks flushing. "We both thought of it! We read a page in the new book together."

"I just thought it would be funny," Pickle says, her eyes wide with panic as they dart between Freya and me. I feel a twinge of sympathy for her; seeing her laugh is joyful, but I don't like to see her looking worried.

"What did you do?" I demand again, raising my voice slightly but consciously keeping my tone steady, avoiding anger.

Freya looks down at her feet, deliberating as if weighing her options. Finally, she meets my eyes. "I turned your Drake into a golem."

"A golem? Aren't they made of clay or something?" I ask, confusion knitting my brow as I grasp for clarity. The concept is familiar from the countless books and Tv shows we have shared over the years, but this is something else entirely.

"Yes, you can make golems from clay, but there's also a way to infuse an inanimate object with life," Freya explains, a hint of pride creeping into her voice. She seems delighted with her newfound ability.

I turn to look at Drake, still sitting there with its big, sorrowful eyes lingering on me, a look I'd never seen before. "Is it dangerous?" I ask, a hint of worry creeping into my voice.

Freya shakes her head vigorously. "Nope! I crafted it as a simple golem and told it that it's your favourite toy that loves to cuddle. It's happy this way and should act just like a normal cat," she assures me, her laughter echoing with Pickles as they exchange glances of shared amusement.

I take a deep breath, contemplating the implications of what they have done. My heart is still beating quicker from a mix of curiosity and apprehension threading through me. I shake my head at them, look back down at Drake, and move slowly towards him. As I do, he starts to look excited, which makes his tail swish faster from side to side. Then, he starts to bounce on his front paws, now looking excited.

I can't help but smile at his reaction and remember all the times when I was sad; he made me feel better when I cuddled him, and I wished he were real. So, I sit down on the edge of the bed, and as soon as I do, Drake jumps onto my lap and snuggles against me. I melt at the sight and feel of him, so I wrap my hands around him, and he still feels soft like he always has, and then he starts to purr just like a real cat when I stroke his head.

Then his hair, fur, whatever you call it, rises up down his back, and he starts to make a cute little growling noise, which is followed by a deep growl that comes from my bedroom door. Beastie has arrived, and they don't seem to like each other.

"Beastie, it's just Drake, Freya, and Pickle turned him into a golem. He's not a threat," I say, and as soon as I do, Beastie stops growling but gives Freya and Pickle what seems like the stink eye. This makes the smiles on their faces drop with concern, and Freya disappears quickly into her room, but Pickle doesn't know what to do with herself.

That is until the front door opens downstairs, signalling Jenny has finally arrived, much later than we expected. She texted to say she had some family issues she needed to deal with. Pickle dashes off in a flash, I guess, to see her so she can escape Beastie and me.

Jenny soon appears in my doorway, and I shake my head when I see Pickle hiding in her hair.

"Chicken," I say, and she sticks her tongue out at me.

"What's going on?" Jenny asks, looking confused about the situation as she glances back and forth between Beastie and me. "Pickle said you two are mad at her, and Freya has left her to shoulder all the blame."

I can't help but raise an eyebrow, "Did she now?" I reply, noticing the hint of sadness in Pickle's eyes peeking out from behind Jenny's tousled hair. Taking a deep breath, I sigh and explain, "Well, you see, Freya and Pickle decided it would be a brilliant idea to turn my beloved Drake into a golem."

Jenny's confusion is evident as she tilts her head. "What's a golem? And are you talking about your panther toy?"

"Yep, that one," I say, lifting the wriggling stuffed toy into the air. Its little limbs flailing, clearly unhappy with the sudden change in its position.

"Bloody hell, it's possessed!" Jenny gasps, her voice tinged with panic. "It's not staying in here, is it?" She says as she stares at Drake with horror in her eyes.

"Afraid so. According to Freya, it's not dangerous; she said she made it, so it acts like a cat, and it likes cuddles," I explain, glancing at Jenny, who is still standing in my bedroom doorway, and I see her gaze is now fixated down the hallway towards the spare room. I know her well enough to sense her discomfort; she doesn't like using the spare room with its old, sagging mattress and the metal bedframe that creaks ominously at the slightest movement. I can tell she is weighing her options, and the thought of spending a night there clearly isn't what she had in mind.

"Are you sure it won't try to smother us in our sleep?" Jenny asks, her eyes darting back to Drake, who is lounging carelessly on my lap. Drake has curled its tail around its paws, blissfully unaware of the tension in the air as I gently stroke its head and back.

"I promise, it's harmless," I reassure her, trying to keep my voice steady while sensing her apprehension. "Now come on, what's really bothering you? You said you wanted to talk?" I urge gently, hoping to coax her concerns out into the open.

Catherine M. Clark

Chapter 15

When Toys Awaken

Jenny stands at the threshold of my room, and she looks concerned and worried, like she is uncertain about something and is weighing her options. After a moment of hesitation, she pushes my bedroom door shut behind her and makes her way to my bed, settling beside me. Her gaze remains fixed on Drake, who lounges innocently, his eyes half-closed.

"Why don't you give him a little stroke? You might find that it eases your worries. He really does behave just like a cat, so far," I suggest, hoping to reassure her.

A flicker of apprehension crosses Jenny's face. "You don't understand," she says, her voice a little shaky, like there is a hint of fear she is trying to hide. "When I was little, I had these terrible nightmares about my toys springing to life and turning on me while I slept. It was terrifying, like they were plotting against me."

I consider what she just told me and start to shake my head to try and distract myself, to stop myself from doing something I don't think I should right now, but *hey*, I'm weak and can't help myself. I burst out laughing, which causes Jenny to give me a dirty look. After a few seconds, though, she joins me in laughing at the situation. When I can finally talk again, I say, "But this isn't the same, not at all," I point out gently. "I really can't picture Freya instructing him to misbehave or cause trouble."

As I tell her this, I glance down at Drake, who seems so unnervingly calm and untroubled. Then I start to wonder if Freya might have slipped in a secret instruction for him to be a little terror later on. Jenny still looks unconvinced as she stops laughing, and then the shadows of her past start to creep back in, and I'm sure she is picturing what happened in those dreams again.

Jenny blows out a breath and sighs. "My brother has had a falling out with my parents, and they kicked him out, so he turned up on my doorstep yesterday. He has nowhere else to go for now, so he wants to stay at mine, but I only have one bedroom in my apartment, so I was wondering," Jenny says, but trails off at the end. I know what she wants to ask. I feel for her, but a shiver of unease runs down my spine at the thought.

"Jenny, it could be dangerous to live here; we just discovered the attacks will start up again," I explain, as my fear for her becomes tangible.

"I don't care. I'm worried about all of you and want to help however I can. My life was dull until you guys moved here, and now I have amazing friends who actually get me. Anyway, if I'm to stay as your friend, then I could be in more danger living alone than I would be living here. You have this strong barrier around the property, so as long as I stay within it, I will be safe," Jenny pleads, giving me her puppy eyes.

She does have a point. "We warded your apartment a few weeks ago, so it's safer than normal, but I guess it's up to you. I'm not your keeper. I'm just worried about you," I say, trying to sound more reassuring than I feel.

"I know you put a ward on my apartment, but I would like to move into your spare room when I can get a decent bed. At least the wards on my place will help protect my brother," Jenny says with a determined glint in her eyes.

"Fine," I say, giving in—how can I not when she still looks at me with those sad eyes? Then I decided to surprise her with something she doesn't know I've done. "You're in luck; this bed will be moved into the spare room next week when my new custom-size bed arrives."

"You ordered it then, that's great. So, I can share it with you until then?" Jenny asks as she sheds the sad eyes, and they turn bright and hopeful as a smile spreads across her face.

"Yeah, that's fine."

"Cool, I'm going to have a quick shower, then you can tell me what's been going on," Jenny says, getting up and heading out of my room, leaving me alone with my newly animated panther. She wasn't here yesterday but was kind enough to come pick up Freya and Beastie.

We spend the evening and morning reviewing the police files, which reveal a disturbing pattern. Most reports say either the mother or father returns home and starts acting entirely differently, like they developed a new personality from what some family members reported.

They also state that they start to become violent in some cases and use it as a game, pushing other family members against each other and driving them out of the house. Then, they systematically emptied bank accounts, sold their homes and any other properties they owned, and quit their jobs, not before, in some instances, violently attacking their boss.

When the police finally track these individuals down, they are invariably found dead with no discernible physical signs of injury. From what the autopsies say, the chilling discovery is that they have all died from an aneurysm.

Luca and Rose explained that this was a typical and terrifying side effect of prolonged demonic possession, as the fragile human mind couldn't cope with such an unnatural intrusion for long.

It's almost time for Sam and me to head to Luna Falls to finally confront the sisters, while I'm still unsure how I will broach the delicate subject of them potentially being witches. We have another layer of complexity now, though. Luca has voiced some serious concerns after we recounted our unsettling encounter with one of the sisters, and Rose could detect the distinct scent of sulphur clinging to my memories of the interaction. His unsettling theory is that perhaps one of the demons plaguing Jackson has somehow made its way to Luna Falls and possessed one of the sisters. Alternatively, he speculated that they might have tried to attack the sisters, or, even more worryingly, that one of the sisters could be a black witch, the very individual responsible for summoning the malevolent shades and dispatching them to Jackson.

Now, I am locked in a tense debate with Luca and Rose about going to Luna Falls without their backup. "The only way we can find out what is happening is by going to the meeting and talking to them. I can't see them attacking us, especially since the sheriff and deputy know we are in town to speak with them. Also, it's far too soon for either of you to head into town right now. If there are shifters in town, we can't risk you going, as it will undoubtedly alert them, and we have absolutely no idea how many they might have here," I explain, trying to inject a note of logic into their palpable anxiety.

"If they are black witches, Ava, you will be in even more danger," Luca counters, his voice tight with worry laced in with his authority of being an alpha.

"Rose, what did you sense from the woman we met? Did she strike you as a black witch? Because to me, she seems more like a typical country housewife, maybe a little too perfect, but certainly not someone who's dabbling in summoning demons," I say, my frustration starting to bubble.

Rose looks between Luca and me before her shoulders visibly slump in defeat. "She has a point, Luca. At worst, the sister she met was a

Stepford wife with questionable blue highlights. Her hair was unnervingly perfect, and she was dressed like a wholesome country girl in a summer dress," Rose elaborates, finally breaking through Luca's staunch defences.

"Fine, just be extra careful. I know you're exceptionally good at reading people, but you haven't had to read paranormal beings before," he concedes, his concern still evident.

"Well, I haven't had an issue reading you, either," I retort with a confident smirk.

Luca and Rose shoot me a playful glare, but Rose can't maintain the stern façade for long. "So, we are all sorted?" Sam interjects, his voice calm as he meticulously cleans his service weapon. I'm doing the same, except my focus is on the gleaming blade of my sword.

"I guess so," I say as they remain silent to his question. I'm not going to mention that I have some lingering unease as I prepare for our departure.

Sam and I are just about to leave when Luca's phone suddenly starts to ring. We all exchange a look of confusion for a split second, as I, for one, can't recall ever hearing his phone ring since we have been together. He wastes no time in answering it, his usual relaxed demeanour instantly replaced by a mask of worry.

"Elijah, what's up?" he asks, looking concerned as I recognise the name; it belongs to Luca's other beta, the one who is in hiding with the remnants of their pack.

"Are you all okay?" Luca asks after listening to whatever Elijah has just told him, while his voice sounds strained. I can't make out the reply, but Rose is immediately on her feet, her senses clearly picking up on something I can't hear. She stands rigidly next to Luca, her expression tight with worry, confirming that whatever news she hears through her enhanced hearing isn't good.

"I'm heading for you right now. Stay safe until I get there, try to get to the Woodlands area in Houston, I will meet you there," Luca says, his voice urgent, before abruptly hanging up.

"I'm coming with you," Rose states immediately, her eyes blazing with determination.

"No, you're not. I need you to stay here for Ava and Sam, as they may need backup," Luca says firmly, his gaze unwavering, and his tone is the most serious I've heard from him so far.

Rose shoots me a quick, worried look before turning back to Luca. "If anything happens to our pack and I'm not there, I won't be able to live with myself," she says, her voice thick with emotion.

"I know, Rose, I feel the same way. I'm the one who decided to do this, hoping it will be for the good of our future. I still believe in this, so I need you to stay and provide help if they need you. We don't know what's going on here yet, but so far, it doesn't seem like this is what we were hoping to discover, as it seems this Cat may be wrong about these sisters. I need you to stay here because I won't risk losing both our packs," he says as his eyes lock with Rose's.

Rose closes her eyes for a moment, and when she reopens them, a steely resolve replaces her raw emotions. "You're right. You better take the Tahoe," Rose concedes, her voice tight.

"Okay," Luca says, then looks over to me. "Do you have everything you might need?" he asks clearly, still concerned about our mission.

"I need to grab my rifle bag just in case," Sam states, his usual quiet demeanour replaced by a focused readiness.

"I have everything I need, except we'd better grab some extra ammunition," I add, a knot of apprehension tightening in my stomach.

We watch Luca race out of the room, his movements swift and purposeful. I turn to Rose, my voice sounding strained, "What's happened?"

"Our pack was discovered and attacked. Luckily, they fought off their attackers, but they called in backup, so they are now trying to get as much distance as possible before they show up," Rose explains, her voice trembling slightly despite her attempt to remain composed.

"Oh! I hope they stay safe," I say, a wave of sympathy washing over me as a practical thought strikes me. "How will you get to Luna Falls if we need you?"

"You're going to drop me off on the outskirts, and then if you need me, I will shift and come running as fast as I can. I can also use the time to scent the area to see if I can pick up on anything," Rose states, a flicker of her usual resourcefulness returning.

"Good idea," I agree, feeling relieved at her proactive thinking.

Rose then pulls me into a scorching kiss, a raw expression of her worry and affection. The intensity of the moment makes Sam visibly uncomfortable, so he busies himself by putting his rifle bag and extra ammunition into the trunk of our rented car and then quietly gets in. We finally pull apart, the lingering tension between us palpable, join Sam, and set off for Luna Falls.

When we drop Rose off on the outskirts of town, she informs us she can't scent any other shifters who have been in the area recently. But I can't help but watch her in my rearview mirror as we drive off, a knot of worry tightening in my chest at the thought of her being out there alone.

As we drive through the quaint, seemingly peaceful town, I keep replaying different scenarios in my mind about what I'm going to say to the sisters. A nagging voice whispers that they are going to look at me like I'm a delusional lunatic. As we approach the turn for the sisters' driveway, I notice an unfamiliar car parked haphazardly on the side of the otherwise empty road. I scan the surrounding area for the owner, but don't see anyone to whom it could belong, and it feels distinctly out of place and suspicious. "Who do you think that belongs to?" I ask Sam, my voice laced with unease.

"I'm not sure. It seems out of place. Maybe once we discuss

things with the sisters, we can casually mention it," Sam says, glancing at me from the driver's seat, his expression mirroring my apprehension.

"I agree. We need to gauge where the sisters stand first. The car might belong to a friend and could be their backup if they are worried about why we are here," I reason, trying to find a logical explanation for the unsettling sight.

"You might be right," said Sam, but it lacked conviction.

As we turn right onto their long, winding drive, a wave of nervousness washes over me. It's an unfamiliar sensation for me as I never feel like this when I head out for a mission. I'm also getting a strange feeling, the distinct prickling sensation of being watched. My mind immediately jumps back to the abandoned car we passed. I try to mentally shrug it off, attributing it to my frayed nerves; otherwise, I know it will drive me crazy with paranoia. Typically, I'm good at objectively assessing a situation before walking into it. I have to admit that since joining this task force, I've been feeling slightly off-kilter, as if my standard military skills aren't entirely applicable in this bizarre and dangerous paranormal world.

We finally pull outside the charmingly rustic house and see a relatively new, expensive-looking truck parked in the driveway. This seems like a good sign that all three sisters are likely present. As I get out of our rental car, I instinctively check that all of my concealed weapons are securely in place, ensuring there is no accidental reveal that might spook the sisters. The magic used to conceal them only works if they are fully and correctly positioned.

Sam and I exchange a quick, silent glance, a shared understanding passing between us, before heading towards the front door. Before we even reach the veranda steps, we hear the same low, guttural growling that greeted us during our previous visit. Then, within seconds, the front door swings open, revealing a strikingly beautiful woman standing in the doorway.

She steps out onto the veranda and descends the steps, effectively blocking our approach to the house. She strongly resembles Maya, whom we met the other day, but there are subtle yet noticeable differences. She has the same dark hair as her sister, but instead of Maya's obviously blue dye, this woman's hair has what looks like natural-looking red undertones.

When I meet her intense gaze, I can immediately tell she isn't thrilled to see us as the same massive dog from our previous encounter appears at her side, its teeth bared in a silent threat. The woman casually scratches between its ears, leans down, and whispers something I can't quite make out—a gesture eerily similar to what Maya had done before. Whatever she said works, as the dog instantly stops growling. It then turns and calmly returns to the front door, where it sits down, its intelligent eyes fixed on us.

I pull out my FBI badge and flash it quickly. "Hey. I'm Agent Bekke, and this is Agent Miller."

"I guess you want to come in and talk to us," she states flatly, her expression unreadable. "Well, come on then," she gestures for us to head up to the front door while she steps to one side, allowing us access. For some reason, I notice her gaze flickers down to our feet as we approach the steps leading to the veranda and the front door. As I watch her, I see a subtle but distinct shift in her expression just as we reach the bottom steps. Her initial guarded look seems to melt away, replaced by a flicker of something akin to relief, all at the exact same moment that the hair on my arms stands on end, as if I have just received a jolt of static electricity. *What the hell was that?* I think to myself, my senses on high alert. I glance at Sam, calmly at my side, to see if he also felt the same, but he shows no reaction as I subtly run my hand over my left arm where the hairs have risen.

When we reach the front door, I stare at the dog. It truly is enormous, easily the size of a bear. It's not quite the same size as Rose in her panther form, but this dog is close, though perhaps a little less bulky than Rose's panther is pure muscle covering her body.

I step through the front door and immediately notice the spacious kitchen to my right. It looks like a typical, well-used kitchen in a ranch-style house. There is a large wooden table, but two chairs seem to be missing. That is, until I spot two identical chairs over in the central living area, where a comfortable-looking couch with two women are seated and watching us. There are also two armchairs and a large television.

One is the sister we encountered the other day, Maya, and the other is a striking blonde with a smattering of freckles across her nose. Despite their different hair colours, the family resemblance is undeniable, so this must be the third and final sister. She looks even less pleased to see us than the one who met us at the door. Maybe this is Reya.

Before I move towards the two chairs I presume have been placed there for us, the massive dog lumbers past us and effortlessly steps onto the couch. It curls up next to the two women, resting its large head on their laps, and watches us with the same intelligent, unwavering eyes as we finally start to move towards the offered seating.

"Please sit down," the sister who follows us back into the house says as she walks past us and gracefully settles into one of two single-seater armchairs which match the plush couch.

I sit down, my senses still on high alert, and do a quick, practised sweep of the rest of the layout. I note a door leading from the kitchen that goes out to the side of the house; there's another door at the rear, and it is also where a sturdy-looking staircase is situated.

I notice a rather peculiar sight under the stairs and see a flicker of movement. I keep my gaze in this direction a while longer in the hope of seeing what is under the stairs. I don't have to wait long as a tiny, pointed face tentatively pokes out from a lower section at the front of what looks like a half-built wooden box. I blink in surprise as I realise it's a fox cub. Then, the adult fox we saw the other day cautiously pokes its head out from the same hiding spot. It also seems to have intelligent eyes, as they lock straight onto mine. It subtly bares its teeth in what I instinctively recognise as a clear warning not to focus on or approach her cub. The sight is something I have never witnessed before, but it seems to be happening with increasing frequency lately.

My attention is drawn back to the sisters when the one who met us at the door speaks again, her voice calm and measured. "So, what did you want to talk to us about?"

I briefly glance around the room again, half-expecting to spot the elusive fairy from before. But I see no sign of her and wonder if maybe I indeed imagined it, despite Rose's confirmation. "We have a few things we need to discuss with you. Some of it may sound strange," I begin, choosing my words carefully.

Before any of the sisters respond, a distinct noise echoes from upstairs. It sounds like something small and quick scurrying across the wooden floor, which is followed by a soft, muffled voice saying, "Drake, come back here; you can't go down there; it might not be safe."

Again, I can't help myself. My gaze flicks upwards, and I address the sisters about whoever is upstairs. "Whoever is upstairs, we won't hurt them. This Drake can come down if they want," I say, my eyes scanning the reactions of the three sisters who had also initially looked up, their expressions ranging from mild annoyance to outright irritation, until I mention the name Drake.

The sister who met us at the door shoots a sharp, almost accusatory look at the blonde, and then all three of their heads snap towards me in unison, their eyes wide with shock. Even the massive dog on the couch lifts its head, its gaze now intently focused on me.

"How did she hear that?" the sister we know as Maya whispers, her voice barely audible but perfectly clear to me in the quiet room. At the same time, the blonde sitting next to her sharply elbows her in the ribs and gives her a pointed "shush."

"Sorry, we are being rude," the sister who greeted us outside says, quickly regaining her composure. "I'm Reya, the blonde is Freya, and you have already met Maya," she says, finally naming the other two sisters. I mentally chide myself for getting Freya and Reya mixed up in my initial assessment.

I'm still slightly distracted by the sound of something small and quick scurrying across the floorboards upstairs, but I reply to Reya, "You can call me Ava, and this is Sam."

The three sisters are really trying their best to ignore whatever is happening upstairs, though Reya continues to shoot pointed, annoyed glances at Freya, as if she holds her solely responsible for this mysterious "Drake."

Then, Reya takes me entirely by surprise. "So, Ava, what kind of FBI agent goes around with swords and blades strapped to themselves?"

I'm so gobsmacked and instinctively look to Sam for some support or explanation for Reya's bizarrely accurate observation. How on earth can she see my concealed weapons when no one else ever has to date?

"Erm," is the only intelligent response I can initially muster. "Well, we are a special task force. Have you been watching the news lately?" I ask as my brain starts to work again and comes up with a reasonable response, seizing the unexpected opening to explain our presence. Reya inadvertently handed me the perfect segue.

Reya looks genuinely confused and glances at her sisters before turning back to me and saying, "Yeah, we have watched the news a few times, but it's mostly doom and gloom. Why?"

"Did you happen to catch any reports about a new special task force being formed?" I ask.

"Yeah, I think I did, actually. Why?" Reya asks, her curiosity piqued.

"Well, I'm the head of that task force," I state, watching their reactions intently. I see a flicker of recognition dawn in their eyes.

Maya then speaks up, her initial shock replaced by a thoughtful expression. "Didn't you not long ago take down a whole gang in that city... what was it?" She looks over at Sam, her eyes suddenly widening in recognition. "Yeah! I saw you do an interview on Tv, the chief of police in the background looked like a complete idiot," Maya adds, then starts to chuckle quietly to herself.

"Yep, that was me," Sam confirms, looking a little proud of himself, which causes me to let out a small, involuntary chuckle.

So far, things are progressing... strangely, but not entirely negatively. So, I decided it's time to drop the real reason for our visit. "It wasn't exactly a typical gang we took out. It was a nest of vampires."

All three sisters try their best not to react to my bombshell, but once again, Maya can't seem to help herself. "No way," she blurts out as her eyes widen in surprise.

Immediately, the other two sisters groan in unison, shooting her exasperated looks while shaking their heads in apparent annoyance.

I smile slightly at their reactions and reply, "Way. I personally killed my first vampire with my sword during that mission."

This time, Freya doesn't seem to be able to contain her curiosity. "Cool," she breathes out, her eyes wide with a mixture of disbelief and fascination.

Reya shoots both of her sisters a look that could have withered flowers; clearly, she is beyond annoyed with their lack of composure. She then turns back to me, her expression serious. "So, you actually believe in all that... stuff?"

"We do," Sam confirms, his voice steady and matter-of-fact.

"And why does any of this concern us?" Reya asks, her tone now laced with a hint of defensiveness.

Before I can formulate a response, Maya again jumps in, seemingly unable to filter her thoughts. "Maybe because a wolf shifter killed our mother." Maya directs the statement at her sister; it's clear this is a painful memory, as I have my own, so I understand. The look Reya gives back is one of pure, unbelievable anger, causing Maya to visibly flinch.

"Nice one, sis. Do you not remember our little chat about the subjects we weren't exactly planning on volunteering, especially that particular piece of information," Freya whispers, but in this quiet room, we can all hear her attempt at subtlety.

"Oh... sorry," Maya mumbles, pleadingly looking at Reya, silently begging for forgiveness.

"As Maya so... helpfully pointed out, we know a shifter killed your mother. We have reason to believe they are either coming here or are already here, looking for you," I say, carefully watching their reactions, and I'm surprised to see that this potentially alarming information doesn't seem to shock them as much as I anticipated.

The sisters don't exchange knowing glances this time. Reya, though, says in a surprisingly calm tone, "Why would you think they would be coming for *us*?"

Sam steps in to answer her, his gaze direct. "Because one of our team badly injured a wolf shifter. In his last moments, he started to ramble about his alpha being in a small town east of Jackson, on a mission to collect his *prize*."

A flicker of genuine panic finally crosses all three of their faces. The massive dog on the couch starts to growl under its breath, a low rumble that sounds disturbingly like it understands every word being spoken. I'm just about to ask about the dog's unusual reaction when its head shoots up, its ears perk, and it fixes its gaze intently on the front door. Then, the low growl intensifies, becoming a deep, menacing rumble that vibrates through the floor, eliciting a primal fear within me. Even Sam, who rarely shows any outward emotion, looks visibly fearful as he stares at the imposing creature.

"Crap! Not now," Reya exclaims, jumping to her feet with surprising agility. Her sisters follow suit, their initial shock replaced by a sense of urgent readiness. The dog continues to growl, its eyes never leaving the front door.

"Beastie, don't run out there," Reya commands, her tone firm. The name confuses me, and I instinctively glance around the room, wondering who or what she is referring to.

Then, a chilling voice echoes from the front of the house, cutting through the dog's tense growls like it has been magically enhanced. "Little girls, little girls, come and get your punishment. He isn't protecting you anymore, and yes, we know it was him, and he will be dealt with soon enough."

"Who are they talking about?" Sam asks, his hand instinctively moving to draw his service weapon.

"Legba," Maya says, her voice surprisingly steady despite the apparent threat.

"Papa Legba? I met him recently," I blurt out, momentarily distracted by the unexpected connection.

"Really?" Reya responds, her eyes widening slightly as she approaches the front door. She pauses and looks at me like she remembered something involving me.

"Now is definitely not the time for a catch-up," Freya retorts, her voice sharp with annoyance.

"Let's just deal with this before they destroy our house or the sheriff turns up… or Jacob," Reya says with urgency, sounding angry.

"Or Duncan," Maya adds, her previous bravado replaced by a worried frown.

"We can help," I offer, my hand instinctively reaching for the hilt of my sword on my back and pulling it from its sheath.

Reya's eyes flick to my sword, a predatory gleam entering her gaze. "I hope you're good with that," she says, a hint of excitement in her voice.

"Let's find out," I reply, my grip tightening on my sword.

"I wish I had a sword," Reya mutters, her *gaze* drifting off into the distance for a fleeting moment, as if she is lost in a daydream. But as soon as that faraway look crosses her face, something utterly unbelievable begins to happen. I watch in stunned amazement as a shimmering, purple, fiery blade materialises in her outstretched hand, as if conjured from thin air.

Chapter 16

Beneath the Blood Moon

When Reya notices the flaming sword, her eyes blow wide. She yelps, instinctively trying to fling it away like it's burning slag. Clearly an unexpected party trick, but damn impressive. Before I can fully process, the purple flaming sword vanishes.

"What the fuck *was* that?" Freya exclaims, gaping.

Reya looks just as stunned, her gaze flicking between her hand and Freya. "I'm not sure," she murmurs, sounding shaken, "One of the other books *has just become* solid…" Books? What books? My training prompts a quick scan of the room – nothing. Freya, sounding practical, cuts her off.

"Worry later, come on!" Reya gives a shaky head clear, then bolts for the door, swinging it wide. Her sisters hang back, letting her take point – tactical caution or letting the *weapon* go first? Reya steps onto the veranda. The dog – Beastie? – follows, instantly more committed than the sisters, who finally edge outside. Sam and I follow, stepping onto the wooden planks.

"What are you waiting for?" I demand, my eyes locking onto the three figures standing a short distance from the house. My breath catches. Flanking the men are two monsters, like heat haze solidified into pure menace, as their bodies are on fire. A cold dread, sharp and professional, floods me. These things are not something I expected to see. "What the hell are those?"

"What are you talking about?" Sam asks, his hand instinctively reaching for his sidearm.

"Those creatures," I say, my voice a little shaky, so it comes out barely a whisper as I point towards the two large creatures flanking the men.

"Those creatures," I manage, my voice tight, barely a whisper despite myself, pointing towards the shimmering darkness flanking the men. They ripple, distorting the air around them, and a low growl vibrates through the soles of my boots.

"They would be hellhounds," Reya states, unnervingly calm, glancing at her own dog with that weird understanding again.

"Hellhounds?" Sam echoes, suspicion hardening his voice. My own mind spins. Hellhounds. The term sits wrong, like something from cheap fiction, yet the *pressure* radiating from those things, the sheer *wrongness* of their presence, makes the hair on my arms stand on end. My hand automatically tightens on my sword hilt.

"How come you can see them, and he can't?" Reya asks me, curiosity momentarily overriding the danger.

"Papa Legba *gave* me a ring," I say, holding up my right hand before remembering it's invisible. Idiot. After Maya's confused question about wedding rings, I snap, "No! A *magical* ring," dropping my hand back to my sword, the solid weight a small anchor in this sea of impossibility.

I catch Reya's eyes fixed on my right hand—her gaze narrowing as if she is deciphering some dark secret. "That's a pretty ring," she murmurs. Before I can question her further, her attention snaps back to the hostile men and monstrous beasts arrayed before us.

"What? You can see it?" I blurt out, disbelief sizzling in my voice. How can she see what I can't even see, let alone my team-mates? The other two sisters confirm with silent nods, their expressions grim as they echo Reya's assessment.

"Ladies, now really isn't the time for discussing pretty rings. What exactly are we supposed to do with our... guests?" Sam interjects sharply, gripping his service weapon until his knuckles go white. His nervous energy is palpable; he clearly doesn't trust what his eyes can't perceive—the invisible threat of the hellhounds.

I fix my eyes on the looming figures and demand, "Do you know who these men are?"

Reya's calm response sends a chill down my spine. "No, but demons are possessing them." Her words resonate with unsettling certainty.

"How can you be so sure?" I press, feeling the tension in the air tightening like a noose.

"Because their eyes are black orbs," she replies, her gaze unflinching. A shiver races along my spine as I observe the men more closely—their eyes are black, like voids that swallow every speck of light.

"Come on, little girls. Stop wasting time and face your punishment for stealing," snarls the man in the centre, his voice thick with malice. All three of them turn their attention to the dog by Reya's side, whose low, guttural growl resonates unsettlingly.

Almost simultaneously, the two hellhounds flanking the men join in the chorus of growls—the sound a ghostly echo of the one I'd just heard. A crushing wave of fear rises within me as I realise it's Rose, and she is coming. "Shit!" I mutter, dread flooding my veins.

Without warning, the three possessed men raise their hands in eerie unison. Dark spheres of swirling smoke burst from their palms, hurtling towards us at deadly speed. Reflexively, I hit the deck, dragging Sam down behind the relative safety of the veranda railing. The sisters stand like statues – unnerving calm or absolute confidence? I peek over the wood just as the swirling black spheres slam into *something*. There's a sharp *crack* like lightning, and the air *shimmers* violently for a heartbeat, revealing a faint, translucent golden web of energy. The spheres detonate against it, imploding into greasy black smoke that vanishes instantly, leaving only the smell of burnt magic hanging in the air. My memory flashes – Reya's focus on my feet, the tingling… a defensive perimeter. Smart. But strong enough?

"Are you ready?" Reya's voice is unnervingly calm as she addresses her sisters.

"I am," Freya snaps, her eyes shining with fierce determination. "Just say the word." I can't grasp what is about to unfold, but it's clear that they have a plan far beyond my understanding already.

"Now!" Reya commands, her authoritative tone cutting through the mounting dread.

In an instant, thick, thorny vines thicker than my arm erupt violently from the earth, their thorns gleaming wickedly. They lash out, coiling around the possessed men with crushing speed, pinning them mid-stride like grotesque insects. With a synchronised surge that speaks of practice, the sisters sprint down the steps towards them, the dog bounding ahead. Then, before my eyes, the dog *changes*. A wave of intense, unnatural heat washes over me as its body is engulfed in swirling black flames that *crackle* audibly, somehow leaving the wooden steps untouched. Bones snap and reform with sickening speed, its form distorting, expanding into a colossal beast of shadow and fire, easily resembling the hellhounds but radiating a different, somehow *controlled* power. It bolts past Reya, launching a torrent of roaring black flame at one hellhound. Simultaneously, Reya conjures crackling spheres of dark fire, hurling them with lethal accuracy at the other as the trapped men writhe against the tightening thorns. The first hellhound vanishes in a silent explosion of black fire and ash. The other *shrieks* – a high, tearing sound that scrapes against my nerves – as it collapses, Reya's fire scorching its hind legs. The stench of burning flesh and something else, something acrid and wrong, fills the air, making my stomach churn.

I stand frozen, my mind spinning from the speed and brutality of the attack. "Ava, help them!" Sam yells from the safety of the veranda, his voice desperate and strained.

Shaking off my numbing stupor, I sprint after the sisters, raising my sword and trembling in readiness, while Sam clings to the safety of the railing. It's the logical place for him when he can't see the full nightmare unfolding. As I descend, I catch sight of Maya at the bottom of the steps, her hands raised and poised for battle, yet unnervingly passive.

I move towards the struggling men possessed, while Reya focuses intently on the injured hellhound—a target that her monstrous beast is now approaching. As I pass by Freya, I see her deeply concentrated on the writhing figures trapped in the vines. She stands at the threshold of the steps, seemingly anchored on this side of an elusive barrier. Meanwhile, Maya's piercing gaze remains fixed on Reya. Unlike her sisters, she neither exudes the same confident power nor possesses their clarity of purpose, but the determination in her jawline is undeniable.

One of the possessed men begins channelling dark energy, his hands igniting with tendrils, meaning to burn through the vines. After a gruelling moment, he breaks free and rises to his feet, his eyes blazing with defiant rage. Smugly, he raises his hands again as if reclaiming dominion over the situation.

"Reya!" Freya's sharp call cuts through the clamour like a knife.

At the sound of her name, Reya instinctively glances back – a rookie mistake, a fatal hesitation in combat. The injured hellhound, playing possum, explodes upwards with horrifying speed. Its massive jaws clamp down hard on her left leg – I hear the wet crunch even from here – yanking her brutally to the ground with a choked yelp. Before she even lands, flickering *orange* flames, the antithesis of the beast's fire, erupt from the hound's maw, engulfing her trapped limb. I brace for the scream, the smell of burning cloth and flesh, but Reya's lips are pressed into a thin white line, her face a mask of silent, contorted agony as the fire crawls up her leg. My training screams *critical injury, third-degree burns, shock*, but the impossible scene holds me for a split second too long.

Driven by pure adrenaline and the need to *act*, I kick into overdrive. My boots pound the drive as I surge forward, sword raised high, the familiar weight balanced for a killing strike. The freed man, ignoring me, raises his hands towards the downed Reya, dark energy swirling, coalescing for a killing blow. "Reya, watch out!" I yell, knowing she can't react, pinned and burning. There's no time for finesse. Lunging the final distance, I put all my strength, training, and desperate urgency into the swing. Aiming for the exposed neck, the blade whistles down. Steel connects with a sickeningly solid *thunk* that jolts up my arm, shearing through vertebrae and flesh. His head separates, rolling away with blank, surprised eyes as the body crumples like a puppet with cut strings, his severed head rolling in a grotesque, lifeless arc beside him.

Then, in a sudden shift of events, I catch sight of Maya altering her stance. Stunned beyond words, I stare as a faint, almost invisible shimmering boundary, like polished glass, envelops Reya just as the dark energy blast hits it and *detonates* in a harmless shower of sparks. My gaze snaps to Maya at the bottom of the steps, hands still raised, her face etched with fierce concentration. *That's* where the shield came from. Not just the house perimeter… she can project them. My tactical assessment scrambles to recalibrate. This quiet one… she's the defence. Heavy defence.

I feel something happening next to me and look down at the body, and a swirling, dark mist peels away from it like smoke escaping a chimney, dissipating into the air. Then, through the lingering haze, I watch in horror as the thorny vines restricting the other two men slacken and die. I strain to focus on them, but my mind is still reeling from the macabre sight of the spectral entity peeling away from the dead man.

I suspect Freya has been controlling the plants all along, so their sudden release must have stemmed from her shock and grief at witnessing her sister being consumed by flames. I can't blame her, terror would paralyse me if it had been my own sister, if I had one, as the dark, ghostlike figure vanishes completely.

Reya is now completely engulfed in the hellhound's orange inferno. I see no movement within the blazing cocoon—she has to be dead. But then, in a twist that defies all logic, Reya's beast roars forward, its black flames surging forth and instantly snuffing out the orange embers licking over her body.

"Ava, watch out!" Sam's urgent cry yanks me back to the present. I'd been dangerously distracted. When I turn towards the remaining two possessed men, one is already facing me, hands crackling with dark energy. I drop into a crouch, adrenaline surging as I brace for the onslaught. In the same breath, a swirling black orb shoots forth from his grasp—but before it can reach me, it's devoured by a burst of black flames.

I pivot, catching sight of Reya now on her knees, hands outstretched as a steady stream of dark fire flows from them and consumes the attacker. Simultaneously, her monstrous beast lunges at the last remaining man, reducing him in a split second to nothing more than a pile of smoking ash—an echo of the fate inflicted on the earlier hellhound. I stare in disbelief at Reya, scanning desperately for any burn marks, only to see blood seeping from around her mangled left leg where the hellhound had bitten her.

"How the hell...?" I mutter, my voice thick with disbelief, as I wonder at her survival amid the inferno. But there's no time to relish my astonishment—the immediate threat is far from over.

Clenching my sword, I watch Reya's sisters hurry over, their expressions marred by concern, while they tend to her injured leg. Her monstrous beast staggers towards me, then abruptly freezes mid-stride, its head snapping towards the dark, dense woods to the right of the house.

That's when I hear it—a deep, guttural growl that resonates right through my body. In an instant, I realise what has roused the beast's attention. "Shit!" I exclaim, alarm warping my voice as every eye turns towards the tree line.

Like a freight train crashing through the undergrowth, Rose bursts onto our scene in a blur, her panther eyes blazing with fury. But she isn't aiming her lethal stare at me—her burning green eyes are fixed on the fiery beast looming protectively by my side. "Shit!" I repeat, panic surging as I scramble to decide my next move.

"What the hell is that?" Freya shouts, shock and alarm intermingling in her voice.

The beast, not long ago a very large dog, lets out a low, menacing growl aimed squarely at Rose. Its black flames flare violently, intensifying, the heat pushing me back a step. I watch, horrified fascination warring with rising panic, as sharp, obsidian horns twist rapidly from its skull, catching the eerie light. Simultaneously, wicked black spikes erupt along the end of its thick tail as it lengthens, whipping back and forth like a lethal scorpion's stinger. The air crackles around it. This isn't Beastie the protective dog anymore; this is something ancient, demonic, and utterly terrifying.

Desperation claws at me as I call out, "Rose, stop!" My voice trembles with urgency as I try to reach her mentally as well, pleading for calm amid the storm of paranormal wrath. But she is either deaf to my reason or too consumed by anger to heed it. Frantically, I scan the scene for any viable solution to stave off an all-out brawl, which I believe Rose will lose.

Then, despite her injured leg, I see Reya tense as if gathering the last of her strength to counter-attack. I know I have only one desperate option left. Dropping my sword onto the ground, I bolt towards the monstrous beast that still hovers near me, its eyes ablaze with deadly intent. It crouches low, muscles coiling like springs, primed to leap at Rose. I have mere seconds to prevent a catastrophic clash that can engulf us all and destroy lives, especially mine.

I position myself squarely in the beast's path, carefully maintaining a safe distance from the intense heat emanating from its flaming form.

Pivoting, I face Rose, who has closed the gap with terrifying speed. Her green eyes narrow and burn with fury and annoyance that I dare block her path. So, with primal desperation, I roar at the top of my lungs, "ROSE NO! THEY ARE ALL FRIENDS!" My defiant scream shatters the tension. The sisters' attention snaps to me from my outburst—Reya slowly lowers her outstretched hands as her black flames flicker and die down. Rose, still in her panther form, blinks in confusion, her powerful gaze wavering from me to the fiery beast snarling menacingly behind.

Rose halts barely a yard from me, the ground trembling slightly under her weight, her hot breath misting in the cool air. Claws like curved knives dig into the dirt. She lets out a low, chest-rumbling snarl, green eyes narrowed to slits, locked onto the demonic form looming behind me. The fiery beast snarls back, lowering its horned head, black fire dripping from its jaws. The space between them vibrates with contained power, two apex predators locked in a standoff that feels seconds away from exploding into lethal violence. My heart hammers against my ribs. I have to do something, *now*. "Reya, do something! She thinks he's a threat to me and won't relent!"

Reya wastes no time saying, "Beastie, *stop*! Come here," she commands, her voice low but imbued with unquestionable authority on the word *stop*. In that instant, the monstrous beast halts its growling and begins a slow, measured walk towards Reya. As it leaves me, its flaming form dwindles until it assumes the size and shape of an ordinary but huge dog, its horns and spikes vanishing as if they were never there. Yet it continues to glare warily at Rose.

Rose's face twists in complete confusion, which is strange to see on a panther. When the now unassuming dog continues to move away, she lowers her massive head and nudges my chest in a silent apology. I instinctively run a hand over her head and scratch gently under her powerful jaw, attempting to convey reassurance.

"It's okay, Rose. The men who attacked were possessed, I'm guessing, similar to the ones in Jackson, we are looking into." I murmur, desperate to explain the maelstrom that has just descended upon us.

Following her gaze, I see Reya cradling her dog—a bizarre, almost tender moment amid the brutality—as her sisters hover by their sister casually, as if the paranormal attack is just a casual Saturday for them. Freya scans the area with a puzzled frown. "Where's the car? The last one had a car."

"There's a car out on the main road," Sam answers, his voice still trembling under the weight of our ordeal. Just then, the shrill wail of a siren pierces the air, growing louder with every heartbeat.

"Crap!" Reya barks, eyes widening in alarm. "We need to hide it, and fast. Freya, can you put a ward on it, so the sheriff doesn't spot it? I'm almost certain he's on his way here."

"Sure," Freya replies coolly, then dashes down the driveway towards the main road, and the dog chases after her.

"We can deal with the car later," Sam says as he extends a hand to help Reya gingerly ascend the veranda steps.

"Thank you," Reya says, gritting her teeth in clear pain as she gingerly puts weight on her injured leg and accepts his assistance. Turning to me, her face hardens with resolve, she states, "Whoever that is needs to be gone before the sheriff shows up."

I glance at Rose, who sits beside me. Her intelligent green eyes scan the sisters with intense curiosity. When our gazes meet, she shakes her massive head ever so slightly. "Rose, you need to hide until the sheriff is gone. We can't afford to put the sisters in danger from the local police," I plead softly, gently cupping her face and locking eyes with her verdant orbs.

She hesitates for a long, tense moment, then, with a reluctant huff, slinks back towards the trees from which she erupted.

Every breath is thick with tension as I struggle to process the torrent of violence—the sound of demonic energy, the fiery explosions, and now, the imminent approach of an even more significant threat to the safety of the sisters.

As I follow the sisters back into the house, picking up my sword as I go, I suddenly remember that Rose wasn't with us when we left the house. I quickly wonder if she remembered to bring a change of clothes with her and then realise she likely has a spare set in our rental car. So, I quickly run for it, pull out Rose's spare clothes from the back seat, and leave them at the boundary of the woods for her before running back to the house so I can get out of sight before the sheriff shows up.

Catherine M. Clark

Chapter 17

Conversations with Shadows

Reya

I hobble back into the house with Maya and Sam's help, my mind still reeling from the fact that I'm somehow not dead. When the hellhound had engulfed me in flames, I'd fully expected to meet my fiery end. Thankfully, I hadn't felt any heat, and even more thankfully, I hadn't had to experience the delightful sensation of my skin being peeled away for the few agonising minutes I would have remained alive. I must be immune to all types of fire because of my own fire ability; at the very least, I now know I'd never burn myself again while cooking, which is a definite bonus.

As they carefully help me onto the couch, I glance back at the floor and see a rather impressive blood trail I'm leaving behind from the wound on my leg. It seems getting injured is just part of my charm these days. Right now, though, we have the sheriff to worry about. He'd undoubtedly demand to be let in, and the moment he spots the blood, he'd put our lives under a forensic microscope.

"I'll grab our new first aid kit," Maya states, already heading towards the kitchen with a determined look on her face. After the last few times I was injured, Freya ordered a well-supplied first aid kit for times like these. Sam grabs a plump cushion off the chair nearest us. He then gently lifts my head just enough to slip the cushion underneath, making me slightly more comfortable, and I use my powers to stop my blood from dripping off my leg and covering the couch and cushion till Maya returns.

I look around for the other agent and see Ava standing by the front door, peering out of the window, probably looking out for her panther pal. The panther had been incredible to see. I'd had a sudden urge to go over and run my hands over its sleek, powerful body, but the thought that it's actually a person made the idea a little… weird. I'd never known there were panther shifters, too; I'd just assumed it was mostly wolves. And this particular panther seems to be on the side of good. Well, I certainly hope so.

Just as Maya returns from the kitchen with the first aid kit and paper towels, Pickle suddenly appears by my head, her tiny form hovering in the air. "Reya, are you okay? I saw you get hurt as I watched out of our bedroom window. When I saw those nasty hellhounds, I was just too scared to come out and help. I'm so, so sorry. Will you ever forgive me?" Pickle begs as her little face crumples with genuine distress.

"It's okay, Pickle. It was definitely better that you stayed inside. I want you to stay safe so I can protect you. I will never expect you to put yourself in danger, especially for me. You have already done more than I can ever ask for when you helped save Maya, okay?" I tell her, and I mean every single word. I'm eternally grateful for her bravery and will always do whatever it takes to keep her safe.

"Who are you talking to?" Sam asks, looking around in my direction, a confused frown on his face.

"There's a fairy by Reya's head," Ava says from her post by the front door, her gaze fixed on Pickle with a mixture of surprise and… was that fear?

"WHAT did you just call me?" Pickle says, her tone one of anger and a level I've never seen from her before. In a flash, she zips right up to Ava's face and hovers there, planting her tiny fists on her hips and leaning her head forward so their faces are mere centimetres apart. This takes Ava completely by surprise, and she stumbles backwards, tripping over her feet and hitting the door frame with a soft thud.

"Oh dear," I say, trying my best not to smile at the comical scene unfolding before me.

"I'm so sorry. Did I say something to offend you?" Ava asks, her voice laced with genuine worry. I never would have guessed that little Pickle could strike fear into a seasoned FBI agent.

"I AM NOT ONE OF THOSE NASTIES!" Pickle shouts indignantly in Ava's face, her voice surprisingly high-pitched, though not actually very loud, to be honest. "Fairies are disgusting, horrible creatures. I am a pixie," Pickle declares, crossing her arms firmly across her chest. "If you don't want me as your sworn enemy, you will never say that word around me again. *Ever*."

"I'm really sorry, I honestly didn't know," Ava says, looking genuinely worried that she has deeply offended the tiny being.

"What's going on?" Sam asks, looking increasingly anxious as he watches the strange interaction, well, Ava's side of it.

"Pixies and fairies have a major beef; trust me, they are horrible things," I tell him, rolling my eyes slightly at the ongoing drama.

"I'll take your word for it," Sam says quickly, then turns to Ava with a slight smirk. "Good first impressions you're making, boss." He then starts to chuckle softly to himself.

"Ha ha, you're so funny," Ava replies dryly, keeping her wary gaze fixed on Pickle, who is still hovering menacingly in front of her face.

Ava suddenly turns her attention back to the window next to the front door and says, "They're back." She then opens the door, and in walk Freya and Beastie, who seem none the worse for wear after the attack. With the door briefly open, the wail of sirens becomes deafeningly close;

it sounds like the sheriff has just turned onto the road leading to our house.

"Beastie, can you clean up the blood, please? Quickly!" I call out. I look down at my leg and see Maya has already efficiently cleaned away the blood on my leg and foot and is now starting to wrap a clean bandage around my calf.

Freya turns to me when she enters and says, "Beastie got rid of your blood outside."

"Thanks, Beastie."

"I can clean up the blood if you need," Ava offers, still looking a little fazed after her encounter with Pickle.

"No need; Beastie has it covered," I tell her with a reassuring smile. We both watch Beastie very efficiently lick up every last drop of blood from the floor. I notice Ava wrinkles her nose in slight disgust at the sight.

"Okay, then. So, your dog, or whatever it is, is called Beastie?" Ava says her tone is a mixture of curiosity and slight apprehension.

"He is; it's the name he prefers. I initially called him Hellboy, but he didn't seem to appreciate it. He used to be a hellhound; I have been told he is now something different after we bonded," I explain to her, hoping that by being honest about our unusual circumstances, she might be more inclined to do the same.

"I got to the car just in time," Freya then informs us as she collapses onto the end of the couch with a dramatic sigh. She then gently lifted my legs and placed them on her lap, as I had moved them so she could sit. Pickle, seemingly having made her point to Ava, settles comfortably on my stomach after her intense face-off.

Just then, we hear a car pull up outside. "Maya, quick, the sheriff can't see I'm injured," I say urgently.

"What are you worried about? I thought you were supposed to be the smart one," Freya says with a mischievous grin. She then runs her hand casually over my injured leg, and in an instant, the visible wound and the fresh bandages vanish entirely from sight.

"That is a fantastic idea! I'll put my momentary lapse in judgment down to blood loss, that's why my usually brilliant brain isn't working at its full power," I state, shaking my head playfully at Freya with a smile.

"Yeah, yeah," Freya says, rolling her eyes playfully as she also shook her head.

Maya huffs good-naturedly and gives Freya an annoyed but fond look before standing up and heading back to the kitchen to put the first aid kit away. Just then, a loud, angry-sounding knock echoes through the house from the front door.

"Help me sit up, please. It will look odd if I'm lying down," I say to Freya, who instantly slips out from under my legs and helps me sit upright just as Maya reaches the front door and waits until I'm sitting up and Freya is settled back down before she finally opens the door to reveal Sheriff Radshaw looking very red-faced and angry.

Maya then greets the sheriff in a way that I never thought she would do, "Afternoon, Sheriff. What can I do for you today? More random stuff you plan to try and pin on us?" Her surprisingly bold remark catches me off guard. I never would have expected her to be so confrontational with the sheriff. I can't help but snicker, and Freya quickly follows suit, both of us trying to cover our amusement with poorly disguised coughs.

We all stare at the sheriff, who is wearing his usual uniform of slightly rumpled brown slacks and a tan shirt, his trusty Stetson hat perched firmly on his head as always. He scans the room, his gaze lingering on the two unfamiliar figures of Ava and Sam sitting on the chairs. The moment he registers their presence, his whole demeanour shifts in a heartbeat, his anger replaced by a more cautious and slightly flustered expression. "I do not try to pin random stuff on you, Maya. I do my job no matter where the information I obtain leads me. If you are implying otherwise, feel free to file a formal complaint," he huffs, clearly taken aback by her directness.

He then turns his attention to the agents, his tone becoming more respectful. "Agents, I wasn't aware you were here." He then looks back out over the front area of our property and adds, "You're not in your government vehicle."

"That's a rental. One of my other agents needed to deal with something else out of town for a few days. What's the problem, Sheriff? We heard your siren and wondered what was going on," Ava says, her tone polite but firm. Clearly, the sheriff wasn't particularly fond of her either, as he gives her the same narrowed-eye look he usually reserves for us.

"Well... you see, I had a couple of rather unusual phone calls. One caller said they were almost certain they heard a lion out this way again. I then got another call from a rather frantic resident saying they saw a huge cat heading in this direction and thought maybe it escaped from a zoo or something," the sheriff explains, looking increasingly flustered under Ava's steady gaze.

"I see. I still don't quite understand why you would roll up to this property with your siren blaring when you weren't given any precise information that something was happening here. Or did you just come here because you told us the other day that these nice women who live here are nothing but trouble-makers, and you can't wait to find something to pin on them?" Ava states, her unexpected defence of us taking me by surprise. I then shoot the sheriff my most withering look and shake my head slowly in disapproval.

The sheriff's face flushes a deep red, and he gets all flustered. "Now, Agent, I don't believe I said anything of the sort. I'm simply doing my job," he stammers, looking somewhat embarrassed. I'm genuinely impressed by Ava's intervention, while Freya bit her lip to keep a straight face.

"Well, for the record, Sheriff, we have not seen or heard a lion. When we arrived, Reya and her sisters were simply playing with their dog outside. Perhaps the acoustics of this area make the dogs' growling during a lively game of tug-of-war sound much more ferocious than it actually is. Instead of considering that possibility, your first thought is that these women must be harbouring an actual lion, which is far more likely to eat them than become a pet. As for a big cat on the loose, why would it specifically head to this property and nowhere else?" Ava says with such a convincingly straight face that I'm now also struggling to suppress a giggle.

"I… I have no choice but to believe you when you tell me nothing illegal was happening here when you arrived. Sorry to disturb you," he says, his shoulders slumping slightly as he starts to turn and head back towards his patrol car. Just then, we hear another car pull up behind his, making the sheriff pause by the front door, a mild irritation crossing his face.

Beastie, sensing my earlier distress, had taken up a protective position next to where I'm sitting on the couch so I can absentmindedly scratch his head while Pickle continues to hover nearby, keeping a watchful eye on me. But as soon as Beastie heard another car door close outside, he showed me rapid flashes of images in my mind—images of Jacob looking worried. "Great, just what we need right now," I mutter, loud enough for those closest to me to hear.

"Jacob?" Freya asks, her eyebrows raised in question. I nod in weary reply.

"Deputy Davids, you can't just walk onto someone's private property like this, even if you are dating one of them," the sheriff says, his voice laced with annoyance as Jacob strides past him and enters our house without so much as a glance. Jacob looks genuinely worried and immediately starts scanning the room with the same intensity the sheriff had displayed moments earlier.

"What happened?" he asks, his gaze settling on me as he walks quickly towards the couch.

"Nothing," I say, perhaps a little too sharply, my annoyance at his unexpected arrival bubbling to the surface. "We've just been discussing things with the agents," I add, trying to sound as nonchalant as possible.

I notice Jacob sniffing the air a couple of times as he approaches, and a knot of anxiety tightens in my stomach as I wonder if he can somehow smell my blood despite Freya's glamour. As he approaches the front of the couch, his gaze drops and zeroes in on my legs. A confused look flickers across his face before he quickly looks back up at me, his eyes full of concern. That's very strange; it's almost as if he somehow knows my leg is injured, and my earlier worries about him start to resurface.

Then Jacob says something that makes the already tense situation significantly worse. "Are you injured, Reya? There's a drop of blood by your foot on the floor."

"There is?" the sheriff instantly says, his head snapping back around, his previous apology completely forgotten.

Crap! I think frantically. "Oh, that. I was just playing with Beastie in the woods earlier and caught myself on a branch that was sticking out of the ground; it's really nothing," I state, hoping my casual tone will be enough to dissuade both the sheriff and Jacob from asking any more probing questions, especially since there isn't currently a visible injury to see.

"That's right. It was actually our fault that she caught herself on a branch. I'm a trained field medic, so I patched her up. It was a very minor cut. It seems we missed a tiny speck of blood when I cleaned her up," Ava says smoothly, her voice so calm and convincing that even I almost believe her.

"Maybe I should just take a quick look at it," Jacob says, his gaze dropping back down to my legs with a persistent, confused frown.

"Oh, it's really fine, the cut is in a… well, it's in a place that I'm not exactly showing off right now," I say, hoping the not-so-subtle hint that the cut might be in a more intimate area will make both Jacob and the sheriff drop the subject immediately. I'm incredibly grateful that Ava is here right now; she is a natural at this.

"Okay, only if you're sure," Jacob reluctantly says, looking a little uncomfortable and unsure of what to do next. It's actually rather sweet how concerned he seems. Maybe I have been wrong about him.

"I'll be fine, but thank you for your concern. You'd better get back to work, Deputy, or the sheriff will be mad at you, too," I say, trying to inject a bit of levity into the awkward situation.

"I guess so, but maybe I should stay for a little while," he says, glancing pointedly at Ava and Sam.

"We still have a few more things to discuss with the agents, so we should probably get back to it, sorry," I say, hoping he'd finally get the hint that his presence isn't exactly helping the situation.

"Okay, I'll leave you to it then. Call if you need anything at all," Jacob says, his gaze lingering on me for a moment. He shifts his weight as if he were going to bend down and kiss me goodbye, but then clearly thinks better of it under the sheriff's watchful eye. So, he turns and heads back out of the house, passing the still-annoyed sheriff without looking at him again. The sheriff gives us all one last lingering look, then follows Jacob down the steps and away from the front door.

Maya has been standing in the kitchen area, having subtly moved into it after she had opened the door to stay out of the sheriff's direct line of sight. As soon as both men leave, she quickly closes the front door and comes to sit back down, a collective sigh of relief washing over the room.

When we hear both cars finally drive away down the road, we all start to giggle nervously for some reason, well, apart from Sam, who still looks slightly bewildered by the whole experience. "Is that your boyfriend?" Sam asks with a mixture of curiosity and amusement.

I'm not entirely sure how to answer his question, but Pickle, as always, has no such hesitation. "Yep, that's her hot, sexy man," she declares proudly and makes those who can hear her chuckle while I cringe and try to hide my face in my hands. Of course, Sam couldn't hear what she said, so Ava relayed what she said.

Sam then follows up with, "If you're dating a deputy, why is the sheriff always trying to pin something on you?"

"I honestly have no idea why he's always trying to find something to accuse us of," I tell him, shaking my head in exasperation and lifting my hands with my palms facing up. After I reply, I notice Ava suddenly looks like she has just remembered something important. "What's up?" I ask her.

"Rose! Oh my god, I need to go and let Rose know it's safe to come out now; I completely forgot about her in all the chaos," Ava says, looking incredibly sheepish as she slaps a hand to her forehead.

"Who is this Rose?" Maya asks, her curiosity piqued.

"The panther. She's also one of my agents and my partner," Ava explains, jumping to her feet and rushing back towards the front door. She cautiously peeks through the window to ensure the sheriff's car is gone, then flings the door open and runs outside, calling the name "Rose" into the surrounding woods.

Freya turns to Sam, a knowing smirk on her face. "You have a panther as an agent? Reya has a bit of a thing for panthers, you know."

"I do not have a 'thing' for panthers. I have a teddy panther, and that's all," I say, giving Freya my best death glare, which she completely ignores.

"Whatever you say. Is it true then? Panther shifters are real, too?" Freya asks Sam, her eyes wide with genuine interest.

"They sure are," Sam confirms with a nod.

"Cool. It's nice to know that not all shifters are the enemy," Freya says, more to herself than anyone else, a thoughtful expression on her face.

"Not many left in the world that are actually on the side of good," Sam replies, his tone a little sombre.

"You have absolutely no idea," Pickle mutters under her breath after listening intently to their conversation.

Except Sam couldn't hear her, of course, so I quickly told him what she said, as it would be rude not to. Sam looks visibly frustrated that he can't see or hear our tiny companion.

Freya looks deep in thought for a moment, then her eyes suddenly widen with excitement, and she turns to me. "Sis! In that new book we got, there's a rune that's supposed to give someone the ability to see things they normally can't. Do you think that would give someone like Sam the ability to see Pickle?" she says, looking genuinely thrilled at the prospect.

"That could actually be incredibly handy. We can definitely talk about it later," I say, trying to put the intriguing idea to one side for now, as we still have more pressing matters to deal with. I shifted my position slightly on the couch and winced involuntarily at the sharp pain that shot up my leg. I glance down at my leg, and of course, I see nothing but smooth skin, having completely forgotten that Freya placed a glamour on it. I lean down and wave my hand casually over my calf, and the illusion shimmers and vanishes, revealing the blood-soaked bandage underneath.

Pickle, who is now nestled comfortably against me, turns to face me with wide, concerned eyes when I wince. "Are you sure your leg will be okay, Reya?"

"Yeah, it'll be fine, Pickle. I heal quickly, remember?" I remind her with a reassuring smile.

Just then, we hear the distinct sound of something small and quick scurrying across the floorboards upstairs again. "Oops, I completely forgot about Drake!" Pickle exclaims, looking up towards the ceiling with a sheepish grin. A moment later, we hear a series of loud thudding sounds coming from the top of the stairs, and we all turn to look in anticipation.

"That bloody thing is a complete menace," Pickle mutters under her breath as she crosses her arms over her chest and slumps against me.

"What the hell is that?" Sam says, his eyes wide with surprise, as we all watch a black, furry object tumble down the last few steps and end up in a rather undignified heap at the foot of the stairs.

"That would be Reya's panther," Freya says with a big, mischievous grin on her face.

"Are you telling me it's actually alive?" Sam asks, his gaze fixed on the furry creature, which is now righting itself, looking around with bright eyes, and then pouncing excitedly towards us, clearly thrilled that it's finally found us.

A voice from behind us makes us all jump. "Oh my god, it looks like a mini-Rose!" Ava says as she re-entered the house, her eyes wide with surprise. She then looks around the room as if she were searching for someone. When she glances back out the open front door, her expression turns to confusion, and she freezes just inside the house.

"You're right, it really does," Sam says, now looking a little happier and less bewildered by the bizarre situation.

"It's not actually alive. Freya and Pickle turned it into a golem," Maya states matter-of-factly, her tone suggesting this is a perfectly regular occurrence.

Our attention is suddenly diverted when Ava, who has moved back to the door, says with concern, "Rose, what are you doing?"

We then hear another female voice, this one sounding slightly strained and echoing from outside, say, "I can't seem to be able to move any closer to the house."

"What are you talking about?" Ava says, stepping back onto the veranda, looking even more confused. Just then, I notice Drake, who had been heading towards us, suddenly swerving and heading for the open front door instead.

"Freya, quick, grab Drake before he gets out!" I say as panic rises in my voice at the thought of the golem panther escaping.

Freya shoots to her feet with surprising agility, runs after the rapidly approaching golem, and manages to scoop him up just as he is about to make a break for it out the front door. When she stands back up, cradling the golem in her arms, she looks out the front door, following Ava's gaze.

Catherine M. Clark

Chapter 18

Whispers from the Pasture

Freya calls out, sounding worried, "Reya, we have an issue. This Rose can't seem to get past our wards." The alarm in her voice confirms what I already suspect. The only reason Rose wouldn't be able to cross the protective barrier is that she is thinking of harming us.

"What's going on?" I demand from Sam, who turns to look at me with genuine confusion etched on his face.

"What do *you* mean? We should ask what you have done to Rose if she can't get any closer to the house," Sam says, his gaze shifting between me and the open doorway.

"There is only one reason someone can't get past our wards, and that is when they intend to do us harm," I state firmly, a knot of unease tightening in my stomach. Even Beastie stirs from his comfortable doze by my feet and looks around, his ears perk with alertness. At the same time, I see a flicker of movement out of the corner of my eye. I turn to find the fox and her cubs, who have woken up and are now cautiously heading for the back door, their eyes wide.

"Maya, can you let the foxes out while you're up?" I say, hoping this small task would give her something to focus on and distract her from the potentially troubling situation with Rose.

"Rose means you no harm," Sam insists, his tone reassuring as he now understands.

"Our wards are telling us differently," I counter, my unease growing. I then hear Freya, who had followed Ava out onto the veranda, telling her the same thing about the wards. They are designed to stop anyone with harmful intentions from getting close to the house. In turn, I distinctly hear Ava relaying the same as Sam.

After Maya quietly lets the foxes slip out the back door, she starts to return, her face falls, and she becomes worried as she glances down at my leg. "I better re-do your bandage properly while you sort out whatever is going on with Ava's friend," Maya comments as her caring nature kicks in.

I hear Ava explaining the situation to Rose outside, then hear Ava calmly instructing Rose to clear her mind of any negative thoughts and think of kittens or something equally benign, which makes me chuckle despite my underlying concern. However, I'm still a little worried that Rose might genuinely have thoughts of harming us until I realise she is likely just intensely worried about Ava and Sam for their safety, for entirely different reasons. This realisation makes me relax slightly, especially when I see Freya saunter back into the living room with a still-wiggling Drake held securely in her arms, her expression showing no signs of alarm.

Moments later, Ava walks back into the house, followed by a very striking woman. The first thing I notice about her is her incredibly vibrant green eyes, which seem to sparkle with an inner light. She also has long, flowing blonde hair that cascades down her back and is slightly taller than Ava.

As Ava walks in, she grabs a spare chair from the kitchen table, places it next to hers, and gestures for Rose to sit down. She moves cautiously and alertly as she walks up to the chair offered and gracefully lowers herself onto it. She then slowly scans the room, her intense green gaze finally settling and zeroing in on Beastie, who is now sitting upright, his ears twitching.

Maya settles down on the floor beside the couch, gently lifting my injured leg and carefully placing it in her lap. Then, she begins to meticulously change my bandage. Rose watches Maya's movements for a moment, then her gaze returns to Beastie, her expression unreadable. My hand instinctively scratches behind Beastie's ears, and I can feel the tension in his body; he is definitely on high alert after Rose's entrance.

"What is *that*?" Rose asks, her voice low and slightly wary, making Beastie emit a low growl under his breath in response.

"He can understand absolutely everything you say," I tell her, meeting her intense gaze with my own.

"You said those creatures that attacked us earlier were hellhounds; he looked exactly like them, well, until he changed and was covered in black flames instead of the normal orange and yellow flames those other hellhounds had," Ava says, her eyes flicking between Rose and Beastie, looking concerned.

"Technically, he is a hellhound, but he's different now. He's mine," I say with a surge of fierce protectiveness washing over me.

"You have a *demon* hellhound. How has it not killed you all?" Rose exclaims, her eyes widening with genuine worry as she keeps glancing nervously at Ava.

"Demon?" Ava says, sounding surprised and now looking genuinely confused. I can also see she is a little worried by Rose's reaction and the mention of a demon.

"Yes, it's a demon," Rose insists, her gaze fixed on Beastie, who responds with another low, rumbling growl.

"If you don't like Beastie, you can leave," I say, trying to inject as much authority into my voice as possible, though I'm starting to feel the exhaustion from the earlier fight creeping in.

"Rose, please," Ava interjects, her tone pleading, finally making

Rose break her intense stare with Beastie and look at Ava. After a tense moment, I see Rose's shoulders relax slightly, her body losing some of its rigidity.

"Sorry," Rose says, directing her apology to the room in general. "We just grew up on stories that weren't very... nice. Stories where hellhounds were always the bad guys." Ava reaches out and places a reassuring hand on Rose's arm.

"For the record," I interject, wanting to clear the air, "I accidentally summoned him. I was messing around trying to cheer Pickle up, and the next thing I knew, he appeared in a flash of smoke, and I promptly passed out. Then Pickle went screaming for help," I tell them, a bittersweet memory of that chaotic day flashing through my mind.

"I did *not* run screaming! I flew as fast as my wings could carry me to get help! Hellhounds have been used to hunt pixies like me for centuries," Pickle declares indignantly to our guests, though it's clear Sam and Rose can't hear her. So, I repeat Pickle's impassioned statement, which causes Rose to look around the room, slightly bewildered, trying to locate Pickle while Ava confirms what I just told them.

I could tell Ava wanted to say something reassuring to Pickle. Then she said, "I'm sorry that moment scared you, but you were incredibly brave to go for help when Reya was in danger. Most people would have frozen in fear or just run and hide, so you did an amazing job."

I appreciate Ava's words, and it seems Pickle does, too, as she beams up at the agent with a grateful smile. "I would never have just left Reya. She is far too important to me," Pickle declares fiercely, tugging at my heart as I feel the same way about her. She then seems to realise she might have revealed too much, and I notice she starts to scratch at her wrist again nervously.

"I'm sure," Ava says, looking a little confused by Pickle's sudden intensity and glancing at me briefly with a questioning look.

"Are you talking to... it again?" Rose asks, her initial

apprehension seemingly becoming annoyed.

"Pickle," Ava corrects gently, giving Rose a look that clearly conveys, '*Are you serious?*'

"What?" Rose says, looking genuinely confused by Ava's correction.

"The pixie's name is Pickle; she isn't an 'it'," Ava says, giving Rose another pointed look that I take to mean '*behave yourself.*' She then subtly gestures towards my lap, where Pickle is now sitting, glaring daggers at Rose with her tiny arms crossed.

"I don't like her," Pickle mutters, making Maya and Freya laugh. Even Sam, sensing the shift in atmosphere, joins in with a chuckle when Freya passes on what Pickle just said, though Rose, who couldn't hear Pickle, stares daggers at me like I'm the one who said it and not Pickle, she then gives us all looks like we have collectively lost our minds.

"I wish I could see Pickle," Sam comments, still smiling.

"I'm sorry, Pickle, if Rose isn't being very friendly right now, I hope you can forgive her," Ava says, shooting Rose a quick, pointed look out of the corner of her eye.

Rose starts to look a little angry, with Ava apologising on her behalf, then digging herself into a deeper hole. "Did you… did you get hit in the head during that fight or something?" she asks Ava, her tone laced with incredulity.

"Of course not. There's a pixie sitting right on Reya's lap, it's also clear she doesn't like you because of how you're reacting," Ava says, shaking her head slightly at Rose. She is also starting to look a little irritated by Rose's dismissive behaviour.

"Seriously, I really don't understand. In your memories, I saw a fairy," Rose insists, her voice rising in frustration, and it suddenly becomes clear why Rose is acting like she is, I'm with Pickle, as I'm not impressed with her behaviour.

As soon as Rose utters the word *fairy*, everyone who knows

Pickle groans in unison. We aren't at all surprised when Pickle, who had been sitting relatively calmly on my lap, suddenly shoots up into the air, her tiny face turning a shade of red I haven't seen before and flies over to Rose and hovers menacingly in front of her face, her small body vibrating with indignation. With a dramatic snap of her tiny fingers, a shower of dead leaves suddenly rains down onto Rose's head, making her jump up from the chair with a startled yelp and frantically brushing the leaves from her blonde hair.

"What the hell was that?!" Rose exclaims, her composure completely shattered.

"You just deeply offended Pickle by calling her a fairy. Fairies are horrible, hideous things," I tell her, struggling to keep a straight face. Unlike everyone else who burst out laughing again at Rose's reaction, even Sam, who still can't see the culprit, joins in this time, his laughter echoing through the room at the sight of Rose now covered in leaves and not fresh green leaves but brown ones that start to break up as Rose tires to get them out of her hair and makes it much worse.

Finally, the penny seems to drop for Rose, and a look of dawning realisation spreads across her face. "Oh! Oh, I get it. Sorry, Pickle! I really didn't mean any offence," she says, directing her apology to the general vicinity of where Pickle is still hovering, looking rather pleased with herself.

"I'm going out," Pickle declares, still slightly huffy as she zips towards the back door. Sensing her mood, Beastie gets up from his spot and follows her.

Seeing that Beastie will join her, she waits for him and lands on his broad back. Just before they both vanish through the closed back door in a shimmer, I call out, "Be safe, you two!"

All three agents look completely shocked as Beastie seemingly disappears through a solid, closed door. "How the hell did he just do that?" Sam asks, his eyes wide with disbelief. I can see that Ava and Rose are equally stunned and want to ask the exact same question.

"It's one of his... abilities. It's what makes him such a good hunter," I explain casually, as if it's the most normal thing in the world.

"I wish I had that ability; it would have made my old job so much easier," Ava comments wistfully, her expression taking on a far-off, nostalgic look.

Rose, still slightly ruffled from her leafy encounter and thankfully, Pickle removed the dead leaves just before she left, looks at me and my sisters, then her gaze settles on the peacefully sleeping Drake in Freya's arms. She points a finger at the golem panther and says, her tone a mixture of accusation and dawning understanding, "So you really are witches, just like we expected."

"You knew we could be witches? How?" I ask, turning to Ava for an explanation.

"Erm... well, this... person... told us that we needed to find these sisters who were in danger. And then we had... other clues," Ava explains vaguely, avoiding direct eye contact. Then she added something that completely took me by surprise. "Because the shifters are after witches... to breed with." A heavy silence fell over the room as we all processed this unexpected and disturbing information.

We then spent the next two hours telling each other our respective stories. The agents found our past heart-breaking and utterly fascinating. At the same time, we were equally captivated by Ava's experiences as an assassin; of course, she couldn't tell us the details of her missions as they were classified. When Ava got to the part about a mysterious voice she had been hearing in her head, and Rose then filled us in on their other partner, Luca, who had also been hearing a similar voice from someone calling themselves Cat, I couldn't help but groan inwardly. Reluctantly, I then confessed to them about my bizarre dream visits from a woman who also called herself Cat. Given the strange similarities, I hadn't planned to tell them about her, but it seemed like the best thing to do.

Freya, ever the enthusiast, repeats something she mentioned earlier. "As I said, in one of the new books we got, there's a rune that's supposed to give 'The Sight.' It sounds like it might do the same thing as that ring on your finger, Ava."

"It might help the rest of your team be able to see enemies that only you will currently be able to see," I say to Ava, who looks genuinely intrigued by the idea.

As I watch Ava thoughtfully consider everything we have just told her, a sudden thought sparks in my mind. I really like this Ava, and I start to wonder if she is the woman Papa Legba had mentioned we would meet soon—the one I am supposed to help find a weapon that, as a human, she can effectively use. An exciting idea begins to form in my mind.

"We'd better discuss it with Luca when he returns," Rose says, her tone a little guarded. I'm not entirely sure I will like Rose, and her slightly wary attitude towards us, coupled with her comment about Luca, gives me a few doubts about him, even though I found out he's a panther shifter too. I'll be honest, when I heard that and his name, something strange came over me. I started to feel a little dizzy for a moment, and for some reason, I couldn't stop thinking about him.

I suddenly had a strong urge to meet him as soon as possible, a part of me even wanting to go and find him immediately, which frankly freaks me out a little. I quickly put it down to the fact that I apparently have a 'thing' for panthers, and Luca is, well, a panther.

Eventually, the agents got ready to leave, promising to keep in close contact as they are currently working on a case in Jackson. They revealed that they are actually investigating the very demon possessions we have just had to deal with when those men attacked us. We, in turn, told them everything Papa Legba had told us about the growing demonic activity in Jackson. Freya also brought up the rune again, emphasising to

Ava that the rest of her team might not always be able to see their attackers, a crucial detail they clearly hadn't previously considered until Sam couldn't see the hellhounds, when the agents left, they said they will take the car out on the road and get there backup team to deal with it.

As I recline against the cushions, a nagging worry begins to surface. What if the intelligence that has led them to our doorstep is linked to when we tragically lost our mother? The thought sends a shiver down my spine. Their intelligence seems to indicate that the wolf shifters want us to bear their children in some twisted attempt to introduce magic into their pack and bloodlines. It reminds me of the descriptions in the ancient diary I've translated, which detail how different magical abilities start to diverge when the gods begin having children with humans.

I briefly wondered if I should have told the agents about the diary, but I quickly dismissed the idea. I still haven't even told my sisters about its contents, and it definitely won't go down well if they find out such a significant secret from complete strangers. Then, my mind can't help but dwell on the bizarre incident earlier, when I somehow produced a fiery sword in my hand, then instinctively recognised when one of the non-corporeal books in my mind suddenly became solid at the time.

As I continue to relax on the couch, I consciously go to that strange place in my mind, I focus on this new book and find something even stranger. On the book cover, the image seems to be in constant flux. It depicts a fan made of multiple different weapons, except all but one of the weapons are fading in and out of existence. The image that isn't fading quite as dramatically, though it still flickers slightly, is that of a sword.

The only conclusion I can come up with is that there is some choice to be made, and for the time being, the sword is leading the charge to become maybe my primary weapon, I guess, thinking about this logically. I figure the few fleeting seconds the sword had been in my hand hadn't been long enough for it to solidify its position as the definitive winner.

I made excuses and headed up to my room, struggling on the stairs with my injured leg. I thought going to my room wouldn't raise suspicion, unlike if I were seen going down into the basement. Then my sisters would know I was planning on doing something, which I am, as I want to conduct a small, private experiment. Once I finally reached my room, I settled on my bed, propped up against my pillows.

I repeat the mental process and try to think and feel the same as when the sword first appeared in my hand, but this time I focus my intention on conjuring a fiery axe in my hand. Within seconds, a shimmering, fiery axe materialises. I kept it there for the same short duration as the sword had been; this time, though, instead of panicking and trying to fling it from me, I just released my grip, and it vanished as quickly as it appeared.

I then close my eyes again and enter the building in my mind to check on the book again. When I see the cover, I instantly see a change; the fan of weapons on the cover now has two weapons that are noticeably more visible than the rest. But this time, the remaining weapons look even fainter than before, further confirming my suspicion that I had to make a conscious choice. Without wasting more time, I focus my thoughts and produce the sword again, the familiar weight and heat settling comfortably in my hand.

I can't think of any other weapon I would rather use. As I hold the fiery sword, the image on the book's cover shifts once more, all the different weapons vanish completely, leaving the sword as the sole, prominent image. This is yet another secret I'm keeping from my sisters, although Freya did catch a glimpse of the sword when I produced it the first time, it seems to have slipped her mind, as she hasn't questioned me about it yet. I have no choice now but to finally tell them everything in one go.

As I mentally debate when and how to best break all this news to them, my mind, despite my best efforts, starts to drift back to the intriguing conversation with Rose. I can't help but wonder what Luca looks like in his panther form. Once I'm done, I head back down and struggle on the stairs again.

Catherine M. Clark

Chapter 19

The Alpha's Shadow

When Jenny arrived at our place after she finished work, she headed for me on the couch, where I had plonked myself down to rest. As she approached, she brandished a walking stick. My sisters must have told her I was struggling to climb stairs, which I had hoped they hadn't noticed. I can't help but cringe internally at the sight of it, as it isn't exactly cool-looking or fancy; it has a very clinical appearance, like something that belongs in a hospital. I must admit that the thought of struggling to get up the stairs to my room is daunting, and I know I'd need all the support I can get right now.

"Here, this is my grandma's spare walking stick; you can borrow it until your leg is better," Jenny said kindly, handing it to me as I lay sprawled on the couch with my injured leg propped up on a cushion. This has been my chosen resting spot after my brief but enlightening bedroom weapon-conjuring experiment.

"Thanks, I think," I said, accepting the walking stick and resting it against the couch next to me.

"Why is it *you* who always ends up getting hurt?" Jenny asks, looking concerned. She studied the bandage on my leg, where a tiny red spot of blood had already started to seep through. She isn't wrong that I'm the one always getting hurt.

I shrug in response, not really having a good answer. But Freya, who is helping Maya set up for dinner in the kitchen, overhears her question. "I don't like it either," Freya calls out, her voice carrying from the kitchen. "She gets hurt because she's our main attacking force. I just wish I could do more to help."

"You do what you can, Freya. It could have been so much worse if you hadn't been able to pin those possessed guys in place while we take out the hellhounds. Beastie told me we had to deal with them first; he should know, right?" I say, hoping Freya doesn't feel too guilty about what has happened. It is what it is; we all played our part.

"I still can't believe they actually brought hellhounds with them. Couldn't you have done something to, you know, turn them to our side?" Jenny asks, still looking at my leg with a worried expression.

That was actually a good point. "I guess I could have tried, but then we would have to deal with having two more hellhounds running around, just like Beastie. I don't think I'd want my time taken away from him by having to manage two more. Also," I add with a shudder, "can you even imagine having three dogs his size in this house? It would be absolute chaos," I state with conviction. I truly believe having three giant hellhounds would cause far more issues than a slightly injured leg.

"Yeah, I guess you're right," Jenny concedes with a thoughtful nod.

"I do have one question for you, Reya," Freya says from the kitchen, her voice suddenly serious. I'm not entirely sure what question she wants to ask. I'd been half-expecting a barrage of questions recently about everything, as my sisters always knew when I was keeping something from them, but she hasn't pressed me on anything so far. Is this finally about the mysterious diary? I wonder nervously.

"What the hell was that fiery sword that appeared in your hand earlier?" Freya shoots at me like a battleship firing its main gun, hitting its primary target dead-on. The sudden question makes everyone in the room momentarily stare at Freya in utter confusion. Then, as if on cue, all eyes swivel to me. *Crap!* Well, here we go.

"What?" Jenny asks first, her jaw practically dropping as she stares down at me in shock and utter confusion.

I realise I have no choice but to come clean. "It shocked me just as much when it appeared in my hand when I watched Ava pull out her sword. I suddenly wished I had a sword too, and before I even knew what was happening, there was this fiery sword just... there, in my hands. I panicked and tried to let go of it, and as soon as I did, it vanished.

Then, this book, one of the non-corporeal ones, suddenly became solid in the library in my mind. It had other images of weapons on its cover, but now it only shows the sword. So, I guess I was able to choose what weapon I could summon subconsciously," I explained to everyone, pointedly avoiding looking at any of them so I couldn't see the undoubtedly incredulous looks they were giving me. Then, I mentally facepalmed. I had just stepped in it big time.

"What the actual hell, sis!" Freya exclaims, dropping a fork she had been holding with a clatter. "What books? Did you find books that could help us, but did not tell us? You know, your sisters who are in this whole crazy mess with you?" Freya adds, her voice rising with each word. She is now sounding and looking very angry as I cautiously peek at her.

"No, I haven't found any actual books, Freya. They're... they're in my head," I say, pointing vaguely towards my temple.

"What are you talking about? Are you losing it?" Freya asks, her initial anger replacing genuine concern as she steps out of the kitchen and moves closer to the couch.

"Remember what Papa Legba said about us eventually accessing our power? Well, before you sprang the whole Drake-is-a-golem surprise on me last night, I discovered I have... a library in my mind with books and statues. Also," I continue, deciding I might as well go all in, "I also seem to have two types of fire now, one large and black, and one small and purple," lifting my right hand and producing my original, familiar purple flames in my palm, letting them dance and flicker for a moment.

"Wow, so pretty," Jenny says, completely mesmerised by the miniature inferno swirling in my hand.

"I'm… pleased for you, Reya, but why on earth didn't you tell us any of this?" Freya demands, her expression now tinged with hurt.

"Well," I begin sheepishly, glancing at what Freya has done to Drake, "with the whole Drake thing. Then I had a chat with Jenny about some stuff, and I was worried about meeting the agents today… It kind of just slipped my mind," I finish lamely.

"Slipped your mind, *really*, Reya? That's the excuse you're going with? You know as well as I do that since all this craziness started," Freya says, gesturing around our living room, "our memory has become ridiculously good. Also, you conveniently forgot to mention that you've apparently become super strong!" Freya adds accusingly.

"You what?!" Maya chimes in, abandoning her dinner preparations to stand next to Freya, her expression mirroring Freya's mixture of shock and hurt.

"Yeah," Freya says, nodding emphatically. "She almost broke my arm last night when she grabbed it!" Freya's dramatic accusation actually takes me by surprise.

"You're both blaming Reya for keeping secrets from us, but Freya, you admitted to doing the same thing with Drake! So maybe don't fling accusations around quite so readily," Maya points out, giving both Freya and me a pointedly unimpressed look.

"Hey, come on, guys. We have bigger issues to worry about right now. How will Reya even cope with doing the full moon ritual tonight with her leg like this?" Jenny says, sounding more logical than the three of us put together. The rising tension in the room suddenly came to a standstill.

"Crap!" I exclaim, slapping my forehead. "I completely forgot all about that."

"Me too," Freya admits, and I can see in her eyes that she now understands how something so important could have momentarily slipped my mind amidst all the day's events. Our memories are indeed so much better now; we seem to be able to recall every single thing we read or said with perfect clarity.

"I'll just have to… hop around, I guess," I say with a sigh, glancing at the clinical-looking walking stick leaning against the couch and blowing out a frustrated breath.

"Just make absolutely sure you use that walking stick, Reya, so you don't fall over and hurt your leg even more," Jenny cautions, her concern evident.

"I'm sure she'll manage," Maya says, ever the pragmatist. "Anyway, dinner is finally ready. Come on, everyone. And can we please try to discuss things without immediately resorting to blaming each other?" Then, thankfully, Maya remembers about Beastie and goes and grabs his dinner of a nice juicy raw steak and a bowl of fresh blood on the floor for him. We are all so used to his unusual dietary requirements by now that it doesn't bother us in the slightest if he eats his dinner while we eat ours instead of making him wait.

During dinner, our conversation revolved around the agents and the surprising revelation that two of them were panther shifters. Again, my mind drifted almost involuntarily to the thought of Luca, and I found myself inexplicably eager to see him in his panther form. I had called Jenny earlier to let her know the bare bones of what had happened that day, but hadn't gone into any real detail over the phone. As we fully recounted the day's events to her, her expression shifted from initial worry to utter fascination, along with the usual worry.

By the time we reached the end of our recap, I realised my mind had kept wandering back to the thought of Luca with an almost obsessive frequency. *What the hell is wrong with me? Why have I suddenly become so fixated on this guy I haven't even met?* Yeah, I had a thing for panthers and dragons, that's true. But that doesn't automatically mean I want to date either one. Besides, I'm kind of dating Jacob.

I've started to consider giving him another chance, but as I think about him now, I've begun to seriously question what I liked about him in the first place. I try to picture an image of him in my mind, but the powerful form of a huge black panther instantly replaces his face. *What the hell is going on?* I thought, trying to appear engaged in my family's conversation about everything that was happening.

I manage to drag my attention back to the conversation, which has now turned back to the mysterious books in my mind. I explained to them in as much detail as possible, and I advised my sisters to try to find similar places within their minds and see what kind of books they might have. I also warned them about the potential ability to summon weapons, and if they discovered they had the same power, they needed to choose wisely which weapon they ultimately ended up with, as I have a strong feeling it can't be changed after you decide.

As we sat there, my sisters attempted to access the doors in their minds, just as I had when we first started exploring whether we were really witches. To my surprise, thanks to my guidance, they both found their doors much quicker than I did. When they shared their experiences, I was taken aback to learn that neither of them had a library with books.

Freya's landscape was filled with plants arranged in unique shapes and images on trees in a kind of grove. She mentioned having a door made of plants and mushrooms in the shape of a circle, which she couldn't open. In contrast, Maya's door led to a bakery filled with food. She described a cupcake adorned with an image of herself kneeling over a fox, healing it. Maya also had a door, but hers was made of light, and like Freya, she was unable to open it. It seems that the landscapes in our minds represent our abilities, while the images, like my own statues and books, reflect the first time we used a new power.

My sisters also tried to create weapons, but their attempts have so far been unsuccessful. We're uncertain whether this is something they cannot do or simply something they haven't achieved yet. However, they plan to keep trying over time.

After dinner, I return to my spot on the couch while Freya helps Jenny bring in a few bags of clothes from her car. We are lucky to have an old, spacious wardrobe in the spare bedroom for Jenny to use. Then they both took the bags upstairs while Maya sat down next to me on the couch, with Beastie and Pickle settling in their usual spots on me. Drake, meanwhile, is happily chasing the fox cubs around the living room under the watchful eye of their mother.

Maya brings her laptop with her as she sits next to me, opens it on her lap, and starts to plan her baking schedule for the upcoming week for our new business, focusing on exactly how much she will need to bake after our successful test run. I'm still a little worried about how incredibly busy we had been during the test run, and that it might be too much for her to handle on her own. I decided to wait and see how the first few days of next week go. If it looks like it's going to be too overwhelming for her, Freya and I will have to figure out a way to get her some much-needed help in the kitchen.

I decide to turn on the Tv and start flipping through the channels until I land on our local news. The channel I chose is partway into a story about our national space agency and their ambitious plans to try yet again to send equipment to the moon. Like most of us, the reporter openly questions the logic behind this persistent endeavour. Since the Russians had first sent a rocket to the moon, which had mysteriously vanished, though, typical of the Russians, they wouldn't officially confirm what had happened to it, so the moon has become a graveyard for rockets as they all disappear.

Then we tried to send our own rockets there, hoping to successfully land a capsule on the lunar surface so we could eventually send astronauts. But just like the Russian rocket, ours had also vanished without a trace. So, since our last ill-fated attempts during 1969 to 1981, our space agency has been more or less put on hold, that is, until they surprisingly managed to send a rover to Mars in 1997, a success that, if I remember correctly from old documentaries I have watched when I was younger, had thoroughly confused the entire scientific community.

Following the unexpected success on Mars, they tried to send another rover to the moon, but again, the rocket either was destroyed mid-flight or vanished into thin air. I couldn't quite recall exactly what had happened to that particular one.

The reporter then starts to talk about some intriguing readings they managed to get just before the last moon rocket was destroyed. The expert the reporter is interviewing explained that all the telemetry reports they had received indicated there were absolutely no issues with the rocket until the very last second before it inexplicably exploded.

However, they did pick up on a strange vibration within the rocket just moments before the catastrophic event. So, in response, they have made significant changes to strengthen this newest rocket, hoping it will be able to withstand whatever caused those mysterious vibrations in the past.

I started daydreaming about being able to travel to other planets. I imagined travelling to the moon and what it would be like. As I imagined myself travelling to the moon on a rocket, I started to get a weird feeling in my back. It was like getting pins and needles, and when I shifted position, the feeling went away.

I mentally wish them the best of luck when I get comfortable again. I've always been fascinated by space and the endless possibilities of what could be out there, even more so now that we have discovered we are witches and magic is real. The bigger, more philosophical question that kept nagging at the back of my mind is, if the ancient diary is indeed true, then whatever this primordial god of the void is, might still be out there somewhere? Is it continuing to create new gods on countless new worlds? And will it ever return to our universe? If it does, will it be pleased with how this world has turned out?

The diary revealed that this entity had created the first gods to oversee our world. However, those gods failed spectacularly and ultimately created their own race—us humans, well, I'm not sure I can call myself human now. We are now attempting to explore the vast universe that this ancient being might have originally created.

A small part of me can't help but worry that if this being ever returns, it could be incredibly angry with us as we are not what it created and who seem to be gone now, apart from the remnants like us witches, shifters, vampires, and god knows what else is out there.

I decided to change the channel, eventually finding a fascinating documentary about animals in the wild. I relaxed against the cushions to watch it until it was time for us to head out for the full moon ritual. After about half an hour, I suddenly felt a strange cold sensation in the area where my leg was injured.

As I concentrate on the feeling, it intensifies and feels distinctly like a hand. A cold hand that is gripping my leg tightly, yet my leg itself doesn't feel cold to the touch. I can also feel the same strange, cold sensation around one of the puncture wounds where the hellhound had bitten me. I turn my head and look down at my leg, my eyes widening slightly, and I have to blink a few times to try to make sense of what I thought I was seeing.

A faint shadow flickers near my legs, a dark, almost indistinct shape. The next time I blink, it's gone, and the cold sensation is gone instantly. *Was that... could it possibly be?* My mind whirls with a multitude of possibilities, none of them particularly comforting. Is it one of the demons from Jackson who had somehow returned and managed to get inside the house? Or maybe... just maybe... It's my shadow, and that weird spell I cast has actually worked after all. Have I really just inadvertently created my very own shadow demon? I glance nervously around the living room, trying to appear calm so I don't freak anyone out.

"What's up, Reya? You look a little worried," Maya says, glancing over at me from her spot on the floor.

Hearing her speak so suddenly makes me jump slightly. "Oh, it's nothing, sis. I just have... stuff on my mind," I say, quickly turning back to the Tv screen, hoping Maya drops her concern and goes back to working on her laptop. Then, trying to sound casual, I add, "If you're worried about anything, you know you can always talk to me, right?"

"I know, sis. I'm okay for now," Maya replies with a reassuring smile.

"Okay, well, when I'm done with this, I'll help you upstairs so you can get changed for the ritual," Maya says, then returns her attention to her laptop screen.

"Thanks," I mumble, my mind already racing back to the fleeting glimpse of the shadow. *Does it need my blood? If I really have created a shadow demon, does it need my blood to survive, just like Beastie does? It was created using my blood, so it kind of makes sense... Why do all these demons seem to have such a thing for blood?* I thought with a sigh.

Eventually, the time arrived when we all needed to start getting ready for the full moon ritual. True to her word, Maya helps me slowly and carefully make my way upstairs. We see Pickle already there when we enter my bedroom, looking rather excited. She's changed into a pretty little white dress she had bought recently because she wanted to join us for the ritual. But what caught my eye was how she nervously scratched at her wrist, like I've spotted her doing now and then.

As soon as we enter the room, Pickle quickly covers her wrist with a makeshift band she had fashioned out of leaves. But just before she manages to conceal it completely, I catch a glimpse of part of a black mark on her skin. I can't see enough of it to make out what it is, but it looks vaguely familiar. I'd tried asking her before if something was wrong, but she always skilfully avoids my questions, becoming unusually evasive. As I try to mentally recall the brief glimpse of the mark on her wrist, I'm almost certain that part of it might have resembled the image of a feather. I have promised myself that I'm not going to push her about it, hoping she will eventually feel comfortable enough to tell me what's going on. She's entitled to her secrets, after all.

    I manage to change without too many issues, carefully pulling on my loose sweatpants over the white smock to provide a little extra warmth and to also cover my body up a little better. It's just a little see-through in the right light, so anyone who might be approaching the house when we leave won't see too much and cause tongues to wag in town.

Chapter 20

Threads of Fate

We all make our way to the clearing, even the fox and her cubs trotting along behind us. And following them, much to my surprise and slight annoyance, is Drake.

"Who let him out?" I say, causing everyone to turn and look at the lumbering golem panther.

"Ooops," Freya says, her tone entirely lacking in remorse.

"Is that all you have to say?" I ask, giving her a pointed look.

Maya decides to answer me this time, "I only warded the one door to stop him from getting out – the one we usually leave open for the foxes. We came out of the door from the kitchen," she explains, sounding slightly exasperated.

"Try and keep an eye on him, please. The last thing we need is him turning up in town and scaring people half to death. I'm sure the sheriff would love to find a way to blame it on us, too," I say, sighing. I do notice, however, that the mother fox seems to be keeping Drake in line, nudging him away from her cubs whenever he gets too boisterous or if it looks like he is about to head off away from us, which surprises me and helps me relax a little.

"I will definitely put up a ward on the kitchen door tomorrow, too, to stop him from getting out again," Maya promises.

"Why not just turn him back into a toy?" Jenny asks, looking at

Drake with a mixture of amusement and concern.

"Well, Freya kind of screwed that up, didn't you?" I say, turning to my sister with a playful glare.

"I said I was sorry!" Freya protests, throwing her hands up in mock defence. She then turns to Jenny and explains, "I warded the mark I put on the toy so it wouldn't accidentally be rubbed off and to stop Reya from rubbing it off herself. I thought it would be funny… well, when I cast the ward, it acted really strange, then the ward was completely absorbed by the golem mark – that's called the aleph. I tried to remove the ward, but I couldn't, and it seems to be permanent now. The only way to change him back is to destroy the toy," Freya finishes, looking slightly sheepish. Freya had told me all this the next day, and since then, I've spent a considerable amount of time searching the internet to see if there's anything out there that might help reverse the process, but so far, I haven't found a single thing.

"Oh," was all Jenny said in response, giving me a worried look that mirrored my own internal frustration.

When we finally reach the familiar clearing we train in, the ancient stone pillars come into view, and like every time we have come here, I wonder about their true meaning and purpose. We have come out here a few times, sometimes even on my own, to try and decipher their significance. I've meticulously traced the runes carved into each pillar, hoping to find some information about them, but again, my research has yielded nothing helpful. I recognise a few of the runes from our book of runes – the familiar protection runes we used on the house and ourselves – but the rest remain a complete mystery.

I carefully sit down and lean against my favourite old oak tree, and within seconds, I am swamped by the fox cubs, who immediately jump onto my lap, vying for attention. Then, Drake, never one to be left out, joins the pile, making it very clear that he expects just as much attention as the cubs and even tries to nudge them off my lap playfully. However, there are more of them, and they hold their ground, eventually winning the battle for lap space, much to his annoyance. I give each of them a little scratch behind the ears and stroke their soft fur. When Beastie finally makes himself comfortable beside me, the cubs immediately jump onto his back until he lets out a low, rumbling growl. At this point, they all scurry off to play amongst the trees.

I watch the mother fox, Red, sitting nearby, calmly observing her playful offspring. The whole scene feels so surreal to me. The fox seems far more intelligent than a normal wild animal should be, and I wonder if she is also a magical creature or if being around so much magic has somehow made her smarter, much like it seems to have done for my sisters and me.

I turn my attention to my sisters, who, with the help of Jenny and Pickle, are carefully creating the pentagram in the centre of the clearing, just as we did before. They then place the candles at each of the five points. It's almost time; the clock is rapidly approaching midnight. Just then, the quiet stillness of the clearing is broken by the distant, mournful sound of wolves howling to the north of us. However, this time, we don't simply dismiss it as wild wolves out in the woods. This time, after everything the agents told us, we all couldn't help but wonder if one of those chilling howls belongs to the very wolf that killed our mother.

We all freeze in our spots, our senses on high alert. It crosses my mind if they might attack tonight; they certainly sound much closer than they had on the last full moon. "Try to ignore them," I say, my voice low but firm. "We need to get this done; it will help protect us better in the long run," I direct my words more towards Maya, as she seems to be the most affected by the unsettling sound tonight. It seems to work as their attention returns to finishing off the last few details of the setup.

When everything is finally in place, everyone starts to strip down until we are all wearing only our simple white smocks. Last time, I felt a little self-conscious about the semi-nudity, but I don't feel that way this time. I'm definitely more comfortable in my own skin and with the whole situation.

My sisters then used their very weak fire powers to light all the candles placed around the pentagram and the main fire we built in the centre a few days ago in preparation. Jenny carefully helps me to my feet, though I don't need much assistance by now, as my leg is feeling significantly better thanks to the accelerated magical healing. I just have a slight, persistent limp left, as putting too much pressure on my leg still pulls uncomfortably at the skin where the deep wound is finally healing over, but is still quite tender.

I keep the walking stick close by, just in case. In the early evening, Pickle decided to decorate the rather drab-looking stick with an assortment of colourful leaves and delicate wildflowers, declaring that it looked "utterly horrible" in its original state. I have to admit, what she had done is a definite improvement; it now looks much more whimsical and less like a medical device.

Like before, we slowly dance around the pentagram's outside. Even though there's no actual music playing, as soon as we begin to move, it feels like I can sense a faint melody in my mind, a rhythmic pulse that I instinctively dance to, well, the best I can with my slight limp and the occasional assistance of the decorated walking stick. As I look at my family dancing around, it seems like we are all moving to the same silent music. I wonder if they can also sense it in their minds. Jenny has even mentioned something about hearing music last time.

Like the previous full moon, I focus my intention and unlock my powers, which feels much easier this time, as we have all learned so much in the intervening weeks. I channel my power into the centre of our circle, which immediately joins with my sisters' energy, creating a swirling vortex of light. I even thought I saw a small amount of power emanating from Pickle as she flew and danced in the air above us, her tiny form a blur of motion. Suddenly struck by an idea, I call over Beastie to join our dance. Everyone gives me slightly amused looks as they continue to move, but no one says anything.

At first, Beastie stood there, looking slightly confused by the ritualistic display. But eventually, he lumbers over and stands by my side, and then, to my surprise, the fox cubs and even Drake join in, all of them moving with us as our combined power continues to flow into the centre of the pentagram.

Moments later, as I glance down at Beastie and the playful cubs, I notice the same phenomenon I observed with Pickle: a small but distinct amount of power has begun to flow from them as well, merging with our own energy and causing the colour of the swirling ball of magic in the centre to shift and change in a way it hadn't done before.

I'm completely mesmerised by our combined, swirling powers, the colours shifting and shimmering like an ethereal aurora borealis, until the distant sound of the wolves howling again breaks our focused silence, causing us all to momentarily lose our concentration, which starts to dissipate the glowing ball of energy. Still, with a concerted effort, we all manage to refocus our minds and continue our dance, which thankfully causes our power to begin flowing strongly again.

We fully expected our ball of power to descend and merge with the ground, just as it had done during the previous ritual. Instead, it remains suspended in the air, hovering directly above the flickering fire in the pentagram's centre. I exchanged puzzled glances with my sisters, trying to see if they had any idea what was going wrong, but they just shrugged in unison, their expressions mirroring my confusion.

Then Freya said thoughtfully, "Do you think it's acting differently because Pickle, Beastie, and the cubs are with us this time? Did you guys see that power coming off them as well?"

"I did see it, Freya, but I honestly have no idea what it means," I reply, worrying that something is going wrong because of me, because I let Beastie, Pickle, and the cubs be with us.

"Have I messed this up somehow?" Pickle calls out, her tiny face starting to crumple with worry.

Before I can even offer her a reassuring word, a sudden streak of bright blue lightning shoots out from the glowing ball of power and strikes each of the ancient stone pillars surrounding the clearing with a loud crackle. The runes carved into the pillars instantly lit up like a bizarre set of Christmas trees, glowing with an intense, otherworldly light as soon as the strange lightning made contact.

Then, as quickly as it appeared, the blue lightning stops, and our swirling ball of power descends as we expected it to do but as it descends though streams of our combined energy shoot out from the ball and begins to funnel into the pillars as well, the ancient stones seeming to absorb the magic with an almost audible hum. When the ball of power finally vanishes completely from the centre and stops channelling into the pillars, the ground beneath our feet starts to shake violently, as if a massive earthquake has suddenly erupted directly beneath us.

The ground continues to tremble and heave for what feels like a full minute, forcing all of us to drop to the ground to avoid being thrown off our feet, especially me with my still-tender leg. Then, with a final, powerful lurch, a shock wave explodes outwards from the pillars deep under the ground, the force of it rippling through the clearing. The ground then returns to its usual calmness, like nothing had happened. I expected some aftershocks, but none came.

The intense light emanating from the runes on the pillars fades back to a soft, almost imperceptible glow until they return to their simple carvings in the stone once more. Then, the entire clearing seemed to become bathed in an ethereal, nearly blinding light, which instinctively causes me to look up towards the sky. I notice with surprise that the full moon seems to be positioned directly above us and appears significantly brighter than usual, almost unnaturally so, until a bank of thick clouds suddenly drifts across its face, momentarily obscuring its brilliance. When the clouds eventually pass, the moon looks precisely as it always does every night, its familiar glow casting long shadows across the clearing.

"What the hell was *that?*" Freya calls out, scrambling to her feet and looking around the clearing with wide, disbelieving eyes. She even looked up at the moon as if she had witnessed the same strange phenomenon I had.

"I… I don't know," is all I manage to say, my mind still trying to process the bizarre sequence of events that had just unfolded. I desperately hope that whatever just happened is what was supposed to happen with the mysterious pillars.

I expected to struggle getting back on my feet, like it had been since the attack, but to my surprise, I can stand up like nothing is wrong with my leg. It's then that I realise my leg feels completely fine. Curious, I pull up the bottom of my smock and peel off the makeshift tape holding the bandage in place. It drops harmlessly to the ground, revealing perfectly smooth, unblemished skin where the deep wound had once been. I just gaped at my leg in utter disbelief.

"That was quite a show," a voice said, startling me. *Did I just think that? It sounded like me, but I'm almost certain I hadn't actually said anything.*

"Did any of you hear that?" I ask, looking around at my sisters and Jenny.

"Hear what? Hey! Your leg is completely healed! How did that happen?" Jenny asks, pointing at my now-perfectly-normal leg with apparent amazement.

"I think the shockwave or whatever it was healed me. Are you absolutely sure none of you heard a voice just now?" I ask again, my gaze sweeping across their faces as everyone stares at my miraculously healed leg.

"Sis, what voice are you talking about?" Freya asks, approaching me with a concerned look.

"It was me," the voice said again, this time more clearly inside my head. Just then, I felt a sudden cold touch on my shoulder, making me spin around abruptly.

"Oh my god, we're under attack again!" Maya screams, her eyes wide with terror, as she points behind me.

I stand there, frozen like a lemon, staring at what I see. A figure is standing there, a shadowy silhouette that vaguely resembles my form, but with eyes that glow with an eerie purple light.

Out of the corner of my eye, I start to see the surrounding plants – the tall grass and ferns–slowly moving towards the shadowy figure as if drawn by an invisible force. Freya begins to shout at me, her voice full of urgency, while Beastie lets out a low, menacing growl behind me. "REYA! Do something! Don't just stand there like a lemon!" The side of my mouth quirked because she said what I was thinking to myself.

I finally engage my brain and shout, "STOP!!"

Freya looks confused as I face her, trying to get her to stop with the plants. "What?"

"It… it won't hurt us. I think it's me, well, my shadow," I say hesitantly as I turn back to face the shadowy figure, looking directly into its glowing purple eyes. An inexplicable feeling of recognition washes over me, and I somehow know I'm right, especially when my connection to the shadow suddenly feels stronger now that I can focus on it to check if I'm right.

'*I am not entirely you; I am me,*' the shadow said, or at least, I think that's what it said. I can't see a mouth or discernible features, but I distinctly hear my voice echoing in my mind.

"If you're you and not entirely me, what do we call you?" I ask out loud, directing the question to the shadow.

"Wait a minute, is it… talking to you?" Freya demands, rushing to my side, her initial fear now mixed with intense curiosity.

"Yeah, can't you hear her?" I reply as I continue to stare at her in surprise.

"Nope. Not a thing."

"Oh. Can they not hear you?" I ask the shadow, tilting my head slightly.

'I am me, and you are my master; only you can hear me unless I take the blood of others but I feel I am unique and if I were to do so I won't be me anymore,' the shadow's voice echoes in my mind, the words sending a shiver down my spine.

"I was afraid you were going to say that," I say out loud so my family can hear my side of this very strange conversation.

"What's going on, Reya? What *is* it?" Freya demands again, her voice sharp and impatient.

"Well," I begin hesitantly, "I… I tried something out of that old diary I found. It mentioned that one of the old gods created shadow people to help protect them, so after what Papa Legba said, right when Madi transported us away, that he had left the diary specifically for me, I went back through my notes again too understand why, it can't have been to give me a history lesson and I found a passage about the shadow people and even copied down the runes. So, I tried it… but I honestly didn't think it had actually worked," I say, trying to explain the situation to everyone. Right then, I fully realise I have yet again been keeping yet another significant secret from my sisters, this time directly related to the mysterious diary.

"Clearly, it *did* work! Why are you constantly keeping things from us, Reya?" Freya says again, sounding genuinely hurt and frustrated with me. Her reaction makes me feel incredibly guilty about my continued secrecy; I'm still unsure why I keep doing it.

'What are your orders, master?' the shadow asks me, its purple eyes fixed intently on mine.

"For now, please don't call me master, it gives me weird thoughts about the master in Doctor Who so please just call me Reya," I say quickly, my attention more focused on Freya's upset expression than the newly manifested shadow, "just stay close to all of us and help protect us if we are attacked or in any danger." I tag on, then the shadow seems to melt into the ground, the darkness vanishing into the night.

"I'm so sorry, guys. A lot has been going on recently. I am truly sorry for not telling you. I think, I just… didn't want to worry you," I say, knowing how feeble and inadequate my excuse sounds even to myself.

"Don't do it again, Reya. Where did it even go?" Freya asks, her anger still simmering beneath the surface, I hate seeing her look at me with such hurt in her eyes. She then starts to pick up the scattered candles, not saying anything else, while Maya and Jenny just stare at me for a long moment before silently following suit, clearing up the remnants of the ritual. The heavy silence speaks volumes; everyone is clearly pissed off with me.

I didn't know what else to do, so I ensured Beastie and the fox cubs were okay, giving each a reassuring pat. I then reluctantly check on Drake to ensure he's still in golem form and hasn't run off into the woods. Thankfully, I spot him by the tree I had been leaning against earlier, fast asleep in the moonlight.

Like the first time we did this, I felt utterly exhausted after the ritual. So, after everything is cleaned up and the clearing is returned to its natural state, we all head back towards the house in silence. No one speaks to me on the way back. When I enter the house, I grab a bottle of water and a packet of biscuits from the kitchen, then quietly head straight up to my room.

After quickly changing into my pyjamas, I climbed into bed, ate a few biscuits, and drank some water. Then, I puffed my pillow and got comfortable as the exhaustion completely overwhelmed me. I drifted off into a deep, dreamless sleep, *thank god*, as I still get weird dreams of being in bed with multiple people. Well, I'm sure there are some creatures in the dream, too, as the dreams have continued, I've started to realise that it's not me I'm dreaming of, it feels more like I'm watching someone else's dreams.

Catherine M. Clark

Chapter 21

Monsters and Men

I've made mistakes keeping things from my sisters. I don't do it to keep them in the dark; I do it to protect them. They mean everything to me. Why couldn't they understand that? My thoughts, though, keep me in bed as I lie there not wanting to move because that will mean facing my family.

Even Jenny looked at me strangely after my shadow had appeared last night. Have I gone too far this time? I instinctively looked towards where Pickle and Beastie usually slept for comfort. I knew they were gone as soon as I woke up, I checked anyway, and yep, they are both gone. I scan my room and see no one. It feels strangely empty to wake up alone. Since Pickle and Beastie have come into my life, they have always been here when I wake, their presence a comforting weight.

"Are you here?" I ask my quiet room as I try to reach out with my mind.

'*I am,*' my voice echoes back to me.

"Can I see you?" I ask, as soon as the words leave my lips, a shadow rises up my bedroom wall, coalescing and solidifying. Those unnerving purple eyes appear, glowing strangely beautiful and so reminiscent of my purple flames. "We need to think of a name for you," I say as I roll onto my left side to get a better look at my shadow and use this to delay having to head downstairs.

'*A name? What is a name?*' she asks, her voice sounding exactly like mine but with a slightly ethereal quality.

"A name is what people call you; for example, I'm called Reya," I explain to my shadow, feeling a bit ridiculous having this conversation with myself or a part of myself.

'*Reya, so my name is Reya too?*' she questions me, a hint of playful curiosity in her tone, which makes me smile despite myself.

"No, that would get confusing pretty quickly. Maybe you can use my middle name," I suggest.

'*What is your... wait, I know this...*' she says, then suddenly freezes, her purple eyes widening slightly as if a memory has just surfaced.

"You do?" I ask, genuinely surprised.

'*I have all these memories that I'm still processing; your middle name is Seraphina,*' she says, the name rolling off her tongue with a familiarity that both intrigued and slightly unnerved me.

"That's right. So, do you have all of my memories?" I ask, my mind racing with the implications.

'I think I do. I was created by you and from you,' she says, her gaze steady. The fact that she possesses my memories will undoubtedly make things going forward so much easier, assuming I can actually trust her.

"Does that mean you can do the same things I can?" I ask, my curiosity piqued.

I watch as my shadow self holds out her hand, mimicking the gesture I would make when summoning my flames. But instead of producing fire, her hands elongate and sharpen, transforming into wickedly sharp claws. Then, taking me by complete surprise, something starts to emerge from her back, growing and expanding outwards on either side.

I can't help but watch in silent astonishment as her shadowy form grows and grows. When her transformation finally stops, I lay there, my breath catching in my throat. Sprouting from my shadow's back are a pair of large shadowy wings.

'*I seem to have other abilities than yours. Is that a good thing?*' she asks me, seeking reassurance, tilting her head slightly, her purple eyes questioning the confusion that she must see in my eyes.

"Erm… I guess?" I reply, still trying to process the sight of the wings. "It would have been cool if you had fire like me. We really need help; well, I need help protecting my family. It seems I'm the only one with real attacking abilities, which means I get hurt a lot," I explain to her, a hint of self-pity creeping into my voice.

'*Yes, I remember. It's good you have the protection barrier, which also helps with healing… and the house, it feels different,*' Shadow me, or Seraphina, as I should probably start thinking of her, says strangely, her gaze drifting around my room as if she were sensing something I wasn't.

I'm not entirely sure what she means about the house feeling different but hearing her confirm that the ritual not only worked again last night but might now be speeding up our already quicker healing abilities, which I need if I continue to get hurt. I'm glad I don't seem to get scared from my injuries either, which is a great bonus; otherwise, I might end up looking like Frankenstein.

'*I will do all I can to help protect your family. I should warn you, though, I have sensed what you call wolves watching this property,*' she says, her tone suddenly serious.

"What?!" I exclaim, adrenaline instantly coursing through me as I shoot up into a sitting position, my heart pounding in my chest. "Where? When?" I ask as panic washes over me, my mind racing. I'm not really sure which piece of information I need more urgently.

'*Right now, in the woods. But they can't get past the barrier; they tried last night, and the wolf killed when your power exploded as it was too close to the barrier as it expanded very slightly; they are furious,*'

Seraphina tells me, her voice flat and devoid of emotion.

"So, the howling… that was them?" I ask, more to myself than to her.

'*Yes, it was,*' she answers me anyway, her gaze unwavering.

"Thank you," I say as a wave of gratitude washes over me. Knowing we aren't wholly unaware of what is happening around us is a big comfort.

'*You are my mast…Reya, I have to protect you and do as you command,*' Seraphina says, catching herself as she was about to call me master again, even thinking of someone calling me master sends a shiver over me, her words, though, echoing what is mentioned in the diary.

"No," I correct her firmly, "you are to protect my family, which includes Pickle, Beastie, and Jenny."

'*I will do as you say,*' she replies, her tone now more subservient.

She starts to fade away, her shadowy form flickering, but I have one more crucial question. "Wait," I call out, and her image solidifies again, her purple eyes fixed on me expectantly. "Do you need blood to survive?" I ask, already dreading the answer but knowing I had to know.

'*I do. You are powerful, so I don't need much. Otherwise, I think I would die, I think I can only survive off you as I was created from you,*' she says, and my heart clenches slightly at the thought of her dying because of me, or without my blood.

"Well, take what you need from me when you need it, okay?" I say, authoritatively, wanting to make sure she understands the boundaries and my willingness to help her survive.

'*I will. Thank you,*' she says, a hint of something akin to gratitude in her mental voice, and then she finally fades entirely from view.

I get dressed for the day, pulling on my favourite pair of well-worn jeans and a comfortable t-shirt Freya had made for me. She thought it would be funny, and like the others she has gifted me over the years, I wear them with pride, *mostly*. This one has a saying I blurted out during a particularly stressful and surprising moment, '*No Witchin Way.*' She thought it perfectly represented our current chaotic situation. Freya thought I wouldn't like it, but I proudly wear it, much to my sister's amusement.

After a quick trip to the bathroom, I head downstairs and find Maya already in the kitchen, the comforting aroma of baking filling the air. She turns when she hears me approach. "It's about time you got up, sleepyhead," she says, a warm smile on her face, not seeming angry with me *at all*. Then she looks down at my t-shirt and chuckles while shaking her head, "One day, Freya is going to get you a t-shirt that you refuse to wear."

"I must have been absolutely exhausted last night. Where are Freya and everyone else?" I ask, ignoring her comments about the tops Freya gets me, as I look around the surprisingly empty kitchen and living area. Even the foxes are gone.

"Freya is out tending to her precious plants, and Pickle and Beastie are outside enjoying the weather along with the foxes. Why?" she asks, giving me a worried look.

"I just found out that wolves are watching us right now," I tell her, deciding that enough is enough with the secrets. It's time to start being more open with them.

Maya's spatula clatters against the countertop as she spins around to face me, her eyes wide with alarm. "What?! How do you know this?" she demands, her voice rising in panic.

"Seraphina – that's my shadow's name – told me they were also out there last night. And apparently, we killed one of them when the ritual happened," I explain, relaying what my shadow had told me.

Maya's eyes widen even further in surprise and a hint of fear. "Can we trust it?" she asks as she starts glancing out the window, I'm guessing, looking for the wolves. She speaks with a whisper, like they might hear her.

"She is me, Maya. She has all my memories, so I think we can trust her... mostly. Also, she's going to use my middle name, Seraphina, and she can only talk to me because I created her, unless she drinks someone else's blood but she said that if she does she won't be her anymore as she was created from me," I tell her not really sure she is listening to me as she is still distracted with looking out the kitchen window that over-looks the front of the house and the right corner, while I'm worried about over-sharing and making things even weirder. This last piece of information did, however, make Maya wrinkle her nose in obvious distaste.

"Well, I think I will definitely pass on that offer. You really hurt Freya's feelings last night, you know? Even Jenny said she's worried this morning before she headed out to check on her brother. Wait, is Duncan going to be safe? He will be here tonight, so don't even think about complaining. I know he isn't supposed to be here on Sundays. Still, I haven't seen him for a few days, what with opening the business on Friday and the new job he got out of town, which he will have finished today, so I told him he could come over," Maya said, her words tumbling out in a rush, a sure sign that she is nervous. Maya's tendency to babble when she's anxious always makes me smile.

"Yeah, that's fine, Maya. I can't see us doing any training today after everything that happened last night and now knowing about the wolves," I said, heading over to the back window to look outside. At least Seraphina has confirmed that the wolves can't get past the barrier, so we should be relatively safe, except for the unsettling fact that the barrier only extends to just in front of the house.

As I peer out the window, I can see Freya in the distance, working diligently in her garden, which is cleverly concealed within the protective wards she has erected. She also uses glamours, a magical camouflage that projects a false image of her garden to anyone looking from a distance, masking what is really going on within the wards. As I scan the surrounding area, I spot Beastie lying contentedly in the long grass, and on top of him is Pickle, lying on her back sunbathing.

Then, a little further away, I see the fox cubs playfully chasing Drake around a bush, which makes me groan inwardly. I miss having the panther on my bed so I can cuddle him whenever possible. He doesn't quite feel like mine anymore, not in the same comforting way.

"Why is Drake outside?" I ask.

"He isn't going to run away, Freya made it so he wants to be around us, so chill, you can shout and complain if he proves us wrong," Maya said, hinting that I have been complaining about him too much.

I move away from the window and absently grab the wooden bannister of the stairs as I turn back towards the living room. I suddenly feel the weight of everything that's happening pressing down on me. I have so much to lose now, with this makeshift family that I love fiercely, and it seems we can't escape the shadow of what happened to our mother. I can't help but think about the unsettling possibility that she might still be out there somewhere as a ghost.

A wave of anger and frustration washes over me, and I grip the bannister harder than I intend. A sharp cracking and snapping sound echoes around me, and I feel my fingers dig slightly into the wood. The sound is eerily similar to when I accidentally damaged a tree out in the clearing during a surge of uncontrolled magic. I look down and see my fingers are embedded in the wooden bannister, splinters of wood sticking up around them.

"What the hell was that?" Maya calls out, sounding alarmed, as she appears from the kitchen moments later, with a dusting of flour on her cheek.

"I… I seem to have damaged the bannister," I whisper, lost in thought and utterly bewildered by what I've just done. "When Duncan gets here, can you see if he can fix it when he has the time, please?" I ask, still trying to process the strange surge of strength.

"Is it bad?" Maya asks, her eyes wide as she stares at my hand still partially embedded in the wooden bannister.

"It's bad enough," I reply, slowly pulling my fingers free, causing more of the already stressed wood to splinter and break away. "I guess it's not that bad compared to everything else that's going on in our lives," I add with a sigh, trying to inject a bit of dark humour into the situation.

Once my hand is free, I move over to the couch and sink into my usual spot, the cushions conforming to my shape. I rub my hand aimlessly, trying to recall the exact moment of the outburst, wondering if I felt any pain, but my mind is strangely blank regarding the sensation. I pick up the remote and turn on the TV, searching for a local news channel to see if whatever happened last night tripped any earthquake sensors. I had the thought just as I was nodding off last night, so I'm surprised I remembered to check.

I really want to go outside and talk to Freya, to try and mend the rift my secrecy has caused, but I'm not quite brave enough yet to face her likely disappointment. So, once I've settled on a news channel, I pull out my phone. I haven't looked at it since waking up; maybe Jacob felt the earthquake and sent a message.

As I check for messages, I find a couple that surprise me. I opened the first one, which is from Agent Bekke. *'Hey, how are you doing? How's the leg? Did you feel that quake last night? The reports say the epicentre was in your area.'*

"Crap!" I say out loud, realising the implications of the earthquake being traced back to our clearing. Maya doesn't seem to have heard me over the Tv as she continues baking in the kitchen. I quickly type out a reply, debating for a moment whether to be completely honest or not. Given everything that is happening, I decide that honesty, however uncomfortable, is the best policy. *'Leg is healed, thanks. And yeah, the* quake was our fault. Also, I just found out wolves are watching us. You were right. And one of them died last night because of our ritual.' I hit send, a knot of anxiety tightening in my stomach.

I then opened the following message, which was indeed from Jacob. I'm not really surprised, as he is usually pretty consistent with his texts: '*Hey, beautiful. Do you fancy joining me for lunch on Tuesday when you're not working?*'

I shake my head, a wry smile playing on my lips. Things really weren't going the way I had hoped they would. For some reason, I completely forgot that he mentioned wanting to meet up this week after he visited our business on Friday.

He isn't going to be thrilled with my response. '*Sorry, Tuesday won't work. I'm going to an estate sale. It's the only day I can go. Again, sorry, maybe later in the week.*' I sent it, feeling a pang of guilt, but knowing I can't focus on dating with everything else going on, I groan to myself as I shouldn't have said maybe later in the week.

I move on to my last message, which is from Jenny. I'm a little worried about what it might say, bracing myself for more disappointment. After a moment of hesitation, I open it to face whatever else I have inadvertently done to upset those I care about. '*Sorry, I ghosted you last night. I was worried about the shadow thing. I shouldn't have been; I know you would never do anything to harm me. See you later.*' She put a few kisses on the end, and my body relaxed from the tension I felt, worried she was still mad at me. *That wasn't too bad*, I thought with a sigh of relief.

"Sis?" Maya calls out from the kitchen.

"Yeah?"

"Can we go buy another car today? With how well Friday went at the café, I really need to be able to go into work early to do my baking. I'm not going to be able to bake enough here to keep up with the possible demand, and I would have to bake all night every night even to try and keep up," she said, sounding genuinely nervous about what my response might be.

"Sure, Maya, whatever you need, as long as you promise to take Beastie with you. I don't want you going anywhere on your own right now, not with these wolves hanging around," I said, keeping my tone light and easy and not saying what I really wanted to say, which was a resounding '*Hell no, it's too dangerous!*'

"I can definitely do that. Thank you, Reya," she said, relief evident in her voice.

"Just let me know when you want to go," I said, putting my phone down on the coffee table next to me and focusing my attention on a news report that had just started with the headline, '*Jackson Quake.*' Crap!

I watch as the news anchor states that scientists are completely baffled by the unexpected earthquake, noting that it occurred without any usual warning, mini-shocks or aftershocks. They also mention that it's a surprisingly strong quake for the area, but overall, it's a weak quake at a magnitude of 3.9. The anchor then reassures viewers that no one should worry, but then she suddenly stops, puts a hand up to her ear, and nods slightly as if she is listening to someone speaking to her through her earpiece.

"I have some breaking news," she announces, her tone shifting to grave concern. "As you know, there have been increasing reports of strange attacks worldwide, not just here in Jackson. We have just received unconfirmed reports about a small town in southern England called Fenrir Hollow that seems to have become a ghost town."

I instinctively reach for the remote and turn down the volume on the television, even though the news is happening overseas. "Early reports coming in state that all of the town's residents have vanished, except for a few bodies which show signs of being violently killed. Local police are reportedly baffled by what has happened and state that even their local police force has also disappeared. We will bring you more on this developing story as soon as we can. In the meantime, it is clear that we all need to do everything we can to help protect our towns and cities, so please help your local law enforcement if you see or hear anything out of place."

The report sends a shiver of unease down my spine. It particularly worries me that it might profoundly affect Maya, as she is the more sensitive one among us and has been managing to keep things together, albeit precariously, since our mother's death.

I must admit that Duncan has been a significant part of her ability to cope, for which I'm incredibly thankful, except for the constant nagging worry that he might have his heart completely shattered when he eventually finds out we are witches.

Catherine M. Clark

Chapter 22

An Uneasy Alliance

Ava

After we left the Harpers, I feel worried for them as they are at risk, and the attack proves it. But it isn't just from the wolves like we expect; it's also from demons. The good thing is that they seem much stronger than we are, which I didn't expect after seeing Rose and Luca in their panther forms. Especially Reya, she seems, *amazing* and I like her a lot, so I can't understand why Rose doesn't. Sam...well, he seems lost as to what to do.

He is intrigued by what Freya said about this rune that can give him the ability to see what I can, like my ring, it would be handy for him to be able to see what I can see. Even Rose can't see everything I can, and she's Paranormal. Rose is kicking off, saying we can't trust them and that it's too risky to let someone cast something permanent on them. Of course, Sam isn't part of Luca's pack, so it's up to him.

I think Rose forgets he isn't paranormal, so he is our weakest team member. Rose sounds the same drumbeat as Luca, as he is positive that Reya is a black witch and that all black witches are evil, as they are the only ones who can summon demons. I don't see it. Her main ability seems to be blackfire, but she doesn't dress or act like black witches are depicted in the media. You could tell they were bad before they did anything. I also don't get that feeling from Reya or her sisters. I've always been a good judge of character. I have to be in my line of work, and my gut feeling tells me Reya is good. I'm willing to fight Rose and even Luca over this.

When we got back to the motel yesterday, I got to work on pinning all the attacks out on a local map to find a pattern to stop any more of these demons from attacking the Harpers and, of course, the locals in Jackson. The only issue is that I'm the only one who can see the demons when they haven't possessed someone, so the rest of my team is at risk if we try to take on these demons. Sam also called Agent Moore to update him when we returned.

He's pleased that we might have found strong paranormals that he hopes might help us. He also advised Sam to take the risk if he wished with the rune. We also heard from Luca this morning that he is looking for his pack around Houston, as they haven't turned up at the meeting area. I hope his pack is safe. The last thing we need is to lose allies, just as we found possible new ones. Rose and I are sitting on the floor with the map in front of us. We both continue to place coloured dots on the map depending on the type of attack or strange event, while Sam heads out to grab us lunch.

As we went through the police files, my mobile phone buzzed with a text message. I pick up my phone and read the message. It's from Reya, which makes me smile. It's nice to have someone else to chat with since I can't really keep in contact with my usual friends. Reading Reya's reply to the message I sent her this morning has really thrown me a bit. I'm completely shocked by what she said, and now I'm seriously worried about how Rose and especially Luca will take this news. It's not going to be easy telling them. "Anything important?" Rose asks.

"You could say that," I say, still debating whether to tell her.

Honestly, I'm finding what Reya said hard to believe. I really wish she had gone into more detail.

Rose finally looks at me with a raised eyebrow, "What is it?"

"Erm…maybe I should keep this to myself till Reya can explain what happened in more detail. She also said she got proof this morning that we were right about the wolves. She states that she has been informed that the wolves are currently watching the property, and one of the wolves was killed last night during a ritual, whatever that means."

"That's not good. My presence in the town might make things much worse now. They will have to deal with it themselves; we have things here we need to deal with, which is our job. What else did she say you don't want to tell me?" Rose pushed, annoying me.

"Our job is also to find others to help us; the Harpers can seriously help. Especially as you, Luca, and Sam can't see everything I can, we are up against demons, and you can't see them unless they have possessed someone, so we need the sisters unless you are willing to let them put this rune spell on you….the part of the message I don't want to tell you is Reya said they were responsible for the quake last night," I say not looking at her directly as I'm worried how she is going to react. "What did you just say?" Rose said as her voice rose an octave.

"We need the sisters," I say, knowing what she is really asking but trying to get her off the subject.

"That's not going to work. After what you just told me, are you still seriously going to try to tell me she isn't a black witch? Luca will not agree to help a black witch," Rose snaps back at me.

"She is not a black witch, I'm sure of it," I say with as much conviction as possible because I really believe it.

"Ava, only a black witch can summon a demon. You're new to this world; you need to trust us," Rose pleads with me.

"I do trust you, but I disagree with you about this. For the record, I'm in charge of this team and will help them. Do you think maybe, after being told all your life that black witches are bad, that you can't think of them any other way? Even if she is a black witch, I don't think she is on the side of bad, especially as demons and wolves are out to kill them," I say, putting my foot down on the subject, which causes Rose to start to look angry with me. Rose really does look angry and remains silent for a few minutes, looking like she is trying to keep herself calm. Then she continues the argument, "You just proved my point. No good witch would cause an earthquake, which puts people at risk. You need to listen to us, Ava. I don't want you trusting them and then getting hurt when they turn on you," Rose said with so much anger in her tone.

"I'm not turning my back on them; I feel it here," I say, resting my hand over my heart, "They are on the side of good."

"We will see," is all Rose says.

"We will. You and Luca need to open yourselves up to the fact that just because you might have a certain power doesn't mean you will use it for evil. Many historical examples show us that not everyone does as you expect; both of you see enemies everywhere now; I'm surprised you both didn't think I was an enemy," I say, getting just as angry as her.

Rose doesn't respond and goes back to going through the files, which pisses me off more. I texted Reya, saying, *'I will do anything I can to help and would like to hear about how you managed to cause a quake.'* I get an instant reply saying, *'Thank you, and I will explain when I see you next.'* If she were an evil witch, she wouldn't care about telling me and wouldn't be interested in messaging me.

Not long after, Sam returns with food. As soon as he enters, he can sense that something is up. "What's going on?" he asks, handing out our food.

"Rose believes Reya is a black witch because she can summon demons. She isn't interested in helping them even after I got a text from her saying she has confirmed wolves are watching them right now," I told him.

"Tell him the rest!" Rose demands.

"Well...Reya said they accidentally caused the small earthquake. She said she will explain the next time I see her. She wouldn't care about explaining if she were an evil witch, right?" I say, begging for him to understand and agree with me. Sam shrugs,

"Yeah, I would agree with your logic." This causes Rose to throw her hands into the air, get up, and take her food over to the only chair in the room. "I think we should help them, which will help us to get to know them better. I am interested in that rune, which will allow me to see everything you can, Ava. I felt helpless during that attack, and if that is what we are up against here in Jackson, then I'm worried we will lose if we stay here. I'm willing to take a chance till they do something proving I can't trust them," Sam said diplomatically.

"Sam, they could do anything to you. Do you know what the strongest smell was in that house? It was the smell of blood," Rose said in the same angry tone she had with me.

"Rose!" Sam exclaims.

"What!" Rose stubbornly replies. It is your choice what you do, but my choice, which I'm entitled to, is to trust them until they break it. If they were bad like most of the paranormal world that is left, why would they invite us into their home and let us leave alive?"

Rose went to say something, but he stopped her by holding up a hand. Then he continues, "Rose, if you and Luca keep fighting your team leader over her decisions, then maybe this task force isn't going to work; I, for one, will be sticking by Ava's side." Sam looks frustrated and annoyed with Rose's attitude, and he continues his rant, saying more than I have heard him speak since I met him, "Why did they sit down with us instead of attacking us? Instead, they told us their story, and then we told them ours. Do you not get it, Rose?"

"Get what? What don't I get?" Rose demands, and I can see she is angry with Sam's attitude towards her as well.

"The same person has been helping us and them; this Cat, even Papa Legba, has helped them and us. Cat has been leading us to the sisters to help them and save them. This task force was created because Luca trusted Cat. Well, it has led us to the sisters, and they might be the only other people who could help us and be on the same side as us. Do you really think the four of us alone can stop what is happening in the world right now?" When Sam finished, he was breathing heavily, as if he had held his breath during his whole statement.

The way I see Rose's expression change, I think he finally might have got through to her, which impresses me because I struck out and I'm her partner. Rose looks defeated, and her angry expression slips away. "You have a point, Sam. Still, it doesn't mean I'm going to trust them," she said stubbornly.

"As long as you give them a chance to prove you can trust them," Sam said, looking tired of the whole argument. Sam then changes the subject, "We need to find something to point us in the right direction to locate these demons if they are holed up somewhere in Jackson. Unless the demons that attacked the sisters were the only ones in town."

"So far, nothing in the files indicates where they might be," Rose replies, taking Sam's cue and accepting the change of direction. The only other option is to drive around the city and hope Luca or I can pick up on a scent.

Then Sam takes Rose by surprise. "Did Ava tell you she took out one of the demons with her sword? She's getting good with it." Sam smiles at me and sounds proud of me. "What?" Rose exclaims. "As I said, Ava took out one of the demons," Sam said, frowning at Rose's expression. He clearly thought it would be good news, but it seems that she isn't happy about this either.

"Yeah, I heard you the first time. Ava, you can't take out a demon with a sword. Especially a shade if that's what is possessing the humans," Rose states, taking me by surprise and making me wonder how the hell we can take out the demons, then if there are more in this city.

"Are you serious?" I ask as I continue to worry about how we will deal with this situation.

"Yes, I'm serious. It's why Luca didn't get us to head straight out to try and track the demons in the city," Rose said, frowning at my expression. She then continued, "Ava, we have no way to take them out except to destroy the human bodies they have possessed and hope they give up and stay in the underworld. Luca hoped the witches would take them out if we tracked them down, but I'm not sure he will be willing to stick to his plan now."

After Rose explained the situation to us, it pisses me off because I'm supposed to be the team leader, and they kept this from me. "What the hell, Rose? Why didn't you tell me this? I know Luca is used to being in charge, so I get why he doesn't always share, but I expected more from you," I said, getting angry with Rose again and Luca.

Rose is the only one here, so she is the one to deal with my attitude. Rose looks taken aback. "You were so gun-ho about finding the sisters that Luca decided to wait till we knew more, and then, well, other things happened. Actually, I was supposed to tell you when you returned after your meeting," Rose tells me, as she won't look me in the eye and looks guilty as hell.

"Unbelievable," is all I said in response. I grab my food, which is getting cold now, and leave the guy's room. I don't go to our room, as that's where she would look for me. Instead, I went to our rental, as I still have the keys on me.

Sure enough, about ten minutes later, Rose leaves Sam's room and goes to enter ours, but she doesn't go in. I watch as she sniffs the air, and then, with no hesitation, she looks right at me, "Damn her heightened senses," I say out loud to myself. Rose heads straight for me and tries to open the passenger door. Except I've locked myself in, so it doesn't open

253

for her and frustrates her.

"Ava, come on. Unlock it, please, I'm sorry," she said, sounding contrite.

"I'm good, thanks," I said, not looking at her. I take another bite of my cold burger.

"This isn't very adult of you. I said I'm sorry. I really am for keeping the information from you," she said, crouching down so her eye level is with me, trying to get me to look at her, probably to try and bat those green eyes at me, which might work if I looked. Just thinking about her eyes makes me cave and have to look, so when I turned and looked into her eyes and saw that they reflected, she was genuinely contrite. I unlock the door, and Rose doesn't hesitate to open it and slide onto the passenger seat.

When she closes the door, I ask, "Are you really or just telling me you are?"

"I am Ava. Please forgive me," Rose begs and gives me the same look cats give when they want something from their owners. I sigh as I look into her eyes, already knowing I would forgive her, but finding it hard to engage my mouth. I continue looking into those eyes as they stare back at me, begging for forgiveness. I finally said the words she hoped for, "I forgive you."

"Thank you, honey, I really am sorry. In my defence, I didn't want to disappoint you. You were so excited that we found the sisters alive. Then, after I found out that Reya summoned a demon, I was scared to tell you that they might not be the good witches we hoped for," Rose said, looking so sad. It made my heart ache to see it all over her face and the way she curved her body into itself like she's trying to protect herself, so my defences fully crumbled.

"Thank you," I say, and after a slight pause, I say, "Please don't keep things from me again; we can't work as a team if we aren't honest." Rose nods in agreement. I then lean over and hug her.

"Before I came to apologise, Sam said he would let them do this rune thing to him. Can you text Reya to arrange it, please?" Rose tells me, looking awkward as she speaks.

I can tell she is worried, but trying not to be for me. I pull away from Rose enough to look her in the eyes, and with a slight smirk, I say, "I already have. I saw how worried he looked after the attack because he couldn't see all our enemies. Part of me knew he would want to try it, and I had to let Reya know that the demon I thought I killed might not have been killed. I explained that you told me these types of demons can't be killed by swords."

"Has she messaged back?" Rose asks.

"Yes, she said she would see if she could do it on Tuesday after she returns from an estate sale, and her sisters don't need help at work," I tell her, watching her face to see if she is okay with everything.

"Why is she going to estate sales?" Rose asks, intrigued as I see her rack her brain for the reason.

"I have no idea. You can ask on Tuesday, as I'm sure you aren't going to let me go back there with just Sam again," I said, chuckling at Rose's reaction and agreeing with my assessment.

"I guess I should also say that as I approached the property, it was like a wall of stink hit me. Wolves have been in the woods around the house a lot," Rose said, looking sheepish. It was something else she hadn't told me right away. She had a chance to say this while we were at the Harpers. I decided not to make a big deal about it, as we have already dealt with this. "Ava?"

"Yes, Rose."

"Are we okay?"

"We're good," I say, and Rose blows out a breath she had been holding and slumps in the seat as she relaxes.

Catherine M. Clark

Chapter 23

Nightmares and Nerves

Reya

I'm having a rough night worrying about Maya, which keeps disturbing Jenny. She isn't the only one, as Beastie took me by surprise, got up in the middle of the night, and left my room because I kept kicking him as I fidgeted. Then I'm worrying about him too, as I have no idea where he went. My mind is racing with possibilities, and none of them are good. I'm particularly worried because when Maya and I looked at cars at a dealership on the outskirts of Jackson, she found a Qashqai she liked and bought it on the spot. I had expected us to look around, make notes, and then discuss what might be best for her. I really thought she would take her usual week to decide. This impulsiveness is entirely out of character.

She's never been this decisive before, so a knot of anxiety tightens in my chest when she left early this morning to bake in the café's kitchen. I knew she was taking Beastie, and my shadow might be looking out for her, too, but my worry persists. I blame Duncan for her newfound confidence; I should probably apologise to him as I was a little off with him over dinner.

When Maya got up to head out, I heard her talking to Beastie, her tone a mix of annoyance and relief, "If you ever do that again, I will throw all your food away. You gave me a heart attack." I couldn't help myself; a giggle escaped my lips despite my worry. After I heard her drive off, I had to get up. I needed to be ready in case something happened, so I took a quick shower, then went downstairs and turned on the coffee maker. I was definitely going to need a lot of caffeine today.

I sit on the couch, flicking through channels aimlessly, hoping time passes quickly. It's only 6am, so I have two hours before I plan to head to town to make sure she is okay, even though she texted me to say she arrived safely after I bombarded her with worried messages demanding confirmation.

Not long after I settled myself on the couch, I heard movement upstairs, followed by the faint sound of water, which I presumed was Freya taking a shower. About twenty minutes later, Freya came down the stairs. She didn't seem surprised to see me. "Couldn't sleep either?" she asked.

"Nope, I've been so worried about her going in alone," I say, glancing over my shoulder at Freya as she heads for the kitchen, undoubtedly, to get some coffee herself. "She isn't alone. Beastie won't let anything happen to her," Freya says reassuringly.

"I know, but he's not unbeatable," I counter, my mind conjuring up all the ways things can go *so* wrong.

"You know, it might not have been such a bad idea to see if you could have turned those other hellhounds to our side," Freya states, making a valid point. However, the thought of having more creatures like Beastie worries me; it feels like it would draw too much unwanted attention to us.

"That's the thing…" I begin, hesitating before deciding to tell her what I realised when we headed out to confront our attackers.

"What?" Freya asks, heading my way with a steaming mug pressed to her lips. Her eyes close in momentary delight as she takes a sip.

"I think I could have. I felt them, even those demons, those shadow people, like my shadow. I could feel them too," I confess, a wave of nausea washing over me. The thought that I might have been able to control all those demons makes me feel incredibly ill.

"Reya, I'm going to kick your arse," Freya said, sitting down next to me and giving me her signature mean-girl stare, though I could see a hint of concern in her eyes.

"Sorry. You have no idea what it's like for me to know I could possibly control these things. Beastie is one thing, but it scares me knowing I could accidentally summon more demons by saying something so innocent. Then we'd be surrounded by demons, and they'd all be looking at me for orders," I say, closing my eyes and lowering my head as my fears crash down on me, causing a few tears to escape and trace paths down my cheeks.

Freya stares at me for a moment, her expression softening with understanding before she surprises me by asking, "Is there anything else you need to tell me while I'm in a forgiving mood?" I give her a guilty smile. "Out with it," she prompts, a hint of amusement in her voice.

"Well, you know that diary I translated?" I said sheepishly.

"Yeah, what about it?" she asks, giving me a look that clearly conveys her frustration with my tendency to withhold information.

"It basically gave me a brief history of the original gods and what happened to them and their descendants," I explain.

"Okay, sounds interesting. That doesn't sound like something you'd need to keep from us," she said, her curiosity piqued, though.

"The part I was worried about telling you – well, Maya, really, as I know you'd be fine – is that as I translated the later years, it started to explain how the angels came into existence," I said, giving my sister a pointed look to see if she could grasp what I was hinting at. I realised then that I sounded so much like Cat and Papa Legba, being just as cryptic.

Freya frowns at me, clearly not understanding. "Okay, there must be more to it," she said, prompting me to elaborate.

I take a deep breath, trying to calm my nerves and face Freya. "It explains that all paranormal beings are descended from these original gods," I tell her, bracing myself for her reaction.

"Oh," is all Freya responds with at first. I brace myself for her to lose it with me, "So you're saying we're essentially children of the gods?" She pauses momentarily, lost in thought, so I don't interrupt. Moments later, she looks back at me and shrugs, "You know, I think I might have already known that. Also, I always knew I was a goddess." Freya then gives me a mischievous smirk that makes me laugh, and she soon joins me. Okay, I didn't expect that reaction.

Our laughter is cut short when both our phones ding simultaneously, causing us to exchange worried glances before grabbing our phones. The message is from Maya, '*All good here. I love these ovens. You can stop pulling your hair out.*' Freya and I visibly relaxed as we both expected the worst.

I need to change the subject before Freya starts asking more questions about the gods. "If you're still going through that new book, can you leave out the section on the rune for this sight thing? Agent Miller wants to give it a try," I say. "I'm thinking of doing it Tuesday afternoon if you guys don't need me at the café."

"No problem," she says, and she doesn't look surprised Agent Miller wants to try it. I think she understands his desperation after witnessing the attack. "I really like this new book; there are a few things I want to try," she adds, a spark of excitement in her eyes.

"Like what?" I inquire, glad our trip to New Orleans wasn't a complete waste.

"There's a potion for protection against the human cold and flu," she said, which triggers a thought in the back of my mind.

"We've never actually had a cold or the flu, have we?" I said, racking my brain to confirm if that is indeed the truth.

"Yeah, I realised that too when I read it, but I want to make it for Jenny and Duncan and maybe find a way to get Duncan's parents to drink it too."

"That's a good idea," I agree.

Freya then starts to smile, her lips twitching in that familiar way that tells me she is about to say something silly. "There's also a… potion to protect your hair against getting wet and stop it from smelling like fish if you go swimming," she said, barely managing to get the words out without laughing.

"Really? That is clearly created by someone who really hated the smell of fish," I said, and we both burst into laughter again.

Just after 8am, Freya, Pickle, and I head to town, with Jenny following in her car. As we pull away, I notice Duncan leaving the house in the rearview mirror. I completely forgot he was in the house. I also see him lock the door, which means Maya has given him her key.

As we drive to town, a knot of anxiety remains in my stomach. I can't shake the feeling of being watched as I constantly scan our surroundings, half-expecting a wolf to jump out at any moment. I also watch Jenny in my rearview mirror until we reach our street in town, where she peels off to park behind her building while we continue to the back of ours.

We let ourselves in through the back door and immediately open the door to the kitchen to check on Maya. We find Maya standing in front of the mixer, its noise masking our entrance as a wave of relief washes over me. I'm sure Freya feels the same as we both slump against the doorframe while Pickle hovers between us, looking relieved to see Maya is okay, before suddenly looking around for Beastie, who makes us jump when he appears behind us, causing Pickle to squeal in shock.

"Bloody hell, you lot just scared the crap out of me," Maya said, clutching her chest.

"Sorry," we all said in unison. Then Pickle points an accusing finger at Beastie, telling Maya it's his fault, to which Beastie just lets out a soft huff of amusement.

Maya shakes her head, a small smile playing on her lips. "I've got so much done in a fraction of the time," she said, sounding genuinely pleased.

"Good, Pickle is going to try and help you later," I say.

"Great, I'll teach her how to put together the sandwich orders," Maya replies, genuinely grateful for the help.

"Yay!" Pickle exclaims, leaning against my shoulder. "Wrap my hands up, please, so I'm good to touch the food," she asks. We haven't found any gloves she can use in the kitchen, so we thought wrapping her hands in cling film might work.

"Let's get set up first, then we'll wrap your hands up," Freya tells her.

When we open the doors at 8:30am, we are shocked to find a queue stretching down the street. It's primarily made up of men, many holding thermoses and what I presume are lunch bags. We know exactly what they want, so Freya and I jump in to help make orders until we get through the rush of early workers commuting to their jobs.

By 9:30am, I'm able to move to my section of the shop as my sisters no longer need my help in the kitchen. My first customers are two young boys wanting to buy a comic book each before school. I then get a trickle of customers wanting a book to take to work or a magazine to read on their break. Even Sarah Turner pops in for a few books, not stopping her enthusiastic praise for the transformation her son has done for us.

When she pokes her head into the kitchen to see Maya, our sister looks adorably awkward under all of Sarah's attention.

Pickle learned how to assemble the sandwiches quickly, making Maya's life significantly easier than on Friday. The cling film we carefully wrapped around her fingers, then her palms, and up her wrists proved effective. The night before, we also fashioned a little head scarf for her by cutting up an old pillowcase that was still in good condition because it had hardly ever been used.

When the lunch period arrives, we are inundated again, but I can't help out in the kitchen as I also have a constant stream of customers in my bookstore. Jacob turned up for lunch again like he did Friday, and with the same deputy. For some reason, as I looked at him, my mind kept drifting back to Luca. When I finally have a spare moment, I reluctantly make my way over to his table, my brain fighting the urge to turn back.

As I approach, thoughts of Luca continue to bombard me until I reach his table. He looks up and says, "Hey, beautiful. I see the business is doing really well."

I try to say, *'Good morning, Jacob,'* but his name won't come out for some reason. After an awkward moment of silence, I manage to say, "Yeah, we've been way busier than on Friday."

"I'm proud of the three of you," he said, but as I looked into his eyes, something in his expression made me doubt his sincerity. "Do you know about tomorrow yet?" he asked, his tone a little strained.

"Oh, right, tomorrow. Sorry, my day has been so jam-packed. I agreed to meet the agents again," I said, feeling incredibly awkward as I realised I was brushing him off after telling him I would give our relationship another try. *I feel terrible.*

Jacob doesn't look happy at all. "Really? Why would they need to see you again?" he asks, his jaw visibly clenching in annoyance.

"They just have a few more questions. They wanted us to take a few days to think over the days before the attack on our mother to see if I remember anything else," I say, wondering why he's questioning it so intensely.

"Did you check their IDs?" he asks, his voice tight with suspicion.

"Yeah, of course we did," I reply, feeling slightly annoyed by his interrogation.

"Good. I'm just confused as to why they would need to see you again; it's not like you saw anything. Maybe I will do my own checks to make sure they are real agents," he said, but it seemed he was saying this more to himself than to me. The thought of him checking on them worries me, as I know the truth, and I hope whoever their boss is has made sure nosy deputies won't discover their true identities.

I stand there, running through past conversations in my mind. I'm almost certain I've never told him any specific details about the day our mother was killed, especially since our minds have become sharper and seem to have the ability to remember everything now, well, almost. The only explanation I can come up with is that he has somehow read the police reports, which means he had to call the Chicago police and request them, which seems like a huge overstep and doesn't sit well with me, *at all*.

I see out of the corner of my eye that someone is approaching my till. "I had better go," I say, starting to turn away when a strange thought crosses my mind. I usually would have given Jacob a quick kiss goodbye, but for some reason, the thought hadn't even occurred to me this time. Just as that thought surfaced, it was immediately replaced by an image of me kissing Luca. '*What the hell?*' I mumble to myself, which I seem to be doing a lot lately, as I hurry back to my section, realising I've completely forgotten about Jacob again.

As I step through the door to my section, I take a quick glance back at Jacob and notice that he looks very unhappy. I can't blame him;

I've been a terrible girlfriend—well, maybe not officially a girlfriend, but we were getting close to that. Instead, I've been acting completely hot and cold, just as he feared when he opened up to me about an ex who treated him poorly. I promised him I was nothing like that, but here I am, behaving just like her.

I try to avoid eye contact with Jacob until he leaves, and when he does, he doesn't come over to say goodbye. After he's gone, I use a spare moment to go to one of our front windows and look across at Jenny's salon. She's busy cutting someone's hair, and Beastie is intently watching something, so I follow his gaze and am surprised to see a shadow on Jenny's wall behind her.

I instantly recognise it as my shadow; the familiar purple orbs looking down at my beloved Beastie. It's like they are having a silent staring contest until my shadow slowly moves towards him, crouches down, and starts to stroke his head. I guess my shadow likes Beastie as much as I do.

As I watched the two, a woman walked in front of our business and opened the door to come inside. It's Dhara.

Catherine M. Clark

Chapter 24

Gifts and Golems

I glance over at Freya as she stood at the counter. When she looks up as the bell above the door jingles, a bright smile spreads across her face as she sees who has entered. It's the biggest smile I've ever seen on her, and when I look back at Dhara, she returns the same radiant smile.

My sister looks completely smitten. I guess the crossroads demon isn't on her mind anymore. As I watch their interaction, a pang of jealousy, sharp and unexpected, shoots through me.

I can't help but watch as they flirt, their easy banter filling the air. I try to focus on my work, but today is much busier than Friday, and I soon notice another customer waiting at my till, so I reluctantly head back. I take one more quick glance at my delighted sister and couldn't help but think, two down, *me* to go. I really need to stop letting the past affect my future.

Things stayed busy until we closed, but during the last couple of hours, I checked on my sisters. They both looked utterly exhausted again, and the counter looked bare, just like on Friday.

When I looked around for Pickle, I had to poke my head into the kitchen, but didn't see her. I eventually found her curled up in the office chair, fast asleep and looking incredibly cute.

We all headed home together. I had to carry Pickle because she was so wiped out that I couldn't even rouse her. Beastie tried to jump into the *car* with Freya and me, but I asked him to travel with Maya so she wouldn't be alone on the drive home. Jenny had one more client before she could leave her salon. I initially asked Beastie to stay with her until she finished, but she insisted he didn't need to, so while everyone was distracted, I asked my shadow to wait and watch over her for me.

When we got home, I fed Beastie and then took him for a long walk. Pickle wanted to come along as well, but she fell asleep just before we left. During our walk, I made sure to stay within the protective barrier around our property, which covered a surprisingly large area of the woods.

We reached the edge of the barrier at the other end of the woods, and I took a moment to gauge its strength compared to the first time we performed the full moon ritual. It felt significantly more potent as I could feel the barriers hum on my skin. I still didn't fully understand what had happened during the ritual this time. At some point, we might learn more about this kind of magic, but for now, it was all trial and error with everything we did; it was a fascinating but also worrying journey of discovery we are on.

We really needed to get more practice with our magic, but we had been so busy with the final preparations for opening our business. Now we are officially open, I thought we might have more time to practice, except we haven't, as we have become swamped.

Soon, when the insurance assessor comes to check out the basement setup, my schedule will become even more packed if I am cleared to work on the high-value restoration projects my old boss occasionally sends my way. We really need these attacks to end so we can finally enjoy our lives and maybe even find some semblance of normality. I hope I can soon join my sisters in finding someone to settle down with.

I had a busy day ahead of me, so when I started to have another rough night worrying about Maya, I decided to use the sleep rune I had successfully used once before.

The rune worked quickly, sending me into a deep slumber. I was so tired and exhausted from yesterday that even my persistent worries couldn't keep me awake. I managed to sleep soundly until my alarm went off at 8 a.m.

I would have loved to have a lay-in, but as I said, I had a busy day planned, starting with Michael delivering my new custom-size bed before he opened his hardware store for the day.

It was also strangely peaceful to wake up in bed alone. I must have been more tired than I thought because I didn't stir when Beastie, Pickle, and Jenny got up earlier. Beastie had gone with Maya to the café, and Jenny had taken Freya and Pickle with her when she left for work at the salon.

Pickle had raved about her time at the café, even though she had fallen asleep in the office. She had made a casual comment about always being bored in Fairie, which provided even more evidence that she might be part of the royal family of the pixies. We weren't entirely sure if pixies even had royal families, but several things she had said and done made us suspect there might be some sort of hierarchy.

Pickle had also mentioned how good it made her feel to be able to help us, as she thought she owed us so much. She believed we had saved her life, although I was pretty sure she would have been fine on her own; she seemed remarkably resilient and had clearly survived on her own before she met us.

I climbed out of bed and stripped the sheets. It was only fair that I put on clean bedding for Jenny, especially since Michael and Duncan will be putting it in the spare room. I already had my new bedding waiting for my new bed.

I had taken a shower last night, which was my usual routine, as I wasn't prone to sweating during the night. So, after a quick wash and brush-up, I got dressed in a purple summer dress, one of my absolute favourites. It had a flattering low cut and an excellent shape that hugged my curves perfectly. I paired it with my trainers, knowing I would be doing a lot of walking today.

When I reached the bottom of the stairs, I froze just before heading into the kitchen. I spun around and carefully examined the bannister for the damage I had caused when I gripped it too hard. I immediately concluded that Duncan had done a fantastic job fixing it, but something felt off as I stared at the spot where the damage had been.

As I studied the bannister, I gently ran my hand over the smooth wood, and the realisation dawned on me. When would Duncan have had time to fix this? It was still damaged when we all went to bed last night, and if he had done it this morning, the noise would have surely woken me.

Also, upon closer inspection, I could see no breaks in the grain of the wood or any variation in colour. It looked absolutely perfect, as if it had never been damaged in the first place. Duncan was good at his work, but even I had to admit, this was beyond his usual skill. It was almost as if the bannister had never been damaged at all.

A sudden noise made me jump, and I spun around to face the kitchen. I cautiously and silently approached the doorway to see what had made the sound. When I got close enough, I saw someone standing with their back to me. My heart started to race until I realised it was Duncan. It then dawned on me that Duncan wouldn't have left this morning because he was waiting for his father to arrive with my new bed.

As I started to relax and moved to enter the kitchen, Duncan turned and said, "Morning, Reya. Are you looking forward to your new bed?"

"I am. It's been getting quite cramped lately," I said with a smile.

"Your dog is rather large," he commented, then took a sip from a mug before him. I'm sure it's coffee.

I glanced at the coffee pot and saw a fresh pot had been brewed, so I headed over and poured myself a mug. "Yeah, he is. Then there's Jenny and Pickle. It really is cramped with all of us," I said, noticing Duncan's eyes widen in confusion. I quickly replayed what I had just said as I leaned against the kitchen counter. "What?" I asked, as nothing I had said seemed particularly strange.

"Who's Pickle? I've heard you guys use that name before, but I haven't actually met anyone by that name," he asked, and I couldn't stop my face from falling in shock for a split second before I quickly regained control of my expression.

'Crap!' I thought to myself repeatedly, desperately trying to come up with a believable explanation. After I mentally curse Maya for not telling Duncan the truth already, I realise I will have to find a way to explain our slip-ups, as it seems we haven't been as careful as we thought.

"Sorry, it's an old nickname for a friend who used to share my apartment with me back in Chicago when she would come to stay over," I said nervously, mentally cursing myself as I knew this flimsy excuse would be exposed as a lie sooner or later. So, I decided to test the waters, partly to distract him but also to gauge his openness to the truth. Jenny swore he would be okay with it because of all the fantastical family stories he had grown up hearing.

"Duncan, can I ask you something?" I asked, feeling as nervous as asking a boy out for the first time in school.

The sudden change of topic caught him by surprise. "Of course, what's on your mind?" he asked, looking slightly suspicious.

"Do you believe in the paranormal?" I asked seriously, ensuring my expression remained neutral so he wouldn't think I was joking.

"Mmmm… strange question. Are you asking because you're going to tell me this Pickle is a ghost or something?" he asked, taking me completely by surprise. I hadn't expected him to jump to that conclusion, though, thinking about it and asking about the paranormal straight after the mention of Pickle, I could see how his mind had gone there.

But how on earth was I supposed to answer that? Of course, my face betrayed my inner turmoil. "Is that what you're getting at?" he pressed.

I had to think fast while trying to maintain a poker face. The only viable option that came to mind was to tell the truth, or at least part of it. Otherwise, I would be compounding lies, inevitably leading to a bigger mess. "You know, last night Maya asked if you could fix the bannister because I somehow managed to damage it," I said, watching his reaction closely to see if he thought I was losing my mind.

Duncan looked at me with clear suspicion in his eyes. "Yeah, I was planning to try fixing it tomorrow if I finish this small job I'm working on. Why?"

"*So*, you haven't already fixed it?" I asked, feeling a little foolish.

"No, as I said, I was hoping to do it tomorrow. What's going on, Reya?" he asked, his brow furrowing with worry.

"Well, it's… fixed. It looks like I never even damaged it," I stammered, watching his reactions intently once more.

"What? I saw the damage last night. That kind of damage doesn't just vanish overnight," he said, looking as confused as I had been when I first saw the undamaged bannister. He glanced in the direction of the stairs, but of course, you couldn't see them clearly from the kitchen table. He then abruptly got up and headed quickly towards the stairs.

Moments later, Duncan's voice echoed from the stairs, laced with disbelief, "What the fuck? How?"

I had to follow him, a wave of amusement washing over me at his bewildered reaction. "So, Duncan," I began, trying to suppress a smile, "do you believe in the paranormal and supernatural?" I asked, barely managing not to laugh at his continued stunned silence as he studied the bannister, repeatedly running his hand over the smooth wood.

"It's funny you should ask that," he finally said, turning back to me, his eyes wide. "Jenny's grandmother used to tell us all sorts of stories while we were growing up. I'm sure Jenny has told you about them?"

"She has. She said she was told she was descended from witches," I replied, keeping my expression serious so he wouldn't think I was making light of the situation.

"That's right. As kids, Jenny used to believe those stories. I guess I did too, back then, but as we grew up, we started to realise they were just stories," he said, his gaze fixed on my face, studying my reaction. Then he glanced back at the bannister, a frown creasing his forehead, before turning back to me and looking me directly in the eye.

A slow smirk spread across his face before he asked, a hint of playful accusation in his voice, "Did you and Jenny come up with this as some elaborate joke to trick me?"

I shook my head slowly, maintaining a serious expression. "Nope, I am just as confused as you are."

He looked back at the bannister, then did exactly as I had done, running his hand over the wood again, his touch gentle and inquisitive. He lowered himself down, his eyes level with the bannister, examining it closely. I guessed he was looking at the grain of the wood, knowing that wouldn't lie, especially to someone in his line of work. "I don't understand. I saw it last night. How?" he repeated, his voice filled with genuine bewilderment.

"It's why I asked if you believe in the paranormal. It's the only explanation I can come up with," I replied, meeting his gaze.

"You might be right, as I certainly don't have a better answer right now. But what could fix wood so perfectly?" he mused, looking back at the bannister and scratching his cheek thoughtfully. A thought flickered through my mind – Freya or Maya could have easily fixed it with magic… but they would have said something, wouldn't they?

Duncan turned back to me, his expression a mixture of curiosity and disbelief. "So, do you actually believe in all that stuff then?"

"I do," I said, keeping my answer concise and direct.

"Really? I bet you and Jenny have had many interesting discussions on the subject." Duncan paused for a moment, a flicker of amusement in his eyes. "Come to think about it, Jenny swore she was cursed once," he said with a chuckle.

I knew exactly what he was referring to. "She told me about that," I said, a genuine smile finally breaking through my serious facade.

"What else do you believe in?" he asked, his curiosity clearly piqued.

I don't know why I did it, the words just tumbled out, "I'm a witch, so I believe in it all."

Duncan didn't react at first, his expression unreadable. Then, slowly, a wide smile spread across his face. "You're a witch?"

"Yep. I believe in Wicca, ghosts, monsters, and everything else," I said, returning my face to a serious expression, wanting to gauge his reaction.

"Does Maya believe she's a witch too?" he asked, finally asking the question I had been expecting from the very beginning.

"We all do, actually. Maya's been a little scared to tell you because she's worried you'll think she's crazy or a freak," I explained, hoping this went as smoothly as Jenny had predicted.

"I wouldn't think that at all. I'm a firm believer in letting people believe in whatever they want. As long as she doesn't believe in sacrificing people or anything like that, then I'm completely cool with it," he said, taking me by complete surprise. Jenny had been right, at least for now. There's a big difference between hypothetical beliefs and real-life actions.

"Good. Now we just have to figure out how the bannister fixed itself," I said, feeling stumped unless one of my sisters had a confession to make.

We reluctantly dragged ourselves away from the bannister

mystery, and we both went upstairs to move my old bed into the spare room. I lifted my end of the heavy wooden frame so easily that Duncan raised a surprised eyebrow at me. I was distracted by the mystery of the bannister and didn't think about trying to appear weaker. I was clearly much stronger than I usually let on, though I didn't feel quite as strong as I had when I had broken the bannister in the first place.

As we awkwardly manoeuvre the old bed frame from the spare room out to the front of the house, we hear a vehicle slow down on the main road. Then, the sound of the engine grew louder, and Michael's familiar van appeared around the bend. When he parked in front of us, he greeted me with his usual warm smile.

He jumped out of the *van* and headed straight for me. I expected him to stop at a polite distance away, but he didn't. He walked right up to me and pulled me into a tight hug. "Morning, Reya, you look very pretty. Got a date with the deputy today?" he asked with a teasing look that made me feel slightly awkward, like I was talking to an overbearing but well-meaning parent.

I couldn't help myself and blurted out, "No, I'm not going on a date with him. It might actually be over. I'm going to an estate sale."

This seemed to surprise him for a moment. He looked like he wanted to say something, a conflict playing out on his face. Finally, he said, "I'm not one for gossip, but my wife has been going on about all the talk around town about your hot kiss with him on Friday."

"God," I said with a sigh, rolling my eyes. "Really!" I exclaimed, my cheeks flushing slightly.

"Don't be surprised if my wife asks you how serious it is. She even mentioned a possible wedding," he said with a cheeky grin that mirrored his son's.

My jaw practically hit the floor in total shock. My brain felt like it was melting from the sheer absurdity of what he had just said. "Wedding?" I croaked out, my voice barely a whisper.

"Dad! Don't tease her like that. That's just mean," Duncan said, though a mischievous grin of his own played on his lips.

Michael threw his head back and started to laugh, a hearty, full-bellied laugh that echoed through the air. I stared at him in utter disbelief. He finally calmed down, wiping a tear from the corner of his eye, and said, "You should have seen your face; it was a picture!"

"Maya left some treats for you and your wife in the fridge. I'm starting to think you don't deserve them," I said, facing him with my hands on my hips and giving him my best mock-angry glare.

"Really? That's how you want to play this? Well then, I guess I can't make this delivery right now. I better go and open the store," Michael said with a playful grin.

"It seems you have won this time," I conceded, then, taking him by complete surprise, I hugged him tightly and, with my mouth pressed against his shoulder, mumbled, "I think I love you. Now, I just need to figure out how to get rid of Sarah."

"That's my father you're declaring your love to," Duncan said, his body visibly shuddering. "I feel grossed out."

"Hey!" Michael exclaimed, giving his son a playful dirty look. He then looked down at me as I eyed them both with my own smile, and he said, "I'm very flattered, Reya. I'm guessing you mean it in a friendly way, but with the way your sister and my son are going, we could actually be family soon."

Now, Duncan looked genuinely shocked, a hint of fear even flickering across his face. "Dad, I think it's a bit early for talk like that. Can we just get on with this, please?"

This caused Michael to erupt into laughter again, and he pulled me into another quick hug. "All I have left to say is, Reya, never go against your elders. We still know how to play the game, and with our vast wisdom, we always win," he said, winking at me as he finally released me.

"Whatever," I said with a fake huff, trying to hide my

amusement. Duncan just walked past us, shaking his head in mock exasperation as he headed towards the back of the van to unload my new bed. It didn't take us long to set up my new bed and load the old one from the spare room into Michael's van.

Catherine M. Clark

Chapter 25

Plans Forged in Shadow

As Michael prepared to head off, another *van* drove up to the house. "Who is this?" I asked, a sliver of anxiety creeping in, hoping it wasn't filled with demons in disguise. Duncan seemed to recognise the driver and said, "It's Dean, the FedEx guy. That's not his usual van, though." This made me relax a little, but the thought still lingered that anyone could be possessed. Dean jumped out of his van, gave us all a quick nod, and then went to the side of his vehicle. Moments later, he reappeared carrying what looked like a large rock in his arms.

"What the hell is that?" I asked, completely bewildered. When he placed it at the bottom of the steps to the veranda, then he spun it around. That's when I noticed the rock had a distinct shape. It was a small lion statue about the size of a medium-sized dog. "Who the hell ordered that?" I asked, staring at it in confusion.

"No idea," Dean said, then added, "I have three more for you. They came from a place in New Orleans."

"Freya," I groaned, rolling my eyes. Of course, it was Freya.

Duncan and I followed Dean to the side of his van. Sure enough, there were three more statues, except two were clearly gargoyles, their grotesque faces staring out at me. *Why on earth had she ordered these?* The delivery guy then handed me a box that looked similar to the one Freya had previously ordered from New Orleans. I took the box indoors while the guys dropped the other statues at the bottom of the steps. I was sure I could have carried one of the statues myself, but I let the guys have their moment of chivalry.

After the delivery guy left, Michael said goodbye and headed off, followed not long after by Duncan. I had a little time before my next adventure, so I poured myself a bowl of cereal and another cup of coffee before heading out to the estate sale. This particular estate sale held extra interest for me because the property was a small horse ranch, and the layout was similar to ours, only much bigger. I was eager to see how our place could potentially look if we ever decided to expand, especially with the growing number of strays we seemed to be taking in, both animal and paranormal. The other reason this place intrigued me was the possibility that if our family had once lived here and were witches, maybe other witches also favoured similar secluded locations.

Freya, Maya, Pickle, and Jenny had all expressed their concerns about me going out on my own. They made me promise to keep my shadow close, just in case. I responded with a casual, "Sure," but I deliberately didn't commit to that promise, as I had no intention of bringing my shadow along. Instead, I instructed her to stay back and watch over my sisters and Jenny. I had a different plan in mind.

As I drove toward town, I pulled over at a turn-off that led east and parked the car carefully so it wouldn't be visible from the main road. I quickly changed my appearance using a glamour. Then I jumped out of the truck, unsure if what I was about to do would work from inside the vehicle. I glamoured the truck, changing its colour to a dull brown and making it look like an older, less conspicuous model. The glamour I cast on myself transformed me into an average-looking man in his late fifties, complete with a receding hairline and a slightly paunchy stomach. I hopped back into the truck and headed off again, merging back onto the main road. I couldn't help but glance in the rearview mirror, and like before, I was still amazed by this ability. I realised that if things ever got really bad, we could potentially change our appearances and disappear, constantly using glamours to hide from the world.

The thought made me feel nervous as I drove through town in disguise. Another aspect of the glamour I had added was a different scent, hoping that if any of those wolves were in town, they wouldn't be able to recognise me. I decided to do this after our conversation with Ava and her team, who explained how shifters could smell someone from a mile away if the wind was right, and even when someone was aroused or lying.

If these wolves were indeed watching us, I wanted to make it as difficult as possible for them to track me. I couldn't help but smile to myself as I reached the main road leading out of town, and no one seemed to pay me any particular attention. I almost forgot to change back when I was nearing my destination. It wasn't until I was about to turn onto the road that led to the ranch that I finally noticed my reflection in the rearview mirror. Once I made the turn, I quickly stopped at the end of the road, hidden from view, and removed both glamours. I checked myself in the mirror to make sure I looked like me again and leaned out of my driver's side window to confirm the *truck* was also back to its normal state.

I set off again towards the house, and as I rounded a curve in the road that also dipped down slightly, the property came into full view. The sheer size of the buildings took my breath away. It was so much bigger than our place; I had expected it to be larger, but not by this much. Several people were moving around the property, presumably setting up for the estate sale.

Then I saw them in the distance, in a large pen to the left of the main house. Horses. Beautiful white horses. I really hadn't expected there to be any still here. I guess my day was looking up. As I drove up the long, winding road, I couldn't stop myself from glancing over at the pen. Four absolutely stunning white horses were in front of a barn that looked remarkably similar to ours. Even from this distance, I could sense they weren't happy. The horses reared up on their hind legs whenever two men tried to put what looked like harnesses on them, their powerful muscles straining against the attempts.

I was so absorbed in watching the horses that I almost drove off the road. '*Geez*,' I muttered to myself, '*I'm a menace behind the wheel today*,' as I straightened the truck. To get to the ranch house, I continued driving to the right, taking me further away from the pen and the captivating horses so I wouldn't be distracted anymore. It was probably best; I didn't want to crash into the house.

I pulled up to the house and recognised the same woman who was running the estate sale that I had visited previously. She had emailed me about this event last week and had been managing it since the day before. I couldn't help but wonder if Papa Legba had left me another unexpected gift somewhere on the property. As I approached Christie, the estate sale organiser, I said, "Hello again," and extended my hand in greeting.

"Reya, how is that beautiful desk working out for you? I'm so jealous," she said, taking my hand for a quick, gentle shake before letting go.

"It's perfect," I replied with a smile.

"That's great. I hope you find something else you like here. I thought you might be interested in this one since you showed interest in the books and furniture at the last sale. This one has both as well," she stated, gesturing towards the house.

"Cool, I better get started and look around in case someone beats me to something I would love," I told her as Christie handed me a familiar clipboard and pen, just like last time. I then headed into the impressive house.

As soon as I stepped into the main foyer, I was stunned by the sheer number of rooms on the ground floor, all branching off from a long central corridor. It looked like the main living room was on the right, so I started there. When I stepped into the room, I was immediately struck by the incredibly high ceilings. The decor was a bit dated for my taste, and you could tell an older couple had lived there for many years. I actually wish we could afford to buy this place.

We could definitely use all this extra space, and the amount of land on the property would be perfect for our growing menagerie, except for the hefty price tag. When I had looked up the property listing to see its exact location, I had seen the price: one point nine million dollars. "Maybe one day, if we survive," I muttered to no one as I slowly walked around the room, taking it all in. You could see where a few items had already been sold, as the patches in the carpet where furniture had once stood looked almost brand new compared to the rest of the slightly faded room. Nothing in this room particularly caught my eye. I wasn't interested in any of the dated furniture, and the few books scattered on a side table weren't the type I was looking for.

I moved on to the next room, a formal dining room. It featured a stunning, long mahogany dining table but not much else, so I quickly moved on. When I finished checking all the rooms on the right side of the house, I found myself at the foot of a grand staircase, so I decided to head upstairs and explore before finishing the ground floor on the left side on my way out. I spent a pleasant hour wandering through the upstairs rooms, most of which were bedrooms and bathrooms, before heading back down to tackle the rooms on the left side of the ground floor. The first room I entered was exactly what I had been hoping to find, a library.

As I gazed at the towering shelves filled with books, I said aloud, "This is going to take a while." Then, I began scanning the titles, looking for anything interesting for our bookstore and, of course, anything related to magic or the paranormal. I also couldn't shake the feeling that I might suddenly stumble upon something significant, like when I had discovered the old diary.

I spent another hour meticulously going through the books on the shelves, but this time, I didn't find anything that particularly grabbed my attention. As I left the library, I kept glancing back, half-expecting to see a hidden compartment or a book tucked away out of sight. I guess Papa Legba didn't have any other literary treasures for me at this particular location.

When I left the house, Christie was engaged in conversation with a couple who looked to be in their sixties. After they entered the house, I approached her and handed back the clipboard, which remained blank.

"Nothing called out to you this time?" Christie asked, noticing I hadn't written anything down.

"Nope, not this time. My main interest right now is in old or unusual books. Most of the books here are about business, horses, and world affairs, so sorry," I explained.

"I'll definitely keep an eye out for you at future sales," she said with a friendly smile.

"Thank you." I was about to return to my *truck* when I suddenly remembered the horses. "Christie?"

"Have you changed your mind about something?" she asked, her smile widening hopefully. She clearly thought she was about to make a commission from a sale.

"No, sorry. What's going on with the horses in the pen?" I asked, which momentarily confused Christie. She then looked over in the direction of the large enclosure.

"I'm not really sure, to be honest. All I know is I wasn't allowed to list them for sale because there are no official records of ownership for them. Also, the last remaining staff member said the horses just showed up around a month ago. The owner simply let them into the pen and even left the gates open so they could leave anytime they wanted, but they just won't," she said, looking genuinely puzzled by the situation.

"Would it be okay if I went over to take a look at them?" I asked, feeling a strange pull towards the animals.

"Oh, yeah, I guess that would be alright. Are you interested in horses?"

"I love horses. I guess they must be wild horses then. You don't see many of those anymore. Maybe I can help in some way," I said, even though I had absolutely no idea how.

"Sure, just don't go inside the pen with the horses, please, as we wouldn't be covered by insurance if anything happened," Christie cautioned.

"Thanks, Christie. Please keep me posted about any other estate sales you have coming up," I said, then set off to go and see the mysterious horses.

When I reached a large horse trailer parked near the pen, one of the men who had been trying to wrangle the horses was leaning against it, looking utterly frustrated. "Hey," I said, startling him out of his apparent misery.

He turned and looked at me, then glanced around as if wondering where I had suddenly appeared from. "Can I help you with something?" he asked, his tone weary.

"What's going on with the horses?" I asked, gesturing towards the pen where the other man was still trying to manoeuvre a harness onto one of the magnificent animals, which continued to rear up in protest.

"Erm… well, they can't sell them, so they hired us to take them to the nearest horse rescue place west of Jackson, but they don't seem particularly interested in leaving this pen," he explained, running a hand through his already dishevelled hair.

Now that I was closer to them, something about the horses drew me in with an almost magnetic force, and I felt an undeniable compulsion to go over to them. "Is it okay if I go and take a closer look?" I asked, unable to tear my gaze away from the majestic creatures.

"Sure, as long as you stay out of the pen," he reiterated.

"Thanks." As soon as I cleared the horse trailer and came into full view of the horses, the nearest one, a stunning white mare, seemed to look directly at me. Then, as if a switch had been flipped, it instantly calmed down, turned towards me, and began to approach the fence of the pen I was walking towards.

The other man in the pen noticed the horse's sudden change in demeanour and began to approach it cautiously, holding a lasso loosely at his side, ready to toss it over the horse's head.

Before he could, though, he also noticed me just as I reached the fence. The white mare leaned her head over the top rail towards me, her soft muzzle inches from my hand. I couldn't resist the urge, so I reached out my right hand and gently touched the horse on the nose. As my fingers made contact, I felt a strange sensation, similar to a mild electric shock. It wasn't strong enough to hurt or make me pull my hand away; I simply assumed it was static electricity, so I continued to run my hand up and down the velvety soft skin of the horse's nose.

I ran my hand up between the horse's wide-set eyes until I reached its ears, gently stroking the soft hair with my fingers and thumb. I then brought my hand back down and started to stroke its nose again. The horse's hair felt incredibly soft and luxurious to touch, and a wave of longing washed over me; I had missed this connection with horses.

For some inexplicable reason, I moved even closer to the fence and leaned forward, resting my forehead against the horse's head. I was almost certain the horse reciprocated the gesture, as I felt a gentle pressure against my forehead.

"Lady, you should be careful, these are wild horses," a man's voice cautioned, but I ignored him, completely confident that this particular horse wouldn't hurt me. I didn't know how I knew, I just did.

"Hey lady, did you hear me?" the man said, his voice growing slightly louder and more insistent. He must be walking towards me.

"It's fine," I finally said, not wanting to break this peaceful moment.

"What the hell, lady, are you some kind of horse whisperer or something? We've been trying to wrangle these horses for hours with no luck," the man said, now almost standing directly in front of me as he continued to move to the horse's side, a mixture of frustration and awe on his face.

I finally pulled my head away from the horse but kept my hand resting on the side of its face. I looked at the man who had been trying to talk to me. To my surprise, the other three horses had also calmed down and approached the fence. They didn't stick their heads over, though; they simply stood there, watching me with intelligent, curious eyes, just behind the horse I was touching.

"How did you do that?" the guy asked, his voice filled with disbelief.

"No idea, they're beautiful," I replied, my gaze still fixed on the gentle giant in front of me.

"They are stunning specimens," he agreed, his initial frustration replaced by admiration.

I don't know what came over me; it felt like I was acting on pure instinct. "So, you were taking them to a horse rescue place?" I asked.

"We are. Maybe you could help us get them into the trailer?" he asked, looking so hopeful that I would assist.

"What if I said I would help you, but instead of taking them to the rescue place, you take them to my place? I have six empty stalls in my barn and had been hoping to get some horses at some point," I said, looking the guy right in the eyes to show I was serious.

"Where do you live?" he asked, taking me slightly by surprise.

"About an hour away in Luna Falls," I stated confidently.

"That's much closer than the rescue place. Do you know much about horses?" he asked next, his eyes assessing me, probably trying to gauge if I knew how to properly care for them.

"I do. I've been riding and caring for horses for most of my life," I told him truthfully as I continued to stroke the side of the white mare's face while the other three horses watched us intently.

"Good enough for me. We've already been paid for the transport, so I don't mind where we take them as long as they're going to be looked after properly," the guy said, a sense of relief washing over his features.

"Fantastic," I said, a surge of excitement bubbling within me. Then I asked, "Is there any spare hay and feed available?"

"Sure is, it's already loaded in the trailer," he replied.

I moved towards the gate of the pen, and the other man, who had been attempting to lasso the horses, asked, "Do you want the rope, or do you want me to rope them?"

"No need for that," I said confidently and unlatched the gate, swinging it open. I don't know how I knew this would work, but I had a strong feeling the horses would follow me. I headed towards the open horse trailer, and sure enough, as soon as I opened the pen, the four horses followed me out and walked calmly beside me to the trailer. Without any prompting, the horses then loaded themselves into the trailer, positioning themselves perfectly so they would all fit comfortably.

Chapter 26

Gifts and Guests

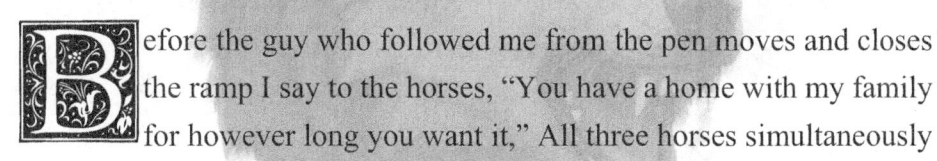

Before the guy who followed me from the pen moves and closes the ramp I say to the horses, "You have a home with my family for however long you want it," All three horses simultaneously jerk their heads up and down, as if in agreement.

"You have one amazing gift, lady," the first guy I spoke to said, his face filled with genuine awe after he and his partner secured the trailer door.

"Thank you," I replied, a small smile playing on my lips. "Would you like to follow me to my place, or do you want the address?"

"We're happy to follow you, but you better give us your address anyway, just in case," the guy who had been in the pen said, extending his hand. "I'm Josh, and this is George," he added, gesturing to his partner.

"Hi, I'm Reya," I said, shaking both of their hands. Then I reached into my bag and pulled out a small diary I kept there, scribbled down my address, tore out the page, and handed it to Josh.

I drive home slowly, mindful of the large horse trailer following behind. I'm not entirely sure if they will make it up our road, as it's still a little overgrown, but they navigate the narrow road carefully, and the trailer manages to squeeze through the overgrown trees and bushes.

It didn't take long to open the back of the trailer once I had directed them to reverse up the driveway on the right side of the house. "Are you sure you don't want to rope them?" Josh asks again, a hint of concern in his voice.

"I'm sure," I say confidently, walking to the now-open trailer and addressing the horses. "This is your new home for as long as you want to stay," I repeat.

After a few moments of hesitation, the horses begin to make their way out of the trailer, their hooves making soft thuds on the ground. I start to walk towards the barn, and when I glance back, I see all four horses following me in a calm, orderly fashion. I also notice the two guys scratching their heads in disbelief, their faces mirroring my own slight bewilderment. This whole situation feels surreal, but a deep sense of rightness resonates within me.

I ensured the horses would be safe from attack by providing the guys backed the trailer far enough down the right side of our house, so they were well within the protection barrier around our property.

Just as I start to lead the horses towards the barn, a familiar car appears up our road and pulls up next to the horse trailer. I recognise it immediately; it's Ava's car. Before I left the ranch, I sent her a quick message letting her know I was heading home if they wanted to come over.

I don't stop for them and continue leading the horses to the barn. When I reach the large wooden doors, I swing them open wide, pinning them back securely. I turn to the horses and say, "This is where you'll sleep at night," gesturing to the spacious stalls inside.

Then I turn towards our largest field, which Freya isn't currently using as she has her hands full managing our medium-sized field and the small one closer to the house. "You can graze on that field," I tell them, pointing as I speak, "but please stay away from the others; those are Freya's." I watch the horses, and there is a strange certainty in my heart that they understand me.

"They can't understand you, lady," Josh said, shaking his head slightly. He had decided to follow me to the barn to make sure I actually had horse stalls, as I had claimed. Behind him, I see George already unloading the bales of hay and bags of horse feed.

I shrug in response, a knowing smile on my face. "Do you mind putting the hay and feed down by the door to the barn, please? I'll give you a good tip for your trouble."

"Sure thing, lady," Josh said, then headed back to the trailer to help George.

When they finish unloading, I hand Josh fifty dollars, which makes his eyes widen in surprise and gratitude. Then I return to the front of the house, where I see Ava, Sam, and Rose waiting for me.

"Hey," I greet them.

"Hi," Ava replies, then nods her head towards the field where the horses are now contentedly grazing. "Did you buy some horses today, or already own them?"

"I actually rescued them today from the estate sale I went to. I've wanted some horses ever since we moved here," I say, looking back at the beautiful animals in the large field, just as I had instructed them.

"They are stunning horses," Sam commented, his eyes full of admiration.

"They sure are, and smart too," I reply, a hint of pride in my voice.

"Horses can be incredibly intelligent creatures. I like horses a lot," Sam said, a genuine smile gracing his lips.

"Then I guess I like you, Sam," I say impulsively, which causes Sam's smile to widen. Rose, however, rolled her eyes dramatically, looking like an impatient child.

"Come on, let's head indoors," I say, turning and making my way up the steps to the front door.

"Hey! I can't get in again!" Rose calls out from behind us as I reach for the doorknob.

Ava turns at the same time as I do to see Rose once again encountering our invisible barrier. "Rose seems to be having some issues again," Ava said with a sigh, a hint of exasperation in her voice.

"I guess she still doesn't quite trust us," I reply, a flicker of worry about Rose's persistent distrust crossing my mind.

"Rose!!!" both Ava and Sam exclaimed in unison, their voices carrying a note of warning.

"What?" she said defensively, sounding frustrated.

"Why are you thinking about hurting Reya?" Ava demands, looking at Rose with a shocked and slightly hurt expression.

"I will only hurt her if she hurts you," Rose retorted, her tone sharp and protective.

"Are you able to let her in? I promise she won't hurt you; she's just very protective of me," Ava pleads with me, her eyes filled with concern.

I felt a pang of sympathy for Ava, but I'm still new to understanding the full extent of our protective barrier. As far as I know, it was designed to keep out anyone with harmful intentions towards us. "Sorry, no can do," I say apologetically. "The barrier seems to be permanent if it detects a threat. If there's a way to let her in manually, I haven't learned how to do it yet." I watch as Rose's face falls, a worried frown creasing her brow.

"Shit!" was all Ava said, looking at the visibly struggling Rose, who was still trying to push her way past the invisible force field. "I guess you're staying out there then unless you can change your thoughts," Ava tells Rose with a cheeky smile, trying to lighten the tense situation.

"Ava! I don't think that's a smart move!" Rose calls out, sounding both frustrated and a little angry as she watches Ava step into the house, leaving her behind.

"I'm with Ava on this one," Sam said firmly. "You've put yourself in this position, Rose. You'll have to deal with the consequences until you can learn to trust new people."

"AVA!!!" Rose shouts from the other side of the barrier, her voice laced with desperation, trying to dissuade Ava from entering my house. I find the situation rather amusing, but I thought it best not to show it.

I pull out my phone from my bag and quickly message my sisters to let them know I'm home and have a surprise waiting for them. I hope everything is going well at the café. After sending the message, I opened a recent one from Freya. It simply says they are busy again and hope I stay safe.

I put my phone back in my bag and find Ava and Sam already preoccupied with the foxes, who are playfully batting at Drake, my once-favourite teddy bear – well, teddy panther, as he once was. I go and open the back door by the stairs, then return to the kitchen, where my guests were standing, watching the unusual scene with mild curiosity.

"Do you want something to drink or eat? I'm sure there's some of Maya's baking in the fridge," I offer.

"I'm good, thanks," Ava says politely.

But Sam had other ideas. "I would love to try some of Maya's baking after what you told us about it." I also notice Sam looks a little nervous, and I wonder if it's because he's about to try food enhanced by magic or if it's something else entirely.

"Don't you dare!" Rose's voice echoes from outside, sharp with warning.

Ava seemed to reconsider after Rose's outburst. "Actually, I think I will join you," she said, then asked, "Do you have any coffee?"

"Sure do; you'll love Freya's brew," I say, pointing to the coffee pot I put on when I first walked in. *I definitely need some myself after my restless night.*

"Thanks," Ava said, then heads over to the counter and grabs a mug from the rack and fills it, then thoughtfully grabs two more mugs and pours one for Sam and me as well.

"You didn't have to do that, but thanks," I say gratefully.

"Ava, please don't do this!" Rose calls out again, her voice laced with panic. We can hear her clearly through the open front door.

We then sit at the kitchen table, and I ask, "Have you had any luck with the cases you're looking into in Jackson?" Their faces fall as soon as I ask, and their earlier light-heartedness vanishes. "What is it?"

"Sam and I have just discovered that we're out of our depth when it comes to dealing with these demons. Luca and Rose were hoping you would be willing to help us, as witches are some of the few in the world who can actually handle demons.... Except now they're hesitant to ask because they think you might be a black witch," Ava said, her expression a mixture of concern and a silent plea for understanding.

I'm taken aback by what Ava said, but Rose's inability to cross the barrier suddenly makes much more sense. I wasn't sure if I was even capable of helping, or if my sisters would even allow me to get involved. The other daunting question was whether I could bring myself to head to Jackson when my own family was still potentially at risk. "I'll have to discuss it with my family, as it could put them in danger if I left," I say, noticing my answer doesn't seem to reassure them.

"Luca and Rose suggested you wouldn't want to help us if you're a black witch, and the fact that you have a demon living in your home has them worried that one of you might even be possessed," Ava said, looking slightly ashamed as she relays this information.

"Well, as far as I know, I'm definitely not a black witch," I begin, my voice steady despite the unexpected accusation. "I understand that I'm a fire witch, and I also have the ability of telekinesis, which allows me to move objects with my mind. Cat once mentioned that I have the ability to summon demons, but that's a path I have absolutely no desire to explore. I thought bringing Beastie into my life was a mistake at first—a reckless act born from a moment of foolish joking when I didn't fully grasp the extent of my powers. Yet, over time, I've come to love him dearly. For a while, after that fateful summoning, I even wrestled with the unsettling thought that I might be part demon myself, casting a shadow of doubt over my own identity. Thankfully, Cat assured me that wasn't the case. That revelation brought me immense relief, allowing me to embrace who I truly am without fear, *finally*," I said, realising I needed to take a few deep breaths, as being this honest with people I barely know makes me feel surprisingly vulnerable. *I don't mention that I might have a bit of a demon within me now that I've bonded with Beastie.*

"Okay, you really don't have to explain yourself to me," Ava said reassuringly.

When we spoke to the three of them on Saturday, we didn't tell them about our specific powers, hoping to maintain some advantage. But now feels like the right time to be more open with them. I decide that from this moment forward, I'm going to be more honest with them. Well, I'm not mentioning everything just yet, though. For example, the fact that I can also see the dead might be something they will find more challenging to believe.

"I want to be completely honest with you, Reya," Ava continued, her gaze sincere. "I like you, and something inside me is telling me that I can trust you and that we can help each other."

As I listen to her heartfelt words, I notice the hilt of her sword peeking out over her shoulder. Then, the fleeting image of the flaming sword I had briefly produced during our previous encounter flashed through my mind, sparking an idea. A strong intuition tells me I can do this, that I can somehow imbue her sword with my magic, giving her the ability to fight the demons and whatever else they were facing. It also feels like it would fulfil Papa Legba's mysterious wish.

"Ava," I say, my voice filling with sudden excitement. I think I just had an excellent idea, and I think it might even fulfil what Papa Legba asked me to do for you."

"What!" Ava exclaims, her eyes widening in surprise. Then, her curiosity piqued, she asks, "What did he want you to do for me?"

"He said I would meet a woman soon, and he was looking for a weapon for her to use. He wanted me to use my abilities on it so that a human could wield it effectively and have the power to defend herself against what's out there," I explained, the pieces of Papa Legba's cryptic message finally clicking into place.

"Really! He did mention something about a weapon to me. What's your idea?" Ava asks, now looking wholly intrigued.

"Ava, don't you dare!" Rose's frantic voice calls out from outside again. I had almost forgotten about her predicament.

"I think I can add my fire to your sword," I say, a surge of hopeful energy coursing through me. I really hope I can pull this off. What I envision is crazy, and I hope I don't look like a complete idiot if I fail.

Ava looks surprised, and then she slowly smiles. She wastes no time pulling her impressive sword out from the sheath on her back and placing it on the kitchen table between us. "Please," she almost begs, her eyes shining with anticipation.

I momentarily stare at the sword, admiring its craftsmanship, then carefully pick it up, holding it flat in my palms. After a brief moment of contemplation, I grip the sword's hilt with my right hand but keep the blade resting gently in my left palm.

The sword is heavier than I anticipated, but surprisingly, it doesn't feel too heavy for me to handle. I move my chair back slightly, causing it to screech against the wooden floor, then hold the sword out in front of me, focusing my intent.

I concentrate on the sword and what I want to achieve, for my black fire to bond with the silver blade. Almost immediately after focusing my intention, I engage my power. But instead of the usual burst of flames erupting from my hands, I watch in fascination as I see my power being drawn into the sword's silver, just as I had hoped and imagined. My power continues to surge down my arms, flowing into the weapon.

When my power touched the sword, a fleeting worry crossed my mind that it might melt or be damaged, so I focused even more intently on the desired outcome. Once my power had spread out throughout the sword, I felt the metal heat up, and my black fire began to emanate outwards from the blade while a concentrated surge of power built up in the hilt.

As I focus on the specific details of how I want the sword to function for Ava, I feel my power begin to truly bond with the metal. I'm not sure if I imagined the next part, but I could have sworn I saw the very structure of the sword subtly shift and change. Then, when I sense the sword is almost ready, I decide to mark it with Ava's nickname. Instantly, as if the sword responds to my will, an even more intense burst of black fire erupts along the blade's centre.

When the fire abruptly extinguishes as quickly as it had appeared, it leaves behind the word *Destroyer* etched down the centre of the blade in what looks like a deep black carving. However, I knew that the word isn't just an inscription; it contains the very essence of my black fire. There was one last crucial step. "How do you want to activate it?" I ask Ava, closing my eyes to better focus on this final enchantment.

"Erm... maybe if I just hold it for more than five seconds? No, that probably won't work," Ava said, sounding a little worried as she considered the possibilities. "Just make it simple. Make it so I have to say in my mind or out loud, 'fire on' and 'fire off,'" Ava said with a nervous giggle.

I then wove a ward into the sword, imbuing it with her desired activation command. I also add a little something extra for good measure. Opening my eyes and looking down at the sword, it looks noticeably different. The blade is now a striking combination of silver, with its intricate engravings on the hilt continuing down the blade's centre. The engravings now have deep black sections, making the details stand out even more beautifully. The most significant change was down the blade's centre, where the word destroyer was now seamlessly integrated as part of the overall design.

As I look closer at the inscription, the word '*Destroyer*' seems to shift and move subtly. When I bring the sword closer to examine it more carefully, I realise tiny black flames are dancing within the letters, flickering and swirling like embers in a fireplace.

I carefully hold out the transformed sword for Ava to take. She hesitates for a moment, especially with Rose's frantic shouts of protest echoing from outside, urging her not to touch it. But Rose's vehement objections seem to spur Ava into action, and she quickly takes the sword from my outstretched hands.

Even with the sword now safely in her grasp, Ava couldn't help but ask, a hint of apprehension in her voice, "Will it hurt me?"

"No, I added a ward to it – well, a few wards actually – to ensure it won't hurt you or your team. I haven't met Luca yet, so I hope I've included him correctly based on what you've told me about him," I say, consciously suppressing the urge to admit that I have been low-key obsessing over every detail they have mentioned about him, like some eager fan girl.

"I've also added a ward so that it can't hurt my family, any member of my family, I added for extra reassurance."

Ava nods in response, her gaze completely fixed on her altered sword. She is mesmerised by the living flames that dance within her nickname. "Try it," Sam encourages her, his eyes full of anticipation.

Ava stands up, moves a few steps away from the table, and holds the sword out in front of her. After about ten seconds of silent concentration, she says, her voice clear and steady, "Fire on."

As soon as the words left her mouth, the sword's blade ignites, erupting in the same mesmerising black flames that dance around my hands when I use my fire magic. Ava jumps slightly when the flames first appear, a startled gasp escaping her lips, but then a wide grin spreads across her face, the kind of pure, unadulterated joy you see on a child who has just received the best present they could have ever wished for. She waved the flaming sword around like a giddy child playing with a lightsaber.

Then, Ava shocks me by putting my newly woven wards to the test when she slowly moves her left hand towards the dancing black flames. "Are you sure you trust me enough to try and do that?" I ask, a sudden wave of concern washing over me that I might have somehow messed up the enchantment.

Catherine M. Clark

Chapter 27

The Sight and the Sword

I really didn't need to worry. Nothing happens as Ava's hand enters the flames, not even a flicker. A shared sigh of relief gusts between Sam and me, but it doesn't reach outside. Rose, still trapped beyond the shimmering barrier, practically vibrates with fury. Her fists are clenched at her sides, visible even from here. Through the open front door, her voice carries, tight and furious as she bellows, "Ava, you are so dead when I get my hands on you!"

"I don't understand," Sam said, looking utterly confused.

Ava and I exchange a glance, and Ava asks him, "What don't you understand?"

"The sword looks almost exactly the same as before. I don't see anything different," Sam said, his gaze shifting between the sword and us.

"Sam, the sword's blade is covered in black flames and has my nickname down the centre of the blade. Can't you see them?" Ava asks, her brow furrowed in confusion.

"Nope," was Sam's simple reply.

Ava turns to me, her expression thoughtful. "Did you somehow make it so only certain people can see what you did to the sword?"

"Erm… no, I didn't actively do anything to make it invisible to humans," I say, equally confused. But thinking about it, it was actually a good thing that Sam couldn't see the flames.

Just then, Rose's voice drifted in from outside. "It's one of those things you need the sight to see."

A light bulb seemed to go off in Sam's head. He turns to me, his eyes almost as wide with excitement as Ava's had been with her newly enhanced sword. "Not to sound all needy or anything, but can you still try that rune thing on me?"

"Of course," I say with a smile. "Let me just check to see if Freya left what I need for it. I didn't have time before I left this morning to look at the note Freya left on that tub of items," I say, indicating the item at the other end of the table from where we were sitting.

I grab the tub and then open the note. Sure enough, it's from Freya and contains a list of items and instructions. As I scanned the list, I realised I couldn't perform the rune today as we were missing a few essential ingredients. I was about to put the note down when I saw a P.S. at the bottom. *'Sis, by the time you get home, a parcel should be waiting for you. Inside, you'll find everything you need.'* It was signed, *'The best sister in the world.'*

"I'll be right back," I say to Ava and Sam, then head down into the basement. I grab the knife, pestle and mortar, and a small piece of wood from our supplies and head back upstairs.

When I emerge from the basement and close the door behind me, I turn and find both Ava and Sam, their jaws almost hitting the floor, wide-eyed. "What's up?" I ask, a little concerned.

"You just vanished from sight," Ava said, her voice filled with disbelief.

"Oh," I said, looking back at the basement door. "I'm sorry. I should have warned you. Our basement is warded, so only those we want to see it can," I explain casually.

"Really? That's so cool," Ava said, her initial shock replaced by fascination.

"It was one of the first things I learnt how to do," I say with a shrug. "There are so many situations where that ability would be incredibly helpful in my line of work," Ava said, and I could tell she was thinking about some of her missions where that would have helped her. Then she refocused and asked, "Well, what are we doing now?" Nodding towards the tub of ingredients, Sam echoed her curiosity with a nod of his own.

I grab the parcel that was delivered this morning and tear it open. Inside are several individually sealed bags containing various items. I pull out a bag at a time and carefully withdraw one item from each that I need for the rune. One dead bee, one small, incredibly white mushroom, a single perfect leaf of ivy, and a small piece of bone that I really, really hope isn't from a pixie.

I also place the piece of wood in the mortar. Ava and Sam watch silently, their eyes glued to my every move, adding a layer of pressure I try to ignore. I focus, using my power to pulverise the ingredients – the brittle crunch of bee exoskeleton, the soft resistance of the mushroom *'releasing a damp, earthy smell'*, the papery tear of ivy, the sharp *snap* of bone. Magically, they reduce to a fine, grey-white ash. I mix them thoroughly with a fingertip, the powder feeling unnervingly soft. Then, steeling myself, I grab the knife. The familiar sharp sting bites as I make a small, clean cut on my palm. Dark blood wells up instantly, smelling faintly of copper. Before the second drop falls, Seraphina coalesces from the deepest shadows beside me, a solid silhouette against the room's light, her purple eyes blazing with protective intensity.

'You're hurt. Are these enemies?' Her voice echoes in my mind, filled with concern and protectiveness.

"No, they aren't enemies," I say aloud, reassuring her. "Please go back and protect my sisters." My shadow glances at Ava and Sam, and then her gaze flickers towards Rose, who is still outside. Then, she seamlessly melds back into the shadows in the room and vanishes.

"What the hell, Reya? That looked just like one of the demons that attacked us! Was Rose right? Are you a black witch?" Ava said, her initial worry clearly visible on her face.

"Who was she talking to?" Sam asks at the same time, looking completely bewildered.

Crap! Their reactions – Ava's shock, Sam's confusion – send a jolt of anxiety through me. "Sorry," I stammer, watching their faces closely, searching for disbelief or fear. "I... I *created* what's called a shadow person. From my *own* shadow. To help protect my sisters." My explanation sounds thin, inadequate, even to my ears. I hold my breath, hoping desperately that this reveal hasn't just detonated the fragile bridge of trust we were only beginning to cross.

From outside, Rose's voice, laced with panic and anger, screams, "AVA! Get out of there! She's a black witch! A shadow person is a shade, just like the demons we're up against in Jackson! She must have created them all!" I can then hear her grunting and growling as she pounds on the invisible barrier, her frustration evident.

"I promise you, I did not create those demons. It was actually Papa Legba who gave me a hint that something in the diary he left for me could help protect us. The only thing I found was a spell to turn my shadow into this shadow person. She has my memories but her own personality and obeys my commands," I say, my voice almost pleading with them to understand.

After a tense moment of studying me, Ava's shoulders relax slightly. Sam, however, got up and moved towards the front door, his hand instinctively resting on his gun. The gesture makes me tense, bracing myself for a potential attack.

"Fine, I believe you," Ava said, her gaze still assessing but less accusatory. She nods to Sam, indicating that he can sit back down, which he does, albeit with a wary look. "You seem to be even more powerful than we initially expected."

I shrug, trying to appear nonchalant as I manage to control myself enough to let a few drops of blood drip onto the ash in the mortar. When there's what I deem enough blood, I pinch the small cut on my hand, as usual, and wait for it to stop bleeding. Then, I mix the ash and blood together until it forms a thick, dark paste.

Rose continues to mutter to herself about a stubborn and reckless woman. I guess she is referring to Ava. I try to ignore her rants and turn to Sam. "Where do you want this rune placed?" I ask.

He stares at me briefly, his expression a mixture of apprehension and curiosity. "What will it look like?"

I turn the piece of paper over, on which Freya had sketched the rune, so he can see the intricate design. Then, I stand up and lift my top just enough to show him the protection rune that was already burned into my skin on my hip.

"Is that burned into your skin?" he asks, his eyes widening slightly.

"Yes," I confirm.

Sam blows out a long breath, nods slowly, and says, "On my upper arm, then, please." He then removes his jacket and begins undoing the buttons on his shirt, revealing a glimpse of a toned physique underneath.

"I hope you're good with pain, as ours definitely hurt at the time," I say, wanting to make sure he understands what to expect.

"I'm sure it'll be fine," Sam said with a nervous smile as he finally took off his shirt, revealing a surprisingly well-built body. He's much more muscular than I had anticipated seeing under his suit. I half-expected a bit of a 'dad bod,' not this lean, fit physique, and I can't help but let my gaze linger for a moment. Again, my thoughts drift to whether Luca possessed a similar physique.

I move closer to Sam and position myself to face him directly. "Ready?" I ask, and he gives me a slight, determined nod in response.

I hold the rune drawing in my left hand and use a finger on my right to scoop up some of the dark ash and blood paste. I carefully begin to draw the intricate symbol onto Sam's upper arm. It doesn't take long to complete the design. When finished, I wipe off my finger and double-check that what I had drawn on Sam's skin matches Freya's sketch.

I meet Sam's gaze once I'm confident the intricate pattern matches Freya's sketch. "Get ready." He gives another tight, small nod, his jaw set. Ava leans forward, utterly captivated. I take a steadying breath and hold my hand hovering just above the dark paste on his skin. Closing my eyes briefly, I channel my magic, focusing my intent, pushing the power down my arm – a familiar warmth building in my palm. *Please work. Please don't hurt him too much. Please don't make them hate us.* I follow Freya's instructions precisely. The paste beneath my hand begins to glow, a faint, sickly green light at first, then brightening. Opening my eyes, I pour my will into the final Latin word, stating with as much force as I can muster, "*Visus!*"

The rune flashes brightly, and I see Sam's jaw clench and hear his teeth grind in response to the sudden pain. Then, just like when we had received our own runes, the sensation stopped abruptly, as if someone had flipped off a light switch.

I remove my hand and look at the now permanently burned rune on his skin. It resembles a typical tattoo, but instead of black ink, it looks like a strange black and grey speckled stamp, slightly raised on his skin.

"You couldn't see my flames during the attack, could you?" I ask as Sam begins to relax, flexing his arm and studying the new mark on his skin with curiosity.

"No, I couldn't. Why?" he asks, looking at me with a questioning gaze.

I ignite my purple flames in my left hand and hold them out between us. Instantly, I know the rune has worked because Sam flinches back slightly, his eyes widening in surprise.

"Wow," Sam breathes out in amazement as he stares at the dancing flames. I then change my flames to my black ones, and for a moment, both my fire powers mix and produce the most amazing effect. I'm so focused on showing off that I haven't felt the extreme drain on my body. When I do notice, I put out the flames quickly and have to take multiple breaths to try to stop myself from passing out.

This surprises Ava, who leans closer to me and asks, "Are you okay?"

"Yeah, I'm fine. I just never mixed them before. It really drained me," I say, starting to feel normal again as my breaths slow and revert to normal breathing.

Then, Rose's sharp and urgent voice pulls the attention away from me. "We have company."

We all rush to the front door to look out. What I see makes my stomach clench with a sense of foreboding. This feels like the moment I have been anticipating, when the wolves, or whatever they were, finally decide to make their move.

I can't allow my sisters to return home to this, so I know I must deal with whatever is approaching before they get home. Also, Rose was still stuck on the other side of our protection barrier, so I know she will inevitably get involved, which in turn will likely draw Ava and Sam into the fray as well.

There are about thirty shadowy figures, spilling across the drive and lawn like pools of unnatural darkness. The air grows noticeably colder, carrying a faint, cloying scent like damp earth and something metallic. They possess the same humanoid outline as Seraphina, but all resemblance ends there. These things feel *wrong*, hollow. And their eyes… they burn in the dim light, pinpricks of malevolent colour: hateful blood red, predatory amber, and a few pairs glowing with a sickly, unsettling orange.

A figure stood at the far end of our drive, partially concealed within the edge of the woods, which serves as our driveway. I couldn't make out many details from this distance, but I can see she has large, dark grey wings and long, flowing hair that shimmers with hints of silver and red. She has to be the one in charge.

"Who is she?" Rose asks, her voice filled with a mixture of fear and confusion. That's when I realise she can only see the winged woman; Ava must have come to the same realisation at the same time.

"Rose, we have a lot of shades here. You need to get out of here. You can't fight what you can't see," Ava demands, her voice low and urgent so our enemy wouldn't be able to hear her, but loud enough for Rose to understand.

Ava then swiftly pulls her newly enchanted sword from its sheath, the inscription gleaming ominously in the faint light. Sam stands slightly behind her, still wearing only the vest he had on under his shirt. His eyes widen with a mixture of fear and morbid fascination as he gawps at our approaching enemy. I also know he's at significant risk, seeing as he doesn't appear to have a weapon that can harm the shadows.

"Sam, you should probably stay behind the barrier," I state, trying to keep him safe. He instinctively places his hand on his gun. "That won't do anything to them," I say, hoping he won't get in the way and distract me.

"I know… I feel completely helpless," Sam said, his gaze darting between Ava and Rose, a look of frustration and worry etched on his face.

The shadowy figures begin to move towards Rose, who stands her ground with her hands raised defensively. Her gaze is still fixed on the winged woman in the distance, but she keeps glancing around, desperately trying to see the approaching shadows. That's when I notice her hands have begun to shift, her fingernails elongating and sharpening into large, wickedly sharp claws.

Ava rushes down the steps without hesitation and joins Rose on the other side of the invisible barrier. I have no choice but to join them. If I don't, these shadows will still be here when my sisters return home, and the thought of them finding a dead Ava and Rose in front of our house is unbearable.

The first thing I do is call out in my mind for my Seraphina. I hope she will hear my mental plea and will not find it necessary to alert my sisters that I was in danger.

Then, I cautiously approached the edge of the barrier, still on our side, to see if I could somehow attack through it, similar to how Maya can manipulate her shields. Of course, she only struggles to produce good shields when she is under extreme stress.

I ignite the black fire in my hands, aiming to send streams of dark fire toward the nearest shadows. However, when my fire reaches the barrier, it erupts in a sudden, violent explosion of flames right in front of me. *Crap!* This isn't going as I had hoped. As the fire dissipates, I realise with dismay that my attack has actually damaged the barrier.

With a sound like cracking ice amplified tenfold, spiderweb fractures race across the barrier's previously invisible surface where my fire hit. For the first time, I see the faint, pulsing golden energy *within* the barrier itself, now exposed and weakened through the spreading cracks. *Gods, no!* Panic claws at my throat. *'I haven't just failed in my attack, I've damaged our only defence! I've made things worse!'*

I have no other option. I step over the damaged barrier just as Ava ignites her new sword ability. The black flames erupt along the blade, and she begins swinging it with a fierce determination at the shadows now rapidly approaching her. I hope the enchantment on the sword will last long enough; I have no idea how much power it can hold or how it will recharge itself.

The sword seems to work effectively. When Ava struck the first few shadows, they instantly burst into black smoke and vanished into thin air. I notice that these shadows also possess clawed hands, just like Rose, who is lashing out blindly with her own claws, unable to connect with the invisible attackers.

As soon as I have a clear shot, I fire streams of black fire at the same group of shadows I targeted before. The shadows at the front of the group see my attack coming and manage to move out of the way just in time, and I do catch two shadows that were behind them. They react too late, and my black fire instantly engulfs the two figures. They then went '*poof,*' the flames seeming to consume them from the inside out, causing them to vanish into thin air.

I glance over at Ava and Rose and see that they both have fresh cuts on their arms. Rose is now wading into a group of shadows, even though she can't see them, her claws flailing wildly, but they don't seem to be affecting the shadowy figures much.

I unleash two more streams of black fire at the shadows advancing towards me and direct one of the streams towards the shadows descending on Rose. They must sense her vulnerability and think they can take her out quickly, which can then distract me and cause me to make a mistake, allowing them to gain an advantage.

My attack scores two more direct hits, removing three more shadows and injuring another. They are so close together that the injured one lost an arm in the blast of my attack. That's when I realise the shadows are making absolutely no noise, especially jarring when I see the injured one contorting as if it were screaming in silent agony. I glance over at the winged woman in the distance and see her flinch, her expression tight with anger. She can hear them; she is definitely their master.

Ava also manages to take out two more shadows. The sword looks incredible as she wields it with surprising grace, leaving a trail of black fire in its wake as she swings it. The scene is almost beautiful, a stark contrast to the mortal danger we are in.

Then, the sun was abruptly blotted out for a moment, momentarily throwing me off. I look up and see another shadow soaring overhead, then descending rapidly into the midst of the enemy shadows, who had, of course, used my distraction to rush me. It takes me a split second to realise that this other shadow is mine – Seraphina. Just then, one of the enemy shadows grabs my right arm, pulling me off balance.

I'm wrenched around just in time to see Ava swarmed, shadowy arms locking hers, preventing her from using the sword. Further off, Rose is a whirlwind of claws and fury in the centre of five flickering shapes, but even from here, the dark stains spreading on her clothes scream danger—too much blood. My focus snaps as icy grips clamp onto my own arms, yanking me violently backwards. I stumble, trying to twist, to face the things holding me, but their strength is unnerving, their touch deathly cold—then agony – sharp, searing, as unseen claws bite deep into my side.

I can't help but cry out in agony, and this involuntary reaction causes my fire to erupt from me uncontrollably. The sudden burst of energy forces the shadows holding me to release their grip momentarily. I then start to feel myself falling to the ground, my body twisting into an unnatural position.

I can't tell which shadow Seraphina is or if she is faring any better than the rest of us. Then I scream out in pain again as sharp claws rake down my back, tearing through my clothes and skin. Even through the intense pain, I feel something familiar about the claws in my back, and a chilling realisation dawns on me. It gave me a desperate idea, but I had to focus on whether it could actually work. It's a difficult task as I feel blow after blow rain down on my body.

Just as I try to put my risky plan into action, which was proving incredibly difficult as I feel more hits land on my body and more claws dig into my skin, I hear both Ava and Rose cry out in pain. This, for some reason, manages to sharpen my focus. Suddenly, the shadows attacking me are ripped away by another shadow with distinctly purple eyes. '*Try your plan quickly, and don't worry about me,*' Seraphina's voice echoes in my mind, her tone firm and reassuring. She must sense my desperate idea through our connection.

The claws in my back also vanish abruptly. This gives me the precious moment I need. I reach out with my mind, focusing all my will. Before fully executing my plan, I see a shadow move in swiftly behind Seraphina. With a surge of adrenaline, I manage to lift my right hand, even though my arm feels battered and weak, and fire off a ball of pure black fire.

It strikes my intended target just as it looks like the shadow is about to rip off Seraphina's head. The shadow burst into flames and vanished into nothingness.

Seraphina knocks another shadow back with a mighty sweep of her dark wings and then immediately heads over to assist Ava and Rose. I can't risk directly helping them with my fire, as I'm more likely to hit one of them accidentally. So, I have to concentrate on my desperate plan. I make sure the shadows that are once again advancing towards me don't get too close and then unleash as much black fire as I can at the ground around me, creating a temporary wall of swirling flames.

I continue to reach out with my mind, and sure enough, I find what I instinctively expect. I really do have some kind of connection to demons. It's like seeing different-coloured dots in my mind. I keep my focus primarily on the dark dots that I knew represented the enemy shadows, but I'm also sure I can see faint dots that could be Ava and Rose, and even a distinct purple dot that I'm certain is Seraphina.

I feel myself getting rapidly tired, and the effort of using so much power to maintain the wall of fire is taking its toll. I know I don't have much time left. I try to establish a mental connection to each of the dark dots, each enemy shadow. It's incredibly mentally draining, like trying to hold onto slippery eels, but I manage to keep each connection in place.

The thought of trying to *control* these things is repulsive; that *was* never the plan. But as I strain to maintain the slippery mental grasp on each dark entity, a disturbing shift occurs. The connections feel… stickier.

Less like holding eels and more like grasping cold, buzzing wires. Faint, alien whispers of malice and hunger seep back along the links, chilling me to the bone. I feel a flicker of *something* from them, colder and sharper than the protectiveness I sometimes sense from Seraphina. This costs me more than energy; it feels invasive and full of malice. *They are becoming mine.*

When I know I have established a connection with all of them, I close my eyes and release the power that was maintaining the fiery barrier. The immediate relief was immense, but now the shadows closest to me are already heading for me, and we will all be overwhelmed soon if I don't take action. I redirect all my remaining power into my mental connections with the enemy shadows. With every last ounce of strength I possess, I send everything I can down those invisible pathways. With my eyes still closed and my focus unwavering on the connections, I start to notice the dark dots in my mind vanishing one by one. I risk opening my eyes and watching as, shadow by shadow, they went '*poof.*' There was no fire, no explosion, no lingering evidence of an attack. The shadows dissipate into wisps of black smoke and vanish as if blown away by a sudden gust of wind.

One by one, each of us collapses to the ground, exhausted and injured. Rose starts to growl, a low, guttural sound of pain and anger. When I manage to focus my heavy eyelids and look over at her, trying desperately to stay conscious, I see she is staring intently in the direction where I last saw the winged woman. She is still here, standing at the edge of the woods, glaring at me with what I can now clearly see were pure black eyes. Unlike my black fire, which holds a strange kind of elegance, the woman's eyes seem devoid of any life, and all her intense anger is focused solely on me.

I glance at Rose, struggling to get to her feet, presumably to go after the winged woman. I raise both hands as I lie on my side and force myself to create two small balls of black fire. The effort is immense, and my body shudders violently, as if I'm about to pass out. With a final surge of will, I quickly send the fireballs hurtling towards our enemy.

A sudden pressure on my arm, cold and reminiscent of Seraphina's touch, draws my attention. When I search for her, I find it isn't her; instead, a new presence beside me is kneeling on the ground and gazing at the woman. Given my weakened state, it isn't easy to discern exactly who I am seeing.

Attached to my arm, where the pressure is, is a figure – translucent, shimmering, but tinted a smoky grey, far darker than Doris's spectral form *looked*. It's a young girl, maybe ten or eleven, her features indistinct but undeniably childlike. Her smoky lips are pressed against a cut on my arm, and I feel a faint, unnatural *tugging* sensation. My breath catches. Is she… drinking my blood? A wave of revulsion and instinctive fear makes me want to rip my arm away, to blast her with fire, ghost or not.

I'm about to instinctively use my power to attack her and get her off me when she suddenly releases my arm and moves away. 'Sorry, I had to,' she said, her voice a faint whisper. *'Please don't hurt her; she was tricked and is now possessed. Please, you have to help her,'* the young girl pleaded with me, her dark eyes filled with a desperate urgency.

I wasn't sure what to do, so I looked over at the others. Sam is now carefully helping Ava to her feet, his gun trained warily on the winged woman in the distance. Ava doesn't look too badly injured, unlike Rose, who is covered in blood and slowly making her way towards the woman, who had somehow managed to avoid the fireballs I sent her way. When the winged woman glances at the advancing Rose and Seraphina, who have joined her, she abruptly flaps her large wings and ascends rapidly into the air.

She flies directly towards me, and when she is just a few yards away, she speaks for the first time, her voice surprisingly clear and cold, but she isn't addressing me. Her intense glare is fixed on the young girl who is still standing hesitantly next to me. Ava and Sam finally seem to notice the girl and start to point at her, trying to get my attention.

"You are a traitor, Kracis. We are going to make you pay for this," the winged woman hissed, her voice venomous. Then she turned and began to fly away, quickly gaining altitude.

I call out to Seraphina in my head, instructing her to follow the winged woman if she can and see where she goes. *'I can do that. Do you want me to deal with this shade first?'* she asks, glancing at the young girl with a curious expression.

"Shade? She's a shade?" I ask, my mind still reeling from everything that has just happened.

'She is, well, maybe not for long. She's changing,' Seraphina said, cocking her head slightly to the side as she studied the young girl with her piercing purple eyes.

"Just follow the enemy, please, and see if you can track where she goes," I demand, my voice weak but firm. Seraphina nods, flaps her dark wings, launches herself into the air, and swiftly follows the rapidly receding speck, now a tiny dot in the distance.

"Why," Rose grits out, pushing herself shakily upright, her body trembling, fresh blood dripping from a cut on her cheek, "didn't you just take her OUT!!!" She stumbles towards me, her face contorted with pain and raw fury, spitting the last word directly into my face, her voice cracking with the force of the scream.

"I… I ran out of power," I gasped, my body aching all over.

"Reya, who is that girl, and who were you just talking to?" Ava asks, kneeling down in the dirt beside me, looking just as exhausted and battered as I felt.

"What are you talking about, and what in the hell is a Kracis?" Rose asks, her brow furrowed in confusion, still trying to catch her breath.

"A young girl is standing right next to Reya. I think she's a ghost or something," Sam said, staring at the translucent figure with an expression of pure disbelief.

"Apparently, this girl is called Kracis, and she told me that the winged woman who just flew off was tricked and is now possessed. Kracis has asked me for help to save her," I explain to the others, my voice weak and breathy.

Chapter 28

Battle Lines Drawn

Sam looks at me with suspicion in his eyes, like I might be making this up, before he says, "I didn't hear her say anything."

I turned to where the girl had been, but she had vanished. "I heard her in my head. She said she had to drink my blood to talk to me, just like my shadow has to," I explain, hoping this information won't cause Rose to start beating the '*black witch*' drum again.

"You what!" Rose exclaims, her voice sharp with disbelief and probably a healthy dose of judgment.

"Rose, please don't start," Ava sighs, rolling her eyes in exasperation.

"Sam, help Ava to the *car*. We are getting out of here," Rose said in a tone that brooks no argument, causing Sam to stiffen slightly. He looks from Ava to me and back again, a flicker of indecision in his eyes, before ultimately doing as Rose instructed.

"Rose, we can't just leave," Ava protests, trying to shrug off Sam's supportive arm.

"I can't even enter the house! I'm not separating from you right now until I can check your injuries properly," Rose said through gritted teeth, shooting me a look that could curdle milk.

"Oh yeah, I forgot. You can't come in because you're so stubborn and pig-headed," Ava retorts, then turns to face me, a hint of apology in her eyes. I knew she felt obligated to leave with Rose.

"Yeah, I'll be fine. I've had worse injuries. Besides, being inside the protection barrier helps to speed up healing now," I say, trying to sound reassuring, even though all I really want to do is crawl indoors and collapse onto the couch.

"That's handy. Message me later to let me know you're okay," Ava said, allowing Sam to guide her towards their *car*.

"I will," I promise, watching them get into their vehicle. Rose and Ava climb into the back, while Sam enters the driver's seat.

Before he closes the door, he looks at me with genuine gratitude. "Thank you. Sorry, we're just leaving like this. I'll grab my shirt and jacket later, I hope." I nod, a wave of exhaustion washing over me as I stand there and watch them drive off. When their *car* has vanished from view, I pull out my phone, hoping it has survived the attack.

I check my phone and am relieved to see it looks undamaged. I promised Freya that I wouldn't keep anything from them again, so I opened Messenger and started to type, '*I was attacked but had the agents here. We won, but we all got a few injuries. We are okay, so don't worry. I'll explain everything when you get home after work. Also, the rune worked on Sam.*'

I'm about to slip my phone back into the side of my bra, where I often keep it when I don't have my bag with me, when I feel a sudden, sharp blow to the back of my head. It feels like I've hit a brick wall, and everything starts to turn black as I hit the ground.

As I lay there, desperately trying to fight the encroaching darkness that is rapidly clouding my vision, I hear Cat's frantic voice screaming in my mind, "REYA, YOU MUST STAY AWAKE! YOU ARE IN SO MUCH DANGER! PLEASE STAY AWAKE AND FIGHT!!!" Cat sounds utterly panicked, and her fear only amplifies the dread that is already settling in my stomach. I see the blurry shadow of someone standing over me just before the darkness finally claims me.

Ava

I passed out again in the back of the car; this was really becoming a recurring theme for me. Going up against paranormals is proving to be much harder than I had ever anticipated. After this latest brutal attack and getting hurt yet again, I'm seriously starting to question whether I'm cut out for this, even with Reya's impressive upgrade to my sword. A nagging feeling tells me we might be completely overwhelmed, especially when facing these demons that half of us can't even see.

Ultimately, I wasn't even entirely sure what had happened to the demons. How did they vanish like that? If it was Reya who had caused it, then it was a seriously neat trick, and it suggests she is far more powerful than any of us had initially expected. Also, she didn't really seem like the stereotypical witch I had seen in Tv shows and films.

After we finally got back to the motel, Rose and I were both too injured and exhausted to do anything other than take a quick shower to wash off the copious amounts of blood and then give our numerous wounds a cursory clean.

Most of our injuries were relatively shallow scratches, but a few were a little deeper than usual, and there were definitely some nasty puncture wounds from the sharp tips of the demons' claws. Who knew shadows could actually inflict so much pain?

Then, we both just collapsed into bed, sleep being the only thing on our minds. The thought of our various injuries rubbing against each other definitely didn't seem sexy or even remotely appealing. Sam said before we went to our room that he was going to update Luca and Agent Moore about what had transpired. He was also eager to inform them that the rune–or spell–or whatever it is–that Reya performed on him had actually worked.

We slept for the rest of the day. When I finally woke up, I was surprised to discover for the first time that I wasn't plastered on top of Rose; in fact, I woke up in the exact same position I had fallen asleep in. When I try to move to grab my phone from the bedside table, I find that even the slightest movement sends sharp jolts of pain through my body—no wonder I haven't stirred in my sleep.

I feel the mattress dip next to me, and then an arm reaches over me, snags my phone, and hands it to me. "How bad are you?" Rose asks, her voice still thick with sleep.

"I think when they dragged me down, I might have pulled a muscle in my back. Otherwise, I feel mostly okay, apart from my entire body feeling incredibly sensitive from all the injuries," I say, glancing at my phone screen to check the time. It's 4am. "Wow, I slept for ages. I must have really needed it," I say to Rose.

"I needed it too. I only woke up just before you," Rose murmured in my right ear. I feel her warm breath against my skin, which, surprisingly, didn't make my body prickle with pleasure like it usually did.

Then I notice a whole bunch of missed calls and messages from Reya and two other numbers I don't recognise. Even with the throbbing pain in my back, I shoot up into a sitting position, my eyes wide as I stare at the countless notifications.

"What is it?" Rose asks, sounding alarmed by my sudden reaction.

"Something's wrong," I say, my voice tight with worry, and open the first message. It read, *'Hey, this is Freya. Do you know where Reya is? Is she with you?'*

I quickly opened message after message, each becoming increasingly frantic and desperate. Rose reads them over my shoulder. "What the hell happened after we left?" Rose said, her voice now laced with concern.

"I knew we should have stayed! It was wrong of us to leave after everything that happened. If anything has happened to Reya, then that's on us," I say, my stomach twisting with a sickening feeling. What if we had just abandoned our best hope of dealing with these enemies? What if Reya was now dead because Rose was too stubborn, and she and Luca were too quick to judge Reya based on their unfounded suspicions about her powers? I should have put my foot down and insisted on staying. It felt wrong to leave at the time, and I knew deep down that I shouldn't have gone. I wouldn't be able to forgive myself if Reya turns up dead, and I would probably leave this entire task force if that were the case.

All I can manage to say right now is, "No idea." I then brought up Reya's number from my contacts and pressed dial. Freya must have her sister's phone. I still have no idea who the other two numbers belong to.

"I bet that other demon circled back and took her out," Rose said, her tone surprisingly nonchalant, as if she wouldn't be bothered in the slightest if she was right. Her callous comment infuriates me and makes me wonder if we were about to have our first serious fight.

"Why do you sound so… happy about it?" I snap, but my call is answered before she can respond.

The voice on the other end was filled with raw fury and screams into the phone, "What the fuck!! Where's our sister? Tell me where she is right now! I don't care if you're with the FBI, I will come and kick your arse!" I was confident it was Freya, and she was so loud I had to hold the phone away from my ear.

"Freya, we don't know where Reya is. We left her standing in front of your house," I say calmly, as I can manage, trying not to escalate the already volatile situation.

"So, where the fuck is she?" Freya demands again, her voice still laced with anger and fear.

"Do you have a way to track her? You know, with magic, like you see on Tv?" I ask, grasping at straws.

"If there is a way, we don't know how! We have no one to train us, and we haven't found a book yet that can teach us that kind of thing," Freya said, her voice filled with disappointment and frustration.

Rose then takes me by surprise. "We could head back over there. Maybe I can pick up on a scent that wasn't there before we left or track Reya's scent."

Maybe she felt guilty after her earlier comment or the fact that she had pressured us to leave. "Really? You would do that?" I ask, a glimmer of hope flickering within me.

"Of course! I'm not as heartless as you seem to think I am," Rose said, looking a little hurt by my question. She has no right to feel hurt, considering this entire situation feels like it's partly our fault.

"Thank you," is all I manage to say. Still on the phone, Freya asks if Rose can track her sister, so I reply, "We're on our way."

"Should we call the police?" a voice I recognise as Maya's asks in the background.

"Do not call the police, the state troopers, or the local sheriff! But is Jacob going to be an issue?" I ask, remembering Reya mentioning a potential date.

"He might be. I think they planned to go on a date on Thursday," Freya relays.

"Hopefully, we find her by then. Anyway, we'll get to you as soon as possible," I say, then hang up.

Before I do, Freya says, rushing, "Thank you."

Rose has to help me get out of bed, as the pain in my back is still quite intense. She also has to assist me with getting dressed, but as soon as I start to move around, I begin to find it easier to walk as my back seems to loosen up slightly. We then wake Sam up and quickly explain the dire situation. Once we are all ready, we head back towards Luna Falls and the Harpers' house, a heavy sense of dread hanging over us.

Reya

I slowly become aware as I start to wake up, but I'm still shrouded in complete darkness. Gradually, I can sense the oppressive darkness beginning to recede. My first coherent thought is a desperate plea. *Am I still alive?*

Then I vaguely remember hearing Cat's voice shouting at me to stay awake and saying that I was in danger. No shit, Sherlock, I thought sarcastically, even in my disoriented state. *And where the hell has she been all this time?* Even though she can be a pain in my arse, she still could have been helpful, even if only a little.

I start to hear voices, which I'm reasonably sure belong to two men. They were arguing about how hard one of them hit me and that their alpha is going to be furious if I don't wake up soon.

Then I hear them talking to someone whose voice sounds vaguely familiar, but my hearing isn't back to normal yet. Everything sounds muffled, as if I'm underwater, making it difficult to understand everything they're saying. For some reason, at one point, I'm sure I hear what sounds like heavy panting, and there's a distinct noise like an animal is walking around, and the sound of nails clicking against a hard floor. The sound vaguely reminds me of Beastie. A fleeting thought crosses my mind, and I wonder if he is here with me. But if I'm in a hospital, he wouldn't be allowed in. However, based on the snippets of conversation I have overheard, something deep inside me tells me I'm definitely with the enemy.

After what feels like an eternity floating in the inky blackness, I start to regain feeling in my body, acutely aware of the many injuries I have sustained during the attack. The throbbing pain is making me feel incredibly drowsy, or maybe it's the lingering effects of the brutal blow to the back of my head.

Eventually, the oppressive darkness completely lifts. I almost miss it; it feels like floating in a sea of black silk. When I finally emerge from that strange, comforting place, I know I can open my eyes, but I'm reluctant to. I know I have to, though, as I desperately need to see where I am and if there's even the slightest chance of escape.

I crack my eyelids open, and all I can initially see is more darkness. But as my eyes gradually adjust, I start to discern a faint light and the barest outlines of my surroundings.

"You're finally awake. They have been worried about you," a weak, feeble voice said. The voice doesn't sound too far away from me and is nothing like the gruff voices I heard earlier.

"Who are you, and what do you want?" I demand, my voice sounding weak and incredibly dry. At the same time, I try to shift my gaze to see if I can locate the source of the voice and who I'm up against.

"I'm no one, and the shifters brought you here. Soon, you will be no one too," the voice replies, its tone flat and devoid of emotion.

"*Crap!*" I exclaim out loud with more conviction this time. Cat had been right; I was in deep shit. I struggle to push myself up into a sitting position, the effort sending waves of pain through my battered body. I eventually manage it and find myself leaning against a cold wall and lying on what seems to be something like a camping bed. Using the wall for support only makes the injuries on my back scream in protest, but I try to ignore the pain as I have far more significant issues to contend with.

I feel nauseous sitting up, and a wave of dizziness washes over me. I wonder if I have a concussion from the blow to my head. I know I need to try to stay awake for as long as possible. I try again to see who's in this room with me when my head stops spinning for a brief moment.

Again, I can't see anyone clearly in the dim light that filters in through a tiny, grimy window that I think is set into a heavy wooden door. As I slowly survey my surroundings, I discover I am in a dank, dirty room that reeks of sweat, stale blood, and other unidentifiable, unpleasant smells.

I can also make out some markings on the two walls I can see; they look like large, intricate symbols, but I can't decipher them in the poor light. At one point, I think I see a flicker of movement in the shadows, which gives me a surge of hope, as I believe Seraphina has somehow managed to find me. Soon, though, I realise she isn't here. I even try to call out to her in my mind, but I can't feel that familiar connection we share anymore. So, the movement must be whoever else is trapped in this hellhole with me.

"Who are you?" I ask again, my voice hoarse.

"I'm no one," the same feeble voice replies, the repetition starting to grate on my already frayed nerves.

"You are someone! Please, what's your name?" I ask, this time, I'm sure I sound just slightly annoyed with their persistent denial.

"I'm no one," the voice said again, but this time, it sounded more agitated, a hint of distress creeping into their tone.

Suddenly, the heavy wooden door bursts open with a loud crash, flooding the room with harsh light that briefly blinds me. I instinctively squint, the sudden brightness hurting my eyes and throbbing head, making it impossible to see anything clearly. However, I hear something scraping frantically against the floor, as if someone is desperately trying to get away from whoever has just entered the room.

I then hear a choked sound, like someone's breath being forcefully expelled, followed by a man's voice, which says with a chillingly casual tone, "Finally, you're awake." As my eyes adjust to the sudden influx of light, I see a man step into the room. From what little I can make out, he's followed closely by an enormous wolf, the biggest I've ever seen. It was more like a large, black bear in its sheer size.

I stare at it in shock, and a terrifying realisation finally dawns on me, this is what attacked our mother. The sight of the massive wolf sends a fresh wave of fear crashing over me as vivid images of our mothers' torn and lifeless bodies flash through my mind. I have a sinking feeling that I might be facing the same gruesome fate very soon.

I'm not surprised our mother didn't survive the attack; this wolf is a similar size to what Rose looks like in her panther form, maybe slightly smaller. As my vision starts to clear, my eyes finally adjust to the sudden light. I look directly into the wolf's eyes and feel a strange flicker of… recognition? No, that's ridiculous. I must still be disoriented. Except the wolf is staring back at me with an equally peculiar intensity.

"How are you feeling, witch?" the man asks, a cruel smirk playing on his lips.

"Just peachy, why do you ask?" I retort, forcing the best sarcastic smile I can muster, which, to my surprise, actually causes the man to laugh. He takes a step closer, his eyes glinting with malicious amusement.

'One more step, and I'm going to engulf this jerk in fire,' I think fiercely. But nothing happens when he crouches in front of me, his face inches from mine, and I try to summon my fire again and again, focusing all my will, but still, nothing.

The man chuckles, a low, mocking sound. "What's up, witch? Lost your mojo?" he said with a smug smirk, making my fists clench.

I thought that once my head stopped spinning, I could figure out how to get myself out of this mess. However, I can't imagine a viable escape route without my powers. I even try to use my telekinesis to send the jerk flying across the room, but that doesn't work either.

That means I must try to survive long enough for my sisters to find me. But they don't have great offensive abilities, and no way to track me unless my shadow, Seraphina, can somehow manage it. But if I can't feel her anymore, can she find me?

"You're going to be our future, witch," the man boasted, his eyes gleaming with a disturbing kind of triumph as his eyes track over my body in a way that makes me feel sick.

"There's absolutely no way in hell I'm going to help you," I spit back, managing a defiant look of my own.

"You won't have a choice," the man says, winking at me in a way that sends a cold, sickening chill down my spine. The massive wolf behind him suddenly lets out a low growl, which causes the man to stand back up abruptly. A flicker of genuine worry crosses his face as he glares at the animal.

Before he can say another word, a woman walks into the room carrying a glass of what looks like water, and hopefully is, a small piece of bread. She shoots me the dirtiest look I have ever received as she approaches, then roughly sets the glass down near me and places the piece of bread on top of it. She gives me one last contemptuous glare and then turns to walk out. As she passes the wolf, she deliberately runs her hand down its back, all while looking back at me with a strange, unsettling smile that I don't understand.

"There's a toilet over there," the man said, casually indicating a dark corner of the room to my left. "I'm sure you and… no one over there will be happy to close his eyes if you ask nicely," the man adds with a cruel chuckle. I finally understand why the other person in this room keeps repeating that he's no one; they have brainwashed him, likely through torture, into believing he is truly nobody.

I finally look over to the far side of the room and see what initially looks like a pile of dirty rags, but as my eyes focus, I see two wide, terrified eyes staring out from underneath the tattered fabric, fixed on our captors, God only knows how long they have been torturing him.

Then, the man who is my captor turns and walks towards the door. "Enjoy the rest of your night," he says with false cheerfulness just before he closes the door. I hear the distinct sound of something large and heavy being moved into place, likely a metal bar being slid across the outside to secure it.

After the door had closed, I realised all sound vanished from the other side, reminiscent of the ward we use at home. The door closing must have triggered the ward, which would explain why I can't use my powers. That means they definitely have a witch working for them, and I wonder if it's Sandra. I wonder who they have managed to coerce or trick into helping them. Even though my mind goes to Sandra, I can't actually see her willingly helping these monsters. Well, maybe she would if it meant getting rid of us. If she has any part in this, then I will make her pay, no matter how long it takes, if I manage to survive this ordeal.

I glance down at the glass of water and the piece of bread. My stomach rumbles loudly in response, and I can't help but wonder if it is safe to eat and drink. I know I need to stay strong if I hope to escape, so I take the chance. I cautiously pick up the piece of bread with my left hand, then reach for the glass of water with my right, hesitating before bringing the glass to my lips.

I'm so incredibly thirsty that I start to sip the water tentatively. It tastes like pure water, and the glorious feeling of it sliding down my parched throat makes me feel instantly better. Once my throat feels less like sandpaper, I take a small bite of the bread. It's surprisingly soft and tastes like it's been freshly baked.

As soon as the bread hits my empty stomach, it feels like it screams at me for more. I don't hesitate and quickly scoff down the rest of the bread. I'm glad I haven't finished the water yet; the bread has made my throat feel dry again, so I finish the rest of the water in one final gulp.

I look over at my silent cellmate. "What did you do to end up here?" I ask, my voice still raspy.

"I'm no one," he repeats, his voice flat and lifeless. This time, his words don't frustrate me as much. I understand now that this mantra has likely been cruelly forced onto him through torture.

I figure trying to have a coherent conversation with him is probably a waste of time, but then he surprises me by saying, his voice barely a whisper, "I was captured when I tried to save the woman I fell in love with."

"Did you save her?" I ask, a desperate hope rising within me that he succeeded, making his current suffering a worthwhile sacrifice.

"I am no one," he repeats again, his voice devoid of any emotion. He follows it up with, "I have no idea. I had just witnessed my oldest friend being killed by a man I didn't recognise. He shouldn't have been able to kill her, but somehow, he did. Then, when I returned to the woman I love, I discovered she and her family were under attack. I tried to get to her home, but there were too many. I'm sure she is dead, and I hope I will see her again in the realm of angels."

I recognise the phrase, '*the realm of angels*,' from Papa Legba's diary. That would mean he might be paranormal, too.

As I process this information, I start to feel an overwhelming wave of exhaustion wash over me. My eyelids feel incredibly heavy, and moments later, I feel myself slide back down the wall, ending up on my side again before I succumb to the beckoning darkness.

Catherine M. Clark

Chapter 29

The Search Begins

Ava

When we reach the Harpers' house, their dog is sitting outside the front door, looking like a four-legged sentinel on guard duty. As we park next to the other vehicles, I can't help but wonder who the Nissan belongs to, as it wasn't here the previous times we visited.

The front door swings open before we even manage to get out of the car, Maya appears, her face etched with hopeful anticipation. But as soon as she sees the three of us emerge, her expression visibly falls as she scans around, clearly expecting someone else. I feel a pang of sympathy for her when I see her disappointment. We make our way towards Maya.

As we walk up the steps of the veranda, I suddenly freeze, stopping abruptly and turning to face Rose, who is right behind me on the steps. "How?" I ask, completely shocked, she has managed to get past the protection barrier.

"What's wrong?" Rose asks, her brow furrowed in confusion.

"How did you get past the barrier?" I demand, my eyes quickly scanning her for any injuries she might have sustained.

Rose looks behind her and then back at me, a sheepish expression spreading across her face. "Oh, I forgot," she said. I'm so distracted. I'm not thinking about how they might hurt you and what I would do if they did."

"I guess you were so distracted you weren't thinking about hurting them then," I quip, unable to suppress a small chuckle.

"I guess that's a good thing, as I can actually come in with you this time," Rose said, a hint of relief in her voice. She continues walking with me up the steps. When we reach the top, Maya turns and walks back into the house without saying a word, so we follow her inside. I can't help but glance down at the dog as we passed it; he gives me a look that clearly conveys, *'You left her all on her own, so this is all your fault.'* I hate it when I have a guilty conscience; thankfully, it doesn't happen frequently.

When we enter the living room, the dog follows us inside, looking like he doesn't entirely trust us yet. He even lets out a small, low growl as he brushes past our legs. As I move towards the *couch* where Freya is sitting, I see that she looks utterly distraught, like she is about to start pulling out her hair. I see Pickle curled up tightly in her lap and hear small, muffled sobs coming from her. The sight of Freya and Pickle causes Maya to immediately burst into tears as she sits down in a nearby armchair. Seeing them all so upset starts to tug at my heartstrings, and I feel tears pricking at the back of my eyes.

When Sam closes the front door behind him and joins us by the couch, he asks, his voice filled with concern, "Did you find any clues at all?"

Freya looks up at him, her own eyes red and watery, and says, "All we found was her mobile phone on the ground just on the other side of the barrier. Also, for some reason, we have four horses out back acting really strange when we went out to check on them this morning."

"When we arrived here yesterday, there was a horse trailer parked outside, and your sister was just leading the horses into the barn. She said she rescued them at the estate sale she went to," I told them, and this piece of news seems to bring a small ray of sunshine into the room, making them all smile faintly. Even Pickle looks up at hearing this, her tear-filled eyes widening slightly.

"That's just like Reya, always taking in strays," Pickle said softly, then curls back into Freya's comforting embrace and starts to cry again, while Freya gently pats her back.

"Well, that's one mystery solved, at least," Freya said with a sigh.

"With regard to where you found Reya's phone, that was exactly where she was standing when we drove off. That means whatever happened to her happened just moments after we left," I explain, then turn to Rose and say, "Do you think you can see if you can pick up her scent or the scent of whoever took her, please?"

"Sure," Rose said immediately, already turning to head back outside.

Freya and her sister watch Rose go, a renewed look of hope flickering in their eyes as she disappears through the front door. Then Freya turns to Sam and me and asks, her voice trembling slightly, "So, what exactly happened yesterday? I got a message from Reya saying there was an attack, and that you were all okay."

I sit on the couch beside her while Sam settles in one of the single armchairs. I start to explain everything that happened, deciding to begin with the horses, as I figure they need to hear every detail from the start. This includes Rose's initial inability to get past the barrier and her subsequent grumbling when Reya enchanted my sword and performed the rune on Sam. Of course, the sisters and Pickle are incredibly curious to see the sword and what Reya had done to it, so I show them.

That's when Pickle suddenly gasps, realising he can now see her, and with a delighted squeal, she flies over to Sam, lands gracefully on his lap, and starts chatting animatedly with him. This unexpected interaction seems to perk her up considerably, and her tears dry up.

When I get to the part about the young girl, it completely surprises Freya and Maya. I recount what the girl had said about the winged woman controlling the demons and that Reya sent her shadow, Seraphina, to follow her.

"Goddammit, I completely forgot all about her!" Freya exclaims, her eyes widening in alarm. She starts looking around the room, calling out the name Seraphina, but she sees no sign of the shadowy figure. We then discuss who could have taken Reya; our main suspects seemed to be the remaining demons or the shifters. We aren't sure which scenario we would prefer, if either, what they might do to her.

When Rose returns a few minutes later, her expression is grim. "I was able to pick up Reya's scent, but whoever took her didn't seem to have any scent at all. I followed Reya's scent, which led me down the side of the house and then out back, continuing to head north. When I reach a certain point, there's a strong smell of shifters; they seem to have been pacing back and forth, like they were walking a specific line. I'm guessing that line is where your barrier ends in that direction. When Reya's scent crosses that line, it vanishes completely. It was the same as whoever took her; it's like a void; there's no scent of anything at all. So, I tried to see if I could follow that void, but as it headed out into an open field, the scents of the shifters also vanished, and I completely lost track of it. Sorry," Rose said, her voice filled with frustration.

At least we now know the general direction Reya was taken. Now, all we have to do is figure out where they would have taken her. It seems more likely that the shifters are responsible, as the demons we fought seem to be coming from Jackson. So, it makes sense that if Reya was taken by force, it would be the shifters, as the demons would have taken her east towards Jackson instead of north.

Reya

    I wake up sometime later, and for all I know, I could have been asleep for an entire day. One thing I do know for certain is that I have been drugged, and whatever they used has stopped me from dreaming, leaving my mind in a disconcerting blankness. When I finally open my eyes, the first thing I see is the empty glass of water right where I left it. Maybe I haven't been unconscious for too long after all. I slowly scan my surroundings and realise it is now daytime, as the room is much brighter than it had been the previous night.

    I can now see details that were obscured in the darkness. There's a small, heavily tinted window high up on the wall, similar to the ones we have in our basement, except this window is tinted a dark, opaque colour. This could be a basement in someone's house, but I can't be sure.

    My gaze drifts to the mere bundle of rags. In this dim light now coming into the room, I can, for the first time, see the face of the man who is currently staring intently at me from the corner of the room.

    I can tell the guy looks severely malnourished. His cheekbones appear sharp and prominent, as if they might break through his skin at any moment. His gaunt appearance is vaguely reminiscent of Papa Legba's, except this man's face is covered in grime, and his eyes hold a strange, unsettling quality. Despite his current state, I can tell he once was a very handsome man, and something about his features seems strangely familiar, though I can't quite place them.

    Looking at the man's dry, cracked lips and what I'm sure had once been bright eyes, I see that they now look dull and lifeless. However, they were the first genuinely golden eyes I have ever seen. They are a mesmerising shade of amber, and I can't help but wonder what type of paranormal being he is.

I try to move back into a sitting position carefully, but the simple movement sends sharp jolts of pain through my back from having slept in an awkward position. I manage to prop myself up against the wall, taking it slow and easy. When I'm as comfortable as I can make myself, I look over at my cellmate again. He's still staring at me with an unnerving intensity.

It's starting to feel like maybe he actually knows who I am, judging by the strange, unwavering way he's still looking at me. I slowly look around the room, and the symbols I glimpsed on the wall last night are in fact, runes, as far as I can tell. There's a different one, each equally intricate rune etched into each of the other three walls.

As my head starts to clear from whatever drug they gave me to knock me out, the familiar tendrils of fear begin to creep into my thoughts. I continue to scan the room, and the stark reality of what they did to our mother starts flooding back to me. I instinctively try to access my powers, but just like last night, I feel nothing. When I enter my landscape and my library, the statues are gone, and so is the strange room with my ghost-self. Most of the familiar books and representations of my power within my mind are gone, vanished as if they had never existed. I still have a few books present in my mental landscape, but they are the ones that weren't fully formed yet, except for one. That particular book is pulsating with a faint, inner light, but I can't quite make out the image on its cover.

What in the hell have they done to me? If Sandra really is helping these monsters, she is so incredibly dead. The thought of Sandra's potential involvement starts to bring my anger bubbling to the surface. Seeing my cellmate still staring at me with those strange golden eyes, I turn to him and ask, my voice still a bit rough, "Are you okay?"

"I am no one," he repeats the same phrase again, his voice flat and devoid of inflexion.

I can't help myself; with my anger still rising, I snap, "Not this crap again!"

"I am the same as every day," he says, his gaze unwavering as he continues to stare directly at me.

"I'm guessing you're paranormal. Do you have any idea what they might have done to me?" I ask, hoping he might have some answers, however cryptic, for me.

"It's in the water," he manages to say, surprisingly, without uttering that annoying '*I am no one*' phrase again.

I stare down at the empty glass of water, and a wave of realisation washes over me. Of course, it was in the water. That would mean every single glass of water they offer me will likely be drugged. I was now faced with a difficult choice. Drink it to try and maintain some semblance of strength, or go thirsty and risk becoming weaker, thereby diminishing any chance I might have of escaping this nightmare.

As he stares at me, I see a subtle change in his eyes. They seemed to brighten for a fleeting moment, a spark of recognition flickering within their golden depths. Then, he asks, his voice barely a whisper, "Are you my Elsie?"

"My name is Reya," I say, my brow furrowing in confusion as I wonder who this Elsie is, but the name sparks a faint flicker of something in my mind, a distant memory trying to surface, but I can't quite grasp it.

Before I can ask anything else, the heavy wooden door to the room creaks open, and the same man and woman from the previous night enter. The man stands just inside the doorway, watching with an unsettlingly calm demeanour as the woman places another glass of water next to the empty one and then sets down a small bowl on the floor. When she puts the bowl on the ground, I can see its contents, which look very much like a thin, watery soup. She then picks up the empty glass and leaves the room without a word or a glance in my direction.

The man just stands there in the doorway, blocking most of the light, as I wonder if I am supposed to get up and approach him. But then the woman returns, carrying another glass of water and another bowl, and takes them over to my cellmate, who is trying to shrink back into the shadows, desperately trying to hide himself from our unwelcome guests.

Once the woman has left the room again, a large, wolf similar to the one from the previous night lumbers in, its massive form filling the doorway, when I can see it more clearly I see it is a dark grey with some light grey as well and some white in places and has strange orange tone around it's snout, at any other time seeing this wolf I would say it was very pretty, right now though all I can think is its one ugly son of a bitch, it looks like the same wolf as before.

"I'm going to give you a choice, little witch, do you understand?" the guy asks, his eyes boring into mine with a predatory gleam.

"What lovely choice are you going to offer me?" I ask, trying to mask the growing dread I'm feeling with a forced air of cockiness.

"Your first choice is that we allow you to contact your sisters and order them to leave the state immediately and never come back. And if they don't cause any trouble and turn out to be good little witches too, we might even let them live. You might even have the chance to return to them in the future, if everything goes according to our plan," he said with a sickeningly sweet smile that makes my blood chill.

"Would the second choice be that I can leave right now and promise never to come back and, oh, I don't know… kill you?" I retort with a sarcastic smirk.

"No chance of that happening, little witch. We will actually kill your sisters and that mutt of a dog you have. And we also know there's something else living in your home that smells strongly of the fae – something that was actually in your house even before you moved in. So, those are your two choices," he said, his smile never wavering, which only amplifies my anger, and I feel my skin start to tingle.

He has some bad news coming his way. Maya would undoubtedly do exactly as I order her to. I'm reasonably sure she would have before she met Duncan, anyway. But Freya? There is absolutely no way she will listen to me. She will stay and search for me until it ultimately gets her killed.

"They won't listen to me," I tell him, my voice flat and resigned.

The guy shrugs, a dismissive gesture that further fuels my rage. "Well, we gave you a choice," he said, as if he had just offered me a fantastic deal.

"I want to see whoever is actually in charge," I demand, my voice gaining a bit of strength despite my weakened state. "I know it isn't you."

"I hope you get the chance," he said, giving me a sleazy, knowing look that makes my stomach churn again. I instantly understand the implication behind his words, and a wave of revulsion washes over me.

"Are you sure you really want to see him?" he asks, his tone shifting slightly, as if he knows something that will make me desperately want to avoid such an encounter. The look he's giving me is genuinely unsettling.

I have to ask, "Why wouldn't I?"

"Because he is the one who killed your mother, of course," he says with the biggest, most triumphant grin on his face. Then, he strangely glances over at the gaunt man huddled in the corner before looking back at me.

My anger explodes inside of me, a raw, visceral feeling that is eerily similar to the intense aversion I feel whenever I get too close to Jacob. Something primal roars within me, a deep, instinctual surge that tells me my power isn't entirely gone. Maybe, just maybe, I can still find a way out of this after all.

"I'm guessing by the look on your face, you would love nothing more than to kill me right now, but we know how to deal with witches. We've been perfecting our methods for almost thirty years now. Anyway, the alpha doesn't want to see you right now, as he has other, more pressing matters to deal with," the guy said and glanced down at the wolf, his expression shifting to one of deep thought, as if he were genuinely considering something.

"I will return later to see if you have changed your mind," he said, then turned and walked out of the room. I desperately hope he forgets to lock the door; he doesn't exactly strike me as the sharpest tool in the shed. But unfortunately, I hear the same heavy scraping sound again as something large, undoubtedly a metal bar, is slid across the door from the outside. Then, just like the night before, all sound abruptly vanishes from the other side of the door after a distinct click of a lock turning follows.

I immediately looked over at my cellmate, and as soon as the door closed, I heard a sudden, frantic noise coming from his direction. He quickly grabbed the bowl of soup and began to gulp it down. Though he had a plastic spoon, he brought the bowl directly to his lips, tilting his head back to drain the contents. The action seemed almost natural for him, like someone accustomed to doing this. It made me realise just how little they must feed him; when he finally gets food, he can't help but consume it as quickly as possible. God, I'm really going to miss Maya's fantastic cooking.

I, on the other hand, don't immediately want to eat the soup. I fully expect it could be drugged, just like the water. But I'm starting to feel genuinely hungry, especially with the adrenaline and anger coursing through my veins. My heart rate is definitely higher than usual, meaning I'm rapidly burning through my energy reserves. If I hope to find any way to escape this prison, I know I need to eat something to keep my strength up.

So, with a sense of reluctance, I pick up the bowl. Unlike my cellmate, I use the flimsy plastic spoon they provided and start to slowly eat the soup, hoping I will notice any signs of being drugged before I finish it. That way, I can stop eating and hopefully reduce the amount of whatever they are giving me, while also providing my body with some much-needed fuel. I finish the thin soup, and thankfully, I don't feel any immediate effects, except that the persistent growling in my stomach has finally subsided.

Catherine M. Clark

Chapter 30

Scents and Silence

Ava

We finally convinced Freya and Maya to go and get some sleep, telling them there was nothing more we could do until the sun came up. We tried to persuade them to open their new business as usual, but Freya immediately responded, "No bloody way. I will be looking for my sister, just like she would be if I went missing."

So, they got Jenny to fix a sign on the door saying, 'Due to an electrical issue, we have to remain closed until it's fixed.' Jenny wanted to come back to the house afterwards to help with the search, but Sam wisely pointed out that if she closed her business as well, it would get tongues wagging around town, which in turn would likely cause the sheriff or even Jacob to come knocking on their door, looking for answers. With obvious reluctance, Jenny agreed to open as usual.

As soon as the first rays of sunlight began to peek over the horizon, the sisters were up, dressed, and practically bursting out the door, with Pickle and their dog, Beastie, I'm really not sure what to call it, hot on their heels, he however, looked like he wanted to tear someone limb from limb, so I made sure to keep a respectful distance from his formidable teeth.

Freya offered us Reya's bed if Rose and I wanted to get some sleep now that they were awake, but I felt a bit strange about sleeping in her bed, so Rose and I decided to stay on the *couch* for a quick nap. Sam, though, decided to claim the spare room, while Jenny, bless her heart, stated that she is going to use Reya's room during the night to keep Pickle and Beastie company until Reya returns.

We are pretty surprised at one point when we overhear Jenny talking to Pickle in a soothing voice, trying to comfort the distraught pixie. I can't help but ask her if Reya put the rune spell on her, too, but she surprises me again when she says no. Apparently, she has always been able to see Pickle, and it turns out witchcraft runs in her family, a few generations back, she explains. She also mentions she has no magical powers herself, as far as she knows, apart from the ability to perceive the paranormal world.

They then surprised us by informing us about another group of witches in town who want them to leave. They explained that Sandra, who they believe is the leader of these other witches, turned up at their business with two of her cronies and tried to curse them again during work yesterday. But this time, they didn't target them directly like they apparently did last time; instead, they focused their efforts on the building itself.

They explained that Reya put a protection rune, the same one Reya showed us, on the building, which visibly lit up when Freya went to check after she felt slight tremors while she saw Sandra and her cronies chanting on the sidewalk outside. Freya said the women stormed off in a huff when nothing happened, and she planned to tell Reya all about it when she got home so Reya wouldn't go and do anything stupid on her own in retaliation.

After we get Reya back, I'm so going to get her to put that

protection rune on me. It can definitely come in handy if we have to go up against other witches. We very well might have to, considering that Sandra wants the Harpers gone so she can get her hands on this property, whatever its significance might be to her. So, even though we might have ruled out the demons as Reya's captors, we can't rule out these other witches just yet, but we have no real evidence to warrant going to question them, nor do we have any protection against them if they are responsible.

So, it's decided that Sam will head out after his nap and stake out Sandra's known locations to see if she is showing any signs of having a prisoner, especially considering Reya has been missing not long after Sandra tried to curse the sisters' new business.

After Rose and I take a short, much-needed nap on the *couch*, we join the sisters in searching the surrounding area. They promised not to venture outside their protection barrier until we join them, just in case the shifters decide to launch another attack.

When we join them, we find Maya standing by the barn, completely mesmerised by the four horses Reya brought home. They really are truly stunning, and I feel a pang of jealousy. Maybe they might let me ride one of them when this is over.

As I watch Maya gazing at the horses, one of them strolls over to her and gently rests its head against her chest. Maya, in turn, rests her head against the horse's forehead in return. They stay like that for less than a minute, a silent connection passing between them, and then the horse slowly walks off and rejoins the other horses in the paddock. It's such a strange and touching sight to witness.

When I look away, I find Freya doing the same with another of the horses. The horse nuzzles against her, and Freya embraces the horse, wrapping her arms around its neck. I look for the other two horses to see what they are doing and find one grazing in the field, but the fourth is missing. As I look for it, I find it in the distance, north of us, staring in the same direction.

I head over to the horse because I'm worried about it being separated from the others. When I reach it, the horse turns its head to look at me and somehow looks... sad. There's no logical way it can possibly know where Reya's been taken; it's just a horse, after all. I really wish I could talk to horses so I could ask her why she looks so mournful and if she knows anything about Reya's sudden disappearance, or where she might be now.

After I leave the horse, I rejoin the others and, as a group, hoping to pick up any signs of where Reya has been taken, we head north. Rose leads us to the spot just outside the protection barrier where she lost Reya's scent. We spread out in a loose line and searched for anything to help us find her.

As we search, Rose explains to us again how incredibly strange it is that there is a complete void of all scents heading north, as if even the natural smells of the nearby woods and the usual smells of the field have been inexplicably erased.

However, she notes that since her initial search earlier that morning, the void is starting to dissipate, and the familiar scents of nature are slowly returning. Rose also mentions that before the void abruptly stops, she hasn't been able to pick up on anything out of place; the area is even devoid of the scents of the other shifters, which is particularly odd considering the area just outside the barrier reeks of them, according to her heightened senses.

As we continue heading north, we pair up. I stick close to Freya, while Rose stays with Maya. Pickle, ever the intrepid explorer, rides comfortably on the dog's back as they join the search effort. Pickle told me about some of her struggles to survive when she first came to our world and all the exploring she did to try and find a safe place to hide while also trying to find others from her world, well, the ones that don't want her dead.

We spend most of the day searching and finding absolutely nothing of significance. We regroup and start to return to the house, hungry and exhausted. Maya looks like she is on the verge of a breakdown as we walk. Pickle must have sensed her distress because she suddenly flies over, landing gently on Maya's shoulder, and starts to whisper something in her ear. Whatever Pickle said only seems to make the tears start to fall faster.

"I don't understand?" Rose says, looking around in confusion as we cross back through the protection barrier.

"What don't you understand?" I ask, equally perplexed by her comment.

"The entire area reeks of wolves, but I didn't pick up on even a single one watching us. We were all completely exposed out there, and I didn't detect even the faintest fresh scent of a shifter. It's like they all just vanished from the area," Rose said, giving me a pointed look. I understand what she's getting at immediately.

"That's good, isn't it? Maybe they have finally given up on us, or perhaps the demons are keeping them away," Maya said, looking utterly bewildered as she wipes her now bloodshot eyes.

"Sis, I think Rose is trying to say that they've probably left because they have what they want, so there's no longer any need for them to keep watch over us," Freya said, her voice tight with barely suppressed fury. "If they have hurt her, I swear I will hunt down every single wolf on this entire planet until they are all extinct," she vows through gritted teeth, her eyes blazing with protective rage.

"We might have our answer as to who has taken Reya. If Sam returns and states that he saw no sign of Sandra being involved, we will know exactly who we are hunting for. We might have to wait until Luca returns before we can actually go after them, though," Rose states, her words immediately sparking a chorus of protests from the sisters.

"I will not wait!" Freya declares, her voice filled with unwavering determination. "If I find even the slightest way to track down these wolves, then I will do absolutely whatever it takes to get my sister back." Her conviction is so firm that I have no doubt she means every single word. Even Maya and Pickle nod in agreement, and their dog lets out a low growl that I take as its form of solidarity.

"Freya, if you go after them unprepared, you are putting your own life at serious risk. Shifters are incredibly deadly," I say, pleading with her to think rationally before acting impulsively.

"Ava, I don't care!" Freya exclaims, her voice rising in desperation. "I'm happy to die to save Reya. She has always been the strong one, the one who got us through all our tough times. Now it's our turn to get her through this situation. You can either help us or stand aside. I honestly don't care!" Freya's fierce gaze locks with mine, a look that typically makes me bristle and immediately go on the defensive, as if I were facing an enemy.

I'm just incredibly grateful that Freya is on our side, as I have no idea if I can take on a determined witch. After Freya's emotional outburst, we all settle down in the living room to wait for Sam to return and see if he has gathered any news that might shed some light on Reya's disappearance. While we wait, Freya orders some food from the local diner as Maya isn't up for cooking. Who can blame her?

During this tense moment of quiet anticipation, I turn to Rose and ask, a strange thought nagging at the back of my mind, "Rose, those horses out back… do they smell like normal horses to you?"

Rose looks at me strangely, thinking I might be losing my mind. "Of course they do. Why would you even ask such a bizarre question?"

I can't help but frown, a flicker of unease settling in my stomach as I contemplate the odd behaviour I witnessed earlier with the horse. Whenever I'm deep in thought, I unconsciously draw up one side of my mouth in a pensive expression, a habit Rose has come to recognise.

"What is it?" she asks, her sharp eyes noticing my subtle change in expression.

"I saw one of the horses acting really strange just before we headed out to try and follow Reya's trail. It was standing there staring intently to the north, almost like it knew exactly where she had been taken. Or maybe it was just a coincidence and I'm starting to see things that aren't really there," I say with a slight, self-deprecating chuckle at the ridiculousness of my thoughts.

"I'm sure it's just a coincidence, but I will definitely check them out more closely next time we head out," she said. I notice her subtly sniffing the air as she glances in the general direction of where the horses would be, even though she can't physically see them from inside the house. I'm sure she can still pick up their scent from here, although it would likely be faint, considering all the other strong scents Rose has mentioned being present.

I can't help but look in the same direction as Rose does. As I do, I catch a fleeting glimpse of movement from a shadow near the top of the stairs, immediately telling me that someone is upstairs. That shouldn't be possible, as we are all downstairs, except for Reya and Sam. "Who's upstairs?" I ask, my voice sharp with alarm as I shoot to a standing position, my hand instinctively reaching for one of the knives concealed on my side in its sheath.

Everyone else in the room immediately shoots to their feet as well, their eyes fixing on the staircase. "I didn't see anything," Rose states, her gaze flickering between the stairs and me, her senses clearly not picking up what I'd seen.

"What exactly did you see?" Freya asks, her voice laced with concern.

"I saw a shadow move across the stairs coming from upstairs like someone was standing up there, then walked off," I explain to everyone, my eyes still glued to the top of the stairs. As soon as the words left my lips, the dog suddenly leapt over the back of the *couch* and bounded towards the stairs, letting out a low, menacing growl as it disappeared from view. This unexpected action causes Pickle to take off after him, flying with a surprising burst of speed. I'm momentarily mesmerised by the shimmering trail she leaves behind as she flies, a faint, watery distortion hanging in the air for a few seconds before slowly vanishing.

    I'm snapped out of my daze when I see Rose quickly follow after the dog and Pickle, her movements fluid and silent. At the exact moment, Maya calls out Reya's name, her voice filling with a desperate hope that her sister has somehow miraculously returned. Just after Rose vanishes from view at the top of the stairs, a deep, guttural growl laced with menace echoes through the house. I know that growl anywhere; it's Rose.

    It takes the rest of us a little longer to get upstairs compared to Rose's lightning-fast ascent. I manage to position myself slightly ahead of the sisters, so I'm the first to see what's happening. What I see initially confuses me. Rose is standing defensively, facing off with the sisters' dog, who is now growling fiercely at something I can't see. Then, the dog moves to the side, and I see it – a distinct, shadowy figure crouching down behind the dog like it had been conversing with the dog. It has piercing purple eyes that glow with an eerie light, and those eyes are currently glaring intently at Rose.

    "Rose, it's okay. They are just protecting Reya's shadow," I say reassuringly. At the same time, I notice Pickle hovering in the air next to the shadow, her tiny fists planted firmly on her hips, also staring down at Rose with an indignant expression. Of course, Rose can't see her either. *I need to persuade Rose to get this rune thing done on her, too; it will make things so much easier.*

    Rose visibly relaxes, her shoulders dropping slightly before she asks, her voice still a bit tense, "Are you absolutely sure it's Reya's shadow and not one of those nasty things from Jackson?"

"I'm positive," Freya said, stepping forward slightly. "It's Seraphina, I promise you," she tacks on with a reassuring nod.

"How can you tell?" Rose asks, her curiosity piqued.

"The eye colour is exactly the same as Reya's original firepower," Freya explains, also visibly relaxing now that she knows who it is. Behind her, however, I see Maya's face fall, her expression shifting to one of complete sadness. She clearly got her hopes up too much that Reya had returned while we were looking for her.

"You really should let Freya put that rune spell on you, Rose. Then you will be able to see everything," I say, hoping to convince her finally. But I immediately regret my words when I see the sharp, almost hostile look Rose shoots my way, so I offer her a placating shrug.

Freya then turns to Rose, saying, "You really should let me do it, Rose. You might go up against an enemy you can't see, like these demons, who can easily take you out. Sometimes, though, I wish I couldn't see everything. I wish I were just a normal human girl." Freya pauses for a moment, a wistful expression on her face, before continuing, "But then these thoughts always disappear the moment I use my powers to make my plants grow strong." She trails off, her gaze distant.

I suddenly have an idea. "If Seraphina is Reya's shadow, does she know how to find her?" I ask, turning to Freya, hope surging within me.

"No idea," Freya said, her voice deflated. "We have one major issue. We can't hear her as only Reya can hear her thoughts." Her words dash my hopes, and my body suddenly feels like it's been drained of all its energy.

"Why is that?" Rose asks, looking genuinely confused.

"No idea. Reya thinks it might be because she created her, or it's because Seraphina has to drink her blood to survive, but she isn't really sure, we are new to all this," Freya explains, shrugging helplessly.

I then remember something from the attack, seeing that girl,

Kracis, I think was her name, and what Reya told us. "It's to do with the blood, that shade, the girl. She had to drink Reya's blood so she could talk to her, too." I say, wondering if Rose will let me be a guinea pig and let Seraphina drink my blood to find out.

"Don't even think about it," Rose immediately says.

"Someone needs to try," I retort.

"Don't bother," Freya tells us. "She told me that she is unique, and if she drinks someone else's blood, it could negatively affect her." Her shoulders slump in defeat, too.

I try talking to her anyway. As I turn, I see Pickle still hovering protectively in front of Seraphina, looking like her own tiny, determined bodyguard. "Seraphina, do you know where Reya is? We think the wolf shifters might have taken her," I ask, my voice filled with earnest hope that she will somehow be able to answer and help us.

As soon as I speak her name, her intense purple eyes snap in my direction, and shadowy wings unfurl from her back. Though I can't quite discern how, she looks… pissed. I still wonder why Reya's shadow has wings when the shades we fought don't. Seraphina then begins to pace back and forth across the wall.

"What's going on?" Rose asks, her voice laced with frustration.

"She's pacing, just like Reya does when she has something important on her mind," Maya observes, her eyes intent on the shadow's movements.

Then, suddenly, Seraphina rises into the air, floating away from the wall she was on. Then moves towards us, becoming a three-dimensional shadow, just like I've seen when she was fighting the shades. She beats her wings with a newfound urgency, then shoots directly towards us, flying low over our heads and causing us all to instinctively duck, except Rose, of course and gives us all a look of, *'What the hell are you all doing?'*

Seraphina's sudden action makes Pickle spin mid-air, creating a shimmering distortion around her, like she's standing under a sparkling waterfall.

Catherine M. Clark

Chapter 31

The Hunter and the Hunted

Seraphina vanishes down the stairs and out of sight. We all race back downstairs, tripping over ourselves in our haste to keep track of where she is going. Maya, being the last one up, is the first one down. "She went out back," she said breathlessly as we reached the bottom of the stairs. However, before we can get out the back door, there is a knock at the front door.

We all freeze and look towards it. No one wants to move, so Rose takes charge and heads for the door. When she opens the door, we see a kid with bags of our ordered food. Immediately, there is a chorus of extinguished breaths being let out. Rose takes the bags of food, gives the kid a tip, and then closes the door.

Before Rose can put the food on the kitchen table, the rest of us scramble out the back door to try and catch up with Seraphina. Once we are all outside, we find Seraphina standing perfectly still, staring intently into the distance.

She abruptly turns and faces the horses, which immediately brings back my earlier thoughts about one of the horses' strange behaviour. I wonder if Seraphina heard what I said about one of them when she was hovering at the top of the stairs. Seraphina then floats down to the ground and turns to face us, her gaze dropping to the dog as he instinctively moves to position himself protectively between us and her. Seraphina then approaches the dog slowly, gently places her hand on the top of his head and follows that by crouching down until she is at eye level with him. The dog then starts shaking his head back and forth, almost as if he is answering a question. He then turns his head and faces Rose as she appears behind us when she walks out the back door, causing all of us to turn and look at her, too. "Why are you all staring at me?" Rose asks, suspicion clouding her eyes as she joins us and looks at each of us in turn.

"Clearly, Seraphina and Beastie can communicate, and something made him look at you, so naturally, we all looked at you," Freya said with a knowing smirk.

"Why me?" Rose asks, her voice laced with irritation. "Why is it so interested in me?" Rose then said, using one of her trademark angry tones. I also don't particularly appreciate her referring to Seraphina as 'it.'

"We don't know, Rose. All we know is that she placed her hand on his head, he shook his head, and then immediately turned to face you. You really do need to get Freya to put that rune on you, so we don't have to waste valuable time constantly explaining things to you," Maya said, sounding angry herself as she shoots Rose a dirty look.

"Don't give me that look, Maya. And to be honest, I still don't trust you enough to let you put something on me that might have some hidden, unforeseen consequences," Rose retorts, giving Maya an equally sharp look back.

"Hey!" I interject, gently squeezing Rose's arm, hoping she will stop being so unnecessarily rude.

"What!" Rose snaps, turning her head to look at me, her eyes flashing.

"There's absolutely no need to be rude, Rose. We are all on the same side here. You really need to start trusting my ability to read people. I trust them implicitly. If you are only here because of me, please feel free to leave and go back to the motel," I say, ensuring Rose knows I'm being completely serious with the unwavering look I give her.

"Are you serious?" Rose asks, her voice filled with genuine surprise.

"Very," is all I say in response, turning my attention back to see if Seraphina and the dog are doing anything else. All they are doing, however, is looking intently at me, making me wonder what I've done.

When we were all facing Seraphina again, she suddenly took off into the air. This time, she flies directly towards the horses. When she lands next to one, just like she did with the dog, she rests a hand on the head of the horse—the magnificent white horse, which I'm sure is the same one I was worried about earlier today.

Moments later, Seraphina turns and flies back towards us, surprising us all. The horse also starts to walk slowly towards us. When they both reach us, Seraphina points a shadowy finger at Rose and then at the approaching horse. The horse, as if understanding her silent command, walks right up to Rose, who, of course, can only perceive the horse's actions and looks at it with utter confusion. "Seraphina seems to want you to get on the horse," Freya said, stating the obvious.

"You what? Absolutely not. I am not getting on that horse," Rose said, shaking her head vehemently in defiance. Just then, the dog takes her completely by surprise. He quickly moves in behind her and shoves his head into her lower back, effectively pushing her forward towards the waiting horse. Rose stumbles, starts to growl, and digs her feet into the ground, stopping all movement. This only causes him to let out a low growl of his own and then attempt to shove her again even harder.

"Rose, I think… I think I've actually worked out what is going on here," Freya said, a look of sudden understanding dawning on her face.

"And what exactly do you think is going on, Freya? Because I am telling you right now, I'm not riding that horse," Rose says as she continues to fight against the dog and increases her growls. She then shocks me when I see her hands turn into claws.

"Rose, don't you dare!" I say, not believing what I'm seeing.

"Get it to stop then," Rose growls at me.

"Hey! Stop this right now, we have more important things to worry about, if you can't play nice Rose I agree you should leave, except I think what Beastie is actually trying to do is get you to go with Seraphina and the horse to rescue Reya," Freya says with so much anger her face is starting to turn red, I don't blame her, then she confirms what I've been wondering, "I think what Ava witnessed earlier today with regard to Reya's horse, I… and don't ask how I know this because it's all speculation, I think Reya's horse knows how to find her."

"I was thinking the same, but thought if I said it, you would all think I'm crazy," I say, while I start to feel excited that we might have a chance of finding Reya.

"Ever since we found out who we really are, crazy has been our life," Freya said with a cocky smile.

The dog has stopped trying to push Rose but he's still giving Rose a look I'm guessing means move your arse. His mouth is slightly open, revealing his teeth; I double-take because the teeth I'm seeing aren't regular dog teeth; they are the sharp razor teeth I saw when he changed into his hellhound form when we were attacked. "Are you two being serious? How can a horse track Reya when I can't?" Rose said, looking offended.

"I think Reya and her horse have a connection," Freya says.

"Why do you think that?" I ask, intrigued.

"Because I'm sure I have a connection with my horse," Freya said, looking a little sheepish.

"Aren't the horses Reya's?" I ask.

"Well, yeah….but since I met the horses, I felt drawn to one of them, and the same horse always comes to me," Freya said, looking more confident about what she's telling us.

I turn to Seraphina and ask, "Do you want Rose to go with you and the horse to rescue Reya?"

She nods her head without hesitation, so I turn to Rose and say, "Yep, she wants you to go with them to find Reya." The dog then gives Rose another shove. Clearly, he wants Rose to get moving. I'm in agreement, as we can't waste time.

"If it's shifters, they will smell me coming from a mile away," Rose says stubbornly.

"Please, Rose, we desperately need Reya back. Are you seriously going just to stand here and let the shifters do whatever they plan to do with her?" Freya asks.

I then look at Seraphina, taking a long shot, and ask, "Seraphina, are you and the horse able to lead Rose in a way so that she isn't downwind, so the shifters can't detect her coming?" I'm genuinely surprised when it looks like she is nodding in response. It's starting to get dark, making it a little tricky to tell, but the subtle up and down movement of her glowing purple eyes indicates a clear 'yes.'

I quickly relayed this to Rose. "Seraphina said that she and the horse can lead you in a way so that the shifters won't be able to detect you. So please, Rose, just go. For me."

Freya then turns to Rose, her expression softening with genuine concern. "Please bring our sister home if you can, Rose. But don't put yourself at unnecessary risk if there are too many of them." I really like Freya for saying that; it makes me like her even more.

"I will certainly try my best, if that is truly where this horse takes me," Rose said as she unclips her bra, a simple action that somehow manages to spark a flicker of jealousy within me as Freya watches with an almost clinical interest.

Rose starts to turn to clearly head for the house. As she starts to walk off while pulling her bra out from under her top, she says stubbornly, "Fine, but I'm not riding the horse." I can't help but smile because I never thought Seraphina wanted her to ride the horse. I think she just wanted her to follow.

As Rose walks off, I can see it doesn't go down well with Freya, but it does with me. I had started to feel a pang of jealousy when I thought she was going to shift in front of Freya. Then I hear Freya mutter, "Damn, I was hoping to see her shift."

"Where are you going? Our sister is in danger," Maya says, balling her hands into fists at her side, giving Rose an angry, frustrated look.

"I need to strip so I can shift. I will be able to keep up with the horse then. Is that okay with you?" Rose snaps at Maya. Again, Rose's attitude gets on my nerves.

Maya doesn't respond, so Rose says, "Thought so." She then enters the house. I shake my head at her, we are *so* having words back at the motel.

Rose left the rear door open, and moments later, her beautiful panther form appears and heads straight for me. When she reaches me, she pushes against my body. I take the opportunity to whisper in her ear as I run my hands over her head, "Check your attitude, or we will be getting separate rooms." Rose snaps her head so she can look me straight in the eyes, and her eyes widen in surprise, but then she lowers her head and strides over to the horse. "Good luck," I call out.

Everyone else calls out similar statements, "Be safe, give them hell." But it's Pickle's words that tug on my heartstrings the most. "Please bring my Reya back. I can't live without her."

As they start to head off, Beastie appears agitated and starts pacing. It seems he wants to accompany Seraphina to rescue Reya. Seraphina likely instructed him to stay behind to protect Freya and Maya, as indicated by his looks towards the sisters and then back at Seraphina. Eventually, his posture relaxes, suggesting he understands the reason for staying behind.

As soon as Rose starts to head in Seraphina's and the horse's direction, they immediately turn and begin racing off, heading north with the singular focus on following the earlier trail Rose indicated to us. Rose gives me a reassuring glance before seamlessly falling into a powerful, four-legged run, effortlessly chasing after the horse, which is now thundering across the field at full speed. I am mesmerised as Rose runs on all fours, her panther form looking absolutely magnificent. I haven't been able to see her many times in this form so far, but every time I do, I think I fall in love with her even more, *except when she is embarrassing herself.*

We all stood there watching them leave, even until we could no longer see them, as they disappeared into another patch of woods in the distance. No one seemed ready to move until a few stomachs began to growl, expressing their discontent. This finally broke the tension in the air, the worried gazes directed northward. We then headed back into the house to eat the food we had ordered, which might be cold by now.

As I step back through the back door, a phone starts to ring. Mine is safely tucked in my front pocket and isn't vibrating, as I habitually keep it on silent. The problem, however, is that the ringing is definitely coming from me, which means it has to be Rose's phone ringing, as I had picked up her clothes off the floor as I entered the house. I laid Rose's clothes down on the back of one of the armchairs and quickly rooted around in the pockets for her phone. When I finally locate it, I see Luca's name on the screen. I quickly answer it before he's disconnected.

"Hey Luca, it's Ava."

"Where's Rose?" he asks immediately, his voice sharp with concern.

I explain the situation as quickly and concisely as possible, hoping he won't be too angry that I've technically pressured Rose into going. As I'm talking, I hear Maya walk into the house, saying with a determined tone, "I'm going to start making Reya's favourite chicken lasagna for when she gets home."

Freya, curious, sees that I'm on the phone and approaches me, but says, "Maya, you need to eat first." She clearly ignores this as I watch, and Freya shakes her head at her and grabs the bags of food as I stand next to the kitchen table. She mouths to me, "Who is it?"

I place my hand over the phone's speaker and mouth back, "Luca." She nods in understanding and listens intently as I continue to explain the situation to Luca, while she sorts the food out and passes me the burger and fries I wanted.

When I've caught Luca up on everything, he says in frustration, "Fuck!" Then I realised it wasn't very considerate to talk about Reya while her sister could only hear one side of the conversation, so I put my phone on speaker, even though I knew Luca would disapprove.

"Can you trust this shadow of Reya's? She has to be a black witch," Luca said, his tone cautious.

"I do trust her, Luca. Even Rose has started to come around." Which causes Freya to snort. I then tell him about Rose's initial inability to get past the barrier around the house, but when she changed her mindset, she can now move freely through it. Then I ask, "Have you managed to find your pack members yet?"

"I have. They were delayed because a tracker was on their tail. They managed to deal with him, and now we are trying to find a safe place for them to go to," Luca explains, a hint of relief in his voice.

"I'm so glad you found them. Are they all okay?" I ask as worry washes over me about what he might say.

"A few minor injuries, nothing too serious to worry about. It sounds like you and Rose were injured, though," Luca said, his own voice tinged with worry.

"We weren't too badly hurt. I've definitely had worse." Then, a realisation struck me. "Actually, for some reason, I've been feeling much better since we got here." I look down at my arm and notice for the first time since our arrival that the cuts on my arms now look pink and significantly healed, like they have had a few days of recovery.

"That would be the ward around our property. It speeds up the healing process," Freya explains casually. It now makes perfect sense what Reya hinted at when she said it would help if we came inside.

"Well, that's incredibly handy," I say, a little stunned that something like that actually exists and immediately wondering if they can somehow put a similar ward on our car. Freya must have been reading my mind.

"It's a very special ward that protects the entire land," Freya clarifies.

"That does sound very handy indeed," Luca echoes, having heard everything Freya said with the phone on speaker.

"With how badly Reya gets injured from all the attacks, we absolutely need it," Freya said, making me wonder just how often they are actually attacked. It makes a certain sense, though, considering how many good paranormals have been systematically killed off over the years, from what Rose and Luca told me.

"Sounds like your sister is incredibly tough," Luca said, sounding genuinely impressed for the first time when it comes to Reya. I half-expected him to say something like, 'Well, most black witches are attacked often,' so I can't help but mentally chuckle to myself at the thought.

Freya then says something that catches me off guard. "Why don't you bring your pack members here until you can find somewhere else for them to go? We have this strong barrier, so they won't be able to be attacked as long as they stay within its boundaries."

It's an intriguing and surprisingly generous proposal, but Luca immediately shuts it down. "I don't think that's a very good idea. It's not exactly safe there right now, either, is it?"

"True," Freya concedes, "But as I said, we have the barrier. So far, no one has been able to get past it since we put it up about a month ago. Also, there is definitely strength in numbers," making another very valid point.

Luca is silent for a moment, I'm guessing, considering her offer. Then, he says, his tone shifting slightly, "Can I talk to you in private for a moment, please, Ava?"

"Sure," I say, then quickly turn off the speakerphone and mouth '*Sorry*' to Freya before heading for the back door, wanting to give Luca the privacy he requests.

Once I'm outside and far enough away so that no one inside can possibly overhear me, I say, "Okay, we're good. You can talk freely now."

"Tell me honestly, Ava, what do you really think?"

"Luca, I genuinely believe they are good people and that they are on our side. Reya has some truly amazing abilities; we haven't had a proper chance to catch you up on everything yet, but Sam allowed Reya to put this rune thing on his arm, and now he can see everything, just like my ring allows me to see."

"That's his choice, Ava. I still don't want you or Rose letting them do anything like that to either of you," he said, his tone firm, making me cringe inwardly. I kind of forgot that by being with Rose, I have essentially agreed to be part of his pack, and now I have to run things past him before making decisions. I'm so used to just deciding things in the moment. No wonder Rose was so resistant earlier, but I'm still glad she was stuck behind the barrier when Reya offered to help me and make my sword so fucking cool and deadly.

I know I have to tell Luca about it, though, for some reason, I have a small amount of fear about actually doing it, going up against terrorists, drug and gun smugglers, no problem, so why am I worried about telling Luca?

"I completely agree, Luca. Also…" I start to say, thinking it's best to get it over with, but again, I hesitate, the words catching in my throat.

"What is it, Ava? What did you let them do to you?" Luca asks, his tone sharp and concerned, clearly sensing my hesitation.

"You know how Papa Legba told me he would try to find a weapon to help me? Well, he also told Reya to help me with it. And well… she came up with this great idea," I explain, bracing myself for his reaction.

"And what exactly did you allow her to do then, Ava, with regard to this so-called '*great idea*'?" Luca asks, his voice now laced with annoyance. Then, he adds pointedly, "I wouldn't have permitted you to do this without you running it past me first." I knew he was going to bring that up.

"I know, Luca, I know. This whole situation is still very new to me, I'm sorry. I'm just so used to making decisions on the fly. Anyway, Reya added her fire ability to my sword. Now, she says it will kill almost anything. She added some protection to it so it wouldn't accidentally hurt me, you, or Rose," I say, hoping that last bit of information will help Luca realise Reya's intentions are good.

Luca is silent for a long moment. Then, he asks a very strange question. "What colour is her fire, Ava?"

"Erm… well, she actually has two different colours. She explained that one is weaker than the other," I start to say, a knot of worry tightening in my stomach as I realise the fire she has added to my sword is distinctly black. He already suspects she's a black witch, so this revelation can potentially add more fuel to that particular fire.

"What colour, Ava?" Luca demands, his voice rising slightly.

"She has purple… and black. She added the black fire magic to my sword." I confess, I instinctively hold my phone slightly away from my ear, half-expecting him to shout at me.

"BLOODY HELL, AVA!" Luca exclaims, his voice booming through the phone, before he manages to bring his tone back down to a slightly more normal level. "As far as I know, there is only one form of black fire, and it hasn't been seen for hundreds of years!"

I honestly didn't know what else to say, so I said a simple, "And?"

"Black fire is commonly known as hell-fire, Ava, and it's a daemon ability," he said, his pronunciation of '*demon*' sounding slightly unusual.

"Did you mean to say demon?" I ask, wondering if I'm hearing things or if something is wrong with our connection that makes what he said sound off.

"No, Ava, I meant daemon. Remember all those stories I told you about the different sides of good and evil? The side of evil was known as daemons, and they were the ones who originally created the demons, naming them after themselves," he explains, finally jogging my somewhat hazy memories. I've had a lot to learn, so he can't blame me for forgetting some of it.

"Oh yeah," I say, remembering the details of his paranormal lore. "Okay, but I still don't really see the big issue. In those stories, you mentioned that the different sides eventually started to mix, so some daemons are actually on the side of good now." I repeat to him what he told me, hoping to point out that he is a bit of a hypocrite if he suddenly declares that all daemons are inherently evil.

Luca is silent again for a moment, seemingly considering my point. "Yes, I did say that, didn't I? But it further confirms that she is a black witch, perhaps a different type of black witch. I've never actually heard of a daemon witch before. Anyway, let's get back to the subject at hand. What do you honestly think of Freya's idea about bringing my pack there?"

I think about it seriously for a moment, weighing the pros and cons, and then say truthfully, "Luca, I actually think it's a really good idea. The barrier here really does seem to work incredibly well, so your pack members will be safe for now. I honestly can't think of a safer place for them to be right now until you manage to figure out a more permanent location. There is plenty of land here for them to camp out on, and they would have access to a proper bathroom and a fully equipped kitchen," I add with a slight chuckle at the end, thinking about the relative luxury of indoor plumbing compared to their current situation.

"I will definitely consider everything you have said and discuss it with Elijah and the others. I will let you know what we decide. I'd better go for now. I sincerely hope Rose manages to find Reya and returns safely," Luca said, his tone carrying a subtle warning that tells me he will be highly displeased if anything happens to Rose.

After I hung up the phone, I couldn't stop thinking about what Luca had just told me about Reya and the implications of her using hell-fire. I wonder if I should tell Freya about it. From everything the sisters have told us, they know next to nothing about being witches, except for a few things they have gleaned from an old book their mother left them and from their own trial and error.

I re-enter the house and see Maya busily gathering pans and ingredients on the kitchen counter, while Freya is patiently waiting for me at the kitchen table, eating her food. Beastie is spread out over one of the armchairs with Pickle sitting on top of him, eating pieces of fruit from a bowl in her lap while they watch what seems to be *'The Fifth Element'* on television.

As I near the kitchen, I smell fresh blood; when I look around, I see two bowls near the kitchen, one of which has drops of blood running down the side. I can't help but wrinkle my nose at the sight and remember that Beastie has to drink fresh blood instead of water. I'm then distracted as two fox cubs and the toy panther playfully chase each other in front of the *couch*. The cubs' mother is curled up asleep on one of the armchairs, but even in her slumber, she looks strangely sad.

"What did he decide?" Freya asks as soon as I reach her at the table.

"He said he would let me know after he discusses it with the others," I tell her, not wanting to reveal the specifics of our conversation just yet. I then sit and plan to eat my cold food, but when I grab a few fries, they are hot. *Freya must have nuked my food for me.*

"Okay. You should probably message Sam and tell him to come back to the house. I honestly don't think Sandra is involved in Reya's disappearance," Freya said, and I have to admit, she is probably right. It's pointless for Sam to stay out there alone now that it's getting dark. So, I pull out my phone and sent a quick text message to Sam, telling him to return.

"Freya, can I talk to you for a moment? In private?" I ask, gesturing towards the *couch*, hoping Pickle and Beastie are too distracted to listen.

She frowns slightly but follows me over to the *couch* and sits beside me after I've sat down. Then she asks, her gaze questioning, "What's up, Ava?"

"Luca just told me something, and I'm not entirely sure how Maya will take it," I say, glancing over to Maya quickly to ensure she isn't eavesdropping on our conversation.

"Just hit me with it, Ava," is all Freya says, her expression serious.

Chapter 32

Truths and Consequences

I try to explain to Freya, "Well, I actually have two things I need to tell you. One is what your sister did to my sword, and the other..." Freya's eyes widen as she interrupts me, her voice filling with sudden urgency.

"What? Wait a second! What did my sister do to your sword?" she demands, leaning forward with an intense look.

"Oh, crap! It happened just before the attack. She took my sword after she said she had this great idea, and she bonded her power of fire to it, with the ability to turn it off and on. She also made it so it couldn't hurt any of you," I say quickly, hoping Freya isn't too upset with what Reya has done, as she seems just as fiercely protective of her sisters as Luca is of his pack.

Except that Freya takes me completely by surprise with her enthusiastic reply. "Really! That sounds incredibly cool! I can't wait to see it in action."

"Anyway," I continue, slightly taken aback by her reaction, "after I told Luca about the sword and after his... little freak out, he tells me something about your sister's power of black fire. He said there is only one type like that, and it hasn't been seen for hundreds of years, maybe even longer," I say, observing her reaction.

"Okay," she says slowly, considering what I have just said. "But why is this important exactly?"

"Not entirely sure that it is," I admit, "but I thought you should probably know what he said, especially since you are still learning about yourselves and your abilities. This information might be helpful in some way. Apparently, black fire is known as hell-fire and is… a daemon ability," I hesitantly say, bracing myself for the worst kind of reaction.

Freya's eyes widen again, this time with concern. "Damn it, Ava, please don't tell Reya it's a demon ability! She's already paranoid that she's part demon because of some of her abilities, although she does technically have a small bit of demon in her now after her accidental bond with Beastie," Freya says, shocking me more than I expect and in a way I never saw coming.

"What?" I exclaim, my eyebrows shooting up. "What do you mean she has a small piece of a demon in her now?" I immediately wonder what Rose and Luca will do if they ever find out about that little tidbit.

"Well crap! It was a complete accident," Freya explains, waving her hand dismissively like it's nothing. "She accidentally bonded herself with Beastie while putting protection wards on our café, apparently, it caused a small piece of themselves to be transferred to each other. Beastie actually got a pretty cool ability out of it; he can now shift his appearance all by himself. We used to have to glamour him to hide his true hellhound form, which now seems like it was a waste of time as Sam couldn't see the hellhounds anyway."

"Okay," I say slowly, trying to process this new information. "That actually sounds like a good thing for Beastie. But what did Reya get out of this accidental bonding?" I ask, genuinely curious and slightly worried about what Luca and Rose will do if they find out.

"We're honestly not entirely sure yet," Freya admits with a shrug. "So far, nothing seems to have changed for her as far as we can tell."

"Okay," I say. "Anyway, I didn't actually say demon. I said

daemon."

Freya's eyes light up with recognition. "Oh! Right, daemons! Reya has actually told us a little bit about them and the original gods of darkness and death. They were known as the daemon gods, and apparently, all paranormal beings are descended from those four original gods, as far as anyone knows," Freya says, surprising me yet again with her knowledge.

"I thought you said you knew next to nothing about all this?" I question, raising an eyebrow.

"Well, Papa Legba left a diary for Reya to find at some random estate sale she went to a while back. Reya spent weeks painstakingly translating it because it was all written in Latin. She actually only told us the rest of the really juicy stuff a few days ago because she was worried about how Maya would take it, especially the part about where we all technically descended from and the fact that all paranormal beings are technically related to each other in some way. Reya worries way too much and is far too overprotective of us," Freya says with a slight, fond smile. Again, though, she completely surprises me with what she has just revealed, as Luca had never mentioned anything about all paranormal beings being distantly related.

"I have definitely noticed that about Reya. Her overprotectiveness can be a good thing, as long as she doesn't take it too far," I comment.

"I'm afraid my sister is exactly the type to take it way too far. I try my best to keep an eye on her and keep her in check, but I obviously can't watch her every single second of the day," Freya says, her face falling slightly, a hint of sadness in her eyes as if Reya might have already done something drastic.

"Well, it's definitely good to find out more about yourselves and your heritage," I say, trying to lighten the mood.

"We actually discovered that I'm part Fae, and Maya is part

angel, not too long ago. Well, we strongly believe so anyway," Freya says, casually dropping another bombshell that completely shocks the hell out of me once again, causing Freya to burst out laughing at my clearly unhidden reaction this time.

"Are you serious? If you keep dropping bombshells, my mind might explode," I say, my eyes widening as I look over at Maya, who's still diligently preparing the lasagna, completely oblivious to our conversation. I wonder what Maya has done to convince them she is part angel.

"We were a little wary about telling you absolutely everything on Saturday, but yeah, it's true. Maya has this incredible ability to heal animals. When I found Red, the fox, she was practically dead. Maya just gently touched her, and there was this bright, golden light, and then the fox was instantly back on its feet, looking perfectly healthy. Apparently, my ability to control plants is a Fae ability. A typical witch can control plants to some extent, but they usually have to use specific spells or potions, whereas I can just… do it," Freya explains, then adds thoughtfully, "It's definitely good to finally find out more about where Reya's unique abilities come from, too."

I sit there silently for a moment, so Freya continues, "You have definitely taken what I've told you much better than how I have reacted to everything you have just told me."

Feeling a mix of relief and utter astonishment, I say, "I honestly thought you might have taken the hell-fire and daemon thing really badly."

"Honestly, Ava, we have had to deal with so much crazy stuff in such a short amount of time that pretty much nothing could surprise me now," Freya says with a shrug, making me think, *'Famous last words.'*

Sam then finally returns, looking tired but thankfully unharmed, and we quickly update him on everything that has transpired while he was gone. Then, we all settle back into the living room, anxiously waiting for Rose, Seraphina and the horse to return, hopefully with Reya safe and sound. Freya, being a good hostess, grabs the food we got for him and heats it up, then she hands it to him as we wait.

Reya

I honestly don't know what they have been drugging me with, but I can't seem to stop myself from constantly nodding off. Unless, of course, I'm still suffering from the lingering effects of the blow to my head. Also, there aren't many stimulating activities to engage in within this bare, depressing room, so all I can do is sit here and contemplate all the questionable decisions I've made recently. Though I absolutely refuse to let my internal panic fully surface and take over. *Not yet anyway.*

My cellmate is proving to be absolutely no help whatsoever. For all I know, it's been hours or days sitting here silently. To be honest, he's been creeping me out something fierce because he simply won't stop staring at me with those wide, unsettling eyes.

Just as I drift off into another unwanted nap, I'm startled awake when the heavy wooden door to our cell slams open with a deafening clang.

The same brutish man from before storms back into the room, his face contorted in anger. He roughly grabs my arm, his fingers digging painfully into my already bruised skin. He has an incredibly strong grip, and I wouldn't be surprised if I'm left with even more bruises on top of the nasty cuts I already have, which his tight grip is currently causing to pull apart, as I see fresh blood start to trickle down my arm.

He roughly drags me to my knees, and just as I'm trying to regain my balance, a deep, guttural growl suddenly erupts from somewhere behind him. The same large wolf appears in the doorway as the menacing growl moves closer. The light today is better, so I can see its details better. Its fur is a patchwork of dark greys and blacks, with strange patches of vibrant orange, especially around its snout, and, of course, some white.

The wolf stalks right up to my face, its hot, fetid breath washing over me as it bares its razor-sharp teeth and lets out a deafening growl directly in my face. I can feel droplets of saliva hitting my cheeks, and all I desperately want to do is wipe them away.

The very thought of anything to do with these disgusting creatures fills me with revulsion and immediately causes horrific images to flash through my mind of our mother and the way she looked when they brought her lifeless body out of our house.

I can't help but wonder how utterly alone and terrified she must have felt in her final moments, thinking she was going to die. I may not be entirely alone in this cold, damp cell, but my fate seems to be mirroring my mother's in a terrifying way.

The arsehole then leans into my face after the wolf backs off slightly and says, "Why are there FBI agents camped out at your house? What exactly do they want? And who is that blonde woman who is with them?" he bombards me with, firing question after question at me without giving me even a single second to respond.

I shrug, a small, defiant gesture that seems to piss both of them off even more. "Tell me right now, witch, or you will start to find out just how bad we can make your little stay with us, on top of what you will ultimately be used for." His words send a fresh wave of icy fear coursing through my veins.

"How in the hell am I supposed to know why the FBI agents are at my home?" I retort, trying to sound more confident than I actually feel. "I would guess it's probably because I have gone missing, you know, since you lovely people decided to kidnap me. And as far as I know, the blonde woman is just another agent." I say, carefully making sure I don't reveal any information they wouldn't already know, to avoid putting anyone else in further danger.

The brutish man's eyes narrow as he stares intently into mine for a long moment. Then, he finally speaks, his voice low and menacing. "If those agents don't leave your property within the next few days, they will meet the exact same fate as your sisters. They will all have to leave that house eventually. We followed one of the agents who started to watch that old crone, Sandra. Do they know about our world?"

That piece of information is certainly interesting. My sisters must have told the agents about Sandra, and they might have even suspected that she had something to do with my disappearance.

The full weight of what he has just said is the best news they could have given me, giving me hope. My body feels like it just downed a Red Bull. It's so good to hear the protection barrier around our property is still working effectively, and these vile wolves can't get to my sisters as long as they remain inside its boundaries.

They damn well better be inside, or I swear I will personally hunt down every single one of these disgusting creatures myself if they hurt my family.

"What exactly is the blonde?" he asks next, his tone giving away the fact that they know Rose is different from the other agents. I've been expecting that question, so I give him my most convincing look of utter confusion.

"She's an agent, just like all the others, as far as I know," I say innocently. "Or are you perhaps referring to the fact that she is a woman? Have you finally figured out what a woman looks like? I guess not, judging by the way you have been treating me. I understand now. I bet they all turn and walk away when they see you coming, don't they?" I turn my head slightly towards the large wolf standing beside him and say, my voice dripping with sarcasm, "They do, don't they? Just give me one small growl to confirm it. I'm sure this idiot won't understand your growl as agreeing with me." When I finish my little sarcastic tirade, I'm almost sure

I see a fleeting hint of amusement flicker in the wolf's dark eyes and see a hint of red around the edges, and as I stare into these eyes again, I have this feeling I recognise them.

Then the man's hand shoots out and strikes me hard across the face, making my already throbbing head feel even worse, and the side of my face instantly flares with pain.

This guy definitely isn't amused by my attempt at humour. He strikes me across the face once more with the back of his hand, the force of the blow sending a sharp jolt of pain through my skull. Despite the pain, I can't help but smirk slightly at his apparent lack of control over his anger. As he strikes me, I notice something else, something strange.

Something deep inside of me reacts to the violence, and it definitely isn't happy, but nothing outwardly happens. I try to lash out at both of them with my magic, but still nothing happens, except I do start to feel a little bit stronger, and the way the man is gripping my arm suddenly gives me a dangerous idea, but I will have to wait for the right moment to put it into action.

"Say anything like that again, witch, and you will get to meet my much meaner side and find out exactly what I can do to you. Then, you will finally understand what your precious mother must have gone through when our alpha killed her." As he spits out those hateful words, he glances at the wolf standing beside him, making the horrifying realisation dawn on me that this is indeed the alpha. This very creature brutally murdered our mother. A fresh wave of intense anger surges through me, making me feel stronger. At the same time, my skin tingles all over, a familiar sensation lately that always precedes when I get angry. The feeling gives me a renewed sense of strength and determination.

I can't help myself, "I'm terribly sorry if you are suffering from a severe case of little man syndrome," my voice dripping with disdain. "Is that why women run screaming when they see you coming? Because when they finally get a good look at you, they can't help but laugh? So, you resort to hitting them like a pathetic man with a small cock." I'm so consumed by rage now, knowing that this disgusting wolf murdered our mother in cold blood, I desperately want to teach this arrogant bastard a lesson, too, that he will never forget.

Of course, he strikes me again, his face contorts in fury, but all it does is make me feel even stronger, and I can feel a strange energy building within me. This hit sends me teetering on the edge of consciousness, especially as my eyes start to roll upwards into my skull involuntarily.

Somehow, through sheer force of will, I manage to stay conscious. The man then roughly flings me back down to the cold, hard floor and starts to walk out of the room, presumably satisfied with his display of dominance.

"What's his name?" I struggle to ask, my voice hoarse and barely above a whisper.

He freezes in the doorway, his hand still resting on the cold metal of the doorframe. He looks back at me as I lie there, I don't even try to move, as I don't want to give him satisfaction with seeing me struggle to push myself into a sitting position.

"Whose name?" he asks, a flicker of intrigue in his eyes.

"The bastard who murdered my mother, Elspeth Harper," I say, my voice filled with venom.

I hear the frail man huddled in the corner of the room suddenly start to mumble something incoherently, and it sounds like he is having a full-blown panic attack. The brutish man in front of me glances over at my cellmate in the corner, a cruel smirk twisting his lips, then looks back down at me. "You will find out soon enough, little witch. At least you got to meet him again today," he smiles at me, "He has enjoyed seeing you in town," with a chilling finality.

Then, he and the wolf finally leave, the heavy door clanging shut and the lock clicking ominously behind them. Before the wolf disappears completely, however, it turns its head back towards me, and its dark eyes glow an unsettling shade of red for a fleeting moment.

The man's last words echo in my mind, making my blood boil with renewed anger as he strongly hinted that I have already met our mother's killer, and he also confirmed that the wolf was the one responsible, his alpha.

I gingerly rub my throbbing face, which is still stinging from the brutal hits, and then glance over at the frail man huddled in the corner. He's still panicking, and his mumbling is starting to get even louder and more frantic.

"Elsie, my Elsie, not again… not to her children… to mine… Elsie, I'm so sorry… I couldn't protect you… or them…" he repeats over and over, his eyes wide with terror as he stares directly at me.

I honestly can't understand what has suddenly set him off like this. The way he keeps staring at me with those haunted eyes is starting to make me uneasy, and it's clear he has been in this awful place for a very long time. As I continue to look at him more closely, the more he reminds me of someone, I'm just not sure who, especially right now, as my vision is blurred around the edges and my head is swimming.

"Can I help you in some way? You have seen me pee a few times now and, well, other things, that practically makes us family in this awful place," I say, attempting a weak joke to break the tension, but it's the wrong thing to say. His eyes grow wide, then he shakes his head vigorously from side to side, his mumbling intensifying.

"No, no, no… this can't be happening again… not to her children… She must hate me… I'm sure she hates me… I would… I thought she died… I had absolutely no idea she had survived… and that her child did…" He continues to ramble to himself, his voice laced with a mixture of fear and despair. But a few things he says make me pause and think.

He starts acting like this right after I mention our mother's name.

Can he possibly have known her at some point in the past? I decided to test my theory.

"Hey," I say, trying to get his attention. "Did you happen to know my mother? Her name is Elspeth Harper." As soon as the question leaves my lips, I start to see a massive reaction from him, but I can't focus on it now as the door to our room bursts open once again.

Catherine M. Clark

Chapter 33

Broken

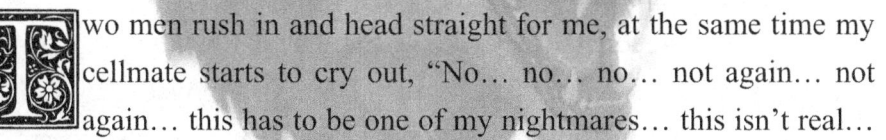

******

Two men rush in and head straight for me, at the same time my cellmate starts to cry out, "No... no... no... not again... not again... this has to be one of my nightmares... this isn't real... it has to be a nightmare... not to her... please not her..." he says, his voice rising in pitch as he starts to freak out completely, and it confuses me why he's reacting like this.

With a savage, precise brutality that steals the air from my lungs, they yank me upright. Rough hands shove a coarse, musty-smelling gag violently into my mouth, scraping against my teeth. Bile rises. Then darkness descends as they force a suffocating hood over my head – the material scratchy against my face, thick with the stale scent of fear from others before me? Without a flicker of remorse, they drag me from the squalid cell, their grips like iron vices under my arms. My boots scrape and stumble over the gritty concrete floor, their callous efficiency a horrifying counterpoint to my rising panic.

We don't seem to travel far, and moments later, I'm flung like a ragdoll onto what I presume is a bed, based on how I bounce and the feel of it. With this realisation, my panic really starts to surface now as the hints of what they want me for seem to be about to put into action, so I begin to thrash and kick, hoping I can do some damage to these two sick bastards.

But it just causes the two men with mechanical, merciless cruelty to drag me up the bed and bind my hands to the bed frame with ropes that bite into my flesh as they tie the rope too tightly around my wrists from my fighting against them.

As my fear increases and deepens, images of Tv shows that I've watched make my fear go into overdrive as I hope I'm not about to experience the same as I watched in those shows. I cry out in fear, hoping someone will hear me, to save me, from this ordeal, but the gag muffles my cry for help, and it starts to sink in that no one is coming to save me, not this time, not from this.

One of the men then yanks my boot from my left foot, while one unbuttons my jeans, and when my second boot is removed, they yank my jeans down my legs. When I feel these monsters' hands touch my bare skin on my legs, I feel like I might puke, as a shiver runs over my body.

As I continue to fight them, still trying to kick out, hoping to catch one of them, they strip away the last remnants of my dignity, ripping off my underwear with soulless precision and chilling indifference. The echoes of their heavy, deliberate footsteps start to fade, leaving me alone in an oppressive, haunting silence, feeling the chill of the air creep over my bare skin. A chilling sound soon breaks it—a scratching, skittering noise coming closer and closer of nails on the concrete floor, echoing just outside the door.

The scraping grows nearer, louder in the confines of the hood. Each *skitter*, *scrape*, and *click* of claw against the floor sends electric jolts of pure terror up my spine. The sound is maddeningly slow, measured, inevitable. I buck against the ropes, sobbing silently into the gag, the rough fibres digging deeper into my raw wrists with each frantic tug. The scraping echoes now, bouncing off unseen walls, a distorted metronome counting down the seconds to violation. My skin crawls, anticipating a touch I can't bear.

There's a hollow thump, like something heavy has thrown itself against wood. Then, the door to the room I'm in slams shut before what I'm sure is a wolf resumes its rap-tap-tapping progress toward me. Almost worse than the cacophony is the waiting, the looming anticipation of what is to come, and it feels like every one of my nerves sparks in terror at what awaits.

My breath comes in ragged, panicked gasps, the gag stifling my cries as the horror stalks ever closer. My thoughts scream with the futility of fighting it, the inevitability of what I know is coming and what I'm going to have to live with if I survive. I twitch like a trapped animal, eyes wide and useless against the hood as the wolf snakes its way nearer and nearer.

A surge of panic electrifies me and moves through my veins as my heart hammers in a frantic rhythm, awakening a desperate something dormant within, and it roars in anger. As the ominous presence slithers nearer, my ears catch the horrific symphony of snapping, popping bones, and grating scrapes against concrete, punctuated by an eerie growl. My blood runs ice-cold when I realise the beast is not just any wolf—I know this is the alpha, the very monster responsible for my mother's death, as her lifeless body flashes through my mind. For the first time since she died, I'm glad she is dead, so she doesn't have to deal with the aftermath of this despicable act.

Terror rockets through me as I register the shift in the air, the subtle sounds of movement near my feet. *He's shifted back. He's a man.* The thought is a physical blow. Bile surges again. Then, with predatory, unyielding strength that speaks of casual power, his hands are on my ankles, forcing my legs apart—a choked scream tears against the gag. I thrash wildly, legs kicking uselessly against his immovable grip – he's impossibly strong. Then the pressure, the intrusion – slow, deliberate, calculated. He pushes himself inside me, violating me not with frenzied lust but with a chilling, almost detached savagery that makes my stomach clench violently and my very soul recoil.

I expect him to just get this over with quickly, but he continues to slowly move in and out of me with a slowness that a boyfriend might do, not a rapist, and he moves his body so even as he releases my left leg I still can't get him off me.

He moves again, and I feel him leaning over me as I feel the bed dip to my left, where I'm sure he has just placed his free hand. I can sense him through my fear and panic as he is now face to face with me, even though I can't see him through this hood. Still, I feel his breath against it. I try to headbutt him, but I hit nothing, whether he sees it coming or he isn't as close as I think he is, but I hear a sickening chuckle in response, which fuels me to continue my struggle to fight against this ordeal and the ropes that bind me.

Within the collapsing depths of my despair, something else sparks – hot, furious, utterly defiant. Incendiary rage surges through my battered core, a desperate, final fuel. My trembling hands claw frantically at the ropes, the fibres digging into bleeding flesh. This bed feels like a sacrificial slab, my soul already dying, fragmenting under the assault. But some core part of me *screams* NO against the intolerable agony. Pain sears through muscle and bone, far beyond endurance, yet I throw my entire being against the restraints with violent, reckless abandon, a cornered animal fighting the inevitable.

Even as terror reaches its vicious zenith, the monster's cruel invasion continues, stretching each excruciating second into a deeply personal, unrelenting torture that leaves me utterly repulsed and horrified by the systematic violation of my body. With each horrifying moment, the animal's slow, unyielding brutality twists my insides further, wringing from my soul any remaining hope.

Using the strength I gain as whatever is inside of me roars and gives me one final act of desperate rebellion, I manage to snap the rope strangling my right hand. With an explosive surge of manic energy, I flail my fists blindly, launching a frantic, hopeless assault against my attacker, whom I can't see. Every furious blow I strike is met with a chilling, mocking chuckle from the monster, who finally withdraws from me with nauseating nonchalance. He then makes me want to rip my skin off my legs as I feel his hands against my legs as he pulls what feels like my underwear back onto my body, then, with brutal disregard, he forces my jeans back onto my legs. He even takes the time to button my jeans back up before departing the room with a sinister, derisive laugh. In the next heart-stopping moment, another pair of figures' dreadful, heavy steps return.

As I feel them move in to either side of me, I lash out again with my waning strength, trying to hit them with my free hand, but they grip my wrist and pin my hand down by my side while another man unties my left hand. They repeat their merciless ritual, forcing me to stand as they drag me off the bed, making my left arm hurt as it's almost yanked out of its socket. The rope is finally removed from my left wrist, and it feels like my skin is removed with it, as pain shoots through my arm again.

The ropes have cut into my now sore, raw skin, and the hateful gag in my mouth stifles my sobs. I fight feebly, kicking with fading energy at the floor and the men's bodies, trying anything to escape. Their grip is unrelenting, and they drag me back to what I'm assuming is my cell, where my cellmate, I'm sure, is still chanting his spiel of being no one. Now I feel like joining him, as I now also feel like no one.

The desperate energy of before is already spent, replaced by a cold, sinking resignation. The world shrinks to the sound of my own weak breathing as my soul curls into itself and withdraws, leaving behind an empty vessel to endure as they drop me to the ground, which I recognise as the same cold concrete floor of my original cell.

When my body hits the ground, it jerks and spasms, struggling against the tightness around my limbs. I collapse into a whimper as hope extinguishes, and I lie pitifully alone in my misery.

But they don't leave me be. They yank me up into a sitting position and callously discard the hood and free me from the gag, flinging my boots back at me with dismissive cruelty. Their departure is accompanied only by scornful chuckles echoing off barren walls, leaving me to curl into a torturous, broken heap as the crushing weight of despair, fear, and unspeakable violation consumes me.

My sobs erupt like violent tsunamis crashing against jagged, unforgiving rocks, and my entire body trembles uncontrollably under the relentless assault of grief. Desperate fingers claw into the skin of my arms as I huddle into my cold, indifferent section of the room, clinging to the unyielding ground that offers no solace. The frigid, merciless concrete pressing against my bruised skin—each icy touch a stark, relentless reminder of the horrors that have been inflicted upon me—while torrents of tears and the bitter residue of snot stream unheeded down my face.

Time dissolves into a maddening blur—a ceaseless loop of excruciating pain and fragmented, nightmarish memories. Every second replays the abuse in searing detail—the repulsive sounds, the acrid stench, and the soul-crushing agony of utter powerlessness.

Gradually, my anguish sobbing dwindles into pitiful whimpers, then fades into a heavy silence punctuated only by my ragged, desperate breaths. The wild roar within me—the spark of strength and rebellion—slowly retreats to its dormant state, leaving behind an empty, hollow shell swallowed by despair.

As endless, relentless hours bleed into one another, I lie unmoving, my body convulsing under the aftershocks of torment. The cold, indifferent concrete serves as a brutal canvas for the raw, searing pain permanently engraved into my flesh and soul. As I lie there, vacant, aching emptiness, my throat is raw from the incessant crying, and my eyes feel swollen with unshed tears. I stare blankly at a wall bathed in a ghostly light, the indistinct glow of dawn or dusk mirroring the shattered fragments of time and my broken soul.

With trembling, blood-slicked fingers from where I re-opened the wounds on my arms as I dug my nails in trying to hold myself together, I reach for my discarded boots. Every agonising movement unleashes fresh, searing waves of pain that ripple ruthlessly through every nerve, dredging up the harrowing memories of my abuse. I sink my teeth into my lower lip until salt and blood mingle on my tongue. I fight desperately to silence any sound, determined that no more cries will betray the depths of my suffering.

In a final, wrenching act of resignation and defiance, I pull on my boots and struggle to a sitting position as fresh pain shoots through my battered body, each movement a brutal reminder of a torment that will forever haunt me. But a renewed strength is starting to rise within me as I plan to get out of here, even if it kills me. I turn to face my cellmate; he thankfully remains quiet since I was brought back, and I find, like always, he is staring at me, but this time he looks more broken than ever.

Chapter 34

Fractured Mind, Fractured Cell

My cellmate continues to stare at me with horror in his eyes. I remember his freak out when I was taken and what he said; he must have had to witness this before, so at some point another girl, woman has been in this room with him. I plan to make it the last time he will have to witness when someone is taken to be used and abused.

He looks tired, more than I've seen on him since I've been here. I wonder if he has been watching over me as I lay here sobbing in my torment. He then starts to mumble something incoherent for a while, his panicked mumbling fills the small, dark space and eventually, exhaustion seems to overtake him. He passes out, his frail body slumping against the cold stone wall. For some strange reason, I'm grateful he seems to care enough to watch over me and makes the decision easy for me, as I plan to make sure he comes with me if I find a way to get out of here.

Now that he's unconscious, I use my time to stare at him to try and keep my mind busy so it doesn't go back to dwelling on the assault. I intently study his features, trying to decipher the familiarity that tugged at the edges of my memory earlier.

His hair is incredibly shaggy and unkempt, and it looks like it might have once been a similar shade of brown to my own, but without the natural red undertones. I'm almost sure there are lighter streaks in his hair, hints of a golden hue that look strangely familiar with the way it makes his face look for some inexplicable reason. However, with his hair being so dirty and matted with oil, it's challenging to be sure.

My gaze drifts to the shape of his nose. Even though it looks vaguely familiar, I still can't place a name or a face to it. I'm absolutely sure I've met him before, but how can that be possible if he's been a prisoner here for a long time, as his current deteriorated state clearly indicates? After considerable time spent trying to force my brain to work in the right way, as images keep trying to creep in, trying to torture me all over again as I try to figure out his identity, I eventually succumb to my own exhaustion of body and mind and nod off into an uneasy sleep.

I wake abruptly from nightmares I can't seem to escape. I gasp to try and breathe and frantically look around, feeling scared that they have come for me again. The room is bathed in the dim, orange glow of early evening. I then notice a fresh glass of water placed carefully beside me and another bowl of lukewarm, watery soup.

Fear washes over me, knowing someone came into the room and left them without waking me, and of course, it makes my mind replay the moments when the monster was leaning over me. I shake my head to try and get the images out, and thankfully, it works this time. I can't believe I didn't wake up when they entered; my body and mind must have needed the rest for me not to wake up as I usually have this thing where I wake when someone I don't know walks into the room where I've nodded off. It hasn't happened since we moved as we haven't had strangers staying in the house; it didn't even occur when Jenny started to stay overnight. Maybe that sense I've always had is now broken.

I reach for the glass of water, my throat and mouth feeling like sandpaper as I feel dehydrated, which must be from all the crying I did. I pause, though, and press the glass so it's resting against my parched lower lip, the proximity only intensifying my desperate thirst.

But I remember my plan, my need to escape this place. I would prefer to die trying than to have to endure it again, by him, the now main monster of my nightmares, so my plan, I started to work out before I was taken to that other room, begins to resurface as it starts to bind, to fit together like a puzzle. I remember the distinct feeling of increased strength that washed over me when my anger rose and rose, especially when I managed to break the rope that was digging into my right wrist.

That surge of unexpected strength could be my only real hope of escaping this hellhole. However, if I drink this water, there's a very high probability that it's drugged, just like before. If I sleep through the night, that will significantly diminish my newfound strength and miss my opportunity, as my plan, I'm sure, will only work during the night if I'm correct about when I've been feeling stronger. I also have the rune of strength I can use from the book our mother left for us. It doesn't seem that my newfound strength is magical in origin, so this drug doesn't seem to be affecting it. The only thing that does is my anger, so as my sisters would say, Ragey needs to come out to play tonight.

So, with a sigh of reluctant resignation, I put the glass back down and decided to take a risk and hope the soup isn't drugged either. I desperately need all the strength I can muster, so I hope the meagre soup will also help quench some of my lingering thirst.

When I've finished the watery broth, I still feel incredibly hungry. I've been spoiled since we moved to Luna Falls, and Maya's new, magically enhanced food is so incredibly good that only getting a small bowl of bland soup twice a day is starting to take its toll on me physically and mentally.

I have absolutely no idea what time it is, but I know it's still far too early to attempt my risky escape plan. I have to wait for as long as possible without falling asleep again. If I do drift off, I might miss my only real chance; my strength has already taken a hit from fighting against the assault, and if I delay, my strength will continue to wane.

Yesterday would have been a better day to put my plan into action, but my brain hasn't been working fast enough to think of it sooner, and of course I didn't know that fucking alpha was going to violate me so soon. I thought I had time, time to find a way to escape or for someone to rescue me. I'm sure my sisters are trying, but how will they find me, and how will they go against so many shifters? So, this must undoubtedly be the best opportunity left for me to get out of here.

If I fail, this will be my fate, and I will soon look just as broken and defeated as my silent cellmate, and I won't be looking for a way to escape. I will be looking to end it before I have to go through that again. I can't bear the thought of going through it again, and who knows what else they have planned for me, and if they plan to put me through it for weeks, months or years. It's a truly sickening and surreal thing to have to come to terms with – the very real possibility of being raped again and by possibly more than one man. The thought alone sends shivers of disgust and terror down my spine, and I know I have to do everything in my power to prevent this from being my life.

While I desperately try to keep myself awake and alert, I decide to attempt something I have never done before. It could very well turn out to be a completely silly and futile effort, but in my current desperate situation, it's certainly worth trying, especially considering my previous unexpected success in making contact with all those shades at once when I could see them all in my mind.

This might not work with the drugs in my system, so why not try? So, I close my eyes and try to focus that same mental energy I used against the shades and send it outward. This can very easily make me fall asleep and end up completely screwing everything up. Still, I feel like I have to try absolutely everything within my limited power, given my dire circumstances; these drugs can't block everything out, surely!

I focus my mind with my eyes closed while sitting cross-legged on the cold concrete floor. I try to concentrate on anything that might be happening outside these thick stone walls. My mind is immediately drawn to the room they took me to. Maybe this is a bad idea. I manage to clear my mind and refocus desperately, hoping my mind plays ball and this will work as it will help with my plan tonight if it does.

As I continue to focus my mental energy outward, a series of strange, unsettling sensations wash over me. I even feel like someone or something is intently studying me, but the feeling passes as quickly as it arrives and makes no sense as it's coming from above me.

It does make me wonder, though, if there is a hidden camera somewhere in this room, silently recording my every move. The mere thought of that possibility makes my skin crawl with disgust, and bile briefly rises in the back of my throat at the thought, as it would mean they could have been watching me in the aftermath of my desperate crying and despair as they laugh at me.

Despite the unsettling thoughts, I stubbornly continue my mental exercise, as I desperately need to keep myself occupied and alert. After what feels like an eternity, I finally feel something. It's a distinct sensation, like the sun is beating down on me with intense heat, but I soon realise that it isn't the sun at all, it's a gentle, cool light.

An image of the moon crosses my mind; it's the moon I'm feeling as it rises. It feels strangely like it's part of me, a comforting presence in the oppressive darkness. I can sense it slowly moving higher into the inky dark tapestry of the night sky. I track its steady ascent for some time, my focus unwavering, and then I suddenly realise the moon is now at its highest elevation, directly overhead. I instinctively know that now is the time to implement my risky plan.

Before I even open my eyes, my focus is abruptly drawn to another distinct feeling. This one feels incredibly close, almost right beside me, and it shines with a bright, nearly blinding intensity, like a miniature star.

What I'm feeling is strangely familiar, but this time it's a familiarity that feels almost too intimate, like one of my sisters is incredibly close to me. My eyes snap open, and my gaze immediately locks onto the exact location where the feeling is emanating from.

My eyes widen in shock as I find myself staring directly into the vast, amber, terrified eyes of the frail man I'm sharing this miserable room with. "It can't be," I whisper to myself in utter disbelief as we continue to stare at each other, a silent understanding passing between us.

I felt something else just before I opened my eyes, but the intense connection with the man completely distracted me. It feels close, too, and it's moving incredibly fast, heading directly towards our location. For some inexplicable reason, the vivid image of a vibrant rainbow flashes through my mind just as I open my eyes.

Whatever that strange feeling is, it's gone now, and I have far more pressing and potentially life-altering things on my mind if my sudden realisation about the man is indeed correct, and if I let it distract me, it could cost me my life in more ways than one.

"I… I felt you just now," my cellmate says, his voice barely a whisper, catching me completely off guard. He sounds genuinely scared. "Do you… do you know?" he asks, his eyes pleading.

"I'm not entirely sure *what* I know yet," I say slowly, still trying to process the implications of our shared connection. "For now, we desperately need to try and get the hell out of here," I say with a newfound determination. I stand up, but my legs feel weaker and shakier than I initially anticipated. After a brief moment, though, they seem to remember what they are supposed to do, and I feel a surge of returning strength, but as I stand there, my body feels awkward and uncomfortable, it's almost like I can still feel him inside of me. *I need to get out of here. I can't go through that again.*

"I'm… I'm no one…" he stammers, his voice full of despair. "We can't get out of here. I've tried for years… countless years," he says, sounding utterly defeated, then goes to the place I don't want him to, especially if he is who I think he is, "Are you okay, did they hurt you, did he hurt you?".

I try to ignore the question, but with the way he's looking at me, it doesn't seem like he's willing to move on until I answer him. "I will survive as long as we get out of here," I tell him.

Then I continue to tell him, "I have a plan," with a tone I hope projects an air of confidence I'm not entirely feeling, especially as I couldn't sense where and how many shifters are out there, but whatever is coming this way might be enough to help us get away. "Just get ready in case it actually works. You're coming with me," I add.

I really hope he agrees. If my sudden realisation about his identity is correct, there's absolutely no way I can leave him behind in this awful place. However, I also know there is no way I will be physically able to carry him if he can't walk properly.

"I can't," he says, shaking his head vehemently, his eyes full of a deep sadness as he looks at me. "I'm no one…this is where I belong…this is my punishment." He then tries to curl up into an even tighter ball, as if attempting to hide himself from me physically.

"You're coming with me, whether you like it or not, even if I have to physically drag you out of here myself," I say as my growing frustration at his self-defeating attitude continues.

He then surprises me by looking up at me, a faint, almost wistful smile touching his lips. "So much like her," he murmurs softly.

I have to consciously force myself to ignore the fact that he has just essentially confirmed my wildest theory about his identity, but I have to continue to ignore my growing realisation about him. I walk over to the heavy wooden door and wrap my hands tightly around the cold, rough handle. Then, I carefully position my feet, keeping one firmly planted on the ground for leverage and placing the other against the wall next to the handle. I take in a few deep, steadying breaths, and then I mentally run through every single thing I can think of that makes my blood boil with anger.

I desperately hope I won't end up transforming into some

mindless, rage-fuelled beast like the Hulk if I get too angry, as I have no idea just what magic can really do with my intent, but right now, I need every ounce of strength I can muster and hope I can imitate the Hulk just a little.

I think about the lies our mother has told us all our lives when she could have been training us. I think about these beasts that then killed her and picture her mangled body as she was brought out of the house, and as we watch her die in the hospital, her final words revealing the truth and her lies. For some reason, my mind then goes to the night of our prom. I go looking for my boyfriend, Harrison and find him in a classroom snogging our school enemy, Nicole, as I watch them through the glass pane in the door, and my heart starts to break into pieces.

I see myself being with him after school, and even let my silly, weak mind think about marrying him.

Following that, I remember all the times people teased us because we were so close in school and how Nicole and her friends bullied Maya and teased Freya about liking girls. My mind circles back to how our lives were restricted because of all the lies our mother told, not being able to go on holiday, not allowed out after dark; we weren't even allowed to stay at school for after-school groups.

When it came the time we left school our mother almost seemed out of her mind as she fought us about going to college and once she got us to give up on the idea she even fought us about getting jobs and forced us to get jobs as close to home as possible and could only work hours during the day, her usual excuse being the rising crime all over the country. My eyes then turn to my cellmate, and now knowing who he is, what we missed out on, and how our lives could have been so different.

Then I allow my mind to go where I never want to go again, to remember, but I need to, as I need the strength I hope it will give me. So, I let my mind skim over the assault. I feel the strength rise within me as I let these final thoughts in and hope it's enough to get us out of here.

When I feel ready, I quickly trace the rune for strength on the back of my left hand when my anger reaches its absolute boiling point. I wasn't sure if it would work without my powers, but I feel it as soon as I've finished tracing it out for the third time, as the book instructed. I feel myself getting stronger.

I pull on the handle with every muscle and ounce of strength within my body. The heavy metal handle groans and creaks ominously, followed by the distinct and satisfying sound of wood splintering and cracking. "How… how did you do that?" my cellmate asks, his voice filled with awe and disbelief.

"Apparently, I'm a lot stronger than I look," I say with a groan as I continue to pull with a small, triumphant smile playing on my lips.

Suddenly, without any warning, something gives way with a violent cracking sound, it almost sounds like lightning, and I fly backwards with considerable force, landing hard on my coccyx with a painful thud. "That's just great," I mutter to myself, wincing. "All I need is to break my damn arse." As I flew backwards, I heard a distinct popping sound. When I prop myself up on my elbows and look back at the door, I see a gaping hole where the handle used to be, the surrounding wood splintered and torn.

"Damn it," I whisper, hoping desperately that no one heard that incredibly loud noise and that whatever ancient runes or wards they were using on this room somehow blocked out most of the sound. I shakily get back to my feet, rubbing my throbbing coccyx gingerly.

I cautiously walk back to the now damaged door and hold my head by the hole in it, listening intently to see if I can hear any sounds from outside. The hole I created is large on this side of the door, but only a tiny hole on the other side of the thick door. When all I can hear is silence from the other side, I breathe a small sigh of relief, realising no one seemingly has heard what just happened.

I carefully study the hole I've made; it's definitely big enough for my hands to get a much better grip on the remaining wood than I managed with the handle. I waste no time and carefully slide my hands into the jagged opening, positioning them so that nothing is digging too painfully into my skin. I'm able to get a few fingers through the hole I made to the other side, so like before, I brace my feet against the wall, preparing to use every last ounce of strength I can muster.

Chapter 35

Escape into Darkness

As soon as I start to pull with all my might, I hear the wood around my hands begin to splinter and crack again, the sounds echoing in the silence, but the door itself doesn't seem to want to budge, stubbornly refusing to give way. I'm putting absolutely everything I have into pulling, my muscles screaming in protest, and I start to feel the rune wearing off. At the same time, I feel my body getting tired as defeat starts to wash over me, along with a growing sense of panic about what my captors will do when they inevitably find the door in this state.

I'm just about to give up, my teeth gritting in frustration and pain as I desperately try to maintain my anger, when a pair of surprisingly strong arms suddenly wrap around my waist from behind and start pulling me backwards with considerable force. It initially makes me jump as my mind makes me think the men have returned for me, but I realise quickly enough who it is. The added pressure against the damaged door immediately makes a difference, giving me much-needed momentum.

I'm able to pull with a renewed surge of adrenaline-fuelled strength.

Then, with a final, deafening groan of protesting wood, the door finally gives way. The entire wooden door breaks from its hinges, allowing the heavy door to rip free and come flying off in my hands. Again, I fall backwards, but this time I manage to avoid landing on my already bruised butt by awkwardly landing on top of my frail cellmate instead.

I quickly scramble off him, apologising profusely, and then reach down to help him to his feet. He's hesitant at first to take my outstretched hand, his eyes wide with a mixture of fear and disbelief, but when he finally does, I feel it again – that same strange, familiar connection that sparked between us earlier. "Thank you," I say softly, finally taking in just how surprisingly tall he is when he stands up straight. Since I was brought to this awful place, I haven't seen him stand up fully, as he constantly moves around hunched over and shuffling when he has to use the rudimentary toilet in the corner.

However, we have no time to dwell. "Come on," I urge him, my voice low and urgent. "We need to get out of here right now." I grab his hand firmly and start to pull him along with me towards the now gaping hole in the wall where the door used to be. I cautiously peek around the door frame to see if anyone is heading our way, but all I can see is a dimly lit corridor that seems to lead only in one direction.

I step over the beam they used to secure the door, taking my first steps into the corridor, still pulling the frail man behind me, desperately hoping he has the strength and will to keep up with me. As we move quickly down the narrow corridor, we come to another heavy wooden door, and my breath catches in my throat, and my heart starts to race uncontrollably. I'm so glad the door is closed, so I can't see where it happened. I'm also glad my companion can't see where they took me either.

We continue to move swiftly down the corridor, our footsteps echoing eerily in the silence. My cellmate is having significant issues with walking. I'm guessing he hasn't been able to walk correctly for a very long time, so I'm actually surprised he is managing to keep up with me as well as he is.

We hear nothing as we approach what I desperately hope is the exit, finally coming upon a narrow set of wooden stairs leading upwards. When we reach the bottom of the stairs and I cautiously look up, I realise with a jolt of hope that we are likely in either a basic bomb shelter or a storm cellar, judging by the heavy, reinforced doors at the top of the stairwell. That means there's a very good chance we are directly underneath a house.

I reach up and gently push on one of the heavy doors. I fully expect them to be securely locked, but to my utter surprise, they move effortlessly. The arrogant arseholes didn't even bother to lock these doors! Typical smug, overconfident bastards.

My cellmate, his eyes wide with a mixture of continued fear and a dawning sense of hope, wordlessly helps me open both heavy doors. As soon as we cautiously poke our heads out of the opening, we're facing the back of a dimly lit house. I quickly scan our surroundings and see that dense woods entirely surround us. Then I hear a voice coming from inside the house, a raised, panicked voice that sends a fresh wave of urgency through me.

"I heard a noise coming from the storm cellar! Get back to the house now and get Lindon and Jasmin, go check the perimeter while I check on our guests!" I don't recognise the voice, so I don't think it's the same arrogant arsehole who hit me.

"Crap!" I hiss. "Come on, we need to move, *now*." We quickly step out of what we now know is a storm cellar. I glance around again, trying to get my bearings in the dim light, and then point in the direction that leads away from the house.

The direction I'm pointing seems to be the quickest way to get into the relative safety of the dense woods, which I hope will provide us with better cover. I also have this strong, almost instinctual feeling telling me we will be heading south, in the general direction of home and whatever is heading this way.

We reach what looks like a small garden shed and use it as

temporary cover, sticking within its shadows as we creep along the outside wall. When we reach the end of the building, we cautiously make our way across a small, open field that separates us from the welcome darkness of the woods. So far, everything is going surprisingly well, and my cellmate, despite his frail condition, is managing to keep going slowly but steadily.

No sooner has the hopeful thought crossed my mind, we hear a man's voice call out from the direction of the house, his tone sharp with urgency. "Lindon! Jasmin! Paul! They escaped! Find them now! They can't have gone far without help, so be careful! I will call it in!"

I try to move faster, pulling gently on my companion's arm, but he can't move any quicker. However, we do manage to reach the edge of the woods just before anyone spots us. The only immediate issue I find is that it's significantly darker under the thick canopy of trees, and the already limited light from the moon is almost completely blocked out.

So, our pace actually becomes even slower as we cautiously navigate the treacherous terrain, constantly stumbling over unseen tree roots, low-hanging branches, and thorny bushes. But we keep pushing forward as best we can, our determination fuelled by a desperate need to escape. In the back of my mind, though, a nagging doubt starts to creep in. These are shifters we were running from, after all. They can likely track us with ease, their heightened senses allowing them to hear and smell us from a considerable distance, and I know in the back of my mind they will be gaining on us with every step.

Despite the growing fear, I force myself to keep us moving, clinging to the hope that this desperate escape attempt is worth the immense risk. It isn't just about trusting in my limited abilities; something deep inside me, an almost primal instinct, tells me we will make it.

Now that we are out of that oppressive room, I can feel so much more clearly. One of those distinct feelings is the vivid image of that vibrant rainbow moving rapidly towards our location and my weak connection to it; I have an unwavering sense that we are on a direct collision course with it. I desperately hope that whatever it turns out to be will provide enough of a distraction for us to make a clean escape.

We start to hear the unmistakable sound of someone moving quickly through the woods behind us, their pace reckless and uncaring with the noise they're making. Then, whoever it is calls out loudly, "This way! They haven't made it far!" Moments later, we hear the distinct sounds of others crashing through the undergrowth, entering the woods at various positions behind us.

They're gaining on us incredibly quickly. I know it's only a matter of moments before the first arsehole is upon us. My companion must also realise this because he suddenly suggests something utterly stupid and self-sacrificing.

"Leave me," his voice full of desperation and a heartbreaking resignation. "You can move much faster without me. I can try to slow them down for you… to give you a better chance." His face looks incredibly sad at the thought of leaving me, and I can see many unspoken questions swirling in his wide, worried eyes.

"Absolutely no chance in hell," I say firmly, tightening my grip on his wrist, ensuring he can't do anything rash or stupid, just like I would, and groan as I now know where that side of me has come from.

"Please… please just let me do this for you," he pleads, choking with emotion. "After… after I failed her before…" he adds, further solidifying the truth about his identity. His words, however, only make me even more determined to keep him safe.

"I will never, ever, leave anyone behind," I say fiercely, my eyes locking onto his. "Please, just stay with me. There's another part to my plan, if my instincts are correct," I whisper urgently to him, hoping to reassure him.

He gives up and allows me to keep pulling him forward as we continue to stumble through the dark woods, putting one foot in front of the other. Our pursuers are now just mere feet behind us. I'm sure that one of them has already shifted into their wolf form and passed us on our left, a silent manoeuvre that I'm sure is part of their carefully orchestrated plan to box us in.

"You can't escape, witch!" the same arrogant fucker who hit me calls out from just to our right. I can hear cruel amusement in his voice. Moments later, before I can react, someone suddenly grabs me from my side and drags me backwards with brutal force, causing me to land hard on my already throbbing and undoubtedly bruised arse. The arsehole has managed to catch up with us while somehow managing cover the ground from where his voice sounded like it was coming from to hide behind a tree we are just passing.

As I lie on my back, staring up at the dark canopy of leaves overhead, my fear rises, and my mind starts to go back to that room as he comes into my line of sight, his face illuminated by the faint moonlight filtering through the trees. He's wearing that smug, self-satisfied smile he sported when he struck me across the face with the back of his hand. "Well, well, well, it looks like you're going to get to experience our full hospitality, after all, witch! I can't wait for it to be my turn. I have to admit, I'm going to enjoy it so very, very much."

"You would, wouldn't you?" I spit back, my anger starting to surge through me again. "It's probably the only way you will ever get to touch a woman in your pathetic little life, you ugly motherfucker."

Fuelled by my rage, I instinctively lift my leg and catch him squarely in the groin with my boot, causing him to double over in agony and fall to his knees right on top of me. It isn't exactly the ideal outcome, as having his disgusting body pressed against mine makes my stomach churn with revulsion, but I do have to admit I thoroughly enjoy the look of utter pain on his face.

"You fucking bitch!" he gasps, clutching his injured jewels. "You are going to pay for that, we only need one specific part of your body, the rest of you is fair game! No one will even be able to recognise you once we are finished with you!" he snarls as his face contorts in a mask of pain and fury.

He looks like he is about to backhand me again when he suddenly snaps his head upwards. He stares intently towards the south, his expression shifting to one of confusion. He quickly scrambles back to his feet, still clutching his groin, just as one of his equally repulsive companions, a woman with short, cropped hair and a menacing sneer, appears beside him, looking similarly bewildered and staring in the same southern direction.

"What the fuck is going on?" the man mutters under his breath. I use his momentary distraction to scan my surroundings for my cellmate quickly. I find him curled up in a tight ball against the base of a large oak tree, rocking back and forth and just barely audible as he mumbles his usual defeated statement of being no one.

It isn't long before I hear the distinct sounds of something significant crashing through the woods towards our position. This isn't another one of his pathetic lackeys; this is a different kind of sound, a powerful, determined force coming from the south.

Strangely, the vivid image of a vibrant rainbow heading our way has abruptly stopped a short distance away, as if it has encountered some invisible barrier. I feel a palpable wave of darkness rolling towards us now, and with it comes a distinct sense of familiarity.

I look up at the man, who is still standing over me, though he's moved slightly to the side now as he tries to figure out whatever is heading our way with such speed and force. I desperately wonder if there's anything at all I can do to defend myself. I still have no access to my magical powers, but when I take a quick glance at the landscape in my mind and enter the library, I find something new. There's a tapestry hanging on one of the walls, it's black but there's a faint image of the woods we are in, there is a pulsating purple light, and by what looks like a tree on the tapestry, there is a golden pulsating light. The two lights must represent me and my cellmate, then a weird pulsating black orb surrounded by a purple light appears on the tapestry and moves towards me with such speed that it's hard to follow.

Then I'm drawn back to the man hovering over me when he abruptly vanishes from my sight, as if he's been snatched away by an unseen force, just as a large, dark form moves swiftly over me. The woman screams, then her mouth falls open as if she is now silently screaming.

I quickly turn my head and see he has hit a tree; he must have hit it hard, as evidenced by the sound he made when he hit it. A sickening spray of blood erupts from his neck as a deep, ragged gash suddenly appears. It's difficult to see precisely what is happening in the dim light, as a swirling darkness intermittently blocks my view as the woman tries to run, but she is suddenly torn limb from limb as I watch her body being tossed into the darkness.

As I continue to stare, trying desperately to make sense of the dramatic scene, part of me enjoys the look on the man's face as he bleeds out while he tries desperately to stop the blood with his hands. Two glowing purple orbs suddenly appear directly above me, their intense glow piercing through the surrounding gloom as they look down at me. "Seraphina," I breathe out in relief. "You found us."

'*I didn't,*' her familiar voice projects directly into my mind. '*Your new horse did. Though it seems you didn't actually need rescuing, did you?*' At least that form of communication still works, and I now know there is a limit to its distance.

"What in the hell did you just call her?" my cellmate asks from his still-cowering position against the tree, his voice a mixture of confusion and awe.

"Seraphina," I say, my gaze still locked on the glowing purple eyes above me.

"How... how did *she* get that name?" he asks, his voice trembling slightly, confusing me as to why that particular detail seems so important to him.

"I named her myself when I created her," I explain in confusion. "I gave her my middle name. Why are you so concerned about her name?"

But he doesn't answer me, instead curling back into his foetal position against the tree and resuming his quiet, repetitive mumbling. Then I remember what our mother said in the letter she left us. She said she gave us the names our father mentioned he would like to call his children if he ever had any. Our middle names are from him.

I put this information to the back of my mind and shakily get to my feet, and just then, another figure comes into view through the darkness of the woods. Seraphina immediately starts to move silently towards him, her dark form almost completely invisible in the gloom, especially when I can't see the telltale glow of her eyes. She takes down this second man just as easily as the first, his surprised yelp cut short as he disappears into the shadows.

She then silently moves back to my side, her glowing purple eyes flicking towards my still-cowering cellmate. Sensing her unspoken question, I quickly say, "He was a prisoner too. He's coming with us." I walk over to him and gently try to help him to his feet, but he instinctively flinches away from my touch, resisting as I try to pull on his arm.

He finally gives in to my gentle persistence and allows me to pull him up, just as a loud, guttural growl and the distinct sound of something large and heavy crashing through the undergrowth reach our ears. I'm almost certain this is the wolf I heard earlier. It then comes bounding directly towards me, its teeth bare in a ferocious snarl, and it looks absolutely furious as small amounts of moonlight flicker across its face. I don't recognise this one. What I can see with our light is that the wolf seems to be light brown with the typical white.

Just then, another loud noise distracts me, this one a deep, menacing growl. It's coming from the south, and another large wolf, even bigger and more imposing than the first, also comes bounding towards us with terrifying speed. This isn't good, and even Seraphina, as powerful as she is, can't possibly take on both of these massive, enraged wolves at once. As the first wolf rapidly approaches my position, its huge jaws open even wider, ready to attack me. I can feel the air around me being displaced by the sheer speed and size of these terrifying beasts, and the strong, coppery scent of fresh blood from the arsehole bleeding against the tree fills my nostrils. I instinctively close my eyes, bracing myself for the inevitable, horrific attack.

Chapter 36

Unexpected Saviors

Nothing happens! Or rather, if something has happened, I would die quickly, my life force extinguished. Maybe I die so quickly I don't even feel it, and I'm now just like Doris – a ghost, tethered to this earthly plane. I desperately don't want to open my eyes and see my own bloody, lifeless body lying there. Still, I have to, especially when the sounds of furious growling and snarling fill the air, which is followed by the sickening thud of something large hitting a tree and the sharp, cracking sound of wood splintering, the noise piercing the tense silence of the night.

I cautiously open my eyes, my heart pounding in my chest. Feeling my heart beating so hard makes me realise I'm still alive, still here. I see a large, dark mass rolling and thrashing through the trees just a short distance away. I stare at it, my mind reeling, wondering what fresh hell we now have to deal with, until the mass abruptly breaks apart and resolves into the forms of two large, fiercely fighting creatures.

One is definitely a wolf, its teeth bared in a savage snarl. The other, though, is harder to make out in the dim moonlight. It isn't until it moves into a small patch of light that I gasp aloud at the sight of a large, sleek black panther.

My mind immediately jumps to the possibility that it's Luca, somehow having finished dealing with his pack and come to rescue me. I quickly realise it can't be him as I'm sure he's not back yet, and why would he come for me just because my mind has been obsessing over him? That means this has to be Rose.

"Rose, is that you?" I ask stupidly, barely a whisper.

Of course, she can't answer me in her current form, but Seraphina's voice echoes in my mind as her dark form effortlessly takes down the remaining wolf. *'Yes, it's Rose,'* Seraphina confirms telepathically.

I realise with a surge of relief that all of our attackers have been swiftly dealt with. I watch as Rose, in her panther form, snaps the neck of the wolf she has been fighting, with a sickening crack. As the wolf's lifeless body falls to the ground, I see its form begin to shimmer and shift, transforming back into a naked human man within a matter of seconds. "We better get moving," I urge, my voice shaky. "They definitely called in backup." I grip my cellmate's wrist again and start pulling him in the direction of south.

Rose quickly shifts back into her human form and joins my side, and she is very naked. She then gives the man I'm pulling a long, assessing look as we both try not to look at her nude form. Just like Seraphina, she clearly has an unspoken question. I quickly tell her, "He was a prisoner, too. He's okay, just…a little out of it."

"Glad you're okay. We better get out of here before we are outnumbered," Rose says.

Just then, another distinct noise breaks through the quiet of the woods, the unmistakable sound of something else large heading rapidly towards us. This time, I have that familiar feeling again – the distinct sensation that a rainbow is moving in our direction. A moment later, a stunning, pure white horse materialises seemingly out of thin air right before us as it steps between large bushes, its coat gleaming in the moonlight.

I'm stunned by its sudden appearance and so incredibly glad to see it. I honestly wasn't sure if my cellmate would have been able to make it much further on foot.

The magnificent horse walks up to me and gently nudges its head against my chest. I hug it around its neck, burying my face in its soft mane, and then ask, "Can you possibly give him a lift home, please?" Surprisingly, the intelligent creature nods its elegant head and lets out a soft, gentle neigh.

Seraphina and I carefully help the frail man onto the back of the horse. I'm not entirely sure how to interpret his reaction, but he has a stunned look on his face and, for once, actually remains quiet as we settle him onto the horse's back. Once he is on the horse, leaning forward so he can wrap his arms around the horse's neck, we start to head south again.

But Seraphina has other ideas. She swiftly swoops down, her powerful arms wrap around my waist, and she effortlessly lifts me off the ground. She flaps her powerful wings, and we lift quickly into the sky. She has to twist to get through some branches; then we are above the trees. Before Rose and my horse disappear from view, I see Rose shift back into a panther, and we all head for home. I just hope my *father* can stay on the horse for the journey. As we head off, I start to feel something happening behind us, a pull on me to go back. I don't like what I'm feeling or sensing, but I ignore it.

The rest of the night passes in a blur as Seraphina swiftly carries me through the air. The sight of our house finally appears in the distance; it's the most beautiful thing I have seen in what feels like a very long time. I never thought I would get to see our new home from the sky, and I might have to see if Seraphina can do this over some famous landmarks if we get the chance.

When we reach the edge of the next grouping of trees we have been flying over, I quickly look for Rose and my horse. When they finally appear, I watch in awe, the sight of them is beautiful as I watch Rose and my magnificent white horse running at full pelt, and somehow, my father is still managing to stay on the back of the horse.

As we approach the edge of the protective barrier surrounding our property, we hear a chorus of chilling howls filling the early morning sky. As I try to pinpoint the direction of the sound, I see three large wolves emerge from the dense woods and begin to relentlessly chase down my horse, rapidly gaining ground.

Without hesitation, Rose peels off and starts to circle back, her black form moving with incredible speed to intercept the wolves. Panic flares in my chest as she can't possibly take on three wolves alone! I instruct Seraphina to take me down so I can go and help protect her.

That is, until the horrifying realisation slams into me. I still have no access to my powers. Instead of dropping me, Seraphina flies me down to just outside the barrier, drops me, and immediately turns back. Her dark form forms a blur against the morning darkness as she races to assist Rose.

I stand there for a moment, feeling utterly useless and frustrated, when I hear frantic shouts coming from behind me, from within the safety of our property. I quickly turn around to see what else is happening, and my heart leaps joyfully.

My sisters are running full tilt in my direction, and as they get nearer, I see their faces etched with worry and relief. And ahead of them, charging at an unbelievable speed, is Beastie, his massive form a blur of black fire and barely contained energy.

But he isn't running towards me, he's heading straight for the wolves. It only takes a few heart-stopping seconds before he races past me and then reaches the wolves just in the nick of time to attack a fourth wolf I hadn't even noticed, who is stealthily trying to sneak up on Rose from the side as it approaches her from a thicket of trees.

Beastie reaches the unsuspecting wolf, and I fully expect him to engulf it in a torrent of his signature fire. Instead, to my utter shock, he goes straight for one of the wolf's front paws. It only takes about two brutal seconds for him to rip the entire leg clean off. The gruesome sight makes me gasp, but Beastie doesn't stop there.

He immediately goes for one of the wolf's rear legs as the injured wolf struggles to remain upright. Seconds later, the wolf finally falls to its side, where Beastie tears it apart, piece by bloody piece. Once finished with the grisly task, he unleashes a torrent of black fire over the scattered remains, incinerating them into nothing but a pile of fine grey ash, then watches as a current of air sweeps up the ash and disappears while Beastie stands there breathing hard, deep breaths.

That's when I realise just how incredibly angry Beastie is – more enraged than I have ever seen him. As I watch him, completely mesmerised by the display of raw power, I haven't even noticed that someone has reached me. Suddenly, I'm lifted off my feet and then unceremoniously dropped flat on my back, a significant weight landing squarely on top of me.

I panic and lash out, thinking the men have snuck up on me; I continue to fight to get away as my panic continues to rise and finally manage to get out from under them. That's when I see Maya move away from me, looking scared, and my heart sinks. God knows what she is now thinking. As my panic starts to subside, I try to smile for her, and Pickle flies over to me tentatively, looking worried about me.

"Sorry, you just caught me by surprise," I say as I try to look happy about seeing them. Then I lose control of my emotions and start to cry—huge, wet, ugly sobs of joy this time.

My sister crawls over to me and gathers me into a hug; this time, I don't flinch or react badly. Pickle joins her and hugs my neck like she does. When Maya pulls away, Freya helps me to my feet, and Maya wraps her arms around me again, this time so tightly that I find it difficult to breathe while Pickle is still plastered to my neck. I expect Freya to wrap her arms around me, too, but she is gone.

Through the haze of my relief and blurred vision from crying, I hear someone almost shouting angrily nearby. "WHO... are... YOU!" the voice demands, laced with suspicion and hostility.

I struggle against Maya's suffocating embrace but manage to turn my head just enough to see what's going on. Freya is standing a short distance away, facing off with my still-dazed cellmate. I see her subtly manipulating the plants around him, causing thick vines to grow behind his back rapidly.

She is making them grow from the ground behind the horse, clearly intending to catch him off guard with a surprise attack. My cellmate looks utterly panicked, his eyes wide with fear, and as usual, he's mumbling incoherently to himself while clutching my white horse as if his very life depends on it.

Before I can even call out to Freya and explain, another one of the horses – not sure which one – races over and positions itself protectively between my sister and my frightened cellmate. It starts to use its head to gently but firmly push Freya away. "What the hell are you doing, Snowdrop!" Freya exclaims, clearly surprised and annoyed as she tries to manoeuvre around the large, stubborn animal, then I gasp, she has named the horse, which means she has picked this one as her own.

Finally, I managed to call out to Freya with enough breath, my voice weak and hoarse. "Freya! Stop! He's with me! He was a prisoner, too!"

Freya looks over to me like I'm being stupid with a mix of confusion and suspicion. "Are you absolutely sure about that, Reya?"

"Y-yes," I say breathily, still trying to catch my breath.

Freya visibly relaxes, her tense posture easing slightly. She looks at the man one more time, her expression still guarded, then comes over and joins my other two attackers and flings her arms around me. Finally, she starts to cry, her tears mingling with Maya's and Pickle's on my face. I can't stop myself; the overwhelming relief and joy of seeing them all again finally breaks through my carefully constructed walls, and I join their emotional outpouring.

Out of the corner of my tear-filled eyes, I see my cellmate peering over at us with a look of utter surprise and dawning realisation, as if he genuinely thought I was the only daughter of Elspeth Harper. As I cry, an old, long-forgotten memory suddenly surfaces in my mind—a vivid recollection of being seven years old and bursting into tears when our mother sharply snapped at me for calling her Elsie.

My mother had turned to face me, her eyes flashing with an uncharacteristic anger that had startled me. 'DON'T EVER CALL ME THAT!' she had shouted, her voice sharp and unforgiving. 'I DON'T WANT TO HEAR THAT NAME, EVER, AGAIN!'

When my sisters and Pickle finally release me from their fierce embrace, my entire body throbs with the lingering pain from all my injuries. I try my best to ensure I don't show any outward signs of how much their tight hugs hurt me, focusing instead on the overwhelming happiness of seeing them all safe and sound. I keep a genuine smile plastered on my face for their benefit.

Once I'm given a little space to breathe, Beastie approaches me and gently nudges his massive head against my leg. His black leathery skin still feels amazingly soft as I run my hand over him. He's in his true hellhound form, and his eyes, even though now black, seem to be glowing with an intense, otherworldly light.

I can sense when he starts to shift back to his dog form. I've never felt that before, but somehow, I can now. He is struggling, though, to control himself, so he can't shift back, and he is having trouble controlling his fire as well, so I'm engulfed in it.

I drop down so I can give him a proper hug, and when I look him in the eyes, I see the first tears start to build in his eyes, I've ever seen from him. Then, I watch as they cascade over his lower eyelid and slowly run down the sides of his face. I guess he is just as emotionally overwhelmed as the rest of us. I give him another hug, the best hug I can manage, wrapping my arms tightly around his thick neck.

He uses this opportunity to show me everything that's happened while I've been gone, including the fact that he desperately wanted to be the one to come and rescue me. Still, Seraphina had somehow managed to convince him to stay behind to protect Freya, Maya and, of course, Pickle. It seems Seraphina can communicate with him like I can through touch.

I'm actually surprised he listened to her. Then, he makes me laugh when he shows me a mental image of himself sitting patiently next to a tiny, very annoyed-looking panther just before Rose starts to follow my white horse into the night. My laughter, however, quickly turns into a painful cough as my throat is still incredibly dry and sore.

When I cough again, I turn my head away from Beastie, and he manages to put out the fire over half his body, so I'm not engulfed anymore. That's when Ava, who has just reached our little group, calls out with alarm as Beastie's fire starts to spread again, "Reya, he'll burn you! Get away from him!"

Freya quickly answers for me. "Actually, Ava, all types of fire don't seem to affect Reya. And for some reason, Beastie's fire doesn't affect any of us – our clothes, our beds, anything to do with us, really."

"Really? Well, I wondered about that," Ava admits, looking slightly sheepish. "It's great to see you, Reya, but maybe we should all get to the other side of the barrier before more wolves turn up," she adds, making a very good point. As we were all currently exposed, the last thing I want is for my sisters or friends to go through what I have.

Chapter 37

Tears and Reunions

We all start to head towards the house, and everyone keeps glancing curiously at the silent, still-dazed man I brought home. Once my sisters, extended family, and guests have all safely entered the house, I turn to Maya and ask, "Sis, can you please look after our guest for me? He desperately needs a good, hot meal to start with." As if on cue, my stomach chooses that exact moment to let out a loud, embarrassing growl of protest, clearly demanding immediate sustenance.

"I've already made your favourite," Maya says warmly. Then she turns her attention to my cellmate and asks gently, "Do you like chicken lasagna?"

"I'm no one," he automatically replies, his voice flat and emotionless. But then manages to add hesitantly, "I don't... I don't think I've ever had it before."

Everyone in the room looks at him, their expressions a mixture of concern and confusion when he utters his usual phrase. Then they all glance at me, their unspoken questions hanging in the air. All I can do for now is shake my head slightly in response, indicating I will explain everything later.

I desperately need a long, hot shower and clean clothes before I drop the massive bombshell about the man's identity on everyone. "I'm going to have a quick shower and change," I announce, my voice still a little rough. "Then we all really need to talk." I notice Ava as she gathers what I assume are Rose's discarded clothes from the back of one of the armchairs and realise I have forgotten all about Rose and Seraphina; they were about to be attacked by three wolves when I last saw them. The fact that Ava is collecting Rose's clothes means she must be okay, so I quickly call out to Seraphina, asking if she is okay, and get a reply instantly, *'I am okay, I am keeping watch to see if the wolves come in force.'* I say thank you and head for the stairs, but catch sight of Jenny hovering just outside the back door.

I can clearly see she has been crying too. When I give her a concerned look, though, she suddenly flings herself at me, wrapping her arms around me in a tight hug and starts to cry all over again. Then, she whispers in my ear, her voice full of emotion, "I thought I had lost you forever, Reya. I was so incredibly scared."

I hug her back just as tightly and whisper reassuringly, "I will always fight to stay here with all of you, Jenny. I promise."

"Will you really?" Jenny asks, her voice laced with a hint of doubt. I know she is subtly referencing the moment when those strange-looking demons attacked, and I thought I was about to lose Maya. I briefly decided to give up as I didn't want to live in a world without Maya.

"I promise you, Jenny," I say firmly, my voice filled with conviction. "I will never give up fighting. Not ever again." I really do mean it, especially now that there is a form of life after death, though I'm not entirely sure what that would mean for me. Now I have another reason to fight, as I want all the wolves dead, no matter what it takes.

"Good," Jenny says, finally stepping back from me, though her eyes were still red and watery. She then wrinkles her nose slightly and adds with a teasing smile, "Now go and have that shower. You really do stink, you know."

As I take my first few hesitant steps onto the stairs, my legs immediately start to shake from exhaustion and lingering weakness, and of course, I'm sore. "Do you need some help getting upstairs?" Jenny asked, giving me a look of concern as she watched me struggle.

"Yes, please," I admit gratefully. "And can someone please find something for him to wear after he has a shower, too?" I ask, hoping someone will take care of it for me.

"I think I have something in the car that might fit him," Sam states, already heading towards the front door. He doesn't go alone, as Ava quickly follows him out, presumably to make sure he is safe.

"Thank you both," I say with genuine gratitude before slowly disappearing from their view as Jenny helps me up the stairs.

"Jenny, do you mind if our guest uses the spare room for now and you continue sharing with me?" I ask as we reach the upstairs landing. I didn't want to ask as I really wanted to have the bed to myself for a bit, but my father needs a bed for now, so I'm going to have to endure it for the time being. It's not like Beastie or Pickle will give me my space anyway.

Jenny doesn't hesitate with her answer. "Yeah, absolutely. Not an issue at all."

Then, from behind us, Pickle suddenly appears, her small face pale and her usually bright eyes still watery from crying. "I was so scared, Reya," she whispers, her voice trembling slightly. "Beastie and I searched all through the woods for you. I thought…I was going to lose another family and someone important to this world."

I'm a little surprised she mentions her family; she has avoided talking about them and has been incredibly cagey and secretive about her past. We strongly suspect she might be pixie royalty, especially after accidentally letting something slip once, but she has never elaborated. I hope she will feel comfortable enough to tell us what happened to them. "Trust me, Pickle," I say gently, giving her a reassuring smile. "I'm not exactly easy to get rid of!" I hope I'm right about that. I'm honestly getting fed up with constantly getting injured and now kidnapped, not to mention other nightmares.

"I know," Pickle says softly, wiping another stray tear from her cheek. "I just… I got really overwhelmed. It brought up some really bad memories." Another single tear escapes her eye and slides down her pale cheek. I reach out and gently wipe it away with my thumb.

"Pickle," I say, my voice full of warmth. "You are my adoptive sister now, you are my sister just as much as Freya and Maya. I will do absolutely whatever it takes to make sure all of you remain safe. And if we find a way, when things eventually get better, I promise I will help you in any way I possibly can to try and find out what happened to the other pixies, even if I have to travel all the way to Fairie to do it myself."

My heartfelt promise makes Pickle start to cry again, and she flings herself at my neck, so I give her a gentle hug, careful not to accidentally damage her delicate wings. "Thank you," she chokes out between sobs, while also scratching absently at her wrist for a fleeting second before she catches herself and abruptly stops the action.

Pickle then gives me a quick, wet kiss on my cheek and heads back down the stairs, presumably to help Maya in the kitchen. She has really enjoyed helping in the café. Jenny then helps me down the hallway to the bathroom. "Jenny," I say, my voice serious. "You need to be incredibly careful now that I've managed to escape. I'm sure they will be coming for all of us soon enough."

"Yeah, I already figured that much out," she says with a sigh, her usual cheerful demeanour slightly subdued. "I will definitely watch my back. The ward you put on my car really helps, but I'm sure there's a way for them to bypass even that protection eventually." She helps me over to the bathroom sink so I can lean against it for support.

"I'm going to make sure that Beastie or Seraphina travels with you and my sisters whenever you need to go into town. Seraphina will constantly watch over all of you to keep you safe. That's one of the main reasons I created her in the first place – because I knew we would be stretched way too thin trying to manage everything, especially with opening the café," I tell her as she turns on the shower, then helps me get undressed.

Jenny can't help herself and gasps when she sees my injuries, especially the bruises I can feel around the top of my legs from where I fought what was happening to me. I don't want anyone else to see the result of what happened to me. "Reya, what did they do to you? Do you need to go to the hospital?" she asks, looking worried and fearful of what they did to me.

"No! I don't want to go to the hospital; it will attract too much attention, and it's not like I can really tell the truth, but please, Jenny, don't mention anything to my sisters, please," I beg of her.

Jenny stares at me for a moment, and I can see the gears working, but finally, she says, "Okay, if you're sure, I still think you should see a doctor."

"You can do one thing for me. Can you get me the morning-after pill, please?" I can't look her in the eyes as I ask, looking down at the floor.

"Sure," is all Jenny says, then continues to help me into the shower, where my body aches in protest with every movement. I'm feeling even weaker now that the initial adrenaline rush from escaping is wearing off, not to mention the effort alone to get out of the room has really weakened me. My body feels like I pulled every muscle.

"Look after yourself," Jenny says softly, her eyes filling with unshed tears. "I'm scared about what's to come; they seem to be obsessed with you."

"I know, but I plan to deal with them, I'm going to make sure they pay, believe me," I promise. "I've actually discovered that I have another new ability I didn't even know about until the demons attacked,"

I say as I slowly step into the welcome warmth of the shower.

When the hot water hits my bruised and aching body, I can't help but let out a long groan of pure pleasure. My body instantly feels like it is getting a second wind as the hot, steaming water runs down my skin, starting to wash away the layers of dried blood and grime that's been stubbornly clinging to me since the demon attack. I'm also happy to wash away the feel of the monster off my body.

"I'll go get you some clothes to change into," Jenny says as she leaves the bathroom.

As soon as she leaves, everything starts to overwhelm me. I quickly place my hands on the bathroom wall and try to put a ward up, but of course, nothing happens, as I still have no access to my powers. As soon as I realise this, I fall onto the shower floor, all my emotions come out as I start to cry uncontrollably, whilst trying to stay as quiet as possible. I hope the sound of water helps block out all sounds from this room.

Not long after, the bathroom door opens again, and Jenny's hesitant voice echoes around the steamy room. "I'm leaving your clothes on top of the laundry basket."

I can't answer her as I'm still unable to control my emotions. The bathroom door then closes, and I'm on my own again as I let out all my feelings and dwell on what happened. When I look up, I see Jenny is actually still in the room with me. I can see her silhouette through the frosted door of the shower. "Are you going to be able to manage getting dressed after your shower?" she asks when I fall silent for a moment as she hovers near the door.

"Yeah, I should be fine now. Thank you, Jenny." I say after a few minutes of silence.

"No probs, I'll see you downstairs when you're all done," Jenny says, leaving the room and quietly closing the door behind her.

Once I've regained control, I thoroughly clean myself as I scrub my entire body raw. I wish I could have enjoyed the shower, but it just brought back too many memories, as all my mind wanted was to get rid of any remnants of the monster.

I finally step out and turn off the water. I honestly could have stayed in the warm, steamy enclosure for hours, but I know I need to leave some hot water for our unexpected guest, and if I stay in here too long, my sisters will come to investigate, which is the last thing I want. When I've dried myself off with one of our ridiculously soft towels, I wrap it securely around my body, walk over to the fogged-up mirror over the sink, and try to look in it. Of course, the glass is completely steamed over, so I use my hand to wipe away the condensation until it is clear enough for me to see my reflection.

I stare at my face, noting the few new bruises that have already started to bloom, then my gaze tracks down to my shoulders and the numerous cuts and scrapes that crisscross my arms. Looking back up at my face and leaning closer to the mirror to examine my eyes, I notice something subtly different about them. I lean in even closer, intently staring into my chocolate-coloured irises, trying to figure out precisely what has changed.

Around the very edge of my irises, I can make out a series of incredibly fine, almost imperceptible marks. They form a delicate band around the outer rim of my iris. I wonder for a moment if I have always had them, but as I continue to stare and mentally flick back through memories of other times I have stared into my own eyes over the years, I know with a certainty that these markings are new.

I tilt my head at different angles, trying to discern the colour of these tiny dashes. They are so fine and delicate, and they are lighter in colour than my normal brown eyes. However, for a fleeting moment, I could have sworn I saw a hint of a second colour. I'm sure I also saw a hint of a deep purple within the brown. Clearly, my mind is tired, and now, it is playing tricks on me. Still, it's definitely something I plan to keep a close eye on.

I study the rest of my face to see if anything else seems different. Thankfully, the rest of me seems the same until I glance at my hair. Again, for a moment, like with my eyes, I think I see a different colour near my roots, but with my hair wet, it's hard to make out anything, so I give up before I drive myself crazy.

I take one final, critical look at myself and how utterly rough I look, then quickly get dressed in the comfortable trackie bottoms and long-sleeved sweatshirt Jenny thoughtfully left for me. Jenny is a mind reader sometimes, as she knew that I would want to cover up my injuries, so they weren't immediately on display.

I'm incredibly grateful that the protective barrier we created by performing the full moon ritual is now actively helping us to heal at an accelerated rate. I hope most of my cuts and scrapes will be significantly healed by the end of the day, if not completely gone. I also can't help but dwell on the fact that the ritual hasn't been exactly as the ancient book described it would go, especially the part about seeing something tangible leave Jenny, Pickle, and Beastie, and even the foxes, and then visibly join our collective magical energy. There is no mention of that happening in the book. I desperately wish I could ask Papa Legba about it, assuming he would even deign to tell me the truth.

Once I brush my still-damp hair, deciding to let it air dry naturally instead of bothering with the hairdryer and brush my teeth, I head downstairs. I've got a lot of serious things that I need to discuss with everyone, and it will be best to do it while our unexpected guest is having his own much-needed shower.

As I make my way down the familiar creaking stairs, I instinctively try to focus on the general location of everyone in the house. Suddenly, I feel a distinct magical signature below me, at the very bottom of the house – a familiar energy that resonates with my cellmate and sisters, too. I can sense it shining like a bright, steady star, just like my sisters and father. That's when I realise it's our book of shadows, our grimoire.

How in the world am I going to explain all these strange changes that have started to happen to me, especially the unsettling new ability I discovered I have as we escaped – the ability to feel the exact moment when the shifters we escaped from died, and what I strongly presume were their souls leaving their lifeless bodies after we put some distance between us?

I felt a distinct, almost magnetic pull towards their departing souls, a strange and unsettling sensation. Part of me, a dark and unfamiliar part, actually wanted to go back to them, to somehow… claim them? It wasn't an overwhelmingly strong pull, thankfully, so I was able to ignore it consciously, but it's definitely something I don't want to experience again.

I have a sinking feeling that I will, however, and whatever strange connection or pull I now have to these departing souls, I really hope it isn't something disgusting or weird. Doris did say something about how she was pulled to me like I sent out a beacon. Again, I wish I could ask Legba about it or even Cat, whom I haven't heard from since I was taken.

Speaking of Cat… I distinctly heard her familiar voice in my mind when I was hit over the head and started to fall unconscious. So why hasn't she reached out to me since? Then, a possible explanation suddenly hits me. I was outside of our protective barrier when I was attacked and heard her. The room I was held in had magical wards just like our home does. Maybe all of the magical protections somehow block Cat from telepathically reaching me. This means I will have to try to fall asleep or perhaps knock myself unconscious with a specific rune outside our protective barrier to test my theory. Right now, though, that's impossible.

Catherine M. Clark

Chapter 38

The Weight of Legacy

As I rejoin everyone downstairs, I know Jenny and my father are watching me as I sit down on the couch. I try to ignore their stares as I watch Maya guide my still-dazed-looking father upstairs, and as they pass, our eyes meet. Sure enough, he is giving me the look I need him to stop doing, as it will pique Freya's interest. The look clearly shows his worry and concern for me, just like Jenny's.

As Maya leads him upstairs, I see she is carrying a pile of clothes; I guess Sam found something in his car that would fit him. Pickle and Beastie immediately join me. Pickle, her usual habit when feeling cuddly or needing reassurance, curls up against my neck, settling herself comfortably on my shoulder. In his massive hellhound form, still, Beastie lies down heavily next to me, resting his large, warm head in my lap, his dark eyes watching me with unwavering loyalty. He's clearly still having issues with shifting back to looking like a dog and reducing his size. I notice Ava and Sam can't help but stare at him; for humans, he seems like a monster from nightmares, not my nightmares, though, as I have something new now that will be there every time I go to sleep.

I'm secretly quite glad that Maya is going to be upstairs for this next bit of news. I want her to have some quiet time to connect with the man before she learns the shocking truth about his identity. I'm not entirely sure how she is going to react to what I have to say, especially in front of all our guests, so I thought it best to tell her in private, after everyone else has been filled in.

I notice Rose has shifted back already and is currently cuddled up with Ava in one of the armchairs by the fireplace we haven't used yet. Their easy affection is a comforting sight.

As soon as I sit down, everyone in the room turns and looks at me expectantly, their expressions clearly showing they are eager to know what happened during my captivity and how exactly I was taken.

I feel uncomfortable with everyone looking at me. I'm worried Rose might scent something on me, or someone might see the state of my wrists. But I'm holding the cuffs of the sweatshirt Jenny left for me tightly, so I don't accidentally reveal their state, as they prove something more has happened to me than what I'm going to tell them. I'm also glad our father is upstairs, so he doesn't blurt out about when I was taken from the room.

I'm about to start explaining the basics when we suddenly hear frantic, distressed voices from upstairs. "I'm no one! I'm no one!" My father's voice echoes down the stairs, filled with panic.

Then Maya's calmer voice tries to reassure him. "It's okay. I won't hurt you. I'm just trying to show you how everything works in here."

"Damn it," I mutter under my breath. "I guess my carefully laid plan isn't going to work after all." I turn to Sam, who is sitting nearby, looking just as curious as everyone else. "Sam, do you mind going upstairs and seeing if you can possibly help him, please? He's been locked away for a very, very long time and might be struggling a bit to be around Maya right now." *Especially as he knows Maya is also his daughter.*

Like everyone else, Sam gives me a rather strange and questioning look at my odd request, but he nods and says, "Sure, Reya. No problem." He then gets up and heads upstairs to see if he can assist.

"What in the world is going on?" Freya asks, her brown eyes narrow on me with suspicion. "Who exactly is this man you've brought back with you, Reya?" she presses.

"When I tell you, I'm not sure you will believe me, I sure couldn't believe it myself when I worked it out, so don't jump down my throat when I tell you, please," I say with a sigh, bracing myself for the inevitable fallout. My attempt to delay the big reveal is thwarted when Maya returns down the stairs a few moments later, looking rather flustered and worried.

Maya walks over to me and says, "Reya." She says my name, sounding so concerned. "Are you sure we shouldn't call for an ambulance? I really think he might need some professional help." Looking at me with wide, troubled eyes.

"He's exactly where he needs to be, sis," I reassure her gently. "We are all the help he needs right now. Please, sit down for a moment. I have something incredibly important that I need to tell everyone, especially you and Freya. This... this changes everything for us." My cryptic words cause everyone in the room to exchange bewildered glances.

"You better just spit it out already, sis," Freya says, her usual patience clearly wearing thin.

"I will, I promise. First, though, I want to take a moment to thank Rose for so bravely coming to help rescue me." I then turn to face the corner of the room to the left of the rear door, where Seraphina is currently hanging out, almost completely hidden within the deep shadows of the room. "Thank you, Sera, for coming too, and for somehow managing to convince Beastie to stay behind and not rush off half-cocked."

'It is why I am here, Reya, to protect your family,' she says in my mind, her voice a comforting presence. *'But why did you just call me Sera?'*

"Because Seraphina is a little bit of a mouthful, even for me," I tell her with a wry smile. "It's why I've never really liked to use it, *if* I can help it."

"Who in the world is she talking to?" Rose asks, her head swivelling around the room as she tries to locate the source of my seemingly one-sided conversation.

"Her shadow," Ava says matter-of-factly, as if it were the most normal thing in the world.

"Oh," Rose says, her eyes widening slightly. "That really creeps me out, Ava. There's an actual shade just hanging out in here?" she says a little too loudly, causing Ava to shoot her a sharp look and shake her head in exasperated response.

Maya, who clearly has something else weighing heavily on her mind, finally speaks up, her voice hesitant. "So, is… is your guest going to be staying here with us then, Reya?"

"Yes, Maya, he is," I confirm without hesitation.

"He can't!" Maya exclaims, her voice rising in panic. "Duncan will be here in two days! I've managed to put him off so far, but he will have so many questions if this man is still here. He might see things he shouldn't be seeing!" She looks genuinely terrified by the prospect.

"I wouldn't be so sure about that, Maya," I say gently. "I might have accidentally slipped up and mentioned Pickle…anyway," I pause for a moment as I know what I'm about to tell her is going to cause fireworks.

"YOU WHAT?!" Maya practically yells, interrupting me, her teeth grinding together as she glares at me.

I continue before she can say anything else, "I actually kind… of tested the waters a little bit while we were waiting for Michael. I found the bannister was suddenly fixed when I came downstairs, and he said he hadn't touched it? So, we talked a little bit about the paranormal world, and… and I even told him that I'm a witch." I brace myself, already cringing inwardly as I watch Maya's face slowly turn a furious shade of red. "He didn't seem all that bothered by it, sis," I say quickly, trying to defuse the situation. "He even talked a little bit about some of the stories he and Jenny grew up with," I say, glancing at Jenny for some much-needed backup.

"Well, I did say he would probably be fine with it, Maya," Jenny chimes in, shrugging one shoulder nonchalantly. "And honestly, the longer you wait to tell Duncan, the more issues it probably would have caused in the long run."

"I cannot believe this," Maya says, completely ignoring Jenny's input. She stands up abruptly and starts to pace agitatedly around the room while flinging her arms around as if she is internally monologuing as she paces.

"Can we please just talk about what actually happened to you, Reya?" Rose asks, looking genuinely annoyed by the detour. "I would really like to know the details so we can head off and return to our motel."

"I do too," Freya agrees, her gaze still intently fixed on me. "And I also want to know exactly who you've brought into our home. There's something about him that seems… strangely familiar."

I welcome the sudden shift in focus, as it conveniently delays revealing to my sisters that the man is our father. I decide to work my way up to the big reveal slowly, starting from the very beginning—from the moment I was hit over the head and heard Cat's frantic mental screams urging me to stay awake.

It takes almost a full hour to recount everything that happened. *Well, not everything*. My story is constantly interrupted by questions and exclamations from everyone in the room. I purposely avoided mentioning who my cellmate was until I explained how we escaped the heavily warded cell in detail. I finally have to tell them what the shifters wanted from me, which, unsurprisingly, didn't shock anyone. I made sure I didn't hint that they put their plan into action, but Freya looks at me when I explain this part, and I can tell she is wondering if they did something I'm not mentioning. Apparently, they have envisioned me in some shifter "bunny boiler," room, their term, not mine, whose sole purpose would be to produce magical cubs for their pack. *They aren't far off the truth.*

I also mention the unsettling fact that they hinted that I have already met their elusive alpha. This particular piece of news causes a significant amount of worry and unease, especially from Freya and Ava.

Beastie lets out a low, guttural growl of displeasure at this revelation, while Pickle instinctively tries to hold onto me even tighter than before, as if she is physically trying to prevent me from going anywhere.

Ava and Rose are both understandably confused about how I managed to escape if I was supposedly being constantly drugged. So, I had to explain my theory – that I believe I was somehow becoming physically stronger, and it doesn't seem to be a magical ability in the traditional sense. I also seem noticeably stronger at night, and I believe it might have something to do with the moon itself.

"That's absolutely ridiculous, Reya," Rose scoffs, rolling her eyes, "wolves are the only paranormal beings that are intrinsically linked to the moon and its cycles. Are you seriously suggesting that you are somehow linked to the wolves now?" she says, giving me a look that makes me feel like I've suddenly become her sworn enemy all over again.

I never thought she viewed me in any other way; I'm pretty sure she is only here because of her deep bond with Ava. Saying I am linked to the wolves, though, causes a reaction out of me that isn't normal. "No, Rose, I am definitely not linked to those disgusting, monstrous, sick fucking wolves," I say almost like I'm a mental patient who is just having a freak out moment. I calm myself when I see all the looks I'm getting, and with a calmer tone, I say, "But I do think the moon has something significant to do with our abilities – well, mine anyway. Even Papa Legba himself told Freya and me that we were born during a very special and powerful moon cycle," I explain, carefully omitting the other rather dramatic detail he mentioned – that there had apparently been a significant earthquake at the exact moment of our birth. Rose still doesn't look convinced by anything I'm saying, and I get a sinking feeling that I will continue to have issues with her sceptical nature.

By the time I finish recounting my harrowing tale, Sam and our father return downstairs, making me groan. I've taken too long explaining and delaying, so now I have to drop the massive bombshell about my father's identity with him present. I've really got no choice.

Once they were both sitting down, Jenny, ever the thoughtful one, gave up her comfortable armchair for him and instead sat on the floor near my legs, gently scratching one of Beastie's large, velvety ears. I notice how much better my father looks now that he's had a shower and brushed his hair. Sure enough, I can now see the golden blonde hues in his hair, and the way it shapes his face reminds me of Freya instantly.

I take a deep breath, look around at everyone gathered in the living room, and finally say, my voice trembling slightly with anticipation, "I'm sure you're all probably wondering exactly who our mysterious guest is." My gaze falls on the man in question, and even though he looks scared, he knows I need to tell them and gives me a very slight nod.

Then he must start panicking as he blurts out his mantra, "I'm no one! I'm no one! I failed her! I failed you all!" The last part of his frantic outburst clearly confuses everyone, and again, all eyes in the room turn back to me, silently demanding answers.

"Out with it already, sis," Freya demands, her voice sharp with impatience. "I can see it all over your face that this is something huge."

"It is huge, Freya, Maya," I confirm, my gaze sweeping over my sisters' anxious faces. "I... I think this is our father. Nathaniel." When the words leave my lips, a collective gasp fills the room.

The man whom I believe to be our long-lost father immediately starts his panicked spiel all over again, repeating that he is no one and beginning to rock back and forth in his chair, his eyes wide with a mixture of fear and confusion.

Nathaniel tries to curl into himself on the armchair, as if attempting to hide from all the stunned and disbelieving glares physically directed his way. "Elsie," he mumbles, his voice barely audible. "Where's my Elsie? It's all Cat's fault."

"Wait, what?" I exclaim, my brow furrowing in confusion. "Did you say Cat? Do you… do you know Cat?" I say shocked, quickly processing what he means by saying it was all Cat's fault.

"Has he not mentioned Cat before now?" Ava asks, looking equally perplexed.

"Nope," I reply. "He's mentioned 'Elsie' a lot, which I figured out is a nickname for our mother, but she hated it. I had a fleeting memory of our old neighbour calling her Elsie once, and our mother had completely lost it. I tried using it myself, thinking it sounded sweet when I was seven. Our mother went absolutely ballistic at me, telling me never to call her that again." I explain, my voice tinged with a hint of lingering childhood confusion.

I look at my remarkably quiet sisters, staring at the man in utter disbelief. Except for Maya, I notice, who is sitting slightly apart from Freya, quietly trying to hide that she is actually crying, tears streaming down her face.

"How can you possibly be so sure, Reya?" Freya finally asks, her voice still filled with scepticism. I knew the question was coming.

"Just look at him, Freya," I urge, gesturing towards the man with my hand. "He has our colouring, our exact same nose. But more than that, I can… feel it inside, you know? I know it's him."

"How long has he been a prisoner?" Freya presses, her mind clearly racing. "Has he been… like this… all this time?"

"He mentioned something about trying to save our mother during the attack," I say, my voice softening with sympathy as I look at the broken man in the armchair. "He said there were just too many of them, and he got overwhelmed and captured." A wave of sadness washes over me, quickly followed by a surge of intense anger. These fucking wolves took him from us, stole our mother, subjected him to who knows what kind of horrors all these years and used my body for their goals.

"Fuckers," Freya spits out, her hands clenched into tight fists at her sides. "I'm going to make them pay for what they've done." I'm right there with her, my anger simmering just beneath the surface, making my whole-body tingle like ants are crawling under it again.

"I think there have been witches helping the wolves," I add, recalling the runes on the room's walls. "The room we were kept in had strange runes carved into the walls, and I'm pretty sure there was some kind of ward on it too, because no sound could get in or out."

"I think you're right about that, Reya," Rose says, her sharp gaze thoughtful. "The trail when you were initially taken was completely wiped clean, as if someone had magically erased it. Around your barrier, the air absolutely reeks of wolves, but when your scent crossed the barrier heading north, there was a sudden void of all scents, like someone had meticulously cleaned the entire area."

"Do we think it could be Sandra?" I ask.

"We don't think so," Ava replies. "Sam actually went and watched Sandra for a while after you were taken, and he didn't see anything that indicates she was involved in your capture."

"That was incredibly risky of you, Sam," I say, full of gratitude. "But thank you for doing it. It sounds like we might also be up against one or two other witches as well, then."

"Maybe," Ava concedes, her expression troubled.

I turn my attention back to Nathaniel, who is still rocking gently in his chair, his eyes darting nervously around the room. "Nathaniel," I ask gently, trying not to startle him. "Do you know any of the witches who might be helping the wolves?"

"I am no one," he repeats automatically, his voice flat. But I wait patiently, knowing he usually follows his initial statement with more information. Sure enough, a few moments later, he continues, "They… they mentioned that the council sent someone to help set up the room where I was kept. They kept me… kept me from Elspeth Harper. I loved her so much. I failed her. This is all Cat's fault."

"What exactly do you mean by 'it's all Cat's fault'?" Freya demands, her voice sharp, causing Nathaniel to flinch visibly in his chair.

"Hey, Freya, be nice!" Maya says defensively, her protective instincts kicking in.

"We need some answers here, Maya!" Freya snaps back, her patience completely gone.

Then, Nathaniel surprises us all by saying, his voice surprisingly clear for the first time since his outburst, "Cat… Cat was the underworld goddess. You might know her by the name… Hecate." We all sit there in stunned silence, completely gobsmacked by his unexpected revelation. Even though I have a vague understanding of who Hecate is, it's Rose who finally breaks the silence, her voice full of disbelief. "She was killed thousands of years ago."

"No," Nathaniel says with a surprising amount of conviction, his gaze finally meeting ours. "A deal was made. The remaining gods… they left this world to the humans. They all agreed that no god would ever walk the earth again, or the others would kill the god who broke the rule. And we… we guardians were left behind to protect the plane doors." It was the most confident I've ever heard him sound since I was dumped in that room with him.

"Wait a minute," Rose interrupts, her eyes narrowing with suspicion. "Did you just say that you were one of the guardians?"

"Yes," Nathaniel says, his voice tinged with a deep sense of shame. "I was… I was the guardian of the underworld." I know exactly why he looks so ashamed; in his mind, he clearly feels he failed in his duty.

"Why does any of this even matter right now?" Ava asks, her brow furrowed in confusion.

"If he was one of the guardians," Rose says slowly, her gaze fixed intently on our father, as if she were trying to decipher some ancient puzzle, "then he absolutely cannot be your father." Her tone is sharp, almost accusatory, and I can practically see the wheels turning in her head.

"I… I don't understand," Freya stammers, completely bewildered by this new information.

"I can't get a proper read on him," Rose admits, shaking her head slightly. "I've never encountered anything quite like him before, and I don't think anyone in my entire lineage has either."

"Rose!" Freya exclaims, her voice laced with exasperation. "What exactly are you getting at here?"

"I'm no one," Nathaniel mumbles, shrinking back from Rose's intense stare. He doesn't seem like he is going to elaborate any further, so I'm just about to nudge Rose to explain whatever's on her mind when Nathaniel suddenly speaks up again, his voice surprisingly clear.

"I… I used to be a daemon archangel. My task was to be a guardian of the gateway to the underworld, to ensure that no demons ever escape. I also used to protect the Fairie gateway, too." The last part of his statement causes Pickle, who has been unusually quiet and looks like she might have been starting to doze off, to suddenly perk up, her wings twitching.

"I was able to sneak into this world because the angel who was guarding the Fairie gate suddenly left his post," Pickle says as she starts to study Nathaniel closer, "He looked panicked when he left."

"That… that was me," Nathaniel says slowly, "I was guarding the Fairie gate when I heard Cat call out to me in my mind. When I got to her, I saw this man… he looked like a regular human man… remove her head. It shouldn't have been possible for a human to kill a god." He then shudders at the memory.

We all stare at him in silence taking in what he is saying which I can't believe because of the implications, before anyone can say a thing, he continues saying more than I have heard him speak since I met him, "I then went to find Elspeth," his voice now filled with remorse. "I was worried that the attacks had started sooner than we had anticipated. That's when… that's when I was caught." He then curls back into himself in the armchair and mumbles, his voice barely a whisper, "I keep… I keep failing." At that last phrase, he looks directly at me.

Pickle suddenly lets go of me and hops into the air, her delicate wings fluttering gently as she hovers in front of Nathaniel. He initially curls even deeper into himself while keeping a wary eye on her as she approached. "I… I'm so sorry that you lost so much," she said softly with so much genuine sympathy. "But you saved my life that day. Thank you."

Nathaniel watches her intently, taking in every word she says. Once she finishes speaking, he slowly sits up straighter in his chair and gives her a small, hesitant smile. "I'm… I'm glad you made it here safely," he says, his voice still a little shaky, "and you found Elsie's girls and are now helping them."

"I try my best," Pickle says with a small, earnest nod. "But it's not always easy. They are all incredibly stubborn, especially Ragey." She then tilts her head and looks at me with a mischievous glint in her eye. "But now I can definitely see where she got her toughness from. Can I ask you a question?" she asks Nathaniel politely.

"Yes, Princess," Nathaniel says gently, his gaze softening as he looks at her. "You can ask me anything you want."

Pickle's head immediately snaps around, looking panicked at all of us, clearly wanting to gauge our reactions to Nathaniel calling her '*Princess.*' Of course, none of us seems particularly surprised to hear this, well, except for Ava, Rose, and Sam, who exchange bewildered glances. Pickle turns back to our father, her small face slightly flushed with embarrassment. "I'm not really a princess," she mumbles shyly. "But thank you for the compliment."

Our father looks genuinely confused by her denial, and I'm not sure if he is about to challenge her about being a princess, but he takes me by surprise and can't help groaning and glaring at Pickle. "I… I don't understand," he says, looking at Pickle, confused, "What do you mean by

'Ragey'?"

"Oh, well, it's Maya's special nickname for Reya," Pickle explains, giggling slightly. "Because she gets all '*Ragey*' when she gets angry and starts to lose her temper. It's actually been a really good thing, though, because it helps her take down all our enemies!" she says, almost sounding proud of me.

"Ah, I see," Nathaniel says thoughtfully. He then turns his gaze to me, Freya, and Maya, studying us intently for a moment before his eyes linger on Maya for a while. "You... you take after me the most, Maya," he says softly, a hint of a smile touching his lips.

I'm surprised by this and try to think about Tv shows with angels and what he might mean, but he continues before I can really get my brain to work on it, "You seem to have inherited my abilities, as far as I can tell." He then seems to remember something suddenly and turns back to Pickle. "Oh, I'm so sorry, Princess. What was it you wanted to ask me?"

Pickle turns bright red again, and her wings stutter for a moment, but she manages to stay in the air and doesn't look at us this time. "If you are an archangel," Pickle asks, her eyes wide with curiosity, "then where are your wings?"

Nathaniel's expression immediately darkens with pain and anger. "The wolves... they cut them off the very day they caught me," he says, his voice full of bitter resentment. "They did it to make sure I couldn't escape. Our wings allow us to travel between planes, you see, and unlike other magical beings, our power mainly resides within our wings. Only my healing ability comes from within me. They... they allowed me to heal myself just a little bit each month, barely enough to keep me alive, purely for their twisted amusement." As he speaks, his anger slowly begins to rise, and I can clearly see a familiar flicker of rage in his eyes, a rage that mirrors my own. Maybe I have got my temper from him after all.

"Will they grow back?" Pickle asks in shock and concern.

Nathaniel slowly starts to shake his head, his eyes filled with a deep sadness. "I'm afraid they won't, and as far as I know, they destroyed my wings, not that I'm sure if they can be re-attached after all these years."

"I'm so sorry," Pickle whispers, then, without hesitation, she floats over and gently hugs him. I'm relieved to see that he lets her and doesn't pull away from her comforting embrace. Pickle then curls up against him on the armchair and stays nestled by his side.

I, on the other hand, have something on my mind, "Are you saying if they have kept your wings there is a chance to re-attach them?"

"Maybe, I don't really know, and if they do still have them, there are too many of them to go searching," he says, looking resigned and worried as he looks at me.

"We will look for them once we deal with the wolves; they will be coming sooner or later," I say, knowing it's the truth and not all of us will survive it. Nathaniel gives me a slight nod.

Freya then looks like she has something on her mind. While Nathaniel seems up for giving us answers, she asks him, "Do you have the ability to wield hellfire?" Her question is directed at our father, but she looks at me.

Our father looks completely bewildered by the question, but before he can respond, I interrupt, my own curiosity is piqued. "Wait a minute. What exactly *is* hellfire?"

"When Ava spoke to Luca," Freya explains, turning to me, "she told him about what you did to her sword before the attack by the demons. He immediately asked her what colour your fire was. When Ava told him it was black, he said it was definitely hellfire, and that only daemons have that particular ability."

"Okay, so are you saying I got that ability from him?" I ask, looking at our father, who immediately starts to shake his head in response.

"I… I don't have that ability," he says, but sounds uncertain. "Hecate was the last being I knew of who possessed that kind of power."

His words only served to confuse all of us even further.

"I don't understand," I say, my frustration growing. "Where did I get it from then?" As soon as the question leaves my lips, Nathaniel's eyes widen with a look of worry, and he starts to fidget nervously in his chair, refusing to meet my gaze. "Where did I get the ability from?" I repeat, my voice now laced with a hint of tension.

"I'm no one," he pleads, his voice barely a whisper. "Please… please don't ask me that."

"Please, Nathaniel," I urge, my voice softening with desperation. "Please just tell me. I know absolutely nothing about my powers. I really need to know."

Nathaniel lets out a long, weary sigh and then reveals something that shocks every single one of us to our very core. "It… it was part of her plan. When we first heard about the planned attacks on the paranormal community, Cat… Hecate… she secretly visited a powerful seer on Earth. And she was shown a terrible vision – a future where the world had fallen into complete darkness and the human race was enslaved, used as nothing more than food and sport for some unspeakable evil. So, she devised a desperate plan to create a being far stronger than herself, hoping that this being would somehow help save the world from that impending darkness. So, Cat… she magically bonded her immense power to my wings, in the hopes that if your mother ever had a child with me, that child would inherit her extraordinary powers as well as mine and the inherent magical abilities of your mother's bloodline."

Chapter 39

Bloodlines and Burdens

Freya explodes at him, "You what?" her voice shaking with a fury I haven't heard from her since the day our mother was killed. "So, you're telling me you only slept with our mother in the hope of creating some kind of powerful being... all for some grand plan?"

"No... no, it wasn't like that," Nathaniel stammers, his eyes wide with fear as he looks at Freya's barely contained rage. "Maybe... maybe at first, there was an element of that, but I truly fell in love with your mother, Elsie. The plan didn't even really work out anyway, as nature clearly decided to create a balance and split all of your mothers, mine and Cat's, powers between the three of you."

His confession completely stuns me, and any lingering positive feelings I might have been harbouring towards him instantly evaporate. I naively thought that finding our father could somehow help us; we might finally have someone who could guide us and teach us about our complicated powers and heritage. Now, though, I'm not sure I want to be in the same room as him, knowing that he and Cat have essentially used our mother as a means to an end, just like the wolves have tried with me; he is just like the monster that raped me.

"Is there somewhere I can sleep?" our father asks hesitantly, his voice barely above a whisper. He clearly wants to escape and doesn't want to answer any more questions.

"Yeah, you will be using the spare room for now," I state flatly, my tone cold. I'm actually quite glad he's removing himself from my immediate sight. Right now, I desperately want to lay into him for what he and Cat have done – for essentially creating me and my sisters for some predetermined purpose, for making me constantly doubt myself and fear who I am and what I can do. They had no right, even if their intentions were to save the world from some unknown darkness.

"I'll take him up," Maya says quickly, jumping to her feet. We all watch in uncomfortable silence as she gently helps support our father as he slowly makes his way up the stairs. I see worry in his eyes as he gives me one last, searching glance before disappearing from view.

"I really worry about her," Freya says quietly once they are gone, knowing Maya couldn't possibly overhear.

"Me too," I respond, a knot of anxiety tightening in my stomach.

"Why?" Rose asks, looking from Freya to me, her expression curious.

"She's always been the sensitive one," we both say in unison, a lifetime of shared understanding passing between us.

"We should probably all try to get some sleep," I say, feeling the exhaustion finally starting to creep back in. "I know I desperately need it." Then I suddenly remember something else I need to tell everyone. "Oh, wait! There is actually something else I need to tell you all first."

"You need to eat something first, Reya," Freya says firmly, her practical nature kicking in. She gets up and grabs a plate piled high with Maya's delicious chicken lasagna from the microwave, handing it to me with a warm smile.

"So, what is it you need to tell us?" Ava asks, looking intrigued.

I take a large mouthful of the lasagna, and I can't help but groan aloud in pure pleasure. For some reason, it tastes even better than I remember, perhaps because there was a terrifying moment when I genuinely thought I might never get to eat my sisters' cooking again.

Once I swallow the mouthful, I look up at Freya and say, "I tried something in that cell, and it actually worked. When the demons attacked, I could feel them, and I'm sure I even felt and saw Ava and Rose in my mind, so I tried to reach out with my mind to see if I could sense what was outside of the room we were held in. It worked; I felt and saw things. Nathaniel shone brightly in my mind, and that's when I started to wonder who he was and what I was feeling from him. I realised he felt familiar, like you and Maya do to me. The issue now is that since then, I can feel everything and sense everything around me," I say, watching Freya's reaction closely to see if she looks worried, as I don't even know what this means now for me. "I can't seem to shut it off completely. I can... I can sense all of you in this room now, but I can't seem to sense the wolves."

"Really?" Freya asks, her eyes widening with interest. "Once you've fully recovered from that horrible ordeal, maybe you can try to teach me how to do that? I would like to see if I can do the same. That can be very handy, and I'm sure you will learn how to turn it off eventually."

"Sure," I agree easily, but I'm not really sure what else to say, as I didn't expect her to be okay with it.

"It will be helpful to know where you are if you are retaken so that we can find you," Freya says, and I agree with her. I understand her concern, especially after what happened to me. If one of us goes missing again, we can locate them quickly to prevent a situation like mine from occurring again.

"If you can sense all of us right now," Rose asks, her expression surprisingly neutral, "how far do you think this new ability might reach?"

"Not entirely sure yet," I reply. "I can only tell we are all here and the horses outside, apart from that, I can't sense anything or anyone else," I tell her as she looks at me suspiciously.

"I don't like that you can tell where Ava and I are," Rose says, looking angry.

"I don't particularly like knowing where you are either, but I'm

445

going to have to live with it," I say as my anger rises at her attitude.

"It could be handy in a battle situation," Ava says, trying to smooth things over by suggesting something I didn't consider. I had only seen it as a way to find my sisters if something happened to them.

"We should probably go. We need some proper rest," Rose states, giving me a dirty look.

"You should definitely leave," I agree, looking pointedly at Rose. "This is our fight, our fate." Before anyone can respond to my statement, Rose's phone buzzes, indicating that she has just received a message.

"Is it Luca?" Ava and Sam ask simultaneously, their expressions hopeful.

"It is," Rose confirms, glancing down at her phone. "He's talked with everyone, and they have all agreed to take you up on your offer, Freya." She looks directly at my sister, her tone neutral, but she gives my sister the same dirty look. Her words completely confuse me. *What offer were they even talking about?*

"Really? That's good news," Freya says, looking genuinely pleased and ignoring the way Rose is staring at her. "Do you need me to do anything at all to prepare?"

"What offer is he talking about, Freya?" Rose demands, continuing to give my sister the same look she always gives me. She abruptly stands up, forcing Ava to get up since she was sitting comfortably on her lap.

It's Ava who answers Rose, "When I was on the phone with Luca, Freya was standing next to me, and when we were talking about where they might go for safety, Freya suggested they come here as they will be safe behind the barrier and plenty of ground for camping."

"You what, are you serious?" Rose says, looking agitated. She starts pacing around, running her hands through her hair. She looks angry and ready to explode, then turns to Ava, "I can't believe you did this behind my back."

Of course, Ava looks hurt by her words and by how she is talking to her. "Hey, don't talk to her like that. It was my idea, not hers, and you weren't here, so she didn't go behind anyone's back, so back off," Freya says, getting in Rose's face. I can see this getting out of control, especially as Rose glares at Freya like she wants to hurt her.

I decide to get in the middle of this before it gets out of hand, "I think it's best you leave before something is said that can't be taken back. If I understand correctly, your pack is coming here to stay for a while. If that's the case, then, like Freya asked, is there anything we need to do?" I then get to my feet as well, waking Beastie; he immediately feels the tension in the room and how Rose looks at us with murder in her eyes, and starts to growl at her.

"As far as I know, you don't need to do anything, so it seems we will be returning later today with your new… guests." Her tone suggests she's worried about Rose's reaction as she tries to pull her towards the front door. "Come on, Rose. Let's go. We can discuss this back at the motel." Sam doesn't say anything and is already heading for the door.

"Okay," is all I say, trying not to provoke Rose anymore, as it's the last thing we need right now. I definitely have a lot more to say about the subject and this insane development.

Sam is out the door and by their car before Rose and Ava hit the steps. But before they join him, Ava turns back to me, her eyes full of genuine affection. "I'm so incredibly glad you're back and safe, Reya," she says warmly. "See you later." She gives me a tight hug, while Rose stares daggers at me.

I walk back inside, sit down, pick up my plate of half-eaten lasagna, which I left on the coffee table, and continue eating it with my left hand while using my right to send a quick text to Ava, saying, *'Please thank Rose again for coming to save me. I really do appreciate it.'*

I don't expect to get a reply anytime soon, so I continue to stuff my face with my sister's food as Beastie makes himself comfortable next to me until a realisation hits me like a bolt of lightning. I'm going to be meeting Luca later today. And for some bizarre reason that I can't quite fathom, I start to picture his naked body in my mind, even though I have absolutely no idea what he even looks like; it's the last thing I want on my mind as I'm done with men! I'm also not happy to be having shifters living here on our property for a while, I really don't want to be living with shifters, especially men, right now.

My mind then takes things a step further as I vividly imagine Luca and me kissing – really hot, passionate kissing – as we fall onto my bed. The intensity of the images startles me so much that I can't eat anymore, as I feel my body start to heat up in a way that has absolutely nothing to do with the food. To distract my suddenly overactive imagination, I turn to Jenny, who is sitting quietly just listening to everything, so I ask, "Are you okay?"

"I'm okay. I'm just shocked by everything, and it's not really my place to say anything. I'm just glad you're back," Jenny says, but she looks just as worried as the rest of us. Finally, but thankfully, my mind stops obsessing about Luca.

"You can say and do whatever you like. You are family now, Jenny, so don't worry if there is something you want to say or ask, okay?" She nods at me as her eyes are drawn to the front door.

Freya and Pickle re-enter the house. I hadn't noticed Pickle had gone out there to see them off. She immediately comes and settles back onto my shoulder as I continue to eat, now that I'm not thinking about Luca. Meanwhile, Freya lets the foxes out the back door, as they start to whine and paw at the door, clearly indicating their need to relieve themselves. Beastie lumbers out after them, and Freya stands at the back door, watching them as they do their business. When they all return inside, she goes around the house, methodically making sure that all the doors and windows are securely closed and locked.

By the time she finished, I had finally finished my plate of lasagna, practically inhaling the food because I was so incredibly hungry. I then head straight to bed without saying anything else, feeling utterly frustrated by my unexpected and unwelcome porn show in my mind about Luca; they were disturbingly real images of him, I don't even know what he looks like, doesn't matter as the images are seared into my mind now.

My sisters and Jenny decide to join me in getting a nap. They are exhausted too, as they couldn't sleep because they were so worried about me. I feel awkward when I get into bed and my usual bedmates get in bed with me; Jenny must sense my unease and sticks to the other side of my new bed, giving me plenty of space, as my new bed is huge.

Even though I'm tired, it takes me a while to nod off because I'm scared to dream, but I finally do. I don't sleep well, though, as I wake up a few times feeling scared and breathing hard from a nightmare, and each time it takes me a while to fall back to sleep. I know I wake Jenny and Pickle each time, Jenny doesn't say anything when I wake her as she knows why I keep waking, but I am surprised Pickle doesn't, as she did when I couldn't sleep when I was worried about Maya.

When we finally managed to drag ourselves out of bed, we were still tired, but we couldn't sleep as long as we wanted with guests arriving. When we all head downstairs, including Freya, we find Maya already downstairs in the kitchen, completely fussing over our father.

I also didn't expect to see him sitting shirtless by the sink, his back to us as we entered the kitchen. His bare skin is a horrifying canvas of old and new injuries – his body is covered in a disturbing tapestry of bruises in various stages of healing and a shocking number of scars, both new and old. Maya gently tends to the mangled stumps, remnants of what had once been his wings, her touch incredibly tender as she cleans them.

This is precisely what I was afraid of. He might be our biological dad and have been a wonderful father to us if he had been around. The harsh reality is that he never would have been a true father to us; we are just a byproduct of some convoluted plan concocted by him and Cat.

Chapter 40

Fractured Family

I want him gone! But I'm conflicted, as he was held prisoner all this time, apparently for trying to protect our mother. He definitely deserves some credit for that, and he also inadvertently helped me escape, so for the time being, I'm willing to offer him a roof over his head. He can stay with us until we figure out if he has anywhere else, he can possibly go – maybe wherever it is that daemon archangels typically live.

I strongly feel Freya will ultimately feel the same way I do towards him – a mixture of pity and cautious acceptance. Maya, though, I'm confident, is going to latch onto him in a big way, desperately trying to fill the gaping hole in her heart left by the devastating loss of our mother.

"Is everything alright?" I ask hesitantly, wondering if his injuries are even worse than I realised.

Maya visibly jumps, startled by our sudden appearance. She spins around quickly, her eyes wide and filled with a primal fear, her hand instinctively raised like when she creates a protective shield. Relief washes over her face when she realises it is just us, and her tense posture immediately softens. When I finally see Maya's face, her eyes are blotchy and red, and fresh tear tracks glisten on her pale cheeks.

"What's up? What happened?" I demand, my voice sharp with concern at the sight of her distress.

Maya struggles to answer, her breath catching in her throat. I quickly pick up my pace to reach her side. When she finally manages to speak, she has to pause for breath after almost every single word, her voice thick with emotion. "They... they... cut... off... his... wings... and... they... beat him... so badly. Why... would they... be so cruel?"

"They did it because they are disgusting, horrible creatures, Maya," Freya says firmly, stepping forward to place a comforting hand on our sister's shoulder.

"All they care about is themselves and what they can take from others. They have absolutely no empathy or compassion." As Freya says this, I notice her looking at me from the corner of her eye.

Then Nathaniel says, "What you said this morning, do you really think they might still have my wings? If they do, there is still a small chance that they could be reattached. But," he adds, his voice grim, "it would be incredibly painful."

"Wouldn't your wings have died and decayed by now?" I ask with genuine curiosity.

"Reya! Seriously?" Maya exclaims, shooting me an exasperated look.

I completely ignore her outburst and wait for Nathaniel to answer my question, which he does, "My wings are made of pure magic and power. Only hellfire, or the angels' equivalent, which has a few different names – some call it grace-fire or holy-fire, we generally refer to it as divine fire – those are the only two ways I know of to destroy archangel wings whereas normal angels' wings are much weaker and can be destroyed by regular magic."

"Well, I guess we're going to have to try and find them then, aren't we?" I say, my mind is already starting to formulate a plan. "Then you can finally return to the angel realm, or wherever it is you normally live."

Maya's tear-streaked face registers complete shock as soon as the words leave my lips. Then, I see a wave of hurt wash over her features, and her eyes begin to fill with tears all over again.

While I'm inadvertently hurting my sister's feelings, I haven't even noticed that Jenny has quietly put on the coffee machine and is busily sorting out Beastie's breakfast. I still find it slightly surreal how comfortable she has become with handling bowls of raw blood and large, bloody steaks.

Then she begins to assemble a small plate of assorted fruits for Pickle, which is a much simpler task. "Thank you, Jenny," I say gratefully, then turn back to Nathaniel and Maya and ask, "How are you feeling this morning, Nathaniel? Are you any better than last night?"

"Reya, why are you being so incredibly rude?" Maya exclaims again with so much indignation.

"What are you even talking about, Maya?" I say, screwing up my face in confusion, trying to figure out how simply asking him if he is feeling okay can possibly be considered rude.

"He's our father, Reya! Not just some random person you know!" Maya says, her voice rising slightly. And then it finally clicks – she doesn't like me calling him by his first name. She probably expects me to call him 'Dad' or 'Father.' Well, she's definitely going to be disappointed then, because there is absolutely no chance of my ever calling him "Dad."

Of course, Nathaniel chooses that exact moment to utter his usual, infuriating line. "I'm no one." Every single time he says it, I want to slap him upside the head to try and knock him out of this self-pitying state. I'm still incredibly angry about the whole situation with him and Cat, while also hating what those wolves have done to him.

"Actually, I'm feeling much stronger already, thank you, Reya," Nathaniel says, his voice surprisingly steady. "This… this energy field you have surrounding your home is quite intriguing. I've never encountered a healing field quite like it before. It has really helped me feel significantly better." He then confuses me by what he says next, "Your house… it feels like your mother, my Elsie. It's very strange. If I had access to my abilities right now, I'm sure I could figure out why I can sense her presence so strongly here. Anyway," he adds with a small, wistful smile, "it's nice. It makes me feel almost at home."

I practically grind my teeth together at his audacity, him calling our home *his* home. There is absolutely no way he is going to be staying here long-term. Then Freya, ever the logical one, asks, "How exactly can our house feel like our mother when she hasn't lived here in a very long time, as far as we know?"

"I honestly have no idea," Nathaniel admits, looking thoughtfully around the kitchen. "It just… it feels like her soul is still here, somehow."

"That sounds absolutely ridiculous," I scoff, my annoyance growing. "Maybe when you have magic and live somewhere for a long time, it leaves some kind of residual magical trace behind, and that's what you're actually feeling." I grab a mug of the freshly brewed coffee, move over to the couch, and plop down heavily.

"Maybe," is all he says in response, his gaze still sweeping around the room.

After that, Jenny pours everyone else cups of coffee and offers to make toast or cereal for anyone who wants it. I silently summon Sera to me. I could sense her roaming the edge of our property since I woke up. In an instant, her dark shadow materialises on the wall to the right of the television and asks in my mind, *'What can I do for you, Reya?'*

Before I can even respond, Nathaniel surprises us all yet again. "I'm not at all surprised that you have shades working for you," he says, his gaze fixed on the shadowy figure on the wall. "Hecate always utilised them extensively, the ones she truly trusted anyway."

What he says is incredibly confusing. Why would he say he wasn't surprised I would be using shades? Was he implying that I'm somehow just like Cat? If he is, I like him even less than I already do, which I didn't think was possible. What he's saying is that I've somehow inherited her affinity for shades and the hellfire ability when she bonded her power to his wings. I quickly get an update from Sera, and then she heads back out to patrol.

Then Nathaniel adds, his voice filled with nostalgia, "She also absolutely adored her hellhounds. She had one in particular that she loved more than any other, which was always by her side. She called him Jax." At the sound of the name, my Beastie, who was returning after his morning constitutional, immediately perked up as he came over to me, his dark eyes fixed intently on Nathaniel.

"You have got to be kidding me right now," I mutter under my breath, shaking my head in disbelief. I place my hand on Beastie's massive head and ask him, "Did you used to be this Jax?"

Instantly, he floods my mind with a series of vivid images – images of who I knew as Cat in various locations, and in every single one, she is affectionately calling him "Jax."

Great! So, not only have I apparently inherited some of Cat's powers, but I have also somehow ended up with her favourite hellhound as my own. Does this mean that none of my choices are truly mine? Has Cat's grand plan predetermined them all?

I keep the unsettling thoughts to myself, as my sisters are already worried enough about me. Then, Beastie shows me a series of images of Cat and Nathaniel together. I can't help but gasp softly at the sight of him in his true form. He used to be absolutely stunning – the most beautiful-looking man, well, angel, I've ever seen in my entire life, which includes Tv angels. No wonder our mother fell for him. Then I immediately start feeling incredibly weird and slightly grossed out because I think of him as a beautiful man.

"What is it, Reya?" Freya asks me, frowning with concern. My obvious reaction to seeing Nathaniel as he used to look is on full display for everyone in the room.

"Beastie just showed me some images of Nathaniel with Cat," I explain, still slightly awestruck. "And he... he used to look absolutely stunning, exactly how you would imagine an angel should look."

"Wait a minute," Freya says, her eyes widening in shock. "Are you actually saying that Beastie... was this Jax?"

"Excuse me," Nathaniel says feebly from his chair, drawing our attention back to him. We all turn to face him, his gaze is fixed intently on Beastie.

"What is it?" I ask, my curiosity piqued.

"Are you saying that *he* is Jax?" Nathaniel asks, his eyes wide with disbelief. "How did you manage to get him?"

"Well, it was actually a bit of a mistake," I say, waving my right hand dismissively to the side, indicating that I really didn't want to go over the entire convoluted story again right now. I have far more critical things on my mind, like the increasingly terrifying possibility that I'm somehow slowly morphing into this Cat, Hecate, the very being I desperately hope I will never have to deal with again. Well, apart from when something new happens to me, then I might really need someone to talk to who will have a clue about what is happening with me.

"Jax... is that really you?" Nathaniel asks as he still can't take his eyes off him. Beastie's body starts to ripple and shift again, he had finally managed to shift back to his dog form just before we went to bed this morning, but now when Beastie shifts back, he shifts back to his original hellhound form of how he looked the very first day we met him, with his red skin and golden eyes. Nathaniel's eyes widen, "Jax... how is it even possible for you to change your form like that? You shouldn't be able to do that." Nathaniel says, sounding astonished and stunned.

"He's been able to do that ever since I, well, bonded with him," I say casually, as if it's the most normal thing in the world, but you can still hear a slight hesitation in my voice.

"You *what?* Bonded with him? That, that shouldn't be possible..." Nathaniel trails off, his mind clearly struggling to process this information. He's silent for a moment, then he finally says, sounding worried, "If he somehow gained the ability to shift forms from you, Reya, who isn't even a shifter yourself, then what exactly did you get from him?"

Before I can even begin to answer, he continues, stunned with a hint of disbelief, "I can't believe you somehow turned him into a hellfire-hound. They were thought to have been wiped out a very long time ago. No one even knows how they were originally created, as they were just... here, when I was created, all the other beings around at the time had no idea either."

"I honestly don't know yet exactly what I got from him," I finally admit, my mind still trying to wrap itself around the fact that my Beastie used to be Jax and Cat's favourite hellhound. Why didn't Cat say anything? "So, are you saying that by bonding with me, I turned him into something that was wiped out? Why?"

"When I was young, there used to be hellfire-hounds and hellhounds, hellhounds used to be the mutts of the race, while hellfire-hounds were feared, deadly, and uncontrollable. Things got so bad with them that Lucifer destroyed them all, and the hellhounds then became the protectors. I never knew that if you bond with a hellhound it turns them into a hellfire-hound, I don't understand how this wasn't known but I do understand now why Lucifer and Hecate were the only ones to have hellhounds, I'm guessing to make sure no one created one," Nathaniel says almost musing to himself about it more than trying to answer my question.

As we sit there in silence, taking in what he has just told us, he says, "Ummm, well, it will be intriguing to see what you got from him when you find out." Nathaniel says slowly, his eyes wide with a mixture of curiosity and apprehension. He then looks around at all of us and suddenly seems to realise just how many people he is in the room with. He abruptly hunches and tries to hide from us, looking slightly scared by his unexpected outburst.

I ignore his reaction and say firmly, "He prefers the name Beastie now, Nathaniel, so please don't call him Jax anymore." Nathaniel gives me a slight nod in response.

We all sit awkwardly in silence for about a minute, the weight of everything sitting heavy on us all. Then, Nathaniel decides to speak again, surprising me with how much he is changing in such a short amount of time. It's like he can't control himself now that he's free. "Of course he does. When a hellhound willingly allows itself to change its owner, they are compelled to go by a different name. When that new name truly sticks and they fully accept it, then the magical bond to their new master is finally complete."

Then, Nathaniel's head snaps up to look at me, his gaze intense after having been staring at Beastie.

"Hecate is going to be absolutely furious that you bonded with him, Reya," he says, his voice a strange mix of awe and concern. "She has everything planned down to the very last detail. She even arranged for you to bond with a powerful shifter, which would have made you so much stronger and even given you the ability to shapeshift. It seems all of her carefully laid plans have gone completely wrong from the moment Elsie gave birth to triplets. Hecate really should have considered that possibility, as it's a well-known phenomenon with witches with strong bloodlines."

"What shifter?" I ask, my anger starting to simmer again at the thought of all these manipulative plans Cat, Hecate, whatever she wants to be called, has put into motion to create us by essentially tricking our mother and using her for her own selfish purposes. The anger I've been feeling lately towards our mother starts to shift again as I begin to realise, she might have done her best with the situation she was dealt, and the ones truly at fault are Cat and our father; now, all I can think about is wanting him gone from our lives. Nathaniel doesn't answer my question as he now looks scared of me, with the way I look at him.

Chapter 41

Revelations and Resentment

When Nathaniel sees my expression, he once again seems to shrink in on himself, reverting back to the weak, feeble man I first encountered in the cell – a man who was scared of his own shadow.

"So, if I'm recapping everything correctly," Freya says, her voice dangerously low and tight with barely suppressed fury, "the '*Cat*' who's been visiting you in your dreams and guiding Ava and her team is actually the goddess Hecate? Who didn't die a very long time ago, but instead died just twenty-three years ago? And before she died, she put this elaborate plan into motion to use our mother as some magical incubator to create a powerful being to take on the entire paranormal world? And she also expects this, *being* that she tried to create using our mother, to then bond with a shifter, effectively taking away all their choices in the matter? That is just… unbelievably sick. You and Cat are almost as bad as these wolf shifters who killed our mother and are now also trying to use Reya to make their pathetic race stronger, too. What a truly fucked up legacy you have given us," Freya finishes, completely out of breath after her furious rant.

"Freya!" Maya exclaims, sounding shocked and looking at Freya disapprovingly. "He was a prisoner, Freya! We can at least try to forgive him for whatever part he might have played in our lives."

"Are you actually serious right now, Maya?" Freya says through gritted teeth, her eyes blazing.

Maya doesn't respond verbally; she simply shoots Freya a scathing look. I decide to stay out of it for the moment, as my involvement will escalate things into a full-blown shouting match, and I will end up on Freya's side. It's been a long time since we've been in a proper screaming match; I really don't want to regress back to those volatile teenage years, as we desperately need to try to stick together right now, not tear each other apart. As I focus on my sisters, I can feel Nathaniel staring at me, and I know why he is, it's because of the comment about using me, because he knows the truth of what happened.

So, I try to change the subject, hoping it will help my sisters and me to cool down a little as I'm just as angry as Freya, if not more so. I then start to realise whilst my anger builds, I feel that strange tingling sensation all over my skin, again, it's a familiar occurrence lately as I try to remember if this has always happened when I become Ragey, like Maya likes to call me. As far as I can remember, it's a recent thing, so I try to ignore it as I have enough to deal with right now. Whatever it is can wait, so I ask my question, directing it at Nathaniel. "Nathaniel, do you have any idea why Cat... why Hecate has suddenly stopped visiting my dreams?"

It takes him a moment to pull his attention away from my sisters' simmering conflict. He looks genuinely fearful about the chaos he has inadvertently caused and finally answers me, his voice still a bit shaky. "The energy field surrounding your property will effectively block her from contacting you. It's not a typical witch's ward; it's far stronger than I would expect you to create, being new to all this."

"That's what I thought," I say, a wave of relief washing over me as he confirms my suspicions. I'm definitely glad that she can't just pop into my head whenever she feels like it anymore.

"So, why has Hecate kept her true identity a secret from us all this time?" I ask Nathaniel, determined to get as many of my lingering questions answered while he feels up to it and while he's here.

It takes him a few moments to consider my question, and then it's like a mental switch flips with how his eyes shift and body moves, telling me he just remembered why. He answers me with a newfound clarity. I hope this particular revelation might not cause any further arguments. "That's actually a fairly simple one to explain. Before you were born, I believe it was what humans would call 1998. Hecate encountered a young girl who was in grave danger because this girl was of her bloodline, and she felt compelled to help her." He pauses momentarily, lost in thought. "The only problem was," he continues with a sigh, "she made the mistake of being completely honest with the girl and told her absolutely everything."

Nathaniel then takes a moment, as I watch him I see his eyes flick side to side like he's trying to remember the order of things, then he continues, "She told this young girl that the people she knew as her parents were actually shifters," he elaborates and frowns as he strains to recall the details, "and that they have been systematically drugging her since she was twelve years old to suppress her emerging magical powers. They continue to drug her for the next four years, I believe… my memory isn't quite as sharp as it used to be," he admits, and we can clearly see the effort he's making to remember by the deep frown lines etched into his forehead.

"Could that possibly be the same kind of drug that they used on me to suppress my own powers?" I ask, giving him time to remember, and a disturbing thought suddenly occurs. This girl's story sounds similar to what's happening to me, the wolves wanting her like they want me.

"I would certainly think so, Reya," Nathaniel replies, nodding slowly. "I'm fairly certain that the shifters have been passing that particular drug around, as most wolf packs seem to share the same misguided plans." He then continues his story, "The shifters planned to use this young girl to try and reintroduce magic back into their own species' genetic makeup."

I can't help myself, so I interrupt him again, my anger flaring up. "That's exactly what they want me for as well!"

"It is," Nathaniel confirms, gives me a look of sadness, averts his eyes from mine, and gives a grim nod. "The major problem, however, was that this girl, Devika, wasn't actually a witch, as the shifters had mistakenly believed. So, their plan was never going to work with her anyway, as she is a unique kind of hybrid; she is the child of a vampire and a reaper," Nathaniel reveals, surprising us all once again with this unexpected piece of information.

"Wait… vampires can actually have children?" Freya asks, her eyes wide with shock. "Is that even something we knew?"

"Yes, they can," Nathaniel confirms, "but only what are known as 'born' vampires can reproduce. Born vampires are what humans often call albinos. They have very pale skin and pinkish eyes and can actually go out in the sun, although it significantly weakens them, making them as vulnerable and slow as regular humans. So, they tend not to do it unless they are desperate. Created or turned vampires, look just like regular humans but cannot go out in the sun as it will instantly turn them to ash," he explains, momentarily digressing from his main story.

"That's actually really good to know," Freya says, filing away this new piece of paranormal knowledge the same as I am.

"So, what actually happened to this Devika?" I ask, a faint spark of recognition igniting in my mind, although I can't place it with the chaos of everything that's been happening.

"After Hecate tells her the truth about her heritage and what the shifters were planning, she promises to help Devika escape. She asked me to come up with a plan to get her away from the shifters' clutches, in a way that would ensure the humans wouldn't be actively looking for her, thus making it impossible for her ever to have a normal life, if I can't. Hecate also sent a shade named Kracis to keep a close eye on her."

I recognise it as soon as he says the name. This Kracis didn't look like a shade to me. Sera said she is one but was changing. I kept quiet, and I could see my sisters recognised the name, too. They also stayed silent, as we all wanted Nathaniel to finish his story.

"This particular shade is quite different from most others; she was a young girl when she died and had been living on the streets, forced to do things she never wanted to do, which had unfortunately darkened her soul. However, despite that, she still possessed a core of kindness towards others. She was on the line between going to the realm of angels and the underworld. When she died, the reaper who got to her first only collected souls for the underworld, so her fate was sealed. So, while she should have become a typical demon, something else happened, just like when she was human, a powerful demon took a twisted fancy to her. It used her for hundreds of years, eventually transforming her into a shade instead of a demon. Eventually, Hecate noticed her unique qualities and took her for herself, primarily using her to watch over humans or other demons," Nathaniel says, once again getting slightly sidetracked from his main story about Devika.

Nathaniel takes another deep breath before continuing, "We only know bits and pieces of what happened next, as Devika was understandably reluctant to talk about it, and Kracis eventually became magically bonded to Devika after Devika allowed her to feed from her. This somehow broke Hecate's direct control over Kracis, which shouldn't have happened, so Hecate couldn't order her to talk."

"Things must have taken a very dark turn because Kracis eventually turned up in Hecate's secret room, badly injured, and frantically told us that Devika was in terrible danger – a Lamia had captured her and a young boy. I don't know exactly what happened to the boy, but his soul was somehow trapped within Devika when I eventually found her. He was desperately trying to keep her alive because she attempted to take her own life; everything became too much for her to bear."

I'm shocked by this latest revelation, and the feeling of

recognition in my mind is becoming stronger and more insistent, but it's still just out of reach. "She was so incredibly close to death when I finally found her." Nathaniel continues, his voice full of deep sadness. "If it hadn't been for this boy's lingering soul, she would have been lost. When I found her in the bath, I sensed the presence of four fresh dead bodies on the property, and I could hear humans outside shouting that they were the police. So, I grabbed Devika and got her out of there as quickly as possible before she was discovered, and I took her to your mother, hoping she could help."

"Oh my god," Freya exclaims, her hand flying to her mouth in shock.

"After that whole ordeal, Hecate vowed never to reveal the entire truth to someone all at once, so that nothing like what happened to Devika would ever occur again," Nathaniel finishes, completely ignoring Freya's outburst.

"So, she's basically being a pain in the arse because of this Devika," Freya says, then adds, a thoughtful look on her face, "So our mother actually helped save her life?"

"Your mother was instrumental in saving her, yes," Nathaniel confirms. "Although it actually took the combined efforts of thirteen powerful witches to save her."

"Wait a second," I suddenly say, my eyes widening as the puzzle pieces finally click into place. I know exactly who the woman who led the demon attack against us is. I turn to Nathaniel and ask him, "What exactly did this Devika look like?"

Everyone in the room looks at me, clearly wondering why I'm asking such a specific question, but Nathaniel gives me the details I knew I would hear. "She is quite unique in appearance. She has striking silver and red hair, unusually bright silver eyes with a slight pinkish tint to them, and a pair of grey wings, which I've never seen before on any other being. Why do you ask, Reya?"

I shake my head slowly, trying to process the implications of this new information. I think back to the events of the demon attack and what the young girl said to me before I finally spoke to my impatient sisters. Finally, though, I tell them what I remember since my sisters weren't present during this particular attack. "The demons who attacked us, well, the army of shades that attacked, were led by a woman who looked exactly like this Devika. And there was also a young girl there, who looked like a ghost, and this Devika called her Kracis and accused her of being a traitor."

As I tell them, Nathaniel starts to shake his head vehemently in denial, but I continue, undeterred.

"When I destroyed the remaining shades, this Kracis told me not to kill Devika, because she has been tricked and is now possessed, and she asked me to save her. I sent Sera to follow her after the attack, and I'm almost certain she knows exactly where to find her, but she couldn't tell me because I was taken by the shifters right after the attack."

"This is… this is impossible," Nathaniel stammers, his face paling. "How can she be possessed? Devika would never intentionally hurt anyone. Wait…" His eyes widen with a sudden, horrifying realisation. "Elsie… there was a contingency plan for her to save your mother if the attacks were to happen, and if your mother… if she couldn't save herself and was killed, she was supposed to save your mother's soul, as the realm of angels could become compromised. Do you… do you know what happened to your mother's soul?" Nathaniel pleads with us, sounding desperate, looking like his entire world has just fallen apart again.

I remember something else, something Madi told us, as Maya's face paled, Jenny gasped in shock, and her hand flew to her mouth at the implications. Freya though clearly remembers what I do, and explains, "Madi mentioned to us that the person who was supposed to keep our mother's soul safe was now lost to them, so they now have no idea what happened to our mothers soul," the weight of this new information settling heavily in the room. Maya looks like she's on the verge of tears. I can see that she was starting to hope we might get answers from this Devika, but she must have just realised that we are far more likely to end up having to kill her, as she is clearly now our enemy.

"Please," Nathaniel begs, his voice cracking with emotion. "You must try to save her if you possibly can." It's incredibly strange to witness this powerful archangel reduced to begging. In all the stories I've ever read that involve archangels, they were never depicted as being this vulnerable; they were usually arrogant and thought they were better than everyone else, and it's their way or the highway.

"I honestly have absolutely no idea how to de-possess someone," I admit, feeling entirely out of my depth.

Nathaniel suddenly starts to look angry, which isn't good for him right now. His face, already sharp from his weight loss, now seems almost deranged with the rising fury. "If I had my powers," he hisses, his fists clenching, "all I would have to do is simply lay my hand on her, and the demon would be instantly expelled."

He then sits there, shaking his head in frustration, muttering something under his breath that I can't quite make out. Then, his head snaps up, his gaze locking onto Maya. "You," he exclaims, his voice urgent. "You might be able to do it. You seem to have inherited some of my abilities. Maybe you can get the demon out of her." He abruptly reaches out and grabs our sister's arm, shaking her roughly.

"Hey! Stop that!" I yell, instantly getting to my feet to get him to let go of Maya, but I didn't need to, though, as Freya moves with lightning speed, her hand flashing out and forcefully ripping his hand off Maya's arm. Maya looks completely shocked by the sudden incident, her eyes finally focusing on Nathaniel with the same wary and slightly hostile gaze that Freya and I have given him.

"Hey, Nathaniel," I say, my voice dangerously low and steady. "Don't you ever touch our sister like that again. We have no idea what we're doing when it comes to our powers, so all we can promise you is that we will do everything we possibly can to help this girl. But we are definitely not promising that we will be able to save her. If you don't like it," I add, gesturing pointedly towards the front door, "there's the bloody door. Feel free to use it."

Nathaniel immediately curls back into himself in his chair, his earlier flash of anger completely extinguished. He annoys me all over again when he starts to repeat his pathetic mantra, "I'm no one. I'm no one."

I turn my attention to Sera, whom I called back to me and has been listening from the shadows, "Did you manage to follow her, Sera?" I ask.

'I did. She went to a large house just north of the city. The house is crawling with demons,' she tells me. I sit straighter in my chair and relay what she told me to the others. Freya and Maya are visibly tense at the news, while Nathaniel stares at me with a renewed hope in his weary eyes.

"Well, it seems these are very likely the same demons that Ava and her team have been trying to track down since they arrived," I say thoughtfully. "I'd better warn them about this when they arrive later." My sisters nod in agreement.

Freya asks as she frowns with concern, "They aren't going to be able to take on that many demons by themselves. Even Ava won't be able to deal with that many after what you told us about the attack and being overwhelmed. On top of that, Sam can only just now see them, and he doesn't have anything that can actually hurt them, and I can't see Rose or this Luca wanting us to put this rune of sight on themselves."

"We can't really offer much help right now either, not while we still have our own issues with the shifters," I point out. "They could attack at any time, especially if we leave the relative safety of our property, from what they told me while they were holding me captive."

"Ava and her team are planning to help us deal with the shifters first," Freya says, ever the optimist. "So then, we can all work together to help them with these demons."

"Based on Rose's less-than-enthusiastic reaction to us earlier, especially to me," I caution, "we absolutely cannot guarantee that they will actually help us, even if Ava says they will. So, let's not rely on that. First and foremost, we need to survive the impending shifter attack before we start making any promises about helping anyone else."

"How long has it actually been for you girls?" Nathaniel suddenly asks, his voice quiet.

"What exactly are you asking, Nathaniel?" Freya says, giving him a confused look.

"Sorry," he mumbles, looking down at his hands as if he were studying them intently. "What is your current age? I honestly don't even know how long I was trapped in that room."

"Oh," Freya says, the confusion still evident on her face. "We are twenty-three years old. Why does it matter?" She isn't the only one who's perplexed by his question.

"You haven't... haven't come of age then," Nathaniel says, his words really starting to confuse me now. We legally came of age at eighteen; apart from that, what on earth is he getting at?

"What do you even mean by 'come of age'?" Freya asks, her voice starting to sound annoyed with his nonsensical statements. "We are twenty-three years old. We have already come of age."

Nathaniel looks incredibly uncomfortable under our combined scrutiny, all eyes in the room waiting for him to elaborate on his cryptic comment. "Of course, you just look so much younger. My mind isn't quite what it used to be," he says, but I can tell he's definitely lying. There's something he's clearly keeping from us, something significant.

I can't really worry about Nathaniel for now, and his strange pronouncements. Once the shifters have been dealt with, if we even survive it. I will definitely have to circle back and try to pry more information out of him about our age and why it seems to matter so much to him. So, to get off whatever bizarre tangent he's currently on, I ask Sera, "Have you seen any more wolves around our property since this morning?"

'Two more wolves have joined the six I already mentioned so there are now eight wolves spread out to the north, patrolling our perimeter, I'm guessing just in case you try and sneak out via the woods. There is also a single wolf in the woods out front, just to the left of the driveway, keeping a close watch on who comes and goes,' she says as I relay this to everyone else.

I'm starting to find her presence reassuring as I get used to her; it's almost like she is my internal monologue. Beastie just lets out a low huff at the news, as if a few measly wolves are nothing to be concerned about. He then helpfully sends me a mental image of himself single-handedly tearing all the wolves to shreds to keep us safe, which, while appreciated, is also slightly disturbing as he shows me in graphic detail.

"Sera, can you please head back out and keep a close eye on them unless you need to rest?" I ask, suddenly feeling a pang of guilt that I've had her constantly working to keep my family safe without asking if she needs a break.

'I don't actually need to rest in the traditional sense, Reya, unless I can't feed,' she replies, surprising me slightly and making me briefly wish that I didn't require sleep. *'Which I will need to do again soon.'*

'Okay,' I say mentally. *'Come and see me later when I'm on my own, then.'* And with that, I sense her presence slip away from the room. When I turn back to face everyone else, Freya gives me a knowing look that clearly questions the look I must have had on my face as I mentally spoke to Sera. "She needs to feed soon." This causes Freya and the others to wrinkle their noses in slight disgust, well, apart from Nathaniel, as he must be used to such things.

"Lovely," Freya says, her tone dry.

We talk for a while longer, the tension in the room slowly dissipating. "I'm going to check on the horses," I tell everyone as I stand up.

"I let them out earlier and made sure they had some food," Maya mentions as I head out.

"I ordered some more hay and feed as I didn't know if you had got round to it," Freya also mentions as I go.

"Thank you, no, I didn't get round to it," I say as I step out the back door.

As soon as I reach the field where our four horses are peacefully grazing, the one I instantly recognise as my horse, that somehow led Sera and Rose directly to where I was being held captive, looks over at me and starts to walk towards me as I make my way over to her. When we reach each other, I wrap my arm around her neck, lean my head against hers, and whisper, "Thank you for coming for me. I honestly don't know how you knew where to find me, but I am so incredibly grateful."

I then add, hoping against hope, "If you are special, like some of my other friends. Can you somehow let me know if you can understand me?" I wait, holding my breath, to see if I will get any kind of response.

I wait patiently, but she only nudges her head against mine a little harder, her warm breath tickling my ear. I'm not entirely sure if that's a response or not; I decide to take it as either she couldn't actually respond to me in words, or she is just a particularly intuitive and loyal horse who has somehow formed a strong connection with me and is able to find me if needed. Maybe my own burgeoning magical abilities have somehow forged that connection between us. Again, it's just another thing that I have no answers for and no one to ask, except for our father, who is apparently a daemon archangel.

The fact that he's an archangel is still incredibly hard to fully believe, and I'm not entirely sure what it means for our own powers and abilities, except that it finally answers one of my lingering questions. I remember the moment when Ava pulled her sword from the sheath on her back and felt a sudden pang of jealousy toward the weapon. When I felt jealous about Ava's sword, I felt a strange sensation in my hand, and then a sword inexplicably appeared in my hand.

From what I've learned in school and from countless books, the ability to manifest a sword seemingly out of thin air, imbued with something called "grace," is a power that some angels possess. So, does that mean that I have this 'grace,' or have I been able to conjure the sword using my own innate magic, whatever it actually is? One tangible change that occurred in that moment was that one more of the previously faded books in the library of my mind suddenly became solid.

I desperately wish I could try to produce another one of those ethereal swords right now, to experiment and learn more about this new ability. But the lingering effects of the drugs they gave me are still in my system, and I still can't feel my power. I really hope the impact of these suppressant drugs won't last much longer, because I know, deep down, that I'm going to need all of my powers and abilities if I'm going to be able to protect my family from the myriad of threats that are rapidly closing in around us.

Chapter 42

Rainbow Horses and Fairie Tales

Pickle makes me jump when she suddenly flies up behind me and says, "They are beautiful."

"They are," I agree once I manage to take a normal breath and steady my slightly frazzled nerves. I seem to be extra jumpy now, which I suppose is understandable after someone managed to sneak up behind me and knock me unconscious, and of course, what happened to me in that storm cellar. If I can't get control of my nerves soon, my sisters will start to ask questions.

"We have horses in Fairie, but they are quite different," Pickle says, fluttering down to settle comfortably on my shoulder.

"How so?" I ask, gently running my hand over her beautiful, silky hair.

"Well… we have horses in a vast array of colours, almost like the rainbows you have here in your world," Pickle explains, her voice full of wonder. "Then we have some with small, delicate horns on their heads, we even have a rare few that actually have wings." As she describes these magical creatures, I can't help but wish I could somehow visit Fairie to see these incredible, multicoloured horses for myself.

As I have this fleeting thought, I feel a strange tingling sensation spread out across my back, and my vision seems to go slightly hazy around the edges. I blink a few times, and the feeling subsides, my vision returns to normal, and the momentary haze is completely gone. I wonder if it's something to do with the wards around the property, or maybe my magic is starting to return.

I focus my attention back on Pickle and say, "I'm so incredibly jealous. We have fairytales about horses with horns, which we call unicorns, and the ones with wings we call Pegasus." I tell her, imagining how utterly cool it would be to have a horse with actual wings that could fly. Except, I'm also a little bit scared of heights, which is probably for the best since we didn't actually have horses that can fly, and the chances of me ever going to Fairie were, realistically, pretty slim even though I promised Pickle I would try and find a way to get there to help her family. I was scared when Sera picked me up and took me into the sky for a moment; my fear couldn't take hold of me at the time because I was so desperate to escape the area.

"What do they have to do with fairies?" Pickle asks, tilting her head in confusion, looking slightly green around the gills, as if the mere mention of fairies makes her feel unwell.

"They have nothing to do with fairies, Pickle," I explain patiently. "Fairytales are just what we call stories about magical creatures and events that aren't actually real… well, some humans still choose to believe they are real, anyway."

"Oh, okay," Pickle says, her expression clearing. She then flies over to my horse and runs her tiny hands over the horse's velvety neck. I see the horse watch her movements with careful curiosity, but she doesn't seem bothered by her touch. And then, I gasp, a sudden realisation hitting me.

My unexpected gasp makes Pickle jump. "What is it? What's wrong?" she asks frantically, her eyes darting around, clearly expecting to see some enemy suddenly appearing out of nowhere.

"The horse… the horse can actually see you, Pickle," I say, my eyes wide with astonishment at this unexpected development.

"Really?" Pickle says, her own eyes widening in surprise. She then flies directly in front of the horse's face, and we both watch in amazement as the horse's large, intelligent eyes track Pickle's every movement as she flits around. "You're absolutely right, Reya. That shouldn't be possible, as far as I know. I've come across other animals since I've been here, and they haven't paid me the slightest bit of attention."

"Maybe some animals can see you, then," I muse, trying to remember if I have ever seen the foxes react to Pickle's presence. But I can't recall ever seeing anything that indicates they can. They definitely see and respond to Drake, but he is my enchanted toy; a spell has been specifically placed on him, so he wasn't exactly a normal magical being.

"We will definitely have to test the foxes later," Pickle agrees, her little forehead creases in thought.

"But these horses… they seem different to me. I've been around horses for most of my life, and I have never met a horse that you can look into its eyes and almost see pure intelligence staring back at you," I say as I study the horse and still can't believe she knew how to find me.

"They do seem remarkably intelligent, don't they?" Pickle says, echoing my thoughts. "Maybe being around, you and your sisters, being on this property which is now surrounded by my magic, is somehow affecting them," Pickle adds, which makes me wonder if she might actually be correct and if it's even a good idea to have these horses here living on our property, especially after the trouble Drake is causing.

As I continue to study the horse, and it studies me right back with an unnerving level of focus, I become increasingly certain that a genuine intelligence shines in those large, gentle eyes. Just then, my phone dings, making me jump yet again. I pull it out of my pocket and read the message aloud. '*Reya, would you like to join me for dinner tonight? I hope everything is okay. I've been concerned about you after seeing your business hasn't been open because of electrical issues. I know someone who can help out with that. Anyway, let me know about dinner. Jacob.'* He even added a kiss to the end of the message. Goddammit, I completely forgot all about him. I'm actually slightly surprised he hasn't shown up at the house already.

"What's going on with your boyfriend?" Pickle asks, her tiny face full of curiosity, as Beastie lumbers over to join us. I automatically start to scratch the top of his massive head, his familiar weight leaning against my leg, strangely comforting.

I feel slightly uncomfortable at Pickle's use of the word "boyfriend." "He isn't actually my boyfriend, Pickle. We were dating, seeing if we liked each other enough to become more serious. To be completely honest, I've kind of lost interest in him recently," I tell her, trying to sound casual. Deep down, the thought of being with any man right now makes my stomach churn, so I have to end things with Jacob sooner rather than later.

Then, like it's been happening far too often lately, I start to think of Luca again, vivid images of him unexpectedly popping into my mind. The images, as usual, feel incredibly real, almost like we are really together. You would think if I'm going to have random, involuntary fantasies about a man I have never even met, I would at least imagine him looking like Thor – tall, blonde, and blue-eyed, which is usually my preferred type.

But the images of Luca that keep appearing in my head show a man with shaggy dark hair, intense dark eyes, and a slightly tanned complexion, which is definitely not a look I have ever consciously gone for. It's unsettling, to say the least, especially since I have no idea who he is or why I keep daydreaming about him.

Pickle has a slightly disappointed look on her face. "So, what are you going to do?" she asks.

Instantly, as if he can somehow sense my internal turmoil, Beastie shows me a series of hilarious mental images of him chasing Jacob away from our property. Jacob looked utterly terrified as he ran away crying. I can't help but burst out laughing at the mental picture.

"What did he just show you?" Pickle asks, her curiosity piqued.

"He showed me him chasing Jacob away," I explain, still chuckling. "And Jacob looks absolutely petrified of him as he runs bawling like a baby." Hearing this, Pickle starts to laugh too, her tiny body shaking with mirth. She even momentarily loses control of her wings and tumbles to the ground in her fit of giggles.

I quickly send a text message back to Jacob, typing, *'Thanks for the help offer. I actually have someone already looking at the electrical issues. I also have some family stuff going on right now, so I won't be free for a while. When we eventually re-open The MoonTree, we can definitely catch up then.'* Once I hit send, I stand there for a moment, watching the screen to see if he replies immediately, but nothing happens. I'm just about to put my phone away when it dings again, and I internally cringe, bracing myself for what kind of wounded or demanding reply Jacob might have sent.

When I unlock my phone to read his response, I see the message is actually from Ava, not Jacob. I quickly read her message. *'We are on our way to you now with the others.'*

"We should probably head back inside unless you two are planning on staying out here," I say to Pickle and Beastie, giving my horse one last affectionate stroke before I turn and head back towards the house, to let the others know that Ava is on her way with what is left of Luca's pack. The thought of Luca sends another shiver down my spine.

"I'm coming too! I want to see these other pack members, even if they can't actually see me," Pickle says, fluttering into the air and flying along next to me, while Beastie walks on my other side, his large form a reassuring presence.

I surprised them both by suddenly saying, "I love you both." Pickle looks somewhat surprised that I said it so out of the blue. Then I lean over and kiss Pickle's cheek, then lean down and kiss the top of Beastie's furry head as he's in dog form.

When I look back at Pickle, her usually pale face has gone slightly red, but she smiles shyly and says, "I love you too, Reya." Still, I wasn't about to tell her that I said it because I have a nagging feeling I might not actually survive whatever happens with the wolves, especially with the numbers Ava said the pack has back in Chicago, and what Rose has explained about shifter packs during one of our previous conversations.

We then continue our walk back to the house in comfortable silence.

Maya gently takes Nathaniel upstairs, as we all agree he shouldn't be in a room full of strange shifters so soon after his ordeal and probably won't be very good for his fragile mental state. Maya said she will stay with him for a while, which isn't at all surprising, as she has barely left his side since we got up.

I noticed something odd on the way back to the house from the field, so while we wait for our unexpected guests to arrive, I ask Freya, "Why exactly did you buy those rather imposing statues of two roaring lions and those rather creepy gargoyles? And why have you placed one lion and one gargoyle by the rear steps?"

"Well," she says with a mischievous glint in her eyes and a wide grin spreading across her face, "after the whole Drake incident, I had a brilliant idea!"

I can't help but groan in response, already anticipating more magical mayhem. "Oh, for the record, Drake was definitely not a good idea, Freya," I say pointedly. As if summoned by the mere mention of his name, Drake comes bounding over to us from where he had been playing with the fox cubs. He somehow manages to jump up onto my lap and starts to paw at me insistently, demanding attention, so I reluctantly start to stroke his soft fur as I wait for Freya to elaborate on her "brilliant" idea.

"Agree to disagree, sis," Freya says airily, completely unfazed by my disapproval. "Anyway, I've also turned those statues into golems. But don't worry, they will only actually come to life if we are directly attacked in their line of sight. I originally was going to put all four of them out front, but then I decided to put two out back as well, just in case we get ambushed from that direction, if anything gets past our barrier."

"Really?" both Jenny and I say simultaneously, our voices sounding with a mixture of disbelief and slight apprehension.

Then Jenny adds, her eyes wide with a childlike wonder, "That's actually really cool, Freya!"

"I know, right?" Freya says, looking smugly pleased with herself. "I've even been thinking about getting some garden gnomes and doing the same thing to them!"

"Absolutely NOT!!!" Jenny and I exclaim again in perfect unison, sounding horrified at the idea. The mere thought of animated garden gnomes running amok on our property makes my whole-body shiver involuntarily. I know I will now have vivid nightmares about hordes of tiny, pointy-hatted terrors.

"Okay, okay! I was just brainstorming ways to protect us," Freya says defensively, holding her hands in mock surrender to our vehement reaction.

"The statues are probably okay, I guess," I concede, "as long as people like Sheriff Radshaw don't happen to see them suddenly come to life and start battling some unseen foe."

"No problem there," Freya says, looking incredibly proud of herself. "I've already worked a little magic on them, so regular humans won't be able to see them at all." I shake my head slowly at her antics.

"If I buy some statues for my business, do you think you can do the same thing to them for me, Freya?" Jenny asks, her eyes sparkling with interest.

"Sure, no problem at all!" Freya replies enthusiastically, and I gape at her in utter disbelief.

"Are you actually serious right now, Freya? Do you really think that's a good idea?" I ask, completely stunned by her nonchalant agreement.

"Why wouldn't it be?" Freya asks, genuinely confused by my reaction.

"You might be able to hide them from human eyes magically," I explain, trying to articulate my concern, "but what if something attacks Jenny's shop, and then these invisible statues suddenly spring to life and start smashing into parked cars and damaging property?

God forbid one of them accidentally hits a passerby! Can you even imagine the chaos that would ensue?" I shudder at the thought of all the ways that particular plan can go horribly, terribly wrong.

"If something powerful enough to warrant animated statues attacking us actually attacked us in town," Freya counters reasonably, "I think we would probably have much bigger issues to worry about than a few damaged cars."

"Oh, whatever," I say, throwing my hands up in exasperation. I cross my arms over my chest and slump down further in my chair, still absently stroking Drake, who is now starting to wiggle impatiently, clearly wanting more than just a few absent-minded strokes.

I shoo him away gently, and he happily jumps back down to the floor and scampers off to rejoin the fox cubs, who are still playfully wrestling under the stairs.

After just over an hour and a half of waiting, we finally heard multiple cars approaching our property. We all immediately got up and headed out the front door, a knot of nervous anticipation tightening in my stomach. We watched as a sleek black SUV and the standard-looking rental car Ava had been using pulled up in front of the house. The SUV then carefully manoeuvred to the side of the driveway, ensuring it wasn't blocking the rental car.

I suddenly feel a strange wave of nervousness wash over me, especially when I feel an inexplicable pull, almost a magnetic force, drawing me towards the SUV. I'm not entirely sure what is going on, and the unfamiliar sensation makes me slightly worried.

But along with the strange pull, I also start to feel a confusing mix of happiness and a deep sense of longing, as if I'm being drawn towards something I desperately want but can't quite reach. I instinctively want to retreat back into the safety of the house, but my feet seem to be rooted to the exact spot where I stand, completely unwilling to move. This feels eerily similar to my pull towards Luca in my daydreams.

I have to consciously fight my body's sudden urge to rush towards the SUV, and I realise that my internal struggle must be showing on my face when Jenny gives me a rather peculiar look and raises a questioning eyebrow at me, clearly asking me what's wrong. I can only shake my head slightly in response, completely unable to explain the bizarre sensations I'm experiencing. After a moment, Jenny shrugs and turns her attention back towards our arriving visitors.

Ava, Rose, and Sam get out of the rental car and head over to the bottom of the steps. Then, another man emerges from the rental car, and under normal circumstances, the sight of him would make me at least slightly swoon. He's tall and ruggedly handsome, looking like a modern-day Viking, which is so my type. He has shaggy blonde hair, stunningly bright blue eyes, and a powerful physique. Again, I think, *'What the hell is wrong with me?'*, I'm completely bewildered by my lack of reaction. It's like the pull towards the SUV is overriding any other attraction I might usually feel.

Freya glances at me, and I instantly know that she thinks this man is my type. Usually, I would have been all over him like a rash, but I feel absolutely nothing. I don't react to Freya's knowing look, which in turn makes her frown slightly in confusion.

It doesn't stop her from whispering loudly, a huge smirk

plastered across her face, "Sis, I think your biggest wet dream just arrived." When I still don't react, she nudges me with her elbow and asks, "What's up with you?"

"I will talk to you later, Freya," I mumble, not looking at her. But I do keep my eyes fixed on the blonde Viking while also surreptitiously flicking my gaze over to the SUV, desperately trying to maintain some semblance of control so I don't just abandon all pretence of composure and rush over to the vehicle to see this elusive Luca finally.

Regardless of my surprisingly muted reaction to this literal god of a man walking towards us, Jenny and Pickle have clearly overheard Freya's rather indelicate comment and started to snicker simultaneously. Crap! I completely forgot that shifters have excellent hearing and must have heard every single word Freya said. The Viking then winks at me, and this time, I finally react, feeling a blush creep up my neck and across my cheeks. Of course, he noticed my reaction and smiled, a rather cheeky and knowing smile.

"Elijah, this is Reya and Freya Harper, and this is Jenny. Pickle is also here, but you probably can't see her unless you let the sisters put a specific rune on you to give you the *Sight*," Ava says, gesturing towards Pickle's general location even though Elijah can't actually see her.

Ava then turns to us and says, "Everyone, this is Elijah. He is Luca's other beta."

I pull myself together, trying to ignore the strange pull towards the SUV, and attempt not to react as Elijah's piercing blue eyes briefly scan over me. "Hello, Elijah," I say, trying to sound nonchalant. "It's nice to meet you finally."

I have no idea what he sees in my expression, but I'm really starting to struggle against this insistent pull on my body and mind towards whatever, or whoever, is inside that SUV. He gives me a rather strange, almost wary look, raises one of his thick blonde eyebrows, then turns his attention towards the SUV.

He glances back at me again, and for some reason that I can't quite understand, he takes a noticeable step away from me. It's almost as if he has just heard something inside the SUV that concerns him. I also notice Rose glance over at the SUV, giving me the same perplexing and slightly worried look. *'What the hell did they just hear?'* I wonder.

Rose stands back slightly, observing the initial exchange until she looks at me again after taking another quick peek at the SUV. Then, she tilts her head to the side thoughtfully and frowns as she starts to study me with an unnervingly intense gaze.

"What's taking the others so long to get out of the SUV?" Ava asks, with a mild impatience as she looks between Rose and the SUV.

"Maybe it's because there's still a shifter watching us from the woods," Rose says, her gaze flicking towards the tree line. "Although they are far enough away, they probably can't actually hear us." Her tone, however, didn't quite ring true, and it sounds more like something she is saying to deflect from the real reason for the delay.

Finally, the back doors of the SUV open, but the driver's side door remains stubbornly closed. The first person I see emerge from the vehicle is another man. He's shorter than Elijah, maybe around my height, and has dark hair that is styled in a swept-back fashion, longer on top and shorter on the sides and back, from what I can see. He also has warm brown eyes and is generally handsome, though not in the same overtly striking way as Elijah. Even though he's shorter than the Viking-looking Elijah, he has a broader, more muscular build.

When he reaches our small group, Rose introduces him while not taking her intense gaze off me. "This is Quinn." She then continues with the introductions, and when she gets to me, Quinn gives me the same curious and slightly wary reaction Rose and Elijah had.

Just like the others, he also glances back at the still-closed driver's side door of the SUV. When he looks back at me, he studies me intently for a brief moment, then moves to join Rose and Elijah, offering a polite, "Thanks for letting us stay here."

"No problem at all," Freya says warmly, finally noticing the strange looks that all the shifters are giving me. She shoots me a questioning look of her own, trying to ask me what is going on silently. I shake my head in response, completely unable to explain the bizarre magnetic pull I'm feeling. I try not to focus on the SUV, but I feel myself starting to lose the internal battle against whatever invisible force is tugging at me. My right foot takes a small, involuntary step forward, as if the unseen magnet has just won the first round.

The following person to approach us is a beautiful woman with long, flowing dark hair. I glance quickly at Freya and am surprised to see she isn't reacting enthusiastically to the sight of such a stunning woman. Rose then tells us, "This is Ivy."

We go through the same polite introductions, and again, Ivy gives me the exact same curious and slightly apprehensive look as the others. This is now starting to piss me off seriously, and I try, really try, to turn around and walk back into the house, but I find that I can't physically make myself move.

Another woman follows Ivy out of the SUV, and Rose introduces her, "Next is Sage." This woman also has long, dark hair like Ivy, but whereas Ivy's hair is an ashy brown with natural blonde highlights, Sage has an unexpected and striking greyish hair. It looks completely natural, which I know shouldn't be possible. I will definitely have to ask her about that later, I think to myself, my curiosity piqued.

The next person to emerge from the SUV practically bounces out of the vehicle and strides towards us with a confident swagger that I can't help but smile at. It's a mistake, though, because I momentarily lose my internal control again. This time, my left foot slides forward a little further until I regain my footing and composure.

Rose introduces him as Echo. He has a youthful, almost boyish charm about him. As he walks right up the steps to us, a bright smile on his face, he says to Rose as he passes her, "Rose, you never mentioned how absolutely beautiful they were." He then takes our hands one at a time and kisses the back of each of our hands in a courtly gesture. This makes Jenny giggle softly, which elicits a warm smile from Echo. And like the others, he also politely says hello to Pickle when Ava introduces her, since Rose didn't, as she can't see her.

Another beautiful woman then gracefully gets out of the SUV. I can see that she is the last one to emerge from the vehicle before she closes the door, apart from whoever is still sitting in the driver's seat, which I suddenly realise has to be Luca.

The unsettling thought then dawns on me that he could very well be why I feel this incredibly strong pull towards the SUV, and perhaps the other shifters already know precisely why.

This last woman, Dawn, has long, flowing dark hair, and it's immediately clear she is of Asian descent. She is undeniably beautiful, and for a fleeting moment, I feel a tiny pang of something akin to jealousy. After exchanging polite introductions, we instinctively turn our attention towards the SUV. We see Rose and her pack members exchange quick, hushed whispers with each other, their eyes flicking over to me every few seconds. Again, I try to *will* myself to turn around and walk back into the house, to escape this increasingly uncomfortable and inexplicable situation, but again, my body refuses to obey my mental commands.

"What in the world is going on?" Ava finally asks, her gaze sweeping between the increasingly shifty-looking shifters. Her attention then focuses expectantly on Rose, clearly wanting her to explain what is happening.

Rose remains stubbornly silent, which is starting to frustrate Ava visibly. She looks like she is just about to approach me when the SUV's driver's side door finally creaks open.

A man slowly gets out, and the very first thing I notice is his shaggy, intensely black hair. And instantly seem to recognise him inexplicably just from that single, rather unremarkable detail. It's him! It has to be Luca! The pull intensifies, almost knocking me off my feet.

Chapter 43

The Unwanted Pull

My body jerks towards the man harder, the unexpected force wrenching my grip from the veranda railing. I gasp, not just from the near fall as I'm forced down the steps and as my feet are dragged over the gravel and dirt ground of the drive area I finally regain control and before it's too late I manage to grab hold of the railing at the end of the steps that help me from moving any closer to the man, but at the sight of him, Luca who's been haunting my thoughts, I mutter, 'It can't be,' my knuckles white as I cling to the railing. Of course, my undignified lurch and my muttering of disbelief aren't going unnoticed. A ripple of curious gazes washes over me before every head snaps towards Luca and then back to me, like spectators at a bizarre tennis match.

As Luca finally turns to face me fully, his intense, dark eyes mirror my own shock and barely contained struggle. He looks like he's also battling an invisible force himself. My body jolts again, and a primal urge to run to him overwhelms me.

My feet shuffle slightly towards him, the gravel grinding under my feet, and it takes every ounce of willpower to plant my feet and stop myself from closing the distance as I desperately hold on to the weak railing, which I can now feel starting to give way under my grip. At the same time, my body starts to heat up, beginning from my core and rapidly spreading over my body, which in turn causes my heart to pick up the beat.

As I try to control my reaction, I see Luca take a few hesitant steps towards me, his hand gripping the open car door so tightly I can see the metal protesting, bending slightly under the strain and then distracting both of us and making everyone jump when the window in the door he is struggling to hold on to shatters. With the distraction, Luca and I lose our grip, and we take unconfident steps towards each other as we both sway as our feet move. *I'm so glad he didn't park closer.*

My gaze remains locked on his, and we both manage to regain control of our bodies. It's like an invisible thread connects us, pulling taut with every breath. A deep, visceral longing washes over me, every cell in my body screaming for him in a way I have never experienced before. This isn't the tentative curiosity I'd felt for Jacob; this is an all-consuming need.

Then, Rose's voice cuts through the charged silence, her words hushed in almost reverent tones as she speaks to Ava, "This is what it's normally like for two shifters to meet for the first time when they have the bond, from what our stories tell us. They try to fight it at first, but all give in to the bond in the end."

The word "bond" hits me like a physical blow. I remember when Rose and Ava told us about their bond, which they described as an unbreakable connection and shared souls. Shock, bordering on horror, surges through me. '*No freaking way is there a bond between this Luca and me; it's impossible,*' I think fiercely, digging in my heels, both literally and figuratively, to fight the relentless pull.

"Rose, are you serious?" Ava asks, her voice a stunned whisper.

It isn't Rose who answers; Quinn's voice, tinged with a hint of amusement, breaks the tension. "It is! Luca isn't happy about it. He started to feel a pull on him just before he left to come to us, and as we got closer to Luna Falls, Luca said the pull was getting stronger the closer we got here. He wanted to stop outside of town so he could get out and wanted to be picked up later, but we wouldn't let him be stuck on the edge of town on his own."

"Wow, I thought this was a good thing. Why doesn't he want to face it?" Ava asks, her confusion evident as I cling to every word, the revelation giving me unexpected strength to resist.

Clearly, Luca isn't thrilled about this either.

This time, Rose answers, her tone laced with exasperation. "Luca mentioned he was starting to see a woman in these...visions, and when he described her, I told him that it sounds like Reya. He freaked out because he believes she is a black witch and can't bring himself to fully trust her."

"Seriously, he still thinks that crap?" Ava says, sounding genuinely annoyed on my behalf. I appreciate her defence, even if I'm still reeling from the "black witch" comment.

"The stories we grew up on and everything that has happened in the world make it hard to trust now, especially when history is telling him black witches can't be trusted," Rose explains, sounding very understanding on Luca's behalf.

"I understand that, but you told me a bond is seen as a gift from your gods. Does he really believe he would get a bond with an enemy?" Ava asks, her agitation growing.

"We need to be quiet and wait for this to happen; we can't interfere or distract them," a woman's voice says softly. I'm not sure if it's Dawn or Sage, but her words add to the already thick tension.

"You are saying my sis has this bond thing with him, and not him," Freya says, her tone a mix of disbelief and a hint of playful challenge as she subtly gestures towards Elijah. "I thought the Viking look is your type, Reya."

"Yes, she and Luca seem to have a bond; it's a miracle to get two in the same pack," Echo says, sounding too enthusiastic about the whole situation, like this is the most exciting reality Tv show ever.

Every word and revelation gives me more strength to fight this unwanted connection as Luca and I remain locked in our silent battle of wills. It feels like an eternity has passed, though I know it's only minutes. My body trembles, exhaustion seeps into my bones, but I refuse to give in. I dig deep within myself, searching for an anchor, a reason to resist. Something powerful stirs within me, answering my silent plea while my mind starts to go back to that room and what was done to me by a shifter. *I can't be with a shifter, not in this life, not now.*

I blink for the first time since our eyes met, and it feels like a shift has occurred, a subtle hardening of my resolve. With a final surge of will, I manage to close my eyes, severing the visual connection. As soon as I do, a strange pang of loss resonates through me, a ghost of my intense longing. It's eerily reminiscent of my ache after my last disastrous breakup with Harrison.

With my eyes still closed, I turn, orienting myself towards the familiar safety of the house. When I know I'm facing the right direction, I reopen them, take a deep breath, and call out, my voice surprisingly steady, "Please come in." Behind me, I hear a collective gasp, a punctuation mark on my sudden action as I walk back into the house.

After I enter the house, a murmur of voices erupts outside, but the sound is muffled, distant as my heartbeat pounds in my ears, a frantic drumbeat that drowns out everything else. A wave of dizziness washes over me, the feeling of loss lingering like a phantom limb.

The pull towards Luca is still there, a faint tug at the back of my mind, but its intensity has lessened, allowing my rational thoughts to resurface. I consciously push the image of his intense gaze away, focusing instead on the immediate need for something grounding. I walk to the kitchen, grab a glass, fill it with cold juice from the fridge, and drink it down in large gulps. I refill the glass, put the juice away, and then I go and sit down in the living room, seeking the comfort of the familiar couch before the others can enter.

Freya and Jenny are the first to follow me; their expressions are a mixture of concern and curiosity as they approach me. Just before anyone else enters, I hear the distinct sound of a car driving away. Has Luca left? Has the intensity of this…bond…scared him off? A part of me doesn't blame him if he has, and I'm glad, as the last thing I want is to be linked to a shifter, especially in a romantic way; the thought sends shivers of disgust over my body.

Elijah walks in, followed closely by Ava and Rose, who are engaged in a hushed conversation with Ivy. As each of them enters, their eyes flick towards me, assessing. Freya, ever the practical one, makes gestures for everyone to find a seat so we can update them. I watch as the rest of the pack files in, a knot of apprehension tightening in my stomach. What will happen if Luca is still here and walks in?

But he doesn't, and neither does Quinn.

Once everyone else is inside, Rose offers a terse explanation. "Luca and Quinn have headed back to our motel to get the camping gear." A wave of relief washes over me at the news—a temporary reprieve.

With everyone finally seated, Freya, ever the thoughtful hostess, even in the face of a paranormal drama, asks if anyone wants a drink. She and Jenny busy themselves fetching beverages while Pickle flutters over to my shoulder and Beastie settles down heavily at my feet, their familiar presence comforting in the swirling chaos of my mind.

While we wait, the fox cubs, tails wagging furiously, trot in, followed by Drake, who bounces with his usual boundless energy, eager to greet the newcomers. When our unexpected guests see Drake, a wave of laughter ripples through the room. I half-expected screams of terror at the sight of the miniature panther, but I guess Ava and Rose have given them a heads-up about Freya's handiwork.

"When you described the golem toy panther, you didn't do it justice, Rose," Dawn says, a smile playing on her lips. Rose shrugs, looking distracted, her gaze flicking towards the front door every few seconds. She is clearly worried about Luca and the…bond…between us.

Once everyone has their drinks, we launch into catching everyone up, especially on what Nathaniel has told us. Our new guests are just as horrified as we were to learn about his clipped wings.

The revelation that our father is an archangel also lands with a significant thud, prompting a flurry of questions about our potential abilities. We admit we are mostly guessing, piecing things together based on what Nathaniel has told us. Still, it seems Maya has inherited a significant portion of his power, particularly her healing touch, even if it seems strangely limited to animals and plants. A peculiar inheritance, but one I'm grateful for, especially after I'd managed to take the front door off its hinges during a demon attack a while ago.

We then recount our encounter with Devika, the subsequent terrifying attack by the shadows, and the unsettling information my shadow, Seraphina, gleaned while following the woman back to Jackson.

As we all talk, I can tell Pickle is bored. She drops down to Beastie and whispers something to him, which causes him to get up. They both head out the back door unnoticed by everyone.

The news that I have my own shadow demon, or "shade" as they call it, is met with varying degrees of unease. Rose remains visibly uncomfortable, but the rest of the pack seems surprisingly accepting, sharing stories of shades and their potential dangers as deadly, unseen assassins.

I still suspect they are more concerned about the looming shifter threat, but they all readily offer their help, a gesture of solidarity that eases some of the tension in my shoulders until Rose reminds them it's up to Luca, while the other beta, Elijah, remains silent on the subject.

Seeing Elijah remain silent, Rose immediately protests, reminding him they are here for safety, not to fight. Elijah, however, firmly tells her to get over her *insecurities* about me, stating he can see the truth of my character, and even if I were a black witch, I'm clearly on the side of good, drawing on his own experience with a black witch to support his assessment. Rose retreats into a sulky silence after that.

I could have kissed Elijah for his unexpected defence, but the thought only served to remind me of the intense, unwanted connection with Luca, effectively killing any nascent feelings of gratitude. However, I do notice that I now feel something for Elijah, like I would expect to feel when seeing him. It seems I may have broken this bond with Luca, which puts a smile on my face for the first time since our guests arrived.

Elijah ruins it when he brings up the elephant in the room, or rather, Luca, which I hoped everyone would politely ignore. I keep seeing everyone give me curious glances, assuming it's all about the Luca situation. *I'm clearly wrong.* "Luca is going to go nuts," Elijah says, confusing me.

Ava turns to Elijah and asks, "Why? What about?"

Elijah ignores Ava and directs his own question at Rose, "Rose, why didn't you tell us?" Elijah asks, his tone carrying a hint of accusation.

"Tell you what?" Ava asks, her gaze sharp as she turns to Rose, whose face clearly displays a guilty flush.

"I'm not sure what you're talking about, Elijah. If you have something to talk to me about, maybe we can chat later," Rose says, offering Elijah a pointedly dismissive look.

I scan the faces of our new guests. They all looked with varying degrees of frustration at Rose, confirming they were all aware of whatever she was trying to avoid discussing. Finally, Rose's shoulders slump in defeat, and she sighs, avoiding eye contact with everyone but me, offering a brief, almost apologetic glance before saying, "I thought it might just be me, that's why I didn't."

"What is going on?" I ask, my own worry and frustration bubbling to the surface at all the evasiveness.

Elijah decides to answer as Rose still looks determined to keep silent. "Reya, as soon as I met you, I started to feel drawn to you. It's hard to explain. I feel like I will be safe around you, and my animal side feels relaxed and calm; it wants to come out so you can give it your attention," he explains. His earnestness makes my earlier embarrassment about Luca seem almost quaint. My internal panic levels, however, are definitely on the rise.

"Are you saying all of you have this same thing as Rose and I do with Reya?" Ava asks, and I see panic washing over her face as she looks at Rose with pleading eyes. I'm guessing that she is hoping what she just asked is wrong.

"No, honey, it's nothing like the bond; it's so different," Rose says, but her reassurance doesn't seem to alleviate Ava's worry.

"Ava, you have nothing to worry about," Elijah says firmly before continuing, "There are other legends in the shifter world. One obscure legend tells us there are magical beings to which our animal side is drawn. It is said that when our race was created, we were drawn to our gods, one of the first pure shifters. Some stories mention the gods as having spirit animals inside them. We don't know anymore, as most of our history has been lost over time. So, of course, this hasn't happened for a very long time, but fragments are still passed down in our genetic memory," Elijah explains, his words sending a fresh wave of bewilderment through me.

Then, a fragment of memory surfaces – something Cat mentioned in one of her cryptic dream visits. It clicks into place with surprising clarity, but I'm unsure if what she was getting at is the same thing. "I know what's going on," I blurt out.

"You are not one of our gods," Rose says immediately, her tone sharp and dismissive, before I can even elaborate.

I frown at her and say, "Of course, I'm not, but I think maybe your legend is wrong."

"How dare you try to tell us you know more about our history than we do. You have only just joined the paranormal world and barely know what you're doing," Rose retorts, her anger flaring as she, predictably, jumps to conclusions.

"Rose, enough," Elijah says, his voice carrying a new weight of authority. "Reya, what is it you were trying to say?"

"I wasn't trying to say I knew better; I'm going to tell you something Cat told me when she visited me in one of my dreams," I say, shooting Rose a withering look. The sooner she and her judgmental attitude are gone, the better.

"What did Cat tell you? Luca and Rose have told us about this Cat, who I believe is actually Hecate, the underworld goddess, before she was killed in the attacks," Elijah says, looking to his pack members for confirmation, which they all readily offer with nods.

"She told me that because of the nature of my power, other paranormal beings on the side of good will be drawn to me. She made it sound like they would be drawn to me because it would make them feel I would protect them. Could this be what you are being drawn to? Which, believe me, I wish you weren't, as I have enough bed buddies," *Crap*. Why did I say that out loud?

A chorus of raised eyebrows and snickers greeted my unfortunate slip of the tongue. "What I mean is I already have Pickle and Beastie and don't want anyone else needing my attention or company." My clumsy explanation does little to quell the amusement, so I slump in my chair, wishing the floor would swallow me whole.

Elijah, thankfully, seems to understand the gist of what I'm trying to say. "You're right, Reya, what Cat told you is correct. The way we are being drawn to you does feel like we will be safe with you, so I have to ask why Rose has been so against being here and not wanting to help. I can only think that Luca has strong opinions about black witches, which have rubbed off on you. I don't have the same judgments, nor do the rest of us."

I can't help but peek over at Elijah. He winks as soon as our eyes meet, sending another unexpected shiver down my spine. A blush definitely starts to creep up my neck this time. Then Elijah, clearly enjoying my discomfort, adds, "Of course, if there is space on your bed, I would be happy to take it."

My cheeks burn so intensely that I feel like I can heat the house during a cold front moving in. I notice that the intense pull I've felt towards Luca seems to be receding even further into the background of my mind. Of course, the pack erupts in laughter again, and even Freya and Jenny join in this time.

"Oh my god," Jenny suddenly says, her eyes wide.

"What?" I ask, my heart leaping into my throat. Has she seen something? Were we under attack…again?

"I feel the same thing. I feel safe around you, and that's why I feel compelled to ask if I can stay with you," Jenny admits, looking a little sheepish.

"I don't understand. You're just human, aren't you?" Rose asks, her tone laced with disbelief, earning her another withering glare from me.

"Well, yeah, but I am descended from witches and can see Pickle without any help," Jenny retorts, a hint of defiance in her voice.

"I guess the small amount of witch blood still in your bloodline is strong enough for you to feel the pull as well," Echo says.

Then Elijah asks, "This Pickle is the pixie you have living here, right?"

"Yes," is my succinct reply.

"Reya and her sisters can help you all to see as they have this rune thing, they can put on you, which will let you all see what I can with my ring, and Sam can now as he has the rune on him," Ava offers, shooting Rose a pointed look that suggests this conversation has happened before.

"We know, Ava; you have already talked about it, and Rose is against it, the same as Luca," Echo says, glancing at Rose with an unreadable expression. I wonder what that's about. Maybe he is keen on getting the rune?

"Well, I was going to talk to you, Reya, about getting that

protection rune put on me as we might go up against witches at some point, and I would prefer not to be cursed," Ava says, her eyes pleading.

"Sure," I say with a smile, which Ava happily returns. "It does hurt, though; Maya sank her teeth into me to stop from screaming," I add, relieved that Maya is still upstairs with Nathaniel and hasn't heard my less-than-flattering description of her when I put the rune on her.

"Really?" Ava asks, her previous enthusiasm waning slightly.

"It's not that bad," Jenny chimes in, standing up to show off her protection rune, discreetly pulling down the waistband of her jeans to reveal the intricate design on her lower back.

"Yeah, Maya just isn't good when it comes to pain," Freya adds with a wry grin.

"I'm so happy to hear people talking about me," Maya says, appearing at the bottom of the stairs, a perfectly timed entrance that drew a fresh round of laughter.

Catherine M. Clark

Chapter 44

Introductions and Intrusions

All eyes turn to Maya as she appears at the bottom of the stairs. "Everyone, this is our sister, Maya," Freya says.

"Hi, everyone," Maya says as she scans the new faces in the room.

Ava then takes it upon herself to introduce everyone, while Maya joins us. "Is this everyone?" Maya asks afterwards.

"Luca and Quinn headed back to get all our camping gear," Sage says, and as she does, all eyes turn to me. Of course, Maya notices and gives me a look, which means she is asking what the look is all about. I wasn't going to bring it up in front of everyone, so I mouthed, 'Later.'

On hearing Luca's name again, I expect that I will start obsessing about him again, but I don't. I can still feel the pull towards him, but nothing like the moment we had outside when I first saw him in the flesh, so I change the subject. "How's Nathaniel doing?"

"Please refer to him as our father," Maya firmly states.

"He's not, sis. It may not have been his fault that he wasn't in our lives, but he is not our father. He's just our bio-dad, especially as we are just the result of his and Cat's plan to try and fix the world," Freya says, taking me by surprise while taking the words out of my mouth.

"Why are you being so horrible?" Maya says, and Freya shrugs in response, which causes Maya to grind her teeth in anger. I knew bringing Nathaniel here was going to cause issues.

Then Beastie walks through the closed door that leads off from the kitchen with Pickle on his back, making everyone jump at the sight of him suddenly appearing. Of course, our new guests can't see Pickle riding on his back like he is her trusty steed.

"Oh my god, did your dog just walk through the door?" Ivy says as she holds a hand over her heart.

"Ivy, remember I explained their dog is a hellhound," Rose says, looking annoyed with Ivy's reaction.

"Oh yeah, that's... a hellhound?" Ivy asks, confused.

Of course, Pickle hears what Ivy says and flies up off Beastie's back, flies over to Ivy, and smiles – a smile that portrays so much. I knew instantly what she was going to do. Sure enough, she turns to Beastie and says, "Show her the new, bigger, meaner you."

No sooner do the words leave Pickle's mouth than Beastie starts to shift into his newer, truer form. Then, he takes it a step up. Just like he did to my sisters to try and scare them, he grows in size, and two small horns on his head start to grow, really grow. So do his large fangs, which he makes look even deadlier and resemble something you would see on a sabre-toothed tiger. Then he starts to swish his now even deadlier tail with massive spikes on the end.

"Fucking hell," Dawn says as she scoots away from where she is sitting on the floor. Then, to make himself look even scarier, he ignites his flames, so he's covered in a sea of black.

I still don't know how either of us doesn't burn everything to ash, especially the chair I'm sitting in, as he climbs onto my lap. Well, a small part of him is on my lap as he's too big to fit. The flames feel soothing as they engulf me, and I hear a couple of screams coming from the women, unless one of the guys has a high-pitched scream.

"Do something!" Dawn cries out.

Beastie shifts back to his dog form, shuts off his flames, and starts chuffing. I join him as I laugh at the look on all the new faces. Freya and Jenny are laughing so hard they have to hold their sides, and even Maya is snickering. Then everyone speaks at the same time, making it hard to understand everything that is said. What I do hear is funny.

"That is impressive."

"My god, that was scary."

"Wasn't expecting that."

Pickle flies over to me when it is safe and lands on my shoulder, chuckling as she watches our guests. "How's it going?" she asks.

"Okay, so far," I say as I lean my head against her. "Well, apparently, I make their animal sides want to be around me," I tell her.

"Great, no one better try to steal my spot. If they try, I will poke them in the eye," Pickle says. Ava and Sam hear what she says as they are closest to me, and they start to laugh at what she said.

"What are you two laughing at?" Echo asks.

"Pickle said something funny," Sam tells him.

"Oh, is the pixie here?" he asks, looking around the room, hoping to see her.

I whisper as low as I can in Pickle's ear. She shoots up into the air and flies over to Echo, then she squeezes his nose, making him jump.

"What the hell!" he exclaims as he touches his nose, trying to work out what just happened—those of us who can see her start to laugh again.

"Getting this rune thing put on me is starting to sound like a good idea," Echo says, and Dawn agrees, while Elijah watches me with a smile. I'm not sure how I will deal with having so many shifters in the house, but they seem like okay people, so far.

Eventually, Luca and Quinn return, and they all help to take the camping gear out back, except when I heard someone say that Luca couldn't get past our wards, which caused me to snicker to myself.

The pack spends a few hours out back setting up their camping gear. I stay away as the last thing I want is to see Luca again so soon, but I can feel how close he is as the pull gets stronger when he returns. My sisters and Jenny do help, but one thing I notice is that Freya keeps pulling out her phone. A sly smile appears on her face before she slides her phone back into her back pocket, and I suddenly realise I have seen her do the same thing now and then for a few days, well, since Friday. She has to be texting, Dhara, it has to be, or it could be Madi. I hope not. The last thing we need right now is more demons being around. If it is Dhara, then we will have a similar issue as we do with Duncan. *'How will Freya tell her we are witches?'*

Luca never comes into the house, and as far as I know, he still hasn't got past the wards. I can feel him outside the whole time, and it starts to annoy me as his presence makes my skin itch. After he has a meeting with his pack, Ava lets me know they have updated him and Quinn about what we talked about.

Sam stays with me as he isn't part of Luca's pack, so he watches Buffy with Pickle and me. Even Beastie watches it and chuffs along with us when we laugh at something. Buffy is Pickle's latest obsession, and she has a crush on Angel even though he's a vampire. Well, I think we all have that guilty pleasure.

Ava and Rose come and say goodbye, promising to be back tomorrow. Then, Ava, Rose, Sam, and Luca head back to their motel. I'm momentarily worried that Luca will be staying here, and I let out a deep sigh when he leaves.

We end up ordering pizzas as Maya is preoccupied with looking after Nathaniel. She has had enough on her plate lately with all the baking she has to do for our new business, which I hope survives once this crisis ends and we can get back to living our lives.

Well, I hope my sisters will be able to, as I'm still unsure if I will survive this one, as I plan to kill every single wolf I can find, especially their alpha.

Our new guests are still outside sorting their gear out. We agree they should set up their camp just outside the back door so they are close and can use the kitchen and bathroom when needed. We also thought it best that they be camped out back so they can't be seen from our drive. The distance to the edge of the ward heading north also gives them cover, as you would need binoculars or something similar to see them.

Nathaniel returns downstairs to join us, insisting he will be okay with the shifters. He sits at the kitchen table and starts to eat a healthy meal Maya has prepared for him, even though we have pizza coming. Once he is settled, Freya starts on me when the rest of us are all settled in the living room. "Reya, what the hell?"

"What's going on?" Maya asks.

"Reya and Luca had a thing," Jenny says, then smirks. She clearly knows I'm trying to avoid the issue.

"A thing? What type of thing?" Maya asks as she looks between us.

"The Reya and Luca thing! You should have seen the way they stared at each other, and what Rose and Ava told me – they said it's basically true love, and our sister turned her back on it like she always does since we left school," Freya says.

"Oh, that kind of thing. Wow, it's about time she accepts love in her life again, right?" Maya says, looking so happy for me. Except she doesn't know everything, so she doesn't understand when I don't give her any look that I'm happy, which I'm not, of course.

"I do not have a thing for him, and what did Rose and Ava actually tell you?" I demand.

"You know, last Saturday, when we shared stories, they mentioned they had this ancient bond that is very rare and is supposed to bring two shifters together as they are perfect mates for each other. They were, of course, shocked when they realised that Rose's perfect mate was a human woman and someone of the same sex, as their legend says the bond also helps maintain strong bloodlines by producing stronger children," Freya looks so excited as she speaks and has to take a few breaths before she continues.

"They explained that when you see your primal mate, you are drawn to them, and you start to think of them constantly until you finally meet," Freya explains, and I'm already shaking my head in response at what she is saying. *No bloody way is this Luca my perfect mate. He isn't even my type, so it can't be this bond thingy. Nope, no way.*

"They are winding you up," I say, not wanting to admit that what they just said seems to be true. Even though I don't want to believe it, what I feel seems to confirm what they were saying.

I'm surprised when Nathaniel speaks up. I hadn't noticed he was heading over to sit with us, so he must have only heard part of what was said. "You have the ancient bond with a shifter, is it Elijah?"

"Why would you mention Elijah? You haven't met them yet?" I ask suspiciously.

"It was her plan for the daughter of Elsie to meet a special shifter called Elijah," Nathaniel says after he sits down on the free armchair.

"I don't understand. Are you talking about Cat? And how would she know our mother would have a daughter?" I ask.

Nathaniel raises an eyebrow at me before he speaks. Clearly, he expects me to know whatever he is about to say. "All witches only have daughters unless the man is a mage, then it can go either way, as mages only have boys."

"Okay, I didn't know that, and it isn't Elijah, it's Luca," Freya tells him, which makes him look confused.

"I don't know this Luca. She also didn't expect Elsie to have identical triplets, and neither did I, for that matter," he says as his gaze washes over us.

"We aren't identical; we are slightly different," Maya says stubbornly. She has never liked people saying we are identical. It's part of the reason Maya put blue highlights in her hair while Freya decided to go blonde. So, I'm the lucky one, as I didn't have to change a thing, except I have natural red in my hair, which neither of my sisters has in their natural hair colouring.

"It seems none of her plans were ever going to succeed, so I guess it was all for nothing, but if you have this bond with someone, you should accept it. Angels also have something similar and are accepted as the miracle it is," Nathaniel says, but when he looks at me with a smile, his face suddenly falls, and I know what he sees on my face.

As soon as he spoke, it became evident to me that I was definitely not interested in accepting this bond. I then recalled our mother mentioning in her letter that she believed our father was religious. A sinking feeling washed over me as I remembered her saying she didn't know what our father truly was. Knowing he's an angel, I still find it hard to believe, even after witnessing the two stumps on his back.

When I first read the letter, I thought she had kept this a secret, but now I wasn't so sure. "Did our mother know you were an angel?" I ask, needing to know if she had also concealed something equally important: that we were witches.

Nathaniel looks ashamed when I ask the question. "No, she didn't. She would have felt my power, but she never asked me. It surprised me until I learned more about their coven and discovered they accepted anyone without question as long as you didn't cause trouble. It also shocked me when I found out the coven had a big gated community the size of a small town," Nathaniel says as his eyes droop in sadness.

"I can't forgive you for what you did, to use our mother the way you did. Even if it's all Cat's idea, you still went along with it," I say as part of me wishes I could rejoice in finding our father, but I just can't be happy about it with the way our mother was used. The reason I can't is that they used her just like the wolves tried to use me, and I hope Jenny manages to get me the morning-after pill, as I'm not currently on any contraceptive right now.

Cat and our father are no better, and I'm never going to forgive the wolf shifters, even those that had nothing to do with killing our mother or what they put me through. Any wolf shifter I meet while I'm alive better start running because I still plan to kill them all.

"Reya, how dare you! He is our father and has been through enough," Maya blows up at me. She is worse than I thought she would be with our father.

"You are right, sis, but maybe it's better to keep your thoughts to yourself and talk to him in private like I planned to do," Freya says, and I can't believe she's on Maya's side with this.

"Whatever," is all I say, feeling annoyed with them both and a little angry.

Everyone is silent for a moment until Jenny decides to take the conversation back to Luca, which I don't want, and she should know better with what she now knows. I give her a dirty look, which makes her flinch. I instantly feel bad, but right now, I can't forgive any of them as I see realisation wash over Jenny's face.

"Sorry, I just wanted to say with this bond thingy, apparently because you managed to break eye contact with Luca and not act on the pull, you have started what is needed to break the bond permanently. I think it was Sage I was talking to, she said all you would have to do now is to say to him while looking him in the eyes that you don't want him, and it will break the bond, and you will never be able to get it back," Jenny says looking sorry for bringing up Luca but I could have kissed her right then and can't help but smile.

"Good, I will get on that when he is man enough to come near me," I say as hope rises within me that I can end this bond.

"Sis, he could be the man of your dreams, although Elijah is more like the type of man you have always gone for and talked about over the years," Maya says, looking hopeful for me.

However, I can see she still looks angry with me. I can see on her face that she believes I'm throwing something special away. What she doesn't realise is that I will never believe what I'm feeling is real, so I can never trust him, or me, for that matter. I don't care if the shifters and angels believe in this crap.

The way my sisters, not Jenny now, stare at me like they can't believe what I'm saying gets my back up, so I let my anger out. "Do you really think I can be with a shifter after what one did to our mother and to…?" I cut myself off and then stand up and head for the stairs. As I head up, Beastie and Pickle enter the house through the back door. They have been watching our guests and now look at me in a way that asks if I want them to follow me up. "Stay down here, please. I want to be on my own for a bit."

Catherine M. Clark

Chapter 45

Waking to Chaos

Ten minutes later, Jenny comes into my room and places a plate and a glass of juice on my bedside table. "Are you okay? I'm sorry for my part in going on about him and that thing," Jenny says and then starts to head out of my room.

"It's okay, I got overwhelmed with all the Luca crap. I've been obsessing about him ever since I heard his name, and then with what happened when I saw him scared me, Jenny. I can't be with a shifter, not after…. so breaking this bond is best. When I managed to turn away from him, I felt this thing between us start to break, until that moment it was in the forefront of my mind; once I turned my back on him, it's still there but is now in the back of my mind like a low hum," I tell her with my head buried in my pillow, so my voice is slightly muffled.

"I know how you feel right now with what happened to you, and I'm so sorry you had to go through that, as everything is still fresh, but maybe don't just go and break this thing. You never know how you might feel in the future," Jenny says, then leaves my room, not allowing me to answer her. It is probably for the best.

I eat my pizza and get changed for bed; even though I got up late, I'm mentally tired and still haven't been able to access my powers yet. Whatever drug they put in my water is strong and is starting to make me worried that I won't have my power back in time when the wolves come for me. I want an early night and use the sleep rune to send myself to sleep, as my mind won't calm down from everything going on right now.

I wake startled for some reason and find my room is still in slight darkness, but the door to my room is open; it shouldn't be, but then I remember when I fell asleep, Beastie and Pickle hadn't been with me, so they might have had to leave the door open. But something feels different in more ways than one. The first being, I sensed before my eyes had snapped open – I felt my power again, humming within me. Having it taken away and then returned has, for some reason, allowed me to feel it better than I ever did before. I had to look for it within me before, and now I feel it there, right at the tip of my fingers, my skin, and my whole body is tingling from it. It's almost like my body wants to change or do something.

The second thing I'm feeling is that my room feels crowded for some reason. Again, before I opened my eyes and now with my power back, I reach out with my mind into my dark room, and what I feel makes me panic and makes me shoot up to a sitting position as my panic goes into overdrive. In the darkness, I see large lumps on the bed around me when I only expect to see Beastie's large lump. My mind goes back to that room, about being taken and being on that bed.

This is what I get for not locking the back door. I scramble for the light switch for the lamp next to my bed, and when I manage to turn it on, I can't believe what I'm seeing, and I start to lose it. Before I can say or do anything, Pickle's voice breaks through the silence, "Hey, give a pixie some warning next time." I don't answer or look at her, but I can feel her struggle to right herself. Then I start screaming, "GET OUT, GET OUT, GET OUT," I then begin to kick my legs out at the large cats that are curled up around and on top of my bed. Deep growling fills my room as the cats are woken suddenly, either from my screaming or from my foot kicking them in the head, body, well, anywhere my feet land, really, and they all turn to face me and show me their teeth as they growl. But one by one, they all start shifting.

Then I hear Pickle swear for the first time since we met her and wonder if she learned it from us, "What the fuck."

Jenny joins the cats in being startled awake along with Beastie who I haven't kicked, thank god; Jenny joins Pickle by swearing, "Oh my fucking god what the hell are they all doing in here."

While Beastie starts to growl at them, I start screaming at them again, "Get Out Of My Fucking Room Before I Kill All Of You," then to show I mean it my hands start blazing with my blackfire. As I shout, I point towards my bedroom door.

All the cats are now humans, and they all look confused about where they are. They all start to scramble off the bed; the ones at the side of my bed start to back off. That's when I notice it's Elijah that had been curled up between my legs and before he can move, as he has to wait for a very naked Sage to get off first, I start to lash out again by kicking him and screaming at him, "Get away from me, get away from me you monster, you fucking monster."

Jenny wraps an arm around me and starts to say, "It's okay, it's okay, you're safe, you're safe, Reya." Then she grabs my face and forces me to look at her, "Reya, you're safe."

I blow out a breath when I see her. I really see her, and I start to calm down as what she says starts to sink in. I notice she can't help herself and is glancing out the corner of her eyes; when I do the same, I see what she is having issues taking her eyes off, very naked people scrambling out of our room as the guys' bits swing as they move. The girls boobs bounce as they also scramble out of our room, and of course bum cheeks wobbling and shaking as they go and I'm right there with Jenny as I stare, then how I reacted sinks in and I groan to myself.

Elijah is the last to leave and pauses at the door and turns back to us, "I'm sorry we invaded your space, I don't know what happened and why we all ended up in here," I am listening to him but I'm not looking at him in his eyes as they are currently fixed on his junk, which is very impressive and slightly aroused, out of the corner of my eye I see Jenny is just as fixated.

"Wow, that is well worth being startled awake," Pickle then says from below me. Before Elijah goes, he gives me a wink when I finally bring myself to look up to confirm who the junk belongs to and I feel my cheeks heat up when our eyes meet even though I'm still extremely pissed off with them all.

Just after Elijah leaves, I hear Freya going off on one at him, "What are you all doing in here and naked, what have you done, if you have hurt any of them, you're so dead." Then Freya appears at our door, and her eyes start to frantically search for us. She sees we are all okay when they land on us, and her body slumps in relief.

As Freya continues to stare at us, her eyes searching for injuries, Elijah says, "We didn't hurt them, as you can see. We are sorry for causing any distress." I then hear him heading down the stairs.

"What's going on?" Maya asks as she also appears at my door. "Was that a naked man? Wait, was that Luca? Have you accepted the bond thing?" Maya says and starts to look excited for me.

"No, it wasn't Luca; it was Elijah and the rest of the pack. I found them all in here asleep in their animal forms," I tell them, feeling bad for waking everyone.

"Oh! Really, all of them, did you have some kind of orgy or something," Maya says as her excited face falls and changes into a confused look as her mind has clearly taken her in the complete wrong direction.

Freya elbows her and gives her a dirty look, "Of course she wasn't having an orgy, if there was one going on it would have been in my room silly, this has to be because the pull thing you have on them," Freya says as she turns back to look at me.

"I guess," I say as I shake my head in response. Then Freya nudges Maya to move; they leave, closing my bedroom door before they go.

Once they have gone, I check on everyone and find Pickle looking over the edge of the duvet. She is very red-faced as she continues to look towards the bedroom door. When I look over to Jenny, she is equally red-faced and fanning her face to try to cool herself down. "Pickle, you are correct; that is a sight to wake up to. That was a once-in-a-lifetime event." I can't help but smile at her comment.

I check on Beastie, and he seems to be okay, but he doesn't look happy. Instead of being around my legs, he is actually between Jenny and me, which means he was aware of what was going on in here. So why the hell didn't he wake me? We are going to have words about it later.

Pickle crawls onto my lap and then asks, "When did they turn up?"

"I have no idea," I say, giving Beastie a look who avoids eye contact with me and then crawls on his belly to the edge of the bed, slides off the end, and sneaks out of the room as he vanishes through the door.

"Whatever it is they feel coming from you seems to have a stronger effect on their animal sides. Is this going to happen every night?" Pickle asks.

"I bloody hope not," I say.

"Why not? It's great to wake up to," Jenny says, then she realises what she just said and eyes me while mouthing, "Sorry."

"If they can't control themselves, I will have to ward the room so they can't enter. And as for Beastie and why he didn't wake me, he had better have a good reason, or he would have to find somewhere else to sleep till I forgive him."

Once I've freshened up, I head downstairs. When I approach the kitchen, I find Freya, Maya, and Nathaniel all sitting around the kitchen table laughing. When they see me approach, my sisters give me a look and start to raise their eyebrows, in an act Maya and I have done to Freya after a new girl has tried to sneak out of the house, hoping our mother doesn't catch them.

"Don't say a thing," I say.

"Say what?" Freya flings back.

"Just don't comment on what happened," I say as I prepare Beastie's breakfast, not that he deserves it. I can sense he and Pickle have gone outside, and I know he will be back soon and will be hungry. Then I grab something for Pickle and me.

"Not sure what you mean," Freya says, acting like she hasn't seen the string of naked people coming from my room. Then she changes her expression to one of realisation, and I knew she is going to go there, "Oh, do you mean about not asking about the orgy Maya said you had?"

Maya looks shocked and gives Freya a dirty look, "Hey, don't get me involved. Yeah, I thought that, like for a second."

"I did not have an orgy," I say, then notice Nathaniel is trying not to laugh. For some reason, I start to feel embarrassed like I've done before when our mother found out I had a boyfriend back when we were in school.

Then Jenny comes down and makes things much worse, "This must be the best morning I've ever had. I'm not sure what to do with myself now." This makes my sisters laugh, and even Nathaniel can't stop laughing.

"I hate you all," I say. "For the record, I woke up and found them in their animal forms, sleeping at the end of the bed and on the floor on my side. Apparently, their animal sides decided they wanted to be near me."

"I guess it's going to happen every night. Maybe I should share with you, and Jenny has my room for now," Freya says looking hopeful; she is such a whore, I think to myself.

"Hey, you have no chance, that's my spot. Find your own pack," Jenny says as she starts to fan her face again.

Before Jenny and my sister can continue this debate, I interject, "Well, if it happens again, I will ward my room so they can't get in or try to make it so they can't feel this thing from me."

"Do you really have to take such drastic action?" Nathaniel says, getting involved where it wasn't welcome. Out of everyone, he should know better, for why I don't want to wake up with a bunch of shifters?

"I do think I should take drastic action, as I have no desire to wake up surrounded by shifters, especially as a shifter killed our mother. I may side with other shifters to protect those I love, but I will never trust them," I say and give Nathaniel a pointed look, finally voicing how I feel and seeing in Freya's eyes that she now understands why I will never be interested in Luca, while understanding also comes to Nathaniel and he looks ashamed.

Now that my sisters understand, they both stop laughing. Nathaniel continues to look ashamed as he hides his face from me. I hate that he knows what happened, and I'm still waiting for him to drop my secret and tell my sisters, whom I never want to find out, what happened to me. If they do, they will start treating me differently, reminding me of it.

Nathaniel and my sisters kept quiet afterwards so I could eat my breakfast in peace, and Pickle and Beastie joined me. Not long after I finished my cereal, Elijah and the others entered the house, dressed, thankfully.

"Again, we are sorry for what happened," Elijah says. I just ignore him, put my bowl in the sink, and leave the house to spend some time with our new horses; only Beastie follows me out after he has finished his food and blood.

I feed the horses and then let them roam our field. As I clean out their stalls, Pickle joins me and starts to help by using her abilities to fill the stalls with fresh hay. We were getting low, but thankfully, we have the delivery Freya ordered while I was a prisoner coming tomorrow, unless the wolves prevent the delivery driver from getting to us.

We also have the issue of our business being closed after we had only just opened. On top of that, Duncan is getting worried about Maya and wants to be here for her. She told him we have some family issues to deal with, which may have been the wrong thing to tell him, as he wants to be here to support our sister.

Of course, I have the Jacob issue; he has been messaging me more than usual. Whatever relationship Jacob and I had is gone, as whatever I felt before isn't there anymore, so I need to deal with that, as I don't want to be one of those girls who leads him on. Even if I didn't have the Luca thing, what happened to me has made it so I can't be with a man for a long time.

Except for some reason, since I turned my back on Luca, I have started to feel what I expected to feel when I see Elijah, especially seeing him naked. I can feel I'm attracted to him, even if part of me is interested I still can't bear the thought of acting on it for two reasons, one him being a shifter and of course what the monster did to me; maybe if I can kill whoever this monster is I might feel different but knowing he's out there and is coming for me I can't think about relationships. So, Jacob has no chance now anyway, even if I still feel something for him.

After we finish in the barn, we head out to the horses. As we approach our large field, one of the horses makes its way over to me. Somehow, I know this is my horse and can't wait to get a saddle and tack so I can ride her.

My sisters can't wait to ride theirs, either. When my horse reaches us, she pushes her head against mine. I feel a connection now, it's different from what I feel with Pickle and Beastie, but it's there, especially now that my powers are back, and I'm able to feel things differently than before. I always felt connected to Pickle and Beastie, but now I can really feel it.

I run my hands over the side of my horse's head and look down at her legs to check that she's okay and has no issues, and as far as I can tell, she has no problems. I'm about to move on to check the rest of her when my eyes catch sight of something, and I have to look back down at her legs and stare at what I think looks different.

Catherine M. Clark

Chapter 46

Whispers in the Woods

Pickle sees my reaction and asks, "What is it?"

"Do her legs look different?" I ask.

"In what way?" Pickle asks as she lowers herself to see the legs better.

"I'm positive her legs *were* pure white like the rest of her, but now the bottom of her legs look darker around her hooves," I state.

"I'm not sure, I haven't spent much time around her," Pickle says after returning to my height.

I reach out with my mind and call Sera, and moments later, she appears by my side. "Hey Sera, do the horse's legs look different to you?" I ask.

'*I'm not sure, why, is there something wrong?*' she asks.

"No, I guess not. I wanted to check in with you. Do we have company?" I ask as Pickle and the horse watch Sera. "Wait, she can see you as well," I say, indicating to Pickle that the horse is also looking at her.

"You're right, she is. This is one special horse," Pickle says as her head swivels between Sera and the horse, whom I should really give a name.

"God, I'm stupid. Of course, she can see Sera. How else *was* she able to find out she could find me?" I say, shaking my head in annoyance from being so stupid, while Pickle smacks her forehead with the palm of her hand, something else I've never seen her do before. I wonder if she has also got that from us, as we do it all the time.

Sera then gives me the update I asked for. *'We still have several wolves around our property on the other side of our wards, and there is still only one out front,'* Sera informs me as I continue to study my horse's legs.

Then I see Sera's posture change sharply, and she looks towards the house. As I follow the direction she is looking in, I see two shifters sitting out back, chatting. Then I see their posture change as well, and they look towards the side of the house, but I don't see anything. "What's going on, Sera?" I ask.

'The wolf out front is heading towards the house,' she informs me as I continue to stare in that direction.

"What's going on?" Pickle asks, so I quickly update her.

As I continue to stare down the side of the house towards the drive area, I notice the two shifters get up from the chairs they are sitting on and head into the house; I'm guessing to let my sisters or Elijah know.

Sure enough, not long after, I see a figure appear, walking towards the house as Sera *mentioned. 'Do you want me to deal with them?'* Sera asks.

"Patrol the rest of our border to make sure the wolves aren't about to attack. I will go and deal with this one," I tell her, and she vanishes out of sight.

I start to head for the front of the house, and not long after, I realise who it is; even at this distance, I recognise them and start to get a bad feeling. Freya *has been trying* to be secretive about being on her phone. I know she must have been messaging a girl. I hope it isn't this one.

I order Pickle to get indoors, and in case she doesn't know, I tell her to get Freya to meet me out front, as we have a guest she is going to want to deal with.

I walk at a clip to the front of the house. I know Freya *has swapped* numbers with her. I just hope it's Madi she has been texting and not Dhara, who is now standing out in front of our house. From what Sera *told* me, she has been in the same spot out front all morning, where a wolf has been watching us since I *escaped*. This is bad because it only means one thing, and it is making my anger rise rapidly within me.

The shifters have reappeared out back, and when they see me, they start to head around the house to join me, but I wave them back; my sister doesn't need an audience for this. I'm not quick enough, as I see Dhara start to talk. I shouldn't have got Pickle to head off so soon; she must have flown as fast as she could.

As I round the corner of the house, ensuring I keep within the wards, I see Freya walking down the steps towards her with a huge smile. *Crap!* "Freya, stop! Don't go near her," I shout, and Beastie starts to growl as he follows me.

Freya freezes near the bottom of the steps and looks at me, confused. Her expression shows slight annoyance as she replies, "It's just Dhara. It's okay."

Freya is about to take the last few steps to join her, but I quickly use my powers to stop her from moving. I watch as she struggles to move, and then she gives me her really angry look, which she doesn't show off that often. "What the hell are you doing?" Freya says through gritted teeth.

"Should I tell her, or are you planning to?" I say as I step up next to Freya, still ensuring my sister can't move.

"I will tell her, but I have something else I need to tell you first," Dhara says.

"Be quick, or I will do it," I say, slowly reducing the power I'm using against my sister. I can feel she has stopped fighting against my hold on her and is now looking extremely confused about the situation.

"What's going on?" Freya demands.

"Freya, when I *saw* you for the first time, I *didn't expect* to feel what I *did*, so I *couldn't help* but return to see you again. Every time I *got* a text from you, I *couldn't help* but smile, the kind that makes your face ache because you're smiling so much, your muscles aren't used to it." *This is not what I expected her to say.*

"Shut it, tell her the truth; nothing you say will change anything, especially how she will feel about you," I say as my anger builds, and my skin tingles. My hands burst into flames as I start to lose control of my anger.

"Reya, what the hell? Why are you outing us in front of her? This has nothing to do with you; please leave and release me before we have a serious falling out," Freya says. She is getting really angry now, especially seeing my hands. Her anger, though, is aimed at me instead of Dhara.

I'm not going to give her a chance to worm herself into my sister's heart anymore. "She's a wolf; she's our enemy," I say as I give Dhara my dirtiest look.

"What are you talking about?" Freya says, her anger still building towards me. I have to reduce my power to hold her almost to nothing so that she can move, just not her legs. I have to do this because trying to maintain both abilities is draining, especially as I've only just *got* my powers back. She grabs my arm and tries to pull me up the stairs, which I allow her to do as it means she is moving away from our enemy.

"She's right, Freya, but I've fallen in love with you," Dhara says.

"WHAT!!! Did *you* just say?" Freya exclaims, freezing in place. She grips my arm harder, but this time, it's to try to keep herself on her feet.

"Why?" I ask.

"I *was ordered* to watch you while you were in town. I *had* no choice, as women have no choice in our pack. Me and some others disagree with what our alpha is doing and *have been trying* to do for years, but he is more determined than ever after his brother *was killed*," Dhara says with pleading eyes aimed at my sister.

"Are you serious? Are you really one of them?" Freya asks, now turning her anger towards the right person.

"When I realised how I *felt* about you, I wanted to tell you everything. And when they *took* your sister, a few of us *were trying* to find a way to get you out without them killing us, but you *managed* to escape before we could help, and we are sorry about what happened to you. How *did* you escape anyway with the drugs you *were given*?" Dhara asks me. But what she says causes Freya to look at me with questioning eyes. I try to ignore her questioning look as my anger goes into overdrive that Dhara has just hinted that more happened to me than I had told my sisters.

"Do you really think I will tell you how and expect us to believe all this?" I say, starting to get worried about my sister as she collapses on the stairs and begins to cry. She still has an angry look as she stares daggers at Dhara.

"It's the truth, and so is the fact I *have fallen* in love with you, Freya, so I asked to be the one to watch the comings and goings today so I could warn you; they plan to attack today and have been trying to find a way to get you off your property. When they do attack, a few others and I will leave and won't be a part of it. I only hope you will forgive me, and hope you feel the same about me as I do about you, and you all find a way to win," Dhara says and gives Freya one last lingering look, then turns and walks back down the drive.

I help Freya to her feet and then help her into the house. Beastie keeps an eye on our visitor as she walks off and shows me an image of himself growling at her like he always does with Jacob. When I get my sister indoors, I find we have an audience, as all the shifters are now inside and clearly have been listening. Maya and Pickle rush over to us.

"Get her upstairs," I tell Maya.

"NO!" Freya shouts and turns to face me. I see that the tears that *had been cascading* down her cheeks have suddenly dried up, and all that's left is pure anger.

"It's okay if you need some space," I say as I look around the room at all the faces watching us, and I can't help but wonder if they all *heard* what Dhara said about what they did to me.

"She said they plan to attack today. We need to prepare and work out how we are going to deal with them, as well as what she meant by what they did to you. What *haven't* you told us?" Freya demands, and I can't help but avert my eyes from hers; this is the last thing I want.

"I've called Luca; they are on their way," Elijah says.

"This is our fight; we don't need him," I snap back.

"Well, they are coming anyway and will help if they can," Elijah says, sounding just as stubborn as I can be.

"Whatever," I say, then face Freya. "I *told* you what *happened*."

Freya shakes her head at me, then barks, "Find someone for me to hurt." Then she continues, "I can't believe she *made* me fall for her; it's such a betrayal."

"I know, sis; I can't believe she would do this if she really did like you. If you did, you wouldn't betray them like this," I say.

"Thanks for that," Maya says.

"What's up with you?" I ask.

"What you just *said* - you basically just *said* I'm betraying Duncan's trust because I haven't told him about me," she says, then continues, "You can't help how you feel. From what I heard, she is against them, which means everything she said is true."

"Are you serious? I *didn't mean* anything towards you; there's a difference between being scared and not telling Duncan. We aren't trying to kill him, so it's different," I say.

"She said she doesn't have a choice," Maya says, then turns to Elijah and asks, "What she said about the women having no choice and having to do what they are ordered to do, is that true?"

"Men run most shifter packs, and women have no say or voice

and have to do as told or die. Wolf packs are the worst for this, but other packs like ours don't agree, and women can be betas or even alphas if chosen, so she *was* telling the truth concerning that," he says.

"She still shouldn't have allowed my sister to fall for her without telling her the truth," I say.

"Have you always done the right thing when you fall in love?" Elijah says back.

"If you want to help, maybe you can give us some space right now," I say, getting frustrated with him.

Elijah nods, and then he and the others head out the back door. "Sis, you *didn't have* to be so rude; they want to help," Maya says, shaking her head at me.

"Don't start," I say, feeling my anger increasing again. Since the wolves *took* me, I have been constantly feeling angry. I'm angry with these shifters, the demons who keep attacking, and still angry with our mother for leaving us in this situation. Now I'm angry at Nathaniel for getting caught and not being here for us. Even though he is here now, I am still angry because he used our mother for a plan. The biggest anger of all, which is keeping me angry, is what the monster *did* to me, and now, for some reason, my skin tingles like ants are under my skin. I'm also angry about what Dhara has done to my sister; she might be angry and want to hurt someone, but I am so angry I feel murderous. Maybe I will become this black witch Luca and Rose believe I am after all.

We hear a car heading towards the house before we can settle down and discuss what to do with the news that the wolves plan to attack today. "Who the hell is that now?" I ask.

Pickle flies to the window by the front door and looks out. "Reya, it's your boyfriend. He still looks hot."

"Why is he here? He isn't my boyfriend; we *were* just dating," I say and head for the front door. I open the door and am surprised to find Jacob already standing there. "Oh, hey, what are you doing here?"

"I've been worried about you, and with Jenny's place being closed as well, I thought I better come to check on you as you've been vague when I've texted you," Jacob says and, as a cop would do, pushes his way in and starts to scan the room, and his eyes fall on Nathaniel.

Because of how angry I'm feeling, I feel annoyed that he just barges in. I'm about to give him a piece of my mind when Nathaniel distracts me. He starts to rock back and forth as he did in the cell, and then begins to say and repeat that same line he always did. "I am no one, I am no one."

"Who is this? Is he okay?" Jacob asks, being rude.

"Oh, he's our father, we *found* him recently living on the streets because he has mental health issues," Maya says, sticking to the story we *thought* up if anyone asks, because of how he looks.

Jacob turns to me and looks so shocked at what Maya has said. "Are you being serious? He's your father?" I notice he looks pissed off for some reason.

I'm about to answer him, but Sera suddenly warns me, 'The wolves are moving towards the house in large numbers.'

"As I *said*, we have family stuff going on right now, so if you wouldn't mind," I say, trying to push him towards the door, which causes Beastie to start growling.

Then the back door opens, and Elijah pokes his head in and frowns when he looks at us. However, when he first appeared, he seemed extremely worried; he must have sensed we had company heading for the house.

When Jacob sees Elijah, he looks at him in disgust. I start to panic as I need him gone. "Please, do you mind going? I will call you tomorrow." *If I'm still alive*, I think. I then start to use my newfound strength to get him to leave before it's too late.

He scans the room one last time, then finally steps outside, and I follow him out with Beastie on my heels. Freya must have *realised* my reaction isn't normal and gets up and starts to follow me out, too.

I get Jacob to the top of the stairs, and then he catches me off guard as I start to see movement in the trees on the left of the driveway. "Please come with me. I need to talk to you," he says, but the tone in which he says it seems really off. I'm starting to panic, so I miss his movements, and he leans down to me. As his lips near mine, I can't help but breathe him in. My body reacts like I have no control over it, and I flinch backwards from him as my whole-body tenses. Fear washes over my body as images push their way to the forefront of my mind. I'm back in that room and I start to remember what I was feeling and worst of all what I could smell when the monster was leaning over me as he continued to violate me.

I recognise the way he smells—it's the same smell I *could smell* through the hood over my head. My eyes go wide, and as they do, a smile spreads across Jacob's face at my reaction. "It's about time," he says.

Then he tries to drag me down the steps as I remain frozen in fear at what I'm realising. He manages to drag me down about halfway when I start to fight back, and I start to see red. "It's you," I say as I try and get my brain to work, to work on whether Jacob is the monster who *raped* me in that room. It can't be, but what he just said indicates it is him. I struggle with this new truth, then, like the other times I've been with Jacob, my magic reacts, and something deep within me roars to life.

I use my power on myself so he can't drag me any further, as I start to see red. Then he says, "I see you're going to make this hard." Then he lets go of me and heads down the rest of the steps, as I stand there still frozen in fear.

"What do you mean by that?" I ask shakily, now noticing he has parked nowhere near the house. *Why would he do that?* I think as my brain is still battling with the truth that Jacob is the *monster, the alpha.*

Beastie continues growling under his breath and starts to break through my frozen state. I begin to remember how Beastie *has* always growled at him, and he did the same with Dhara; he *has been telling* me all this time that Jacob is the enemy. Also, my magic *has been warning* me *too*, that he's the enemy when it roars inside of me whenever we *get* close. I then feel Freya move in behind me and stop in the doorway as I feel so stupid, why didn't I push Beastie to explain why he kept growing at him?

Then, in the background, I hear Elijah going on about something, probably warning the others that the wolves are here. Then I hear him say, "There's something off with that guy; he has no scent at all. Who is he?"

Once Jacob is at the bottom of the stairs, he stops and faces me. He has a smile on his face that doesn't seem like a friendly smile at all. Then it all crashes down on me, all the little signs I've missed. What I *heard* Elijah say about no scent at all finally puts all the pieces together for me. I remember what Rose said when I returned home after being a prisoner to the wolves. She said there *was* a lack of scent.

"It's you?" I say again, not believing it.

Jacob smiles at me and says, "Yep, it *was* me. Now I find out it might have been a waste of time, as it wouldn't have worked, as you're not a pure witch. At least I *enjoyed* it, so it *wasn't* a complete waste." He then turns and heads for his police cruiser.

Chapter 47

The Beast Unleashed

My fury erupts like a violent inferno, and before I can even register my own actions, I'm sprinting after Jacob with reckless abandon. I hurtle down the stairs as my ears catch the desperate cry of Freya, her voice laden with terror and pleading, "Stop, Reya!" Meanwhile, I sense Sera moving stealthily towards the wolves she tells me are entrenched deep in the woods. Jacob is already at the midpoint to his cruiser when I surge faster, crossing our wards with one singular, burning determination to reach him and exact the revenge for what he had inflicted on me.

Freya's anguished cries ring out again, this time shrill and desperate, "Reya, no!!" The raw panic in her tone brushes past me like ashes in the wind, but my fury eclipses all reason as I press on, my heart set solely on retribution. As I tear across our drive, I feel the pulsing weight of Beastie at my heels, a relentless presence in the maelstrom. Then, I notice something amiss from the corner of my eye, a mass of bristling movement. I turn sharply and see a pack of enormous wolves barrelling towards me, their eyes blazing with primal hunger—it's clear they will overtake me long before I can catch up to Jacob.

My pulse hammers a frantic drumbeat against my eardrums as I skid to a halt, pivoting to face the snarling wall of fur and teeth. The metallic tang of bloodlust—theirs and mine—thickens the air. Rage surges through every fibre, a nauseating heat that tightens my chest and makes me want to *roar*. It isn't just Jacob I hate; it's these hulking, hot-breathed beasts blocking my path. My skin *prickles* violently, then seethes as if doused in liquid fire, an uncontrollable tremor racking my frame. Ignoring the screaming protest of my own nerves, I force my trembling hands up, palms forward, and unleash orbs of pure, searing fire—the air *crackles*. The incandescent blasts hit the two lead wolves with a sickening *thump*, engulfing them in a sudden, ferocious conflagration. Their pained yelps cut off abruptly as their forms blacken and collapse into drifting cinders within heartbeats.

In the midst of this chaotic inferno, I notice Jacob's cruiser beginning to roll away. Desperation fuels my resolve—I extend my telekinetic force to seize the vehicle, and in an explosive moment, the cruiser shudders to a dead halt as if caught in an invisible vice. But fate is not on my side; Beastie comes crashing into me before I can regain my balance. In the confusion of a wolf's sudden lunge, Beastie's powerful form collides with mine, sending me spiralling off my feet, and I am airborne.

I hear the sickeningly loud *crunch* of bone, a sound that vibrates through the air – Beastie's jaws clamping around the wolf's neck. Splinters fly. In that stretched second, I'm airborne, soaring over the snapping jaws of another wolf. Time seems to slow just enough for me to see the yellowed fangs, the saliva dripping, the murderous red glint in its eyes as it lunges for my legs. Then reality snaps back. Panic flares, instantly scorched away by overwhelming fury. *Idiot!* I curse myself for chasing Jacob, for this vulnerability, as the world tints, then floods, with a blinding, searing red.

Amid fiercely spinning limbs, I catch sight of the wolf I had just flown over, trying desperately to alter its trajectory and clamp its jaws onto me. It snaps with a menacing snarl, but my rapid movement sends it skidding across the rough terrain, barely missing me.

I slam into the ground, scattering stones that cut into my flesh, yet my anger renders me numb to pain. Scrambling upright, I survey the scene—a veritable tide of wolves advances on me like an endless ocean of snarling fury. I quickly dispatch the wolf as it regains its footing and starts bounding towards me again.

Five wolves descend like a stampeding frenzy when I look towards the woods. I raise my right hand, intent on unleashing another torrent of fire. Suddenly, a thick, twisting vine erupts from the earth below, lashing out to ensnare one of the snarling beasts and pinning it to the ground. The other wolves collide in a chaotic tangle, sprawling helplessly before me. Without missing a beat, I summon a swift and violent blaze that devours them one by one. The agonised cries of the wolves fill the air, a symphony of torment that ends in silence as their forms turn to ash before my eyes.

One wolf, cruelly trapped in the vine's suffocating coil, is left to its fate—crushed mercilessly until it collapses like a damp sack of potatoes. Peering around in a frantic haze, I search for Jacob only to find his car vanishing into the distance. Curse him—he had forsaken the fight by fleeing, likely to avoid being outed if the all-too-impatient sheriff turns up.

The pounding of heavy, relentless feet reaches my ears. As I turn around, a group of enormous big cats rush out of the house, charging into the battle. Their sudden appearance, though unintentional, offers a much-needed ally amid the overwhelming tide of wolves. Despite my simmering disdain for their involvement, the ferocity of our enemies leaves no room for pride.

I release two controlled streams of my signature purple fire—a containment measure to conserve my strength. One burst catches a wolf squarely, and it writhes in searing agony as flames dance along its hide.

However, the other wolves nimbly dodge my firestorm. I try frantically to track their lightning-quick movements, launching two additional streams which, though initially missing, somehow force one wolf crashing to the soil after an unseen force collides with it. It's grey—a figure that isn't one of our felines—and I have no time to dwell on its identity as the pack closes in around me.

With relentless determination, I hurl two more streams of flames. Sensing the urgency, the wolves scatter in a calculated attempt to divide my focus. I manage to scorch one on the right, yet my left, less practised and unaccustomed to such furious exertion, fails to connect, allowing a wolf to pounce onto me and drag me forcefully to the ground. I barely have time to elevate my hands to fend off its snapping jaws before its bite latches onto me.

The wolf would have overpowered me instantly if I *were* any less powerful than I used to *be*. Yet, I manage to hold it at bay as it snaps viciously, its razor-sharp teeth aiming for my head. My concentration wavers under the assault, and before I can ignite it into flames, a massive, clawed force intervenes—a swift strike from a big cat tears the wolf from my grasp as it lunges. In that split-second, I recognise Elijah's cheetah; I recognise it from finding him on my bed as I watched him shift back to his human form. He is surprisingly compact yet ferociously potent, devouring the threat with a strength that belies his size.

As the chaos swirls, I glance back towards the house. Freya and Maya stand on the other side of the wards. Freya's face is etched in intense focus as she commands the surrounding flora. Ensnaring wolves with creeping vines and thorned branches effectively immobilises them for a subsequent, lethal strike. Maya, on the other hand, throws up shimmering shields—force fields that pulse with protective energy, fending off the relentless assault, giving the cats the time to strike with ease. Their unified efforts underscore the desperate unity of our ragtag band.

Nearby, Beastie fights a furious battle of his own—each savage swipe aims not at killing but at crippling the wolves, maiming them so they can't rise again. I can see the anguish in the eyes of the transformed men and women—injured souls, their wolf forms faltering as limbs are lost, their agonised cries mingling with the cacophony of battle.

Then I turn to see Elijah in his full glory; my jaw drops as his cheetah morphs fluidly into an enormous eagle, wings spread wide as it soars skyward before plummeting in a fearsome dive-bomb attack on a wolf, a spectacle that surpasses even the wild chaos of the melee.

The barrage of attackers seems endless as three sleek panthers and a stealthy leopard strike at the wolves emerging from the dark woods. The relentless tide of predatory creatures surges like a maddening, surging sea. Determined to turn the tide, I rise to my feet and race to lend my aid. I see two wolves converging on one of the panthers; rushing past, I channel my power and set one ablaze while using telekinesis to spin the other out of balance. The panther immediately capitalises on the opportunity, clamping its powerful jaws around the exposed wolf's neck—an audible crunch heralds the breaking of bone.

Amid the ongoing battle, I hear the shriek of a screeching engine—someone's car screeches to a halt on our embattled road. The abrupt sound of braking sends a chill down my spine; I silently pray it isn't the sheriff. But with three wolves barrelling towards me, I have no time to glance to find out.

I fling one of the frontal attackers skyward with a burst of energy and then let loose a rapid salvo of fireballs, finding their mark on one wolf after two missed attempts. I then freeze another wolf in place, my focus splitting as I rush past it, my hand trailing over its fur and channelling my incendiary power so that the fur darkens ominously along my path—crippling it eventually even if not killing it outright.

The wolf I sent flying has now become ensnared in thick branches from a nearby tree, its tangled limbs echoing Freya's rapid efficiency. Suddenly, a sharp, popping sound splits the air—a noise more delicate than a gunshot—drawing my attention until I catch sight of Sam crouching behind a car door, brandishing what appears to be a silenced machine gun with grim resolve.

Then my eyes catch Ava's flaming sword dancing in an elegant yet deadly arc as she spins gracefully through the fray, each strike a fluid motion of lethal beauty. I long to summon my own weapon in that moment, but I know I lack the grace—and the energy—to do so elegantly as Ava does.

I continue my deadly ballet, attacking and dispatching another wolf that lunges at me, only to find myself face-to-face with a wolf trying to take me out. Its head jerks unnaturally as it nears me before collapsing in a heap. Then, almost as if by magic, a shimmering blur flashes before my eyes and vanishes. Looking towards the house, I see Maya's mischievous smirk through her protective shield—she had erected it at the last desperate moment, causing the wolf to collide with it and break its neck with fatal precision.

I press on, unleashing wave after wave of attacks as wolves pour out from the dark woods. I try to mimic Beastie's technique of crippling their legs, but precision evades me in the maelstrom. Instead, after pinning a wolf into immobility, I conjure a surge of my ominous black fire, which consumes it entirely until nothing but a pile of ash remains.

Just as I lock onto my next target, agony explodes in my left arm. Searing, blinding pain. I'm yanked violently off balance, hitting the ground hard enough to steal my breath. My concentration shatters; the fire I was summoning fizzles into nothing. Disoriented, looking down through a haze of pain, I see it – massive grey jaws clamped tight around my forearm, hot, fetid breath hitting my skin. It's dragging me, scraping my body along the unforgiving, stony ground.

A wet, sickening *snap* echoes, horrifyingly close. It's my bone. The pain flares from searing to an impossible, white-hot nova that consumes everything. My arm goes instantly, terrifyingly limp and useless below the bite. Then, in a moment of grotesque horror, something *slams* down beside me. It's the wolf's head – severed – sliding off the ragged stump of my upper arm but *still attached* to my forearm, its dead weight pinning my destroyed limb to the ground, jagged teeth buried deep in my flesh. Bile rises in my throat.

Ava appears over me, sporting a grin that is as unsettling as it's triumphant—an expression that hints at the dark pleasures of her past life. Her nickname is no idle moniker; she thrives in the midst of battle. I silently thank the heavens she isn't obliterating everything with explosive force, for that will attract far too much unwanted attention.

Crouching down with swift efficiency, Ava pries the wolf's grotesque jaw apart just as the severed head begins its ghastly transformation back to human form. Then, with a mix of urgency and tenderness, she helps me to my feet. "Are you okay?" she asks, her voice threaded with concern as she examines my mangled arm.

"I'll live. Thank you," I manage to say, my voice strained with both agony and determination.

"Good. Let's get back to it. I think we're starting to win," she says before darting off towards three wolves that have ensnared Rose in her panther form. I recognise her immediately—emerald eyes gleaming with feral intensity—as Ava swiftly fells one of the predators. Unlike any I had seen before, a larger, more imposing panther decimates another wolf with terrifying speed. And then I feel a magnetic pull drawing me irresistibly towards that very panther.

It has to be Luca. Our eyes meet briefly; he turns his head in my direction, and the panther acknowledges me with a subtle, regal nod before it charges off towards another pack of wolves as Rose eliminates the last threat attempting to corner her.

A soft whimper pulls my attention behind me. I turn to find one of the leopards in dire straits. One wolf *has* its vicious jaws wrapped around its neck, another clutching its tail between its teeth, and a third has it pinned mercilessly to the ground, poised to break its ribs. Rushing to assist, I conjure a precise fireball, carefully aimed so as not to harm the cat if I miss. My shot strikes true—the wolf instantly releases its grip on the terrified feline and collapses in a burst of ashen flames.

Before I can ponder the sudden, grey blur of a small object colliding with another wolf, I realise it's a statue turned golem by Freya. I cast off two more streams of fire while the desperate and cunning wolves attempt to divide my focus by spreading out again. I manage to catch one of the wolves, but now, with only one hand to fight, the other wolves advance on me quickly. In a flash, a wolf pounces, driving me harshly to the ground again.

Time slows as I raise my only good hand in a last-ditch effort to block the snapping jaws from latching onto any vulnerable part of my body. I would have been overwhelmed in mere seconds if not for my considerably increased strength. The wolf relentlessly snaps at me, its teeth clashing in a painful rhythm as I struggle to concentrate enough to call forth my fiery powers.

Then, almost miraculously, a huge, powerful blow disrupts our deadly tango—a massive cat tears the wolf right out of my grasp. I watch, stunned, as the assailant is revealed to be none other than Elijah's cheetah again. I'm still amazed by his modest size compared to the panthers. His strength is awe-inspiring, though, and if I survive this, I am going to owe him big time. The cheetah rips at the wolf's side with precise savagery, ensuring my survival.

My eyes dart around the besieged battlefield. Looking back towards the house, I see Freya and Maya standing vigil on the far side of our wards. Freya, her entire being concentrated, manipulating the surrounding vegetation—twisting branches and piercing vines—to immobilise every wolf straying too close, while Maya, ever vigilant, bolsters protective shields to secure our flanks. Their resolute determination is nothing short of inspiring amidst this maelstrom of blood and flame.

Nearby, Beastie continues his brutal assault, methodically

disabling wolves—crippling limbs so they can never regain their feral stance. I watch in grim satisfaction as several of the injured transform back to men and women crying out in anguish, their howls muted by the overwhelming sound of destruction.

Simultaneously, three panthers and a sleek leopard emerge from the oppressive darkness of the woods, launching savage assaults on the advancing wolves. The ceaseless influx of enemies sweeps over me like a tidal wave. With no time to ponder, I leap back into the melee; as I run past, I encounter two wolves vying for a panther's attention. I unleash a torrent of flames that engulf one, while a telekinetic spin sends the other reeling.

Glancing over to check on my sisters, I notice Freya's concentration faltering; the onslaught is overwhelming. Maya frantically attempts to shield Freya from the wolves as she has stupidly crossed over the wards and is now surrounded. I curse inwardly as the protective plants she commands begin to falter, motionless and ineffective. Freya's panic is mounting as the wolves play with her fear by slowly moving in on her while baring their teeth.

Hearing Maya's terrified cry echo as I barrel towards her, I start to feel my energy dwindle—though anger still fuels each desperate step, I fear I might collapse if I don't shield my family. Just then, a dark, imposing figure tears a wolf away and dismembers it with clawed hands. I gasp in disbelief as my hero is Sera as she protects Freya.

Without hesitation, I hurl a series of fireballs at the remaining wolf, striking true and watching it vanish into a smouldering heap. In that brief moment, Sera's voice resonates in my mind, calm but insistent, '*Stay strong; we can do this.*' Then, as if shedding mortal constraints, she unfurls majestic wings, soars skyward, and disappears into the tangled woods where the fighting is, as we seem to be pushing the wolves back.

Reaching Freya in a final mad dash, I bellow, "Get Back Over To The Other Side Of The Wards Before I Put You There Myself!"

She hesitates, her gaze full of guilt, then rushes to me, ignoring self-preservation. "What's wrong with your arm?" she demands, alarm lacing every word.

"It's broken; get behind the wards, now!" I insist, panting with raw urgency.

Freya's stubborn voice answers, "I'd prefer to stay with you—I can help, you're vulnerable with that arm."

"No, please, go back behind the wards. I need to know you're safe so you can keep attacking with your plants instead of distracting me," I plead. Eventually, her determination fades, and she retreats towards the relative safety of our fortified boundary.

As I track Freya heading for our wards, I spot a gargoyle golem methodically dispatching a wolf that threatens Maya, also exposed after crossing the wards. My sisters, I think bitterly, will ultimately be the death of me.

Then a bone-chilling scream erupts from behind me. I pivot to see a snarling wolf pinning Ava, then shaking her like a ragdoll. "NOOO!!!" I scream, charge surging through my veins. I race towards her, unleashing wave after wave of fireballs. On my third desperate try, one of my blazing projectiles strikes its mark—a deep, fiery wound mars the wolf's flank, forcing it to drop Ava in a crumpled heap. I rush to her side; she lies still, her once vibrant form now limp and eerily silent.

Collapsing to my knees, I gather her slender frame, my only uninjured arm trembling as I pull her onto my lap. I cradle her head against my chest, feeling her ragged breathing and the shudder of her fragile heart. Chaos reigns for a moment, all around us—but in that intimate instant, nothing else matters. Ava manages to open her eyes, and in their depths, I see resolve; she knows she's dying. I whisper hoarsely, "You're going to be okay. We will find a way." My voice breaks as a hot tear smudges my cheek—an echo of the raw, unyielding sorrow of this unending battle.

Ava's feeble, trembling voice emerges, "It's too late. Please tell

Rose I love her."

"Where is Rose?" I demand, scanning the melee desperately, but the identity of each panther blurs amid the carnage.

"She was with Luca last I saw," she manages before falling silent.

I cling to the hope that Rose will soon realise Ava's peril and rush to her aid, sparing her from a lonely, agonising death. Suddenly, a chilling call of my name echoes, and I sense a cold menace behind me—a wolf poised above, ready to strike. It opens its grotesquely gaping maw, presumably aiming for my head, but at the last miraculous moment, it is wrenched away. However, not before its snapping jaw clips my ear; pain explodes through my head as crimson droplets stain my face.

The wolf coils around itself once more, sinking its lethal fangs into something—more blood gushes as the beast feasts, and then a body collapses beside it. Rage floods my senses as I raise my arm and engulf the attacking creature in seething flames.

As the wolf crumbles into ash, the figure of the victim emerges from the dissipating ash. I gasp at the sight of Nathaniel, lying crumpled, his hands clutching at his throat as blood cascades in a grim fountain around his fingers. One of his hands falls away from his throat as his eyes start to flutter closed. I know he was going to *die*, especially as there isn't much left of his neck.

This cruel twist of fate is almost too much to bear, Ava dying in my arms, and now Nathaniel—the archangel our father—dying mere feet away. For a moment, I cling to the futile hope that his archangel nature might spare him, only to recall the bitter truth he had confided: without his wings, his immortality is a memory of the past.

Catherine M. Clark

Chapter 48

Fates Entwined

I stare at Nathaniel, his face slackening from resignation into stillness as the last faint puff of air leaves his lips, a sound barely audible over the frantic hammering in my own chest. An icy cold, utterly separate from the night air, seeps deep into my marrow. Time seems to stretch thin. *He's stopped. He's not breathing.* The realisation hits like a physical blow. He's gone. I watch, lungs frozen, helpless horror rooting me to the spot. Then, impossibly, his form *shivers*. It's as if I *have channelled* my own destructive power onto him; his flesh begins to subtly flake, then crumble faster, dissolving not into soot but into ash that *glows*—a pure, brilliant white that seems to absorb and refract the surrounding chaos into particles of ethereal light, like crystallised snow catching a phantom sun.

I remain frozen in disbelief as the fine, luminous ash vanishes, carried on an unseen breeze. I wait with bated breath for the return of his soul, longing to see it take form—just like Doris—but nothing stirs. Instead, the ominous words of Papa Legba echo in my mind, 'The gods just vanish.' In that moment, the harrowing truth strikes me—souls only reside within those who bear human blood; Nathaniel, with a lineage untainted by mortal influence, has no soul to leave behind. Unlike Hecate, he must have been much older than her, and she must have had a human descendant at some point in history.

The pain of our collective loss intensifies as I recall that we *have* now *lost* both our parents to these monstrous wolves. I hear a blood-curdling scream shatter the stillness—a scream that sends shockwaves through my heart and mind. An empty, numbing despair engulfs me as I recognise the scream of Maya, and then a new dread takes hold as I sense Ava's pulse, continuing to wane. I can't let her slip away, too.

Desperation forces my mind to search for an answer, to recall anything that can help me save Ava. Then the words of Cat—words now echoing like a long-forgotten incantation—*'Your blood has healing abilities.'* With nothing at hand to cut my skin, I summon my silent ally, "Beastie, I need you!"

In a heartbeat, Beastie materialises at my side. His eyes, dark pools of shared anguish as they fall upon Ava's trembling form, betray the depth of his feelings—he cares for her as fiercely as I do. "Quickly," I implore, voice trembling with urgency, "sink one of your fangs into my hand." I hold up my outstretched, shaking hand towards him.

Without a moment's hesitation, his sharp fang bites into my skin, drawing a fresh stream of blood that surges like a ruby river. I press my bleeding hand into Ava's open mouth, forcing it apart so that my vital essence can cascade down her throat like a desperate lifeline.

In that frantic moment, a storm of emotions batter me—anger, heartbreak, and panic all converge as if tiny, biting ants scurry under my skin. The heat of my burning blood is matched only by the intensity of my fear; I'm uncertain if this meagre offering will suffice to keep her alive. Summoning the remnants of my power, I channel it into my bleeding hand. I feel it flow with my blood and with it my intent for what I need to happen, as it flows into her with a faint shimmering glow. For a few agonising seconds, Ava convulses, her body betraying the struggle within, then falls eerily still.

Moments later, I feel her heartbeat slow perilously, its faint rhythm barely resonating against the chorus of my own mounting despair.

Suddenly, her body jerks violently against mine as if waging a desperate, uncontrolled battle against its fate, and in that chaos, another scream-this one rough and desperate—pierces the air, calling her name. I ignore it, forcing my hand to remain over her mouth and ensuring my blood continues its course, hoping Cat is right about my blood.

As I cradle her, the very ground beneath us begins to tremble, a vibration that promises imminent change. Out of the corner of my eye, a sleek panther charges into view, nearly colliding with me before coming to a stop beside me, then shifting, with sinuous grace. "What the fuck are you doing to her?" Rose screams, her voice a mixture of fury and desperation as she yanks me away from Ava. Her anger and grief are palpable, and as my back strikes the hard ground, I try desperately to crawl back to her. But Rose, stark naked and seething, glowers at me with burning contempt, making every movement a battle against both physical pain and emotional exhaustion.

"If she dies, you die," Rose snaps, coldly, her words slicing through the chaos.

"I didn't do this to her. A wolf did," I protest, struggling to rise on my broken arm while my body throbs with weariness. Glancing about, I note the destructive tableau around me and see we have the wolves in hand, mostly. We have pushed back against the wolves' onslaught, and everyone seems to be in the woods.

My thoughts swiftly turn to Jacob. If Rose is to act on her dire warning, my only path left leads straight to him—and I'm not one to delay. The mere thought of his name ignites an inferno of rage within me, so fierce it threatens to make my body burst. Amid these searing emotions, memories flash unbidden—Nathaniel's anguished final moments, and our mother's broken, lifeless body and face as she *passed* on.

I know Jacob is responsible for her death. Then I can't help but remember what he did to me, how he violated my body, and I picture every moment I had with him before he raped me, how he pretended to be a good guy and wanting to date me. The realisation of his plan unfurls in my mind: he hoped to date me and get me pregnant while he hid the truth of who he really was. But how did he know we would come here? Maybe I will never know.

I search desperately for my sisters amidst the pandemonium. I see Maya collapsing on the steps of the house, sobbing uncontrollably, while Jenny offers quiet comfort, her touch gentle against the backdrop of raw sorrow. My anger swells, as if fuelled by the injustice that Maya *had loved* our father in ways I never *had* or *could*. Then Freya emerges, her eyes blazing with fury as she glares daggers at Rose, who cradles Ava in a fit of tearful mourning.

Amidst the dizzying rage of my thoughts and the vivid tableau around me, my body convulses abruptly, which I'm sure is from my exhaustion. I turn towards the direction of the community Jacob once *took* me into and wonder if, perhaps, that is where he has *fled*.

With grim determination, I begin my journey towards the lake, its shores promising an encounter, however delayed, with the man who haunts my every thought. I need my revenge before I pass out.

But fate has one more cruel twist. After only a few stumbling steps, my body locks in a brutal convulsion, pitching me forward onto my hands and knees. The impact jars through me. I gasp, pressing my palms into the gritty earth as an agony unlike anything before rips up my spine like a serrated blade. Then, my hands *ignite*. Not my usual purple, but roaring flames of fierce red, orange, yellow – colours that feel alien, *wrong*. I *feel* the heat sear my skin, yet somehow not consume it, as the fire crawls relentlessly up my arms, engulfing my vision in a dizzying, wild dance.

The fire spreads, and the pain becomes supernova. It's everywhere, feeling like my very bones are on fire, twisting, reshaping. A scream tears from my throat, raw and inhuman. Over the roaring in my ears, I distantly hear Freya and Maya crying my name – their anguish a thin counterpoint to my own agony. My broken arm *jerks* with impossible force, a sharp, grinding torment. The world greys at the edges, consciousness fraying. But beneath the pain, beneath the fire, a new sound emerges – not voices, but a cacophony of heartbeats, a thousand frantic drums pounding *inside* my head, insistent, overwhelming.

Through the haze of agony, I feel a bizarre knitting sensation deep within my shattered arm. Bones *grind*, then fuse with impossible speed, the searing pain momentarily overridden by a wave of unnatural strength. Is this healing? It feels too violent. Both arms jerk again, harder this time, and impossibly, I feel myself *lift*, hovering inches off the ground as if gravity is merely a suggestion. My arms twist, muscles bunching and elongating, the bones popping sickeningly as they reshape into something... else. My hands swell, skin darkening to polished ebony, fingernails thickening, sharpening, lengthening into gleaming, lethal claws. Reflected dimly in the firelight on the ground, I see them—not hands anymore, but paws. Like Beastie's. A surge of raw power floods me, terrifying and horribly, instinctively *right*.

A sudden, sharp sting breaks my reverie—a pointed sensation digging into my lip, compelling me to part my mouth. I feel a strange movement within; my jaw shifts, my nose seems to rearrange itself, and my entire body writhes in a transformation entirely out of my control. Amid the disordered symphony of my metamorphosis, someone's sardonic voice breaks through: "I guess we now know what Beastie gave her."

And then, in this moment of chilling clarity, I understand. Delving into the library in my mind, where the secret books of my abilities dwell, I discover a new tome has taken its rightful place. Its cover bears the unmistakable image of Beastie, albeit altered ever so subtly. Then I'm shoved out of the landscape and unable to find the door again to re-enter.

Whatever just happened, I will have to deal with it later, so tentatively, I test my new limbs. To my astonishment, my once-broken arm has healed completely. Tentatively, I press my transformed, clawed hands—well, paws that are like hardened wild animal paws—into the fertile earth and propel myself forward with speed and newfound strength. Like a beast reborn, I race around the glistening lake, feeling the rush of the wind as I join and follow the winding road heading north.

Within minutes, as I race along the road and pass a few cars, I come upon large, weathered wooden gates standing before me like an ancient threshold. Unsure if my current form can vault such an obstacle, I seek to test the limits of my elemental power. Concentrating fiercely, I feel an intense heat build in my throat until fire erupts from my mouth in a burst of raw energy. The flames lick the gates mercilessly, quickly carving a smoking hole through the wood.

I dash through the smoking hole, landing lightly on the other side where two men stand frozen, mouths agape. Instinct, raw and predatory, takes over. I launch myself at the nearest one, the world narrowing to this single target. My teeth, suddenly feeling longer, sharper, sink into the yielding flesh of his neck. The sound is wet, tearing. Hot, coppery blood floods my mouth. A part of my mind recoils – *disgusting!* – but another, deeper part, the part that is now more beast than human, *revels* in it. It tastes… vital. Good. Like raw electricity, a jolt surges through me, replenishing some of my spent energy. *Oh gods, do I have to drink blood just like Beastie now?* Shaking my head to clear the disturbing thought, I spin away. The other man is fumbling, trying to shift, but a blast of fire erupts from my jaws – standard orange flames, not my black fire, just like Beastie's – engulfing him instantly. His agonised scream cuts through the air. I try to find the door to my landscape again, to switch the fire, to do *anything* else, but it's still gone, inaccessible. I'm forced to listen as he burns, turning away because I can't bear to watch. The act of breathing fire, however, sends another unwanted surge of pure, animalistic power through my transformed body.

The power surge leaves me intoxicated as I scan the desolate compound searching for Jacob. A lone wolf charges at me, and I dispatch it with ease. The silence is almost palpable until I spot him around a corner of a modest building. He looks like he is searching for something himself, and I remember what Dhara *said*: that she and others are going to sneak away. He halts abruptly, his voice dripping with condescension as he sneers, "She *sent* her mutt. I *should have known* she is too scared to face me."

A guttural growl, raw and fierce like Beastie's own, bubbles from deep within me as I advance deliberately, cautious of any hidden threats. "Mutt, your fire won't hurt me. I am protected," Jacob declares haughtily, as he caresses a heavy chain around his neck from which a mysterious pendant swings. "This charm allows me to breach those bitches' wards and hide my scent from you and your pack of shifters masquerading as agents. So, what are you going to do, mutt? You should head back to your bitch and tell her to face me."

I growl low and step closer, only to feel two snarling wolves encircle me from either side. Before they can attack, Jacob raises his hand, his tone mocking as he notes, "You are outnumbered. Not even you can take on all three of us. God, I doubt you can even understand me." He then offers a peculiar comment, "I don't remember reading about hellhounds having purple eyes—very strange, even stranger is that I can see you. Maybe you are something different."

Barely a few feet from him now, he brazenly positions himself directly in my path. "If you don't head back to your bitch soon, I'll order them to kill you," he threatens with venom in every syllable.

Desperation surges through me—I don't want this confrontation to be like this; I want to face him as myself. I close my eyes, trying to summon the memory of who I am, hoping it will trigger the shift back to human form, to regain some semblance of humanity amidst the beastly transformation. But nothing comes at first; panic grips me as I fear I might remain like this, an eternal aberration. Amidst my inner turmoil, I wonder fleetingly if Beastie was once human. Surrendering to inevitable change, I sit down, feeling exhaustion and sorrow wrest control of my body.

Jacob's jaw drops as he observes the miraculous reversal. Slowly, my hands and arms revert to their original form, and the fire I'm covered in dissipates into nothingness. With a smug grin stretching his face, Jacob remarks, "Well, what do we have here? You *brought* yourself to me, and whatever you are, we can still give it a try. If it works, you will make us strong. Being a shifter of sorts, you will increase the chances of our triumph. I *did enjoy* our time together."

I stand shakily, only to become painfully aware of my nakedness—a humiliating state that makes my skin crawl with vulnerability. Jacob's smirk deepens as he inches closer, his eyes glinting with mischievous malice. "I'm going to enjoy this, again," he murmurs, his fingers trailing slowly over my exposed cheek.

I manage a weak smile and raise my right hand, knowing that speed is essential as darkness tugs at the edges of my awareness. My mind teeters on the brink of oblivion—I *have pushed* myself beyond endurance. Then, without warning, the sword I conjure shoots forth from my outstretched hand, piercing Jacob's body with an unerring precision.

For a harrowing moment, his eyes stay fixed on me as life begins to seep away, and he collapses, head tilting back as his eyes dim and start to become vacant as his body slides off my sword, and I can smell his flesh burning from the purple flames.

Turning instinctively towards the wolves' retreating figures, I see them scrambling towards the back of the compound—fear evident in their flight at the loss of their leader, their alpha. I hold the sword too long for a moment, transfixed by the encroaching darkness that fills my vision. Eventually, I relinquish it, but my body betrays me; I sink forward, collapsing beside the fallen Jacob, his vacant eyes a final, haunting image as despair whispers that my end is also near.

I don't expect to wake again as I expect a wolf to kill me as I lie here, yet here I am, roused by a familiar voice. "Miss Harper, you need to wake up." The words repeat several times, growing in insistence until I manage to pry open my heavy eyelids. I find myself staring at Jacob's lifeless eyes once more—an eerie grin creeping onto my lips against all reason.

"Miss Harper, I don't think this is a matter to smile about, do you?" The voice, formal yet disturbingly familiar, cuts through the haze. I try to turn my head, but every movement brings searing pain as I realise my hands are pinned behind my back. My neck throbs with the memory of the fall, each slight movement a fresh agony.

Finally, I see a figure standing over me, visibly uncomfortable and reluctant to meet my gaze. The recognition is immediate—Sheriff Radshaw, his stance stiff and his expression a grim blend of duty and satisfaction.

I groan, "What do you want now?"

"Miss Harper, you are under arrest for the murder of Deputy Davids, and for the murder of whoever is lying over by the gates, and for arson," the sheriff proclaims, his tone laced with an unsettling glee that makes my internal scream echo silently.

Crap! I feel a surge of dread with every beat of my racing heart as I lie there, overwhelmed by the realisation I won't be able to protect my family. I almost wish I had died like I expected after I passed out. I also can't help but wonder if Ava finally *died*, as it seemed at the time, my blood wasn't helping her; I'm sure Rose will be coming for me now, as I'm still alive.

OTHER BOOKS BY CATHERINE M. CLARK

The Harper Legacy Series

No Witchin Way – Book 1

Ava the Destroyer Series

The Mission – Book 1

Bloodlines & Chains Series

I Think I'm A Monster – Book 1

My next book will be:
Ava the Destroyer – Book 2

You can contact the author via the following means:
Email: authorcatherinemclark@hotmail.com
TikTok: www.tiktok.com/@catherine.m.clark
https://www.facebook.com/groups/themoontree

Printed in Dunstable, United Kingdom